AVENGER OF BLOOD

A Novel

BOOK TWO: THE APOCALYPSE DIARIES

JOHN HAGEE

THOMAS NELSON PUBLISHERS®
Nashville

A Division of Thomas Nelson, Inc.
www.ThomasNelson.com

Published in Nashville, Tennessee, by Thomas Nelson, Inc.

Library of Congress Cataloging-in-Publication Data

Hagee, John.
    Avenger of blood : a novel / John Hagee.
        p. cm. — (The apocalypse diaries ; bk. 2)
    ISBN 0-7852-6789-1
    1. Church history—Primitive and early church, ca. 30–600—Fiction. 2. John, the
Apostle, Saint—Fiction. 3. Christian saints—Fiction. 4. Apostles—Fiction. I. Title.
    PS3608.A35 A96 2002
    813'.54—dc21   2002008943

Printed in the United States of America

02 03 04 05 06 BVG 5 4 3 2 1

1

November, A.D. 96

JACOB SAT AT THE elegant mahogany writing desk, intently focused on two goals: composing a letter and ignoring his brother, who was leaning against one of the tall marble columns in the spacious room that had served as their father's library and home office. Ordinarily, ignoring his brother was not a difficult task; this afternoon, however, Peter seemed determined to distract him with questions.

"What are we going to do about Rebecca?" he asked for the second time.

Jacob finally looked up. "What do you mean?"

"Rebecca," Peter repeated. "I'm worried about her."

Peter shifted his weight and limped clumsily toward the desk, obviously fatigued after a full day at the harbor, and Jacob frowned. He didn't want to deal with his brother's worries about their younger sister right now. He wanted to finish his correspondence and then finalize his plans to travel to Rome.

"Marcellus is worried too," Peter said, and the older man nodded his agreement.

"Haven't you noticed how despondent she is?" Peter continued. "She mopes around the house, doesn't talk much—doesn't even come downstairs for dinner some days. I'm very concerned. Rebecca is not the same person she used to be."

Neither am I, Jacob thought. He set the pen down and moved a leather weight on top of his unfinished letter. A picture flashed through his mind of his father sitting at the same desk, his bulky frame perched on the same backless chair covered in striped brocade, his massive hand clutching a fragile reed pen as he scratched words and numbers on an unrolled parchment with a flourish. His mother, Elizabeth, entered the mental picture, gently chiding her husband: "Put your work aside, Abraham; dinner is ready. The family is waiting." But the family was not waiting for Abraham anymore. In fact, both of Jacob's parents were dead now.

Clamping down on the enormous sense of loss that swept over him, Jacob said curtly, "You wouldn't be the same person either if you'd spent the last year on Devil's Island instead of living like this." He looked around the lavishly furnished room in the sprawling villa his father had built in the hills overlooking the harbor of Ephesus.

Jacob was reluctant to admit, even to himself, just how much he resented the fact that Peter had escaped the previous year's persecution. Granted, Peter had not forsaken his faith and sacrificed to Caesar as their older sister, Naomi, had; instead, Peter had cowered and hidden while the rest of the family was arrested and forced to either make the imperial sacrifice or be sentenced to hard labor. And Jacob did admire the way Peter had overcome his physical disability and his timid personality to take over the daily operation of one of the empire's largest businesses. Still, while Rebecca had endured the living nightmare of Devil's Island and Jacob had been sentenced to backbreaking work as an oarsman on a Roman warship, Peter had enjoyed the benefits of the family's vast wealth. A palatial home, the finest food, luxurious clothes—all the things Jacob had once taken for granted before he lost them in an instant.

"It's not necessary to keep reminding me that you and Rebecca suffered a great deal while I didn't." Peter started to leave, taking a few stiff steps, then he turned back around. "Our quibbles with each other aren't important," he said after a moment. "What *is* important is Rebecca. We need to do something so she doesn't become a recluse."

"I'm sure Rebecca will be fine." Jacob attempted to soften his tone as well. "She just needs time to adjust to the idea of being home again, to being free."

"She's been home over a month and she hasn't adjusted," Peter pointed out. "Instead, she's becoming more and more withdrawn."

Marcellus finally joined the conversation. "And more fearful. As much as she went through on Devil's Island, Rebecca wasn't as afraid then as she seems to be now. The least noise startles her, and she is so protective of Victor that she will scarcely let him out of her sight."

"That's not necessarily bad, is it?" Jacob asked the retired medical officer. "After all, he's only three months old."

Marcellus answered, "It goes beyond maternal instinct, I think."

"Another thing," Peter said. "She never cries anymore." He eased himself onto one of the long settees. "There was a time I would have considered that good news, but somehow it's not."

Jacob silently agreed that the changes in his sister were not good news, and he realized just how much he missed her stormy outbursts of tears as well as the sunshine of her quick laugh. These days her behavior, as well as her appearance, was dull and flat. Rebecca truly wasn't the same person. None of them were, really, but especially not Rebecca. And her suffering hadn't ended once they'd been set free. When they returned home, she'd endured yet another crushing blow.

That thought galled Jacob, and he suddenly gave the desk a resounding thump with the heel of his hand. "How I'd love to get my hands on—"

"That won't help," Peter said quickly. "You know how we all feel about not seeking revenge."

"I wasn't referring to Damian this time, although I'd like a piece of his hide as well." Jacob clenched and unclenched his fist reflexively. From the moment he'd been released, Jacob had been determined to pursue his family's persecutor and to exact vengeance for the deaths of his mother and father, not to mention what Damian had done to Rebecca. But the apostle John had reasoned with Jacob and, when that failed, had argued with him and pleaded with Jacob not to seek revenge. John had eventually worn him down, but Jacob's anger still boiled over from time to time, and his relationship with John had become strained.

Now there were not only Damian's atrocities to consider, but someone else had wounded his sister, and Jacob's instincts were to go after him as well. For the moment, however, he suppressed those instincts and conceded to his brother's original question.

"All right," Jacob said. "What are we going to do about Rebecca?"

"She needs to be distracted from her situation," Marcellus suggested. "To get involved with something outside of herself."

Peter spoke slowly and thoughtfully, as was his custom. "She often accompanied Mother on visits to the sick and needy. Rebecca's very good with people—at least, she used to be."

"That's a wonderful idea." Jacob drummed his fingers on the desk, then abruptly stood and began giving directions. Once his mind latched onto a solution to a problem, he saw no reason to delay its implementation. "Instruct the household staff to prepare additional food, and find out which of the church members are in need. Then tell Rebecca she's to carry on Mother's ministry of good works."

"Not so fast," Peter objected. "You don't just *tell* someone to take over a ministry like that. Besides, Helena has been coordinating the charitable efforts Mother used to oversee, and she's already tried to enlist Rebecca's help. Rebecca wouldn't do it."

Jacob groaned and sat back down. "If Helena's involved, I pity the poor and needy more than ever. The woman's spiritual gifts must be confusion and calamity."

With a smile that momentarily widened his thin face, Peter said, "Helena can be rather flighty sometimes, but she's a good-hearted soul. Her compassion manages to overcome her confusion, and she gets the job done." His face resumed a somber expression. "And it's been quite a job. There have been far greater needs in the church body since the emperor's persecution."

"The *late* emperor, thank God." Jacob shuddered slightly. If

Domitian hadn't been assassinated, he and Rebecca and John would still be prisoners.

Peter explained to Marcellus that a number of families had been split up when one or both parents were sent to Devil's Island. "The consequences have been devastating," he said.

"All the more reason for Rebecca to get involved in helping the prisoners' families." Jacob spread his hands in an appeal to the other two. "So how do we persuade her to do it?"

Marcellus rose and stretched. The late afternoon sun streamed in through an unshuttered window, highlighting the few streaks of gray in his dark wavy hair. "I can talk to her if you like. Perhaps she'll listen to me."

Jacob nodded. "Then do it." He knew Rebecca regarded the retired soldier as a father figure, and, sad to say, she'd be more likely to listen to him right now than she would to Jacob. He'd been separated from his sister for almost their entire imprisonment, and their relationship had not quite gotten back to its original footing.

Jacob watched as Marcellus clapped Peter on the shoulder and the two of them left to find Rebecca. Then he picked up the reed pen and returned to his letter, thinking of what Peter had said about so many families being torn apart.

All the more reason for me to go to Rome, Jacob thought. Dozens of Christians from Ephesus and Smyrna and the surrounding cities were still being held on Devil's Island. The new emperor, Marcus Cocceius Nerva, had indicated that Domitian's political exiles would be recalled. Jacob had a few contacts in the higher echelons of Roman politics, and he intended to go there and plead the case for the religious exiles as well.

Just as you interceded for me, he silently promised his late father.

✝

Marcellus knew where he would find her: at the top of Mount Koressos. Like a tortoise reluctant to stick its head out of its shell,

Rebecca seldom left the house. When she did, it was only for an afternoon walk in the high hills surrounding the villa.

It grieved him that she no longer showed any flash of spontaneity
or stubborn endurance, qualities Marcellus had seen her exhibit under
the direst of circumstances. He had been stationed on Devil's Island as
the medical officer for the prison camp. It was not a posting he relished, but one he had endured with a certain stoicism. His long stint
in the army had ended about the time Rebecca, her brother, and the
apostle John were released, and Marcellus had returned to Ephesus
with them. He had been so openly welcomed into the family, and into
the family of believers, that it seemed he had been there for years, not
a matter of weeks.

He reflected on Rebecca's despondency as he climbed, praying
silently that he would be able to encourage her. He was still wondering how to coax Rebecca out of her shell when he topped the hill and
found her sitting in a clearing just off the main path.

"Hello, Marcellus," Rebecca said evenly, with no trace of a smile.

Marcellus returned the greeting, only slightly winded by the quarter-hour climb, and sat down beside Rebecca. She rocked the infant
she held swaddled in her cloak, which she had draped around her like
a sling to form a carrier.

They fell into an easy silence, enjoying the spectacular view. The
city of Ephesus, third largest in the Empire, sprawled below them. Off
to their left, in the distance, was the busy harbor, now quiet at the end
of another long workday. Marcellus shaded his eyes against the
reflected glare of the sun, which was about an hour from sinking
below the watery horizon. He could make out the lines of a number
of cargo ships moored along the docks; several of them, he knew,
belonged to Rebecca's family.

"Not so long ago we spent many hours like this, sitting on a hill-
top, looking out over the water," Marcellus finally said.

Rebecca didn't respond for a moment, then softly said, "It's why I
come here, you know."

"No . . . I didn't." Her statement puzzled Marcellus.

"It reminds me of Devil's Island. Not the bad part," she hastened to add as he turned toward her in surprise, "but the good part."

"You mean there *was* a good part?" He looked in her direction and smiled. In spite of all the misery, he had enjoyed some good times with Rebecca and John, times of laughter and sharing memories of the lives and families they'd left behind. The two unlikely prisoners—an elderly preacher and a sweet, innocent girl—had also spent many hours discipling Marcellus in his newfound faith. Yes, there had been good times on Devil's Island, Marcellus recalled, and he was encouraged that Rebecca seemed to want to talk about them.

"The good part was finding you," Rebecca said. "And finding myself, in a way."

"What do you mean?"

Rebecca paused while she bent over and tucked her cloak around Victor, who had fallen asleep. Then she brushed her long, chestnut-brown hair back across her shoulders. "Like the work I did for John," she said. "Copying his letters to the churches about the revelation. It seemed I had a purpose for being there, that what I was doing really mattered."

"It did matter. And it does. We'll be delivering those letters—God's messages—to the churches soon."

"It's more than that, though . . . it's . . . I don't know exactly." Rebecca shrugged and grew quiet.

Marcellus sought for a way to draw her out; she was more talkative than she had been in days, and he wanted her to continue. If nothing else, he was just glad to hear her voice; more than that, he thought perhaps if she could put what was bothering her into words, she could conquer it.

"So you come here," he said, "because it reminds you of Devil's Island and the meaningful work you did for John. Anything else?"

"The rest of it is more like a feeling . . ."

"What kind of feeling?" he prompted when she hesitated.

Rebecca looked down and stroked the baby's cheek for a moment before answering. "When I was on Devil's Island—after I recovered, anyway—I seemed to have an inner strength. Even when things were really bad, and I had no hope I would ever get off the island, I could somehow manage to be strong. But now that I'm home and everything is fine, it's like I'm falling apart inside."

Her beautiful brown eyes moistened as she continued speaking. "I'm more scared now than when I was a prisoner, and I don't know why. I keep waiting for something else to happen, but I don't know what. Something bad, I suppose.

"I know that's not acting in faith," she added quickly, "but I can't seem to help it." She dropped her head, looking embarrassed. "I should be a better example. Sometimes I think I'm not much of a Christian."

"Not much of a Christian? Let's see, as I recall the circumstances that sent you to Devil's Island, you stood in front of an entire cohort of Roman soldiers and refused to sacrifice to the emperor—proclaiming instead that Jesus Christ is Lord. I wouldn't call a person who does something as courageous as that 'not much of a Christian.'

"You're just human, Rebecca. You've been through a lot, even since you've been home, and it's taken a toll on you."

"I thought I would feel safe again when I got home, but I don't. The house I grew up in doesn't seem safe anymore—instead of comfortable and familiar, it just seems big and scary."

"Perhaps your fear is understandable," he said. "You spent almost a year in a small enclosure—spacious, as far as caves go, but still a very small place."

Marcellus leaned backward, bracing his arms on the hard ground for support. "A Scripture passage comes to mind. The twenty-seventh psalm, I believe. 'The LORD is my light and my salvation; whom shall I fear?'. . . You taught me that psalm, remember?"

"Yes, and I remember who taught it to me." A brief smile flitted across her face, the first he had seen in days. It hinted at the spark of vitality that still smoldered somewhere beneath the surface of her sadness.

"As a little girl," Rebecca said, "I never wanted the lamps to be extinguished at night. My father explained that we couldn't leave them burning because they might start a fire while we were sleeping. He said it was the job of our steward, Servius, to snuff out all the lights—but only after he had checked each room to make sure it was safe and that nothing could harm us. That comforted my fears as long as my father was in the next bedroom. I knew that if I cried, he would hear me.

"But when I was five, Papa sailed to Rome on business. He was gone for several months, and I got scared again. So Servius included me in his evening ritual while Papa was gone. He would carry me in one arm and a small clay lamp in the other. We would go from room to room, snuffing out the flickering lights of the lampstands one by one, quoting Scripture the entire time. Psalm 27 was one of his favorites. Then he would carry me upstairs to my bedroom, and I would go to sleep saying, 'The Lord is my light. The Lord is my light.'"

Rebecca grew quiet again when she finished her story, and Marcellus knew she must miss Servius, who had died on Devil's Island a few months after being sentenced.

Marcellus gave her a moment to let the memories fade, then he said, "A few minutes ago you were talking about how you had found your purpose on Devil's Island. I'm sure there's a purpose for you here, as well. A ministry God has for you—perhaps something only you can do. But you can't find what that is if you don't look beyond yourself, Rebecca."

She looked doubtful. "What could God possibly have for me to do?"

"Perhaps the same kind of work your mother did. Peter says she visited the sick and took food and clothing to those who needed it."

"Mother always took care of the less fortunate."

"Peter also said you used to go with her sometimes and that you were good with people, just like she was. I already know how you took care of John every day for the last year."

"The truth is that neither one of us could have survived without you, Marcellus. You're the one who risked your career, and probably your life, to hide us, bring us food."

"All of which simply proves that we need each other. And from what I understand, there are many believers in Ephesus who need help, especially the families of prisoners."

"Helena has already talked to me about that."

Her voice was flat but a glimmer of interest seemed to light up her eyes, and Marcellus pressed the advantage. "Evidently she could use your assistance. According to Jacob, she has the gift of confusion."

Rebecca rewarded him with another fleeting smile. "That sounds like Jacob . . . and Helena." The baby fussed in his sleep, and Rebecca comforted him until he quieted. "But I can't traipse all over Ephesus with Victor, and he's too young for me to leave him."

Marcellus was ready for this objection, and he had already thought of a solution. "You could leave for a few hours. Agatha is always saying that she'll watch Victor for you." Peter had hired Agatha, a recent convert, as part of the villa's housekeeping staff. Agatha had a young infant of her own, so she could nurse Victor if need be.

"I suppose," Rebecca agreed, yet she looked pained and almost panicked. "But even if I weren't worried about Victor, I still couldn't do it."

"Why not?"

"I'm afraid. Afraid of what people would say. Or what they wouldn't say. Some of the other Christians think I'm a bad person. Oh, most of them won't say it to my face, but they talk about it behind my back. I don't know who my friends are anymore." Her face fell as she admitted, "And I'm still too sad to be around people most of the time."

Now, there was a problem, Marcellus acknowledged silently. A few people had been upset when Rebecca returned from Devil's Island with Victor. Instead of rejoicing over a fellow believer surviving the ordeal of a brutal prison camp, they had wagged fingers at an unwed mother. *If they only knew the whole story,* Marcellus thought. He'd been the one to find Rebecca after she had been sexually assaulted and savagely beaten.

"I understand," he said. "But hiding at home all the time won't quell the gossip. And I'm sure the people who need your help won't really care that you came back from prison with a baby but no husband."

Marcellus stood and offered his hand to Rebecca. The brilliant fireball of sun had faded to a burnished glow that shimmered over the Aegean waves.

"Let's go home before it gets dark," he said as he helped her stand and secure Victor for walking down the hillside. "Just promise me you'll think about it, all right?"

✝

Rebecca had thought about their conversation for several days, then she had decided to help Helena, who urgently needed her.

For the past week Rebecca had risen early each day to help coordinate their efforts to minister to the needy. The first day she'd been so upset about leaving Victor that she'd fretted constantly and had tried to rush Helena out of every home they visited. But when she'd returned to the villa, Victor was fine, sleeping contentedly in the handcarved crib that had once been hers, with Agatha and her baby girl close by.

After a few days Rebecca was still trying to hurry Helena along, but simply because the woman had no concept of what it meant to keep to a schedule. The needs had indeed multiplied far beyond anything Rebecca's mother had overseen. In their area of the city alone, some twelve families were in dire economic situations. In households where someone was sick, they tried to visit every day, and at one place

Helena had taken several children home with her because their mother was too ill to care for them.

Rebecca's worries about people being unkind or thinking she was sinful had also evaporated. In home after home she had been embraced warmly, grateful men and women telling her how much they missed her mother, what a kind person Elizabeth had been, and how glad they were to see Rebecca following in her mother's footsteps. Rebecca's spirits had lifted immeasurably, and she was beginning to feel much more hopeful about life.

One afternoon as they returned to the villa, Helena commented on the changes in Rebecca. "It's good for you to be with people," she said.

"I enjoy your company, Helena." It was true. In spite of the air of confusion that sometimes surrounded her, Helena brought a lot of joy to people. She was warm-hearted and generous to a fault.

"I was really talking more about people closer to your own age. In fact, I was thinking you should get to know Antony."

Rebecca noted that Helena's hazel eyes—which were beautifully tinted but too large for her small heart-shaped face—always sparkled when she talked about Antony.

"My son is a good man," Helena said, "even though he is not a believer—yet. He will be someday, I know in my heart. And Antony has never opposed my charitable work, though he sometimes complains that I spend so much of my household budget to feed others that my own pantry is empty. But I notice that he's taken more of an interest in good deeds since you've been helping me."

Helena chattered on about her oldest son for a moment, and Rebecca frowned when she finally realized that her friend was trying to play matchmaker.

"Have I said something wrong?" Helena asked, then didn't give Rebecca a chance to reply. "I don't mean to be insensitive, and perhaps it's not the right time to bring this up, but you don't want to spend the rest of your life alone . . ."

She would have to think of a way to stop Helena. Antony seemed to be very nice, even though she had only met him a couple of times.

An attorney, he was helping Peter and Jacob through the legal morass of getting their father's will probated. However, nice wasn't the issue. Rebecca simply was not interested. She would have to find a polite way to tell Helena.

When they arrived at the villa there was no bustle of activity as they entered the atrium, the large central room of the home. Rebecca was looking forward to a quiet hour or two. Peter and Jacob would not have returned from the harbor yet, and Marcellus was usually visiting John at this time of day. Perhaps she could even take a nap before dinner.

"We'll talk about this later, Helena," Rebecca said firmly as she headed upstairs. "I need to check on Victor right now."

"Oh, bring him down if he's awake," Helena called after her. "I love that precious boy. It's been so long since mine were babies, and I do enjoy holding them . . ."

Helena's voice trailed off as Rebecca reached the top of the stairs. She was glad to get back home to her son. Until this week Victor had never been out of her sight for more than a few minutes, and she missed him.

Rebecca tiptoed into the bedroom and closed the door softly behind her, in case the baby was sleeping. She had taken only a few steps into the room when she stumbled and almost lost her balance. She looked down to see what had tripped her and found Agatha lying crumpled on the floor, bound and gagged, a deep gash on the back of her head. Blood had pooled and caked on her face and neck.

Rebecca knelt down beside the housekeeper. Agatha was alive but unconscious.

Instinctively, Rebecca loosened the gag and was starting to untie Agatha's hands when an icy fear gripped her heart. *Victor!*

Stifling a sob, Rebecca stood and looked around frantically. Then she ran to the other end of the room, where Victor's crib stood next to her bed.

A long, gleaming sword lay across the empty crib.

2

"FOR ALL PRACTICAL PURPOSES, it's over." Antony was delighted to deliver the good news to his clients. He sat across from them in their office at the harbor, the sounds of the cargo handlers drifting in from the dock outside as the three of them conferred over the case.

He marveled once again that the brothers were actually twins. Peter and Jacob were physical opposites—Peter, thin and frail; Jacob as muscular and sturdy as a plow ox. Antony had quickly learned they had opposite temperaments, as well. Peter was cautious and deliberate, while Jacob was impulsive, a man of constant action. He was pacing the floor, in fact, as Antony spoke.

"There will be an official ruling by the court," he continued, "but I can assure you that it is just a legal formality."

"You're positive?" Jacob asked. "I don't want to leave for Rome until I know everything's settled."

"About as positive as I can be. Both the law and public sentiment are on your side. Your father was well respected in this community, while the late emperor was not only despised but has now been officially dishonored by the new government in Rome."

The case was certainly unlike anything Antony had ever seen. He had handled fairly complicated wills and estates for a few prominent citizens, but nothing that could compare to this. To begin with, the size of the estate was enormous. Abraham had been one of the wealthiest men in Asia. But politics, not to mention treachery, had complicated the situation.

Abraham had been caught in the web of Domitian's religious persecution of Christians and executed in Rome. Abraham's oldest daughter, Naomi, the wife of a top-ranking senator, had betrayed her father, knowing it would lead to his death. And then, with the help of her powerful husband, no doubt, she had managed to get herself named as sole heir to her father's estate.

Antony had seen the decree presented to the court; it had been issued by Domitian shortly before his death. The document stated that because Abraham had died as a traitor to the Empire, all his possessions were to be confiscated by the state and then subsequently awarded to Naomi and her husband, Senator Mallus.

"The codicil to your father's will was properly executed, and it clearly disinherits Naomi. Naturally, it was dated prior to Domitian's decree, which the court will set aside *pro forma*. The Senate, working with Emperor Nerva, is trying to undo much of the damage Domitian did in the last few years, and the court has signaled it will take notice of that. Even if Naomi appealed to Caesar, he would not uphold Domitian's ruling; it's well known that the emperor is behind the move to publicly vilify his predecessor.

"So your legal worries with your sister are over. We should have a formal ruling in a few days, and then your lives can go back to normal."

"Our legal worries may be over," Peter said, "but somehow I doubt Naomi will just pack up and leave."

"What else can she possibly do?" Jacob asked. "Besides, she doesn't even need the money. Mallus is ridiculously wealthy in his own right. When Naomi finds out her little scheme has been defeated, she'll hurry to reclaim her place in Roman society."

"You're probably right." Peter's brow wrinkled in obvious concern. "I just can't shake the feeling I had the last time I saw her."

Antony knew that Peter had stood up to her then, vowing to fight Naomi if she tried to claim the estate. She *had* tried, of course, which was when Antony had gotten involved in the case.

Now, thankfully, it would soon be over.

†

Helena wished her body would move as fast as her mind, but at forty-four her agility was not what it once was. When she heard Rebecca's bloodcurdling scream, she ignored her usual aches and pains and scrambled upstairs as rapidly as she could.

What she found astounded her. She didn't know whether to go to Rebecca, who was holding a heavy saber, a look of sheer terror on her face, or Agatha, who appeared to have been mortally wounded and lay bleeding on the rare Persian carpet.

"Victor's gone!" Rebecca trembled as she looked around frantically.

Helena stood paralyzed for a long moment, then she went in six different directions at once. "Go get help and search the house," she said to Rebecca while stooping down beside Agatha's still form.

Rebecca dropped the sword on the bed and started to run out of the room as Helena cried, "No! Wait!" She left Agatha, retrieved the sword, and clumsily handed the heavy weapon to Rebecca. "Take it with you," she ordered. "The attacker could still be in the house."

Helena knelt beside Agatha again and untied her hands. The woman was breathing but didn't respond. Realizing there was little she could do for her, Helena ran to the hall. *Where was everyone? Why hadn't there been any servants around when this happened?*

She ran back to Agatha, thought about trying to get her off the floor and onto the bed, but couldn't do it by herself, so she started downstairs. But when she got to the landing, she saw Rebecca charging upstairs with the chief steward close behind her, wielding the sword over his head.

After that, everything seemed to happen at once. Rebecca and the steward led a search of all the rooms upstairs while the cook and the kitchen crew searched through the many downstairs rooms. Helena sent one of the servants to the harbor to notify Jacob and Peter, and another one to John's house to fetch Marcellus. Perhaps there was something he could do for Agatha.

Helena went up and down the stairs several times to check on the progress of the search, then she finally collapsed in the bedroom where the pandemonium had started. Her legs, unaccustomed to that much exertion, shook with pain and exhaustion; her hands trembled as she placed them on the empty crib and began to pray.

✝

Antony had never been on the upper floor of the villa, where the bedrooms were located. He ran upstairs behind Jacob, and Peter followed, climbing much more slowly and with great effort.

When a messenger had interrupted their meeting to deliver the news that Rebecca's baby was missing and a housekeeper had been attacked, Peter had told the others to leave the waterfront without him. But then Jacob had spied one of the company's delivery wagons that had just unloaded and was about to leave the pier. He commandeered the vehicle and Antony helped Peter climb in, then they drove the horses at breakneck speed through the city.

Now about a dozen people, most of them servants, were assembled in what appeared to be Rebecca's bedroom. Helena had her arm around an ashen-faced Rebecca, and a woman, who must have been the injured housekeeper, lay at an odd angle across the bed. One of the other maids was tending to the bloody wound on her head.

"What happened?" Jacob demanded.

"Any sign of Victor?" Peter asked simultaneously.

Helena shook her head. "No, we've searched the house thoroughly. Some of the servants are combing the grounds, but I don't think they'll find anything. Many of them were in the garden when it happened, and they didn't hear any unusual noises."

"Why not?" Jacob shouted. "Why wasn't someone here with Victor? How could this have happened?" He kept firing questions and people kept trying to answer, but with everybody talking at once, nobody could be heard.

Finally, Antony stepped forward and raised his voice. When he had everyone's attention, he said, "It would help if we heard the story in an orderly fashion. Jacob, if you don't mind, I'd like to ask some questions. You're too upset—understandably—to think clearly at the moment."

Jacob scowled, but he sat down and listened.

"Now," Antony said, "who discovered that Victor was missing? Mother, you seem to have been here the whole time. What do you know?"

"As soon as we arrived, Rebecca came upstairs to get Victor. Almost immediately, I heard her scream, so I came up to see what was wrong."

Antony walked over to Rebecca and knelt beside the large chest on which she was seated. "What did you find when you came upstairs?"

She looked at him with such obvious agony in her dark eyes, luminous with unshed tears, that it tugged at his heart. Rebecca didn't speak for a moment, and Antony realized he was staring at her. She was a very beautiful woman, no doubt about it. He looked away quickly and cleared his throat. "Can you tell me about it?"

Her voice was quiet but steady. "When I came into the room, I tripped over Agatha. She had been tied up and it looked like she'd been hit in the head with something heavy." Rebecca paused to take a deep breath. "Then I looked over at the crib and saw that a sword had been placed across the top."

"A sword?" Jacob asked, then he quickly muttered, "Sorry," in Antony's direction.

"Yes, I picked it up. Victor wasn't in his crib, and we couldn't find him anywhere."

One of the servants held out the sword. "Here it is."

Antony exchanged a long look with Jacob; no doubt he also recognized the insignia on the hilt.

After a few more questions directed to the staff, they learned that the cook and a few workers had been preparing dinner in the kitchen, at the very back of the house, when the child disappeared. The housekeeping staff—except for Agatha, who was watching Victor—had been in the gardens adjoining the main part of the house. The steward said he often allowed them to take a break in the afternoon, after they had finished their cleaning chores and before the family arrived for dinner. An intruder had apparently entered the villa at the quietest time of the workday.

Once they'd learned the gist of the story, Peter dismissed the staff and they filed out, their heads down. Several of them looked cha-grined because they had failed in their responsibilities and evil had managed to invade the home. As far as Antony knew, however, there was no reason for them to have suspected anything like this.

It must have been a simple abduction, Antony reasoned. There appeared to have been no robbery involved, and no one had known anyone who could possibly have wanted to hurt Agatha—and if someone did, why would they want to take Victor? No, someone must have been watching the villa and learned the family's routine. If Agatha survived, perhaps she could identify her attacker.

When everyone had left except Rebecca and Helena, who didn't want to leave Agatha, Jacob told the others, "Meet me in the library." He headed downstairs, taking the sword with him.

$$\dagger$$

Peter laboriously made his way downstairs with Antony following close behind, ready to offer a steadying hand if needed. Peter's was the only bedroom on the ground level, and he seldom visited the upper floor because it was so difficult for him to navigate the stairs.

When they entered the library, Jacob was still holding the sword. He set it on the desk, then turned to ask, "Do you know whose this is?" His voice was barely under control.

Peter winced in pain as he sat down behind the desk. "Of course not."

"From the insignia I can tell it belongs to a Roman soldier," Antony said. "It's odd, though. The only time troops were ever sta-tioned here was last year, when you and the other Christians were arrested. But the troops left months ago."

"I know whose it is," Jacob announced.

That the sword belonged to a Roman soldier was an ominous sign, Peter thought, but he had no idea why Jacob would believe he knew the weapon's owner. "You recognize it?" Peter asked his brother.

"Look closely at the insignia."

Antony moved the sword closer to Peter and stood behind him so they could both inspect it. The insignia was an eagle's head, the symbol of the Roman army; above it had been engraved a numeric inscription: X.

"The Tenth Legion?" Peter asked. It was a cohort of the Tenth Legion, he recalled, that had carried out the orders for a mandatory sacrifice to the emperor.

Jacob nodded. "And this sword belongs to the commander of the first cohort. A living devil named Damian," he added for Antony's benefit, "who raped Rebecca and left her for dead."

Antony grimaced at the disclosure, then asked, "How can you tell it's Damian's sword? Maybe one of the soldiers left it behind and some common criminal found it."

"Some common criminal who hatched a plot to steal my nephew and then was stupid enough to leave his sword behind? I don't think so. It has to be Damian. No one else would want to hurt us like that."

"But Damian is off serving with the army somewhere," Peter objected. He thought Jacob was jumping to an unwarranted conclusion simply because he had wanted vengeance against Damian for so long. "As Antony said, no troops have been here in months."

"Think about it. Whoever did this didn't just drop his sword in haste. You heard Rebecca. The sword was carefully balanced across the top of the crib—it was left intentionally, like someone wanted us to find it."

"I agree," Antony said. "It didn't appear to have been left behind accidentally."

Jacob turned to Peter. "Earlier you said that you felt Naomi wouldn't just pack up and leave. I thought you were wrong, but maybe she's out to retaliate against us because she knows she's lost the battle over the estate."

"Slow down, I'm lost." Antony held up a hand toward Jacob. "You just said you thought this Damian character was the guilty party. Now you think your sister is behind this?"

"My guess is, they're in this together," Jacob said.

The sinking feeling that Peter had had earlier returned. He had been worried that Naomi would not give up easily, and he knew that she had never taken defeat well. But this was beyond anything he could have imagined.

Peter explained to Antony, who still looked perplexed, "If Damian has returned, it's likely that Naomi would know where he is. She's his stepmother."

Antony landed on the nearest settee, his head in his hands, as Peter continued, "Naomi's husband, Senator Mallus, is Damian's father."

Another thought was assaulting Peter's mind, and he spoke it out loud. "If this *is* Damian's sword, then . . ."

Jacob finished his brother's sentence. "That's right. It's the sword that murdered our mother."

Peter pushed the weapon away and stood up from the desk. His ankle was throbbing and he badly needed to lie down. He couldn't bear to think about his mother's death; he still missed her terribly. And now Victor was gone. It was incomprehensible.

" I'll tell you something else," Jacob said to Peter's retreating back. "If I'm right, and if Damian dares to harm that baby, I'll kill him with his own sword. And nobody is going to talk me out of it this time."

3

PETER NEVER MADE IT to his bedroom to lie down. As he left the library, he met Rebecca, who was outwardly calm but still visibly shaken.

"Marcellus is with Agatha," his sister said. "She's awake and trying to talk."

"Does Marcellus think she'll recover?"

"He said the wound wasn't as bad as it seemed, and he sounded reassuring." In spite of the great effort her words seemed to require, Rebecca touched his arm in concern. "You don't look well," she said.

"I'm all right, just hurting some. I'm much more worried about you. And Victor."

The tears Rebecca had been holding back finally started to spill over. "Why would somebody want to take my baby?" she asked in a voice that wavered with anguish. "Who would do a thing like that?"

Peter wrapped his arms around her, offering what comfort he could. "We'll find Victor," he said, "and we'll get him back." Peter certainly wasn't about to tell her Jacob's theory that Damian had taken the baby. He still thought Jacob was overreacting, and he didn't want to alarm Rebecca any more than she already was.

He led Rebecca into the main room on the lower floor of the house, the *triclinium*, where the family took their meals. Soon the servants would begin preparing to serve dinner, but the room was quiet for the moment. Peter stretched out on one of the sloping sofas, easing the pain in his badly misshapen ankle. Rebecca sat beside him, holding his hand, her shoulders trembling as her tears subsided.

A few minutes later Marcellus came to find them. "We moved Agatha to her quarters," he told Rebecca, "but she needs to rest quietly. Perhaps you could look after her baby for the time being; Aurora is fussing for her mother."

Rebecca hesitated for a moment, then said, "Of course. I'll move Aurora into my room." She gave Peter's hand a squeeze as she stood to leave. "Did Agatha say anything?" Rebecca asked. "Does she know who did this?"

Marcellus paused slightly before he answered. "She saw the man, but she didn't know who he was."

When Rebecca left the room, Marcellus sat down on one of the other sofas. His jaw was set in a grim line.

"What is it you didn't want to say in front of Rebecca?" Peter asked.

"Agatha got a good look at her attacker. Her description sounded familiar—too familiar." He paused, shook his head, then stared at the floor as if carefully inspecting the elaborate pattern in the mosaic tile. "I don't know. Maybe I'm jumping to conclusions."

"Jacob is convinced he knows the attacker's identity just by looking at the sword," Peter said. "However, I'm afraid he's letting his imagination run wild."

Marcellus looked up. "Agatha mentioned a sword. What about it?"

"It's army. Tenth Legion."

"Tenth Legion?" Marcellus repeated, and Peter nodded yes.

From the look on the other man's face, Peter knew the retired army officer had reached the same conclusion his brother had: Damian.

"I don't think it's a coincidence," Marcellus said. "My instincts tell me Jacob isn't imagining things."

Peter rubbed his eyes wearily. *His* instincts told him they were about to have a confrontation with Naomi. And if he'd thought the last encounter with his sister had been unpleasant, he knew that it would be nothing compared to this one.

✝

Rebecca balanced the nine-month-old on her hip while she walked. Several times she had tried to place Aurora in the crib, but the infant had wailed so forlornly that Rebecca gave up the effort.

Why did Marcellus have to ask me *to take care of Agatha's baby?* she wondered. Perhaps he had thought it would take her mind off the kidnapping. Instead, every time Aurora cried, Rebecca thought about what had happened to Victor and worried whether someone was comforting *her* son when he cried for his mother. Just when she had almost conquered her unidentified fear—the vague sense she'd been harboring that some other catastrophe was about to befall them—this had happened. And now each pitiful little cry of another woman's child brought a knifelike pain to her heart.

It was impossible to concentrate on consoling Aurora when her own baby was gone, Rebecca decided; she would find someone else to care for the child overnight. But as she started to leave the room, she recalled how Agatha had been injured trying to protect Victor, and she felt a twinge of guilt. She reached for the door and then stopped.

You're stronger than this, Rebecca told herself, shifting Aurora to the other hip. *You can do this one thing for a woman who tried to save your child.*

The baby nestled against Rebecca now, her ragged little sobs diminishing as Rebecca patted her back and tried to soothe her. In days past she had occasionally been able to coax a shy smile out of the tot, but most of the time her large gray eyes held a solemn expression; even at such a young age Aurora was a very serious child.

"Don't be sad, little one," Rebecca said. "Everything will be all right." It was more of a prayer than a statement.

She wondered if Agatha, like her daughter, had been somber as a girl. Rebecca didn't know Agatha that well; she had not been part of the congregation before Rebecca had left home. She had found their newest maid to be a pleasant person. Mostly Agatha was quiet, respectful, hardworking, and private. Of course, she was a servant, so that would be considered appropriate behavior; but Rebecca was used to more of a family relationship with the household staff.

Many of the family's servants, like their former steward, Servius, had helped raise her. They had always been a part of Rebecca's life, and she missed them now. Most of the household staff had been believers, and the majority of them had been sentenced to Devil's Island at the same time Rebecca had.

Six weeks ago, when Rebecca had returned, the changes had been jolting: not only were her mother and father gone, but she no longer saw other familiar faces around the house. She was home again, yet everything was completely different.

Rebecca tried putting Aurora in the crib again, but she immediately started whimpering.

"You miss Victor too, is that it?" Rebecca asked, remembering that Agatha often put the two babies in the crib together. It was an oversized crib that had originally been built for her twin brothers, then it had been Rebecca's.

She also recalled that Aurora was getting teeth, which was probably why the baby was crying now, and it was why Aurora had not been in the crib with Victor when the kidnapper entered the house. When Antony had questioned the servants earlier, one of them had said that Aurora had been fussy all afternoon, and Agatha had taken her out to the garden for someone else to watch so Victor could go to sleep. Then when Agatha had gone back upstairs to check on Victor, she had encountered the intruder.

What if the kidnapper intended to take Aurora and got Victor by mistake? Rebecca suddenly wondered. Rebecca didn't know anything about Agatha's former husband or his family. What if one of them had wanted to steal Agatha's baby?

She immediately felt guilty for such a thought. It was useless to speculate, she told herself, and she should be grateful that only one child was abducted and not both of them.

No one had cleared the room after Marcellus had examined

Agatha, and now Rebecca noticed a cup of *mulsum* on a tray near the bed. She poured some fresh water into a small basin and added a few drops of the honey-sweetened wine to it. Then she soaked one end of a clean handkerchief, in the liquid and gave it to the fussy infant to suck on. Aurora settled down, and after a few minutes fell asleep, one plump little fist resting against a damp cheek.

Earlier, Rebecca had asked for a maid to bring dinner to her room. She wasn't hungry at all and knew she wouldn't be able to eat more than a few bites, but she also knew she had to eat something. She had to keep her strength up, for Victor's sake.

Instead of a maid, however, it was Jacob who knocked on her door to deliver the meal. He was wearing a cloak over his tunic, as if he were about to leave the house. It would soon be dark outside, however, so if Jacob were leaving, it could only be for an important reason. Perhaps he intended to search for Victor.

"Are you going somewhere?" she asked.

Jacob sat the serving tray down and looked at her for a moment, evidently choosing his words carefully. "We think we may know where Victor is," he said.

"Where?" Rebecca's heart soared with hope.

Again Jacob paused before speaking—not a trait he was given to. "I'm not sure exactly where," he said, "but based on Agatha's description, we have an idea of who might have done this. So we'll start from there."

"Just let me find someone to watch Aurora, then I'll get my cloak and be ready to go."

"You can't go!" Jacob blurted out as Rebecca rushed toward the door.

Rebecca stopped suddenly and turned to face him. "Why not?" she demanded, hands on her hips. "He's my son, and he needs me."

"But you're a . . ." Jacob caught himself before he finished the thought.

"I'm what? A woman?" Rebecca stared up at her brother, angry at his patronizing tone.

"Well . . . yes . . . and it might be dangerous."

"And you think Devil's Island wasn't?" At the moment Rebecca didn't care about potential danger; all she could think of was that she wanted her baby.

Jacob looked flustered when she didn't back down. "That's beside the point," he said. "Look, we're wasting time arguing. I've already had to talk Peter into staying. He wanted to go with us to Naomi's, but it truly could be dangerous, and if we had to make a run for it, what would he do?"

"Naomi? You think *she* did this?" Rebecca took a step backward, stunned.

"Rebecca . . ." Jacob sighed in frustration and ran his hands through his thick black hair.

So that's what he had been trying to avoid telling her. Jacob thought Naomi was involved in Victor's kidnapping.

"Just stay put. Please," Jacob said as he turned to leave. "I have to go now. Antony and Marcellus are waiting for me."

Rebecca caught his arm. "You didn't answer me. Do you think Naomi put someone up to stealing my baby?"

"That's what we're going to find out," he said, grim determination lining his face. Jacob paused at the door. "I won't rest until we get Victor back. I promise you that, Rebecca."

When Jacob left she stared at the door, then she tucked the blanket around Aurora and sat down on the bed. *My own sister.*

✝

Two hours later Rebecca snuffed out the lamp and tried to sleep. She had managed to eat some of her dinner, then she had paced the floor and prayed, pleading with God for the safe return of her son.

With heightened senses, she strained to hear every sound, alternately thinking that the least noise must be Jacob and the others returning, then wondering if an intruder had managed to enter the villa. Gradually the large house grew quiet, and Rebecca's mind finally gave up the struggle to stay alert.

Her sleep was not peaceful, however. Victor's disappearance invaded her dreams in disturbing images as Rebecca groped her way through an endless series of dim caves, searching desperately for her baby. She stumbled and fell, stumbled and fell, as she wandered through the cavernous realms of unreality on her frantic pursuit.

Finally, a beam of light appeared in the distance, and she recognized it as the entrance of the cave. She made her way toward the light and emerged into the bright sunshine, blinking at the vista that had greeted her every day of her life on Devil's Island: a rugged mountain peak with a sweeping view of the surrounding ocean.

Standing a few yards in front of her, staring out at the water, was a man. Even with his back toward her, Rebecca recognized him, and a profound mixture of relief and joy washed over her.

"Galen!"

At the sound of her voice he turned around, and Rebecca saw that her fiancé was holding Victor. She gasped. "Oh, Galen, you found him for me!"

"Yes," he said sadly, fixing his familiar, intense gaze on her. "But you know I can't keep him."

Before Rebecca could answer, Galen swiveled back toward the cliff and swung his arms in a wide arc, releasing Victor into the air. Rebecca watched helplessly as her baby sailed over the barren trees and plunged down, down, down toward the brilliant-blue water below.

She woke and sat straight up in bed, clutching the bedcovers, her heart pounding. For several long minutes Rebecca was barely able to breathe. The vivid image had been frightfully disturbing, but she was aware that that's all it was: a nightmare.

Rebecca knew Galen couldn't possibly have Victor; Naomi did. Galen was a gentle man, a complete stranger to violence; he would never kidnap her son, let alone throw him off a cliff.

Yet Galen had thrown away something cherished, something Rebecca had treasured for years . . .

4

REBECCA HAD JUST CELEBRATED her twelfth birthday when she decided it was God's will for her to marry Galen. Naomi's wedding the previous year was still fresh in her mind, and Rebecca adored her new brother-in-law, Crispin, who worked with their father in the shipping business. Ever since their wedding Rebecca had been praying that God would bring the right husband into her life. She was in no rush; she wanted to wait until she was eighteen, as Naomi had, even though many girls married at thirteen or fourteen.

Even now, Rebecca could remember the precise moment she knew Galen was the one. It happened the night he came up to her and smiled—a rarity in itself—and asked if he could sit beside her at the *agape* feast. Although she had known him for several years, she looked up now as if seeing him for the first time, registering every detail: the slight cleft in his chin, the whiteness of his evenly spaced teeth, the lock of straight jet-black hair that fell over his forehead, obscuring his brooding black eyes, which were ringed with long dark lashes. Something in her twelve-year-old mind said, "This is the one."

Galen was gifted; everyone knew it. And most of them admitted that his talent would someday surpass that of his father. But no one ever knew what Galen was thinking. His ability to express himself was found not in his voice but in his hands, as he deftly worked molten strands of silver and gold into shapes of graceful beauty.

And no one, except for Rebecca, ever knew what was in his heart. For some reason, which she could only attribute to God, she had always been able to communicate intuitively with the budding artisan, who, like her twin brothers, was two years older.

It took a while longer for Galen to realize they were meant to be together. The first time they had talked about it was two years later, when Rebecca was recovering from a serious illness. She had run a terribly high fever for days, and Galen had come to see her every afternoon, after he finished his work. As she began to get stronger, he would visit with her in the garden, sometimes sitting quietly beside her on one of the stone benches surrounding the central fountain, and sometimes making an effort at the kind of light-hearted conversation he knew she would enjoy. He described the various people who had come into the silversmith shop, and he made her laugh by imitating the accent of the Anatolian traders he'd overheard in the *agora*.

Rebecca had learned that with Galen, what he didn't say was as important as what he did say—more so, perhaps. One day she knew something was on his mind. She could tell by the intense look in his eyes when he thought she wasn't watching him.

"I had an offer for a big job," he told her when she finally decided to pry into his secret. "But I turned it down."

That's what I would have done too."

Galen pushed away the long shock of hair that habitually fell across his forehead as he told her about the temple official who had wanted to commission new serving pieces for the banquet hall at the Temple of Artemis. "It would have meant a lot of money,," he said, since I hope to be married someday, I've started thinking about what it would take to support a wife."

Rebecca suddenly felt flushed, and it had nothing to do with her recent fever. She was proud of his principal decision and intrigued by his mention of marriage.

"Lucrative jobs like that are hard to come by," he continued, "so it was naturally tempting." Galen looked away quickly, staring into the fountain. When he spoke, his voice could barely be heard over the gentle roar of cascading water. "Especially when the girl I want to marry comes from a very wealthy family. I could never provide the kind of life she's used to living."

"Perhaps material things don't matter to her as much as you think they do. Perhaps love and commitment are much more important." This time Rebecca reached over and pushed back the hair that had already fallen over his eyebrows. "You should ask her about that sometime."

He looked up and saw her smile, and there was no mistaking the happiness in his expression. "That's good advice," he said.

†

She had intended to let him be the one to bring up the topic again, but several days after their conversation her father had received news that one of his ships had been lost at sea, and Crispin along with it. Rebecca felt deeply for Naomi, who had lost her husband after only three years of marriage. And it made her consider her feelings for Galen even more carefully.

After several days of dropping hints—all in vain—she had finally confronted the issue directly. And she had gone all the way to the silversmith shop to do it.

When she entered, Galen was putting away the hammers and tongs and other implements of his profession. She regretted not arriving a few minutes earlier; she loved watching him work. However, she had wanted to time her visit so they would have a chance to talk.

"Rebecca, what are you doing here?" Galen scowled as he pulled the heavy work apron over his head and hung it on a peg.

"Is it all right?" she asked quickly. "I . . . I thought you'd be glad to see me." Had she come at a bad time? Why was he upset?

"Of course I'm glad. It's just that you've been sick recently, and it's an awfully long walk from your house to Harbor Street." His face relaxed in a near smile. "I was worried about you, that's all."

"I'm fine now—I needed the walk. I haven't been anywhere in

two weeks." She exhaled in relief. "But I am a little winded. Perhaps I should sit down."

"Yes, but not in here. It's too hot."

The fires, used to heat precious metals until they were pliable, had been extinguished, but it was still quite warm in the shop. Galen guided her outside and they strolled toward the waterfront, stopping to buy some fruit from one of the vendor stalls lining the colonnade.

Rebecca loved the varied noises and smells of the marketplace. Many of the merchants had already closed for the day and most of the pedestrians were headed away from the center of the city.

They found an unoccupied bench near the river and watched a cargo ship dock while they ate their snack. When the silence had deepened beyond her endurance, Rebecca prodded Galen.

"The other day," she began, "when you said there was this wealthy girl you wanted to marry . . ." She hesitated, hoping he would pick up the cue, but he just looked at her, patiently waiting. "Anyway, I said that maybe money wasn't that important to her."

She paused again, and still he remained silent. "I know it's only been a few days," she continued, "but you haven't mentioned it again, and, well, with everything that's happened, I keep thinking . . ." This time she paused not for his reply but to summon her courage for the question that really mattered.

"Galen, am I that girl?"

A slow, deep smile parted his lips and a hint of amusement flashed in his eyes. "Of course. I thought you knew, Rebecca."

"I did. Or I thought I did. I mean, I usually know what you're thinking." She fidgeted with her tunic, arranging the skirt in folds. "I guess I just needed to hear it from you, that's all."

"Yes," he repeated. "You are the girl I want to marry."

Rebecca was silent then, basking in the overwhelming relief she felt at his words and the happy sight of his smile. But then a new concern stirred her, and since she'd gone this far, she decided she might as well take things a step further.

"Have you talked to your father about it?" she asked. According to custom, Galen's father should be the one to approach her father about the union.

Galen's smile vanished. "I've talked to him about it."

"Is he opposed to it?"

"No. But he's not enthusiastic about it, either. He doesn't think your father would find me suitable."

"Because your family is not as wealthy as ours?" That was the obstacle he had implied earlier, when he talked to her in the garden.

"We're not even close. No family is as wealthy as yours."

"That's beside the point," she said. "If you follow that line of thinking, then there would never be a suitable husband for me."

"Then I guess the question is, *would* your father approve?"

"My father wants what's best for me," she said confidently. "And you're what's best for me, Galen." Her voice wavered with the emotion of saying the words out loud. "I've loved you for a long time."

"I've loved you longer."

The statement surprised Rebecca into complete silence.

"You didn't know that?" he asked. "And here I thought you always knew what I was thinking."

She looked at him in amazement as he continued, "I've been in love with you since almost the first day I met you."

"But that would have been . . ." She finally found her voice, but her mind wasn't quite working yet. "I was just eight years old when your family started coming to our house for church."

"And I was ten, and not the least bit interested in girls at the time. But then I'd never seen a girl as beautiful as you. And then I discovered you were as sweet as you were beautiful. I think it took me two years just to work up the courage to speak to you. And when I did, and you smiled at me, I thought my life had ended—or that it had just begun. I was so confused, I wasn't sure which; I just knew my life would never be the same." He reached for her hand, bringing it to his lips. "And it hasn't."

Rebecca left her hand in his after he kissed it. She couldn't remember when Galen had said so many words at once. And what sweet words they were.

"I'll speak to my father again," he told her.

†

When she was seventeen, Rebecca and Galen had received their parents' blessing. But by then the Tenth Legion had arrived in Ephesus. That autumn had been a time of great uncertainty, but Rebecca and Galen continued to make plans for a wedding the following spring. They promised that nothing, not even the threat of persecution, would ever separate them. Of the two of them, Rebecca had thought it would be Galen who faced the greater danger; his shop was in the crowded marketplace that lined the main avenue of the commercial district, and soldiers were often in the area asking questions.

Of course, it turned out that she was the one who became a prisoner for her faith.

On Devil's Island her dream of marrying and raising a family with Galen had been utterly destroyed, and she had had to come to terms with the grievous loss of that dream.

But then a miracle happened. Almost one year into her life sentence, Rebecca had been released.

As she sailed home to Ephesus, Rebecca had dared to let God rekindle her dream. She couldn't wait to see Galen.

When she got home and got a good look at herself in the mirror, however, she was horrified. Her well-proportioned curves had turned into bony angles. She was thin and gaunt, her eyes sunken. Her once lovely hair was lackluster, her hands were callused and rough.

But it wasn't just the changes in her appearance that concerned her. Rebecca also had a baby, and she didn't know how her fiancé would react. Could he accept Victor and learn to love him? What if Galen hadn't even waited for her? What if he had given up hope and married someone else?

Word of their return had spread quickly. Just before noon on the day following their arrival, Galen appeared at the villa. When the steward had told Rebecca that Galen was waiting for her in the garden, she was filled with joyous anticipation as well as a good deal of apprehension.

The low noise of the fountain covered the sound of her footsteps on the tiled walkway, and she approached without his notice. She stood to one side and took a moment just to look at him. If possible, Galen was more handsome than ever. And just as preoccupied. He was leaning forward, elbows on knees, staring intently into the fountain; but his eyes, she knew, were looking beyond the water, his subconscious mind creating objects that only he could see.

She walked into his field of vision and he slowly sensed her presence. " I closed the shop and rushed here as soon as I heard . . ." His voice trailed off when he looked up, and his eyes clouded over as he took in her appearance. "Oh, Rebecca."

He stood and reached for her and she fell against him, relieved. There had been love in his expression as well as shock. They clung to each other, both of them too overcome to speak.

After a while Rebecca pulled back, embarrassed. "I look awful," she said, patting her still-damp hair. She had pinned it up before it dried completely, not wanting anyone to see how unevenly she'd had to trim it to get rid of the impossibly tangled ends. "You look beautiful to me," he said gallantly. But Rebecca could see the pain in his eyes as he looked at her. The evidence of her suffering wounded him.

He asked her about it rather awkwardly, and she found for once that she couldn't talk about it. So she asked him questions instead, making him talk about his work, about the church.

After a few minutes, conversation with her fiancé began to seem more normal to her, and he appeared to have recovered somewhat from the initial shock of seeing her.

Tears filled her eyes as he held her hand and told her how much he had missed her. This was what she had waited for, hoped for, dreamed for—and God had brought her back for this.

Finally she was able to speak about Devil's Island, but only the less painful things. She told him about John's glorious vision of Christ, and how the Apostle had called her "Scribe" because she worked for months making copies of his letters for the churches in Asia. And she made him laugh about the previous occupants of their cave, who had remained frequent visitors even after John had tried to forcefully evict them: two rats he had named Damian and Domitian.

As their laughter died down, she thought she heard Victor crying. She looked up and saw Marcellus standing on the colonnaded walkway. He was holding the baby. "I'm sorry to interrupt," he said, "but Victor's hungry. It's time for you to feed him."

The stricken look on Galen's face pierced her heart. She hadn't had a chance to tell him about Victor yet; they'd only been talking for a short while. But when she looked at the sundial, she discovered they had been sitting on the garden bench for almost two hours. Rebecca's heart sank. She should have prepared Galen for the news; finding out this way was all wrong.

She glanced at her squalling son and then back at her fiancé. "We still have a lot to talk about," she said.

"It appears so." Galen's face had turned to stone but his dark eyes flashed, and she sensed a hint of anger brewing beneath the surface. She didn't blame him. How could he help but feel betrayed? But he would understand as soon as she explained it.

"I'll be right there," she called to Marcellus.

"Galen, don't think the worst until you've heard my story." She stood and put a hand on his shoulder. "Will you stay for dinner? We can talk again afterward."

He nodded morosely. "Of course."

†

As customary, the main meal of the day had been served at mid-afternoon. For Rebecca, who had been eating all her meals seated on the hard ground in front of an open fire, it now seemed extraordinary to recline on comfortable sofas while servants scurried around the *triclinium* waiting on the family and their guests.

That day the diners had tried to maintain an air of celebration, yet the atmosphere was strained. Jacob and Peter had been glad to see each other yesterday but were already at odds twenty-four hours after their reunion. Marcellus was a stranger to everyone except Rebecca, but he managed to make polite conversation with Quintus, the second-in-command at the shipping business—not an easy feat, as Quintus was a man of few words. He was, however, a man of great appetite, something no one would guess from his long, lean build.

Galen, who had positioned himself on the sofa to her right, was subdued. He had never been a brilliant conversationalist, and now it was almost impossible to draw him out, even though Quintus made a vain attempt. Rebecca had such butterflies in her stomach, she found it difficult to eat.

After dinner Rebecca and Galen went for a walk, and without really intending to, she gravitated toward the grassy knoll just west of the villa. It was a pleasant spot with several large shade trees and an elliptical-shaped structure that had been set into the hillside, its outer facade of polished Italian marble extending in a wide arc.

"I haven't been to the mausoleum since I got back," Rebecca had said. "Do you mind?" She motioned toward the heavy vaulted doors, and Galen propped them open.

Entering the family tomb, Rebecca did not feel uneasy as she once would have. Instead, she felt oddly comforted.

It was dim inside, but enough light filtered in through the open doors that her eyes gradually adjusted. In that aspect, it was not unlike the cave she had lived in for the past year. The mausoleum was much more luxurious, of course, with its smooth, gleaming walls. And much more fragrant. The aroma of spices permeated the thick air.

She walked over to the matching pair of carved limestone ossuaries that bore the names of her mother and father. The one marked *Elizabeth* contained her mother's bones. Peter had moved her remains from the funeral bier, which had been placed in a niche in the inner wall, to the ossuary just the previous week.

"If I'd had any idea you would be coming home, I would have waited," he'd told Rebecca earlier.

But he couldn't have known, and it had been time to complete the burial process. Most of the Empire had adopted the Roman practice of cremation. But the Christians, following the Jewish custom, prepared the body of the deceased for burial and placed it in a crypt. After a year, when the body had decomposed, the bones were gathered and stored in an ossuary, a rectangular box about three feet long.

Rebecca touched the cool stone and whispered brokenly, "Goodbye, Mother." She had witnessed her mother's murder but not her funeral; by the time Elizabeth was buried, Rebecca was on Patmos. Now, she blinked once but didn't cry. The sadness was not as overwhelming as she had expected, perhaps because she had had a year to grieve. Or perhaps because Galen was with her now. Rebecca reached for his hand and he twined his fingers through hers.

Lifting her free hand, Rebecca lightly ran her fingers over the raised letters of her father's name. His ossuary, she knew, was empty. Because he had been killed as part of a grand public entertainment at the Colosseum in Rome, his friends had not been allowed to reclaim his mutilated body; it had been dumped in the Tiber River. Even though there had been no body to bury, no funeral with friends and family to mourn for him, Peter had prepared an ossuary to honor their father's memory. She loved her brother for that gesture.

"He faced death bravely," Rebecca said.

Galen had squeezed her hand. "I know. I heard the story."

After a lingering moment of silence, she said, "I'm ready to talk."

They walked back outside, and Rebecca leaned against the cool marble while Galen closed the cumbersome doors. When he came and stood beside her, she began, "There's been so much death around me. Victor was like a gift of life.

"It didn't seem like much of a gift at first. He was conceived on the worst night of my life, a night I barely survived, and most of the time I was carrying him I felt I was walking through 'the valley of the shadow of death'—although I never left the mountaintop cave where I was hiding."

She had told him then about being raped. She didn't tell him all the gruesome details but neither did she gloss over the facts.

When she was finished, Galen turned his face to the wall and wept. Rebecca came up behind him, wrapped her arms around his waist, and pressed her cheek against his back. She was touched by the depth of his sorrow for her.

"It's all right," she had said. *"I'm* all right. I survived."

In a moment he lifted her hands so he could turn and look at her. He leaned forward and she thought he was going to kiss her, then he bent down and simply placed his forehead against hers. He put his hands on her waist but didn't embrace her, and she sensed Galen was struggling to comprehend what had happened to her and how it had changed both of their lives.

He didn't say anything for so long, it began to worry her. "Do you still love me?" she finally asked.

"Rebecca, I could never stop loving you."

†

Galen might not have stopped loving her, but he had grown more and more distant. He didn't come to see her the rest of the week. When he joined the Christians who met at the villa for worship on the Lord's Day, Galen had greeted Rebecca affectionately and sat by her. Several times he acted as if he wanted to say something but couldn't quite get the words out. He left when the others did, so she never got to speak with him privately.

The same thing had happened the following week, and the week after that. A few times her brothers had asked why Galen hadn't been around much, and Rebecca found herself making excuses that he was busy. But the truth was, she didn't know why Galen was keeping his distance, and it was killing her. She alternated between being angry with him and being wounded by his absence. She thought of a number of errands that would take her right past his shop, but pride kept her from seeking him out. He would have to come to terms with the changes in their relationship in his own way, in his own time.

A month after Rebecca's return, she had finally been propelled to action when her mother's longtime friend, Helena, had cornered her one Sunday. "When are you and Galen getting married?" Helena asked bluntly. Rebecca didn't have an answer, and she realized just how much she needed one. She *deserved* an answer.

She found Galen in the atrium as he was leaving and managed to get him alone. "I need to talk to you," she said. "Now."

He looked trapped, and she felt a brief moment of sympathy. It passed quickly. He had treated her badly.

"I have some questions, and I deserve some answers," she said when they had walked outside, away from the others.

"Yes, you do." He glanced at her briefly, then looked away. "I just don't know if I have any answers yet."

Find some soon, she was tempted to say. Instead she took a deep breath. This was definitely one time she didn't want to have to pull Galen's thoughts out of him, especially because she was more than a little afraid of what those thoughts might be. But she'd gotten to the point at which not knowing was worse than knowing.

"You said you'd never stop loving me, Galen. What kind of love is it when you don't want to be alone with me, when you won't even talk to me?"

"You know I'm not very good at talking sometimes."

"That's not an answer; it's an excuse. You may not have been the most talkative person, but you were always good company—and you were always here, with me, every spare minute you had." Bittersweet thoughts of those happy times flooded her mind, but she didn't stop to dwell on the memories. "You haven't been to see me since that first night after I returned, and when you are here for church, you try to avoid me. Why, Galen? Why?"

He pushed his hair back with both his hands, holding it off his forehead for a moment, then letting it drop with a sigh. "Every time I look at you, I think about how much I love you, then I think about what he did to you, and I just can't get over it. I think about him touching you, and it makes my skin crawl. I can't stand the thought of your being with another man—"

"I wasn't 'with' another man, Galen. I was raped!"

"I know."

"But do you understand that? It wasn't an act of love. He touched me because he assaulted me."

"I understand that. I just don't know how to deal with it, how to keep from thinking about it, how to . . ." He looked down at the ground, and Rebecca knew there was something else he wasn't saying. Something that bothered him a great deal.

"What else?" she asked.

"You have his child," he said without looking up.

Rebecca lost all the air in her lungs as suddenly as if he'd punched her. "Yes, I have a child," she said slowly. "And I love my son dearly." She took another deep breath and held it an extra beat before asking, "Is that something else you can't get over?"

Galen didn't reply, and Rebecca realized his silence was an answer in itself.

"You don't want to marry me now." She didn't even bother to phrase it as a question.

He reached for her hand, and the wistful look in his eyes nearly broke her heart. "Maybe I just need more time, Rebecca."

"Or maybe you need more love."

✝

As she thought about it now, Rebecca realized that she should have reached that conclusion earlier. She always had understood Galen better than he understood himself.

He did love her; perhaps he always would. But Galen had idealized her. When she returned from Devil's Island, she no longer fit the ideal, and he was unable to accept a less-than-perfect version of love.

Rebecca punched the pillow and lay back down, trying to get back to sleep after her nightmare.

It didn't matter now. None of it did. The only thing that mattered was Victor.

Galen was gone, out of her life. She'd had a dream and lost it, then found it and lost it again. Her heart was broken, but it would mend. And when it did, she wouldn't ever make the mistake of falling in love again. The risk of losing another dream was simply too painful. No man was ever going to accept the fact that she'd been raped and borne a child, and she might as well face that now.

Rebecca decided it was God's will for her to remain single. She would devote herself to a ministry of works, and to her son—just as soon as she got him back.

5

"THIS IS NOT a social visit," Jacob said, cutting off Naomi's patently insincere greeting.

From the moment she had swept into the room in one of her typically grand entrances, Jacob had known she was expecting them. Naomi did not look the least bit surprised. She did manage to look regal, however, even though she had already unpinned her hair for the evening. Voluminous waves of deep auburn fell over her shoulders, which were draped in an emerald-green *stola* that sparkled with threads of spun gold. Jacob couldn't help thinking of what her tunic and *stola* must have cost; Naomi had always taken great pride in her wardrobe.

"Then tell me why you and your . . . friends . . . are here at this late hour." As she spoke, Naomi looked Marcellus and Antony up and down, finally dismissing them with an irritated look and a wave of her hand, as if she were shooing away a couple of unwelcome flies at a banquet table.

"I think you know why we're here," Jacob said testily. It was late, he was tired, and he was angry. They'd walked the better part of an hour—down Mount Koressos, across Ephesus, and up the hill past the Temple of Artemis—to get to the house Naomi had rented. If there hadn't been a full moon, they would never have been able to see the way. He also resented Naomi's arrogance, and he was in no mood to play games. A life was at stake. Jacob was almost certain she knew who had abducted his nephew, and he was determined to drag the truth out of her. His voice rose with his temper. "I want some answers, Naomi. And I want them *now*."

Antony stepped forward, positioning himself between Jacob and Naomi, and introduced himself. "I represent the family in legal matters—" he began.

Naomi interrupted him. "I'm part of the family and you don't represent me."

"You are *not* part of our family." Jacob was almost shouting now.

"Your sister's child is missing," Antony continued diplomatically, "and we simply wanted to find out if you knew anything about it."

"I didn't even know Rebecca was married." Naomi's mouth curved in a slight smile.

"You cold-hearted—" Jacob had had enough. "Where is Victor?" he demanded. "Where is the baby?" He started to lunge toward the conniving woman—he no longer thought of her as his sister—but Marcellus held him back.

Jacob was angry enough to throttle her, and Naomi must have realized it. She blanched and took a step backward.

"Calm down," she said, "and I'll tell you what you want to know."

The slave who had let them in suddenly reappeared in the doorway. Naomi said, "It's all right, Lepidus. You may wait in the other room. If I need you, I'll call." The tall, well-built man bowed almost imperceptibly toward his mistress, then backed out of the room.

"Start talking," Jacob said. He shook off Marcellus's restraining hand, nodding to indicate he had himself under control.

Naomi sat down, carefully arranged the folds of her skirt, and took a deep breath. For the first time, Jacob realized that she was not quite as collected as she had first appeared. Beneath the cool surface, she was deeply troubled.

"You're right," she said. "I do know what happened." When Jacob gave her another murderous look, she quickly added, "The baby is not here. But I can assure you that he's safe and well cared for."

The news that Victor was all right brought Jacob a bit of relief, but it raised as many questions as it answered. "Where is he? Who took him? Who has him now?"

Again, Marcellus put a friendly hand on Jacob's shoulder and squeezed, urging him to slow down. "You can imagine how worried Rebecca is," Marcellus said to Naomi. "Please tell us where we can find the child, and we won't disturb you any longer."

She did not look at Marcellus but continued staring at her brother. "That information will cost you."

Cost me? Jacob wondered. He should have known that whatever information Naomi had, it would come at a price. He started to verbally assault her, then held back, gritting his teeth in frustration. The important thing was getting Victor back; after that he would say whatever he wanted to Naomi.

Assuming a polite but official tone, Antony said, "I suggest you tell us where he is immediately. You have no legal right to the child."

"But I do have a legal right to my share of our father's estate."

Jacob was outraged. "Father disowned you."

"Father was a traitor who forfeited his entire estate to Caesar."

"You're the traitor!"

Jacob would gladly have continued the shouting match with his sister, but Antony again intervened. "The court will decide how to settle the estate," he told Naomi, "but I think you know that you're on very shaky legal grounds. It's unlikely you will ever see a *denarius* of the family fortune."

"Give up, Naomi." Jacob managed to say the words without shouting, but bitterness kept a bite in his voice. "You have a piece of paper signed by a dead emperor—a dictator who was despised and has now been dishonored. A worthless piece of paper, that's all you have."

"You're wrong. I have something else." Naomi had regained her composure. Her smile was malicious, and it made him go cold inside. "I have Victor."

She stood again and this time looked directly at Antony. "Tell the family you represent," she said, heavily emphasizing the word *family*, "that I will drop my legal claim against the estate, and I will see that Victor is returned to his mother. But I want something in return."

"And what is that?" Antony asked.

"I want the shipping business."

Jacob exploded. "You want *what?*"

"I want control of the shipping business. You and Peter and Rebecca can have all the rest. The villa here, the one in Rome. The vineyard in Gaul, the olive groves on the Mediterranean coast. You can have all the bank accounts. I'm sure there are substantial amounts stashed away—more than enough for all of you to live in luxury the rest of your lives. All I want is to run the shipping business."

"You're out of your mind." Jacob could not believe what he had just heard, even though he knew Naomi was right: even without the shipping income they would have no financial worries. But money was not the issue. The shipping empire had defined his father. It was quintessentially Abraham, and the thought of Naomi seizing it—by kidnapping Abraham's grandson, of all things—was beyond comprehension.

"And you're out of time." Naomi turned and called for Lepidus. He returned, accompanied by another slave. "Please see these gentlemen out," she instructed them.

"Go home," she told Jacob. "Talk it over with the *family*. You can let me know tomorrow. Or the next day. Or whenever you finally decide you want Rebecca's baby back."

Naomi turned and started to walk away. "You'll never get away with this," Jacob said.

She left without responding.

He looked at the others, wondering what they should do next. He was so furious, he could barely resist shoving Lepidus and the other slave out of the way and charging after Naomi. *We outnumber them,* Jacob thought. *Three of us to two of them.* The second man was not as big and foreboding as Lepidus, but he looked plenty tough.

Jacob's fingers were itching for a fight; Marcellus and Antony, however, shepherded him toward the door, the two slaves following to make sure the trio left.

Once outside, Jacob started to say something but Antony shushed him. When they'd gone a distance from the house, they stopped.

"I know you wanted to tear into them," Antony said, "but it wouldn't have accomplished anything."

"I won't let her get away with this," Jacob replied in an angry whisper.

"I'm not saying you have to. But there's no sense risking our lives without knowing where Victor is."

Marcellus said, "I listened for any sounds that would indicate a baby was nearby, but I didn't hear anything. Do you think she was telling the truth about Victor not being there?"

"I don't know," Jacob answered. "But I'm not taking any chances. I think we should stay and watch the house."

For the next few minutes, the three men talked it over and made a plan to spy on Naomi, in the hope she would lead them to the kidnapper.

"I'll stay with Jacob for now," Marcellus said to Antony. "You go back to the villa and get some rest. Let Rebecca know that Victor is safe—at least, we think he is."

"All right. I'll meet you back here in the morning and we'll trade places."

As Antony left, Marcellus and Jacob stepped off the road and into the shadows, trying to remain unseen as they walked back to Naomi's house. They had already agreed that the stand of juniper trees just a few yards from the front door would be their hiding place, and they crept toward it.

Jacob crouched behind one of the trees and stretched out on the ground, drawing his cloak around him. He lay on his stomach, watching the house and thinking back over the meeting. Even though she had obviously been expecting them, there had been something odd about Naomi's behavior. *Not that her behavior could ever be considered normal,* he reflected. Still, it puzzled him.

Gradually his thoughts drifted from Naomi to Damian. Jacob

knew he had to be somewhere nearby. With every thought of Damian, Jacob seethed.

Over and over his mind returned to the biblical accounts of the cities of refuge. They had been part of the ancient Hebrew legal code. If a man committed manslaughter—that is, if he killed another person accidentally— then he could flee to one of six designated cities for protection from those who would otherwise seek vengeance and bring upon him a disproportionate punishment. But if he intended to kill someone—if he committed murder—then he would receive the death penalty. "The avenger of blood himself shall put the murderer to death," Scripture said.

Jacob's first goal was to find his nephew. But after that, when Victor was back in his mother's arms, Jacob had a score to settle with Damian. He knew John's feelings on the matter. He knew what Rebecca and Peter and Marcellus thought. He knew they no longer lived under the ancient Hebrew legal code but the vaunted Roman system of justice. And he knew, as John so often quoted, that vengeance belongs to the Lord.

Jacob knew all of that, but he still could not help thinking of himself as the avenger of blood. He vowed silently, *I will make sure there is no refuge for you, Damian.*

†

"I can't believe you did this to me." Naomi rubbed her temples. Her head was throbbing after the nerve-wracking meeting with her brother.

Damian strutted back and forth in front of the chair where she sat. "You certainly weren't getting anything done on your own," he said.

"So without even consulting me, you kidnap my sister's baby. And then you just show up here this afternoon with him." She didn't bother to disguise her disbelief or her profound irritation.

"As I told you earlier—you need leverage. Something to bargain with."

Naomi silently acknowledged that her case needed bolstering; she hadn't needed Jacob's lawyer to tell her that. But she had certainly never imagined that a squalling infant would be the solution. She'd gone along with Damian's unannounced plan—what else could she do when Jacob had shown up before she'd had time to think things through?—but she wasn't happy about it.

She wasn't happy about much of anything these days. Naomi missed Rome, and she missed her elderly husband. Lucius was attentive and devoted, even though, as a prominent senator, the demands on his time were enormous.

"And it worked," Damian continued. "Or it will. They'll do anything to get that baby back, you wait and see. Then you can have your little shipping business to run."

"And you can go back to Rome, or wherever the emperor sends you." That thought certainly appealed to her. Naomi could not abide the rude, conceited—not to mention cruel—soldier who had become her stepson. Before he arrived in Ephesus ten days ago, she had only met Damian once, and that was the day he'd forced her family to make the mandatory sacrifice to Caesar.

He was here now because Lucius had been unable to make the trip with her and had thought Damian would be helpful in pursuing her case. He might be useful, she admitted, but he was certainly distasteful, and she would be relieved when he was out of her life again.

"Perhaps I will leave then," he said, "although I have no assignment. The new emperor is not much enamored with my unique abilities." Damian's narrow eyes beaded in an amused yet ominous glare. "Or perhaps I'll stick around and make sure my son gets his share of your new business. I'll have to manage it for him, of course, until—"

"What?" Naomi could not have heard right. Surely that was not what he'd said. "Rebecca's baby is your son?"

"That's right. The boy is mine." Damian smiled, but it was not the expression of a proud father that creased his face. It was the oily smile of a greed-obsessed man whose behavior knew no boundaries.

Naomi did not shock easily, and she certainly had no scruples about manipulating a situation to her advantage. But somehow this kidnapping had crossed the line. Damian was not just deceitful, he had a decidedly barbaric streak—and he was the baby's father? Impossible.

With a shudder, Naomi thought of her sister. Rebecca would never have let him touch her willingly—not simply because he was repulsive, which he was. But he was the man Rebecca would hold responsible for her mother's death and her own suffering. Which meant, Naomi realized, that Damian had forced himself on Rebecca. And as much as Naomi disliked her family, as much as she wanted to wrench part of her father's fortune from them, that thought turned her stomach.

Naomi stood and approached Damian. He was barely taller than she was, and she pinned him now with an angry stare. "You neglected to tell me that important little detail."

"We didn't have time to get around to discussing fatherhood this afternoon," Damian said. "You had me too busy hunting down a wet nurse for the lad. I suppose we do need to keep him fed until we get what we want."

"I know what *I* want. I want that child, and you, out of my house."

Damian did not back down from her threatening stance. "Naomi, where are your maternal instincts?" he asked with pretended dismay. "Victor is not just your nephew; he's your grandson."

That thought sent him into peals of laughter. "You don't like the thought of being a grandmother, do you? You think you're much too young and beautiful."

"I don't like the thought of you being under my roof." She could dwell on the ironic fact that she was a grandmother at the age of twenty-five later. All she could think about now was getting rid of Damian. She should never have agreed to let Lucius send him to her.

"Besides, even if I go along with your scheme," she told him, "we can't keep the baby here. Jacob and his friends will continue looking for him, and you can be sure they'll come back. I was petrified the entire time they were here that the baby would cry and give us away. Then there would have been some kind of fight, and no telling what would have happened."

"I wouldn't have minded that. I owe your brother for a nasty knot on my head. He almost killed me once."

"You would have minded if they had managed to get Victor back. Or if he'd gotten hurt or killed in the process. Then your extortion scheme would have been over immediately."

They argued hotly for a while, then much to her relief, Damian finally agreed to leave. "I know somewhere I can take the child," he said. "Some place away from Ephesus, where Jacob and the others will never find him."

"Good. You can leave first thing in the morning."

"And you can continue negotiating with your family. They'll come around. But keep one thing in mind, Naomi." He reached out with an index finger and lifted her chin. "I'll be back to check on you. Don't disappoint me."

Naomi recoiled, slapping his hand away from her face. "Don't ever touch me again."

"And don't think of cutting me out. Like it or not, Naomi, we're partners now."

6

PETER STIFLED A YAWN. Antony had roused him and Rebecca from bed well before daylight to report what had happened at Naomi's. The three of them had gathered in the dining room, and like Rebecca, Peter was both relieved and dismayed to hear the lawyer's news.

"At least we know who took him," Antony said, "and that he's all right. She won't let anything happen to Victor—not if she's going to use him for negotiation."

"Thank God for that," Rebecca said, her relief expressed in a long exhalation that made her shoulders drop noticeably. "But I won't be able to rest until he's home with me."

"What do you think we should do next?" Peter asked.

Antony relayed their intent to watch the house and follow Naomi. "She could lead us to wherever Victor is. Or . . . " He hesitated, looking at Peter to gauge his reaction. "Or we could make some kind of offer, find a way to meet her demand—if that's what you want to do."

Lost in thought, Peter did not answer. He recalled the last time he had seen Naomi, the day she had arrived in Ephesus to try to claim the estate entirely for herself. When she had discovered that, for the very first time, she was unable to intimidate him, she had offered to share the estate with Peter, casually saying that since Jacob and Rebecca would never return from Devil's Island, the two of them could divide the assets. Infuriated at her callous dismissal of their brother and sister, not to mention her betrayal of their father, Peter had spurned Naomi's offer and ordered her off the premises. Just thinking about it now tied his stomach in knots.

"Absolutely not," Rebecca said quickly. "We can't cater to Naomi. She has gone against everything our family stands for." Then she sighed, and her voice lost its adamant tone as she asked, "But what will happen to Victor if we don't . . ."

"We could go to the authorities," Antony suggested, "although I'm not sure how much good it would do. Even though the persecution has ended, there are lingering hostilities toward Christians from some quarters. So I don't know if official help would be forthcoming, or how effective it would be. They're likely to view it as a mere family dispute and not want to get involved."

"I vowed I would not let Naomi so much as set foot in Father's office ever again," Peter said. "But if it means getting Victor back, well . . ."

Rebecca shook her head. "No, Peter. As much as I want my baby, you can't just hand over the business to Naomi. It wouldn't be right."

"I would never hand over the business completely," Peter said thoughtfully. "But we could offer her a compromise."

"What do you have in mind?" Antony asked.

"It's not really the money she wants," Peter said.

"She isn't after one of the largest businesses in the Empire?" Antony asked. "I find that hard to believe."

"That's not the ultimate issue with Naomi." Peter noticed Rebecca's raised eyebrows and explained, "Oh, she loves all the privileges of wealth, and she spends money as if every grain of sand on the seashore was a gold coin. But that's not why she wants the shipping business."

"Then what does she want?" Rebecca asked. "Is it just to torment us?"

"No. She wants control. Recognition. And she wants to prove Father was wrong."

"Wrong about what?" Rebecca frowned, obviously not following Peter's point.

"Naomi is bitter," he said, "because Father refused to consider her as his successor. She learned the business before Jacob and I were old enough to read and write, and she was inherently smarter at it than I'll ever hope to be. But she's a woman, and therefore Father never appreciated her business acumen. 'Women run households,' he once told her, 'not worldwide enterprises.'"

"I imagine that didn't set well with her," Rebecca acknowledged. "Naomi could never abide being told no."

"I almost—*almost*—felt sorry for her when she came back to Ephesus. She proposed splitting the business with me. 'We could work together,' she said. 'You could run the office here in Ephesus, and I'll run the office in Rome.'

"Of course, I figured she would try to make the Rome office the main headquarters for the business and turn Ephesus into just another branch office. And eventually she would try to cut me out altogether. So I wouldn't have any part of it." He turned to Antony. "I still don't like the idea one bit," Peter said, "but you asked if I would be willing to make an offer to Naomi. I guess that would be it. Perhaps she would settle for running the Rome office."

Antony contemplated the suggestion for a moment. "Jacob would have to agree to it. And Rebecca, of course."

Peter noted the way Antony's voice seemed to soften when he said Rebecca's name, yet he couldn't help wondering why Antony never looked directly at her when he spoke. Did he have some kind of problem with Rebecca?

"I'll do whatever you think is best," Rebecca said. "But I doubt Jacob will ever agree."

Peter turned his attention back to his sister. "He might if you asked him."

"I'll mention it to Jacob," Antony said, "and you can talk to him when he gets home." He stood and reached for his cloak, preparing to leave. "I should go now, in fact. I promised to spell Jacob and Marcellus first thing this morning; they've been watching Naomi's house all night."

"I'll recruit some others to help, as you requested—" Peter broke off as Marcellus entered, his cloak thrown back and his face red from exertion.

"I ran all the way here," he said, then stopped to catch his breath.

"What happened?" Peter was instantly worried.

"Where's Jacob?" Antony asked.

"Following Damian," Marcellus announced, still gulping for air.

"Damian?" Rebecca jumped to her feet. "What's going on?" she demanded. "I didn't know Damian was here."

"At daybreak," Marcellus said, "a carriage pulled up to the house." He unfastened his cloak and tossed it on one of the *triclinia*. "Shortly after that, Damian came out, followed by a woman. She was—"

"Was it Naomi?"

Just like a lawyer, Peter thought wryly as Antony spoke. Always interrupting with a question. Always probing the facts.

"No, she looked like a servant," Marcellus said. "Probably a wet nurse. She was carrying a baby."

"So Victor was there, after all." Antony blew out a long breath.

Rebecca gasped. "Damian has my baby?" She looked suddenly ill, and Peter moved to put an arm around her.

"They got into the carriage and drove off. Jacob and I followed, running as fast as we could. Naturally, we couldn't catch them, but we managed to run far enough to tell which road they were taking. They were headed north, out of the city."

Antony filled a goblet with water and handed it to Marcellus, who drained the goblet, then said, "Jacob left to find transportation, and I came here to tell you that he's going after Damian."

"Do you have any idea where they were going?" Peter asked. He tried to summon a mental picture of the road they would have taken, but since he seldom ventured farther than the office at the harbor, he wasn't familiar with the outlying areas.

"It was the highway that goes to Smyrna and on to Pergamum, although we don't know their destination. Jacob has probably gotten a horse by now, but I don't know if there's any way he can catch up with them."

"He will eventually. And I think you and I should follow him," Antony said to Marcellus. "I'll go into town and find a couple of horses for hire."

"I'll take care of that," Peter said. "My litter should be ready by now." When he had started working at the shipping office, Quintus had arranged for eight of the company's cargo handlers to arrive at the villa early each morning. They hoisted the canopied sedan's long poles and transported Peter through the hills to the harbor, then repeated the process at the end of the workday. With his lame ankle, Peter would never have been able to manage the long walk there and back each day. "When I get to the office," he said, "I'll send a couple of our delivery horses to you."

"No!" Everyone turned as Rebecca raised her voice. "Send a carriage instead," she instructed Peter. "I'm going with them."

After a startled moment when no one spoke, Antony asked, "Are you sure that's what you want to do? It's a long journey, and we may not even . . ." He paused briefly to rephrase his thought. "And we may have trouble finding the baby."

"My son needs his mother," Rebecca said, her shoulders squared in a determined stance, "and I intend to be there when you find him."

✝

It was past noon when Jacob reined in his horse and dismounted. He had reached the first of two halts between Ephesus and Smyrna. They were small outposts, located every dozen or so miles, where military couriers carrying official dispatches could change mounts. Over the centuries, the conquering legions of Rome had been supported by a vast corps of civil engineers. The partnership had resulted in a system of well-traveled roads that not only allowed for the movement of large numbers of troops but also linked the far reaches of the Empire commercially. At every mile along the fifty thousand miles of high-way and two hundred thousand miles of lesser paved and gravel roads, a round stone pillar marked the distance to the capital. Indeed, all roads eventually led to Rome.

Knowing he was at least an hour behind the kidnappers, Jacob had not intended to stop until his horse could go no farther. He had stopped now, however, because it had occurred to him that if Damian had wanted to stop for some reason, he would likely have done so at one of these army halts. Although, Jacob had noticed, Damian had not been wearing a uniform when he'd left Naomi's that morning. Had he quit the army? Perhaps he was simply on leave; tribunes often wore their own clothing when they were not serving a commission.

The soldiers told Jacob they had seen quite a few carriages on the road, but none of them had stopped at the outpost.

Jacob mounted again and continued riding toward Smyrna. He could not imagine where Damian would be taking Victor. Why was he leaving Ephesus in the first place? If Naomi wanted to trade Victor for the shipping business, why would she send him away? It didn't make sense. But then, very little in life made sense anymore, and hadn't since the day he had dusted the ground with the imperial incense and refused to say two little words: *Lord Caesar.*

He pushed the animal as fast as he dared, trying to make up the lost time as he continually searched the wide road ahead. A cool front began blowing in, and the wind whipped around him, chapping his face.

Two hours later Jacob stopped at the second halt, again inquiring about a carriage that was carrying a man and a woman with a baby. He began to describe Damian in some detail when the soldier stopped him.

"What makes you think they would stop here?" the soldier asked. "This is an army outpost, not an inn for travelers."

"I know that," Jacob replied, "but the man is a military officer. I need to get a message to him, and I'm not sure what his next stop was supposed to be." It wasn't a lie, Jacob thought. He intended to deliver a message to Damian in no uncertain terms.

Unsuccessful again, Jacob pushed on. It was almost nightfall by the time he reached Smyrna. The wind had died down, but the overcast sky had turned into a fine fall mist. Like it or not, he would have to stop.

Even if Damian were traveling past Smyrna, he would also have to break for the night, especially traveling with an infant. He hadn't been that far ahead of Jacob, so Damian was probably somewhere in the same city right now. *But where?* Jacob wondered. How was he supposed to find Damian? How was he supposed to rescue Victor?

Exhausted, chilled, and famished—he had not eaten anything since dinner the previous evening—Jacob stopped at a rundown inn at the edge of town. He turned his weary mount over to an unreliable-looking stable boy and went inside. Perhaps things would look better after he had a warm meal and a few hours' sleep.

✝

The absurdity of the situation struck Antony as he looked at his traveling companions: a white-haired preacher, without doubt the oldest man Antony had ever seen; a middle-aged, recently retired medical officer whose stern demeanor and ramrod bearing gave away his previous occupation as a soldier; and a beautiful young mother who managed to maintain a quiet dignity in the midst of turmoil. The diverse group was headed to an unknown destination, without any notion of a plan to execute upon their arrival. *Absurd.*

"Ouch!" The Apostle rubbed his head where it had struck the side of the coach as the vehicle hit another uneven patch of pavement. "My innards haven't been jostled this much since I rode out storms on the Sea of Galilee in a small fishing boat."

"I'll tell the driver to slow down." Antony started to rap on the wall of the enclosed vehicle to get the driver's attention, but hesitated when the old man grunted again. He quickly looked over at John, who was grinning.

"Tell him to go faster," the Apostle said.

Antony returned the smile and settled back, leaving it up to the driver to determine the speed. It was the first time he had met the elderly preacher. He had heard about the legendary leader of the Christians in Ephesus from his mother, who had often talked about John, but Antony had to admit he hadn't paid much attention. Helena tended to ramble, and he frequently found himself nodding at his mother without really hearing what she was saying. He did recall, however, a striking description: she had referred to John as "an ageless treasure in an ancient container."

He was beginning to agree, although he'd originally been disgruntled to discover the Apostle would be riding with them. When Peter had left for the office, Marcellus had gone to tell John what was happening and where they were going—or where they thought they were going. The old man had been infirm when they first returned from Devil's Island, and even though he had regained his strength, Marcellus still checked on him every day.

"I'll be back before the carriage arrives," Marcellus had assured Antony. He had indeed returned on time, but with the Apostle in tow. "I've been promising John that I would soon accompany him to Smyrna," Marcellus had explained when he drew Antony off to the side. "He has an important letter to deliver to the church there, and he insisted on going now. I couldn't say no."

"But he'll slow us down," Antony had protested.

"Not John. Besides, if we learn Jacob has followed Damian beyond Smyrna, we can leave John there and continue our journey."

Now Antony silently admitted that the elderly man had not slowed them down at all; on the contrary, he was trying to speed them up.

John leaned over and patted Rebecca's hand. "You mustn't worry," he told her. "Do you remember the prophecy the Lord gave me before Victor was born?"

She nodded, and a shadow of a smile stole across her face. "You said God had a message of comfort for me. Then you said that the child I was carrying was a son, and that he would become a great servant of the Lord."

"Do you believe that?"

She held the old man's steady gaze. "Yes."

"Then God will preserve Victor and give us success in finding him."

Antony listened to their exchange without comment. He hoped the Apostle was right, although he had never put much stock in prophecy. After all, Ephesus was full of supposed oracles who would gladly prophesy the future for a paying customer.

His opinions about Christians were hazy. Except for his mother, Antony hadn't actually been around that many. And until he had met Peter and Jacob, he had considered it a woman's faith. A faith for the weak and dispossessed elements of society. Now he was discovering that their beliefs cut across boundaries of class and gender, and he still wasn't sure what he thought about it.

Glancing quickly away from Rebecca, however, he was certain of one thing: he was inexorably drawn to her, and had been since the moment he'd met her. Antony had avoided looking at her all morning because his thoughts were entirely inappropriate. She'd been distraught yet determined, and he'd fought the urge to take her in his arms and reassure her that everything would be all right. For one thing, he couldn't promise her there would be a positive outcome. And for another, he barely knew Rebecca; such close physical contact would be offensive to her, not reassuring.

So he'd tried to ignore her at the villa. Now here he was, sitting beside her on a hard bench seat, bouncing along an uneven stretch of highway at top speed, and it was impossible to ignore his feelings for her at such close proximity. He felt her eyes on him again and risked another quick peek.

"You didn't have to get involved in my problems," she said, "but I'm glad you did." She paused and then looked away. "Or is it just because you're working for my brothers?"

John cast a knowing look in Antony's direction. "I don't think you'll be getting a bill for his services this time."

Was it a warning? Antony wasn't sure.

He cleared his throat. He couldn't explain to Rebecca that his primary motivation was a strong physical and emotional attraction to her. "Peter and Jacob have become more than just clients to me," he said. "I count them as friends." That, Antony thought, was certainly true. He relaxed a bit and smiled. "And I fear my mother would take a switch to me if I didn't do whatever I could to help you. She dotes on you, Rebecca."

She looked at him and smiled then, and he nearly gulped at the way her dark eyes came to life. "You're the one she dotes on," Rebecca said. "She's always talking about 'my Antony.' Helena is a very proud mother."

"I only hope I live up to her expectations . . . and yours."

Antony forced himself to look away. He couldn't dwell on his feelings for Rebecca right now or he wouldn't be able to think clearly. And someone needed to come up with a plan for what to do when they caught up with Jacob. He thought about rescuing Victor for only a moment before his thoughts inevitably returned to the woman sitting beside him.

He couldn't help comparing Rebecca to her older sister. There was a noticeable family resemblance between the two, yet they were quite dissimilar. It had taken only a moment to size up Naomi. As Antony had heard, Naomi was one of the most beautiful women he had ever seen; but outside of a glorious mane of hair, hers was an artificial beauty, achieved with cosmetics and clothes. Rebecca possessed a natural beauty, a loveliness that could not be eradicated even when her face was etched with worry, as it was now.

Yes, Rebecca was quite beautiful, Antony acknowledged. Yet the attraction she held for him went far beyond that, though if someone had asked him exactly what it was, he could not have defined it. He simply knew that Rebecca had an intangible quality he didn't have, a quality he wanted to possess.

As he often did, Antony began thinking in two different directions at once. He was used to jumping ahead and seeing the conclusion of a matter while simultaneously figuring out all the minute details, patiently working toward a goal he had first pictured in his head as a vague possibility until it emerged as a full-blown reality. With the carriage racing toward Smyrna, Antony looked into his future, and he clearly saw Rebecca there.

Now all he had to do was work out the details.

7

ANTONY HELPED REBECCA out of the four-wheeled coach, in one easy swoop lifting her and setting her on the ground, then he steadied the door as Marcellus gave John a hand. They'd been riding for hours, and it felt good to get out and walk around.

"Hear that? I think my joints are still rattling." John shook one leg in front of him and then the other.

Marcellus chuckled. "That was the driver unhitching the horses."

"It has been a bone-jarring ride," Antony admitted. The custom carriage Peter had sent for them had been designed for flexibility over comfort. The two passenger benches could be folded up against the sides of the enclosed coach to allow room for cargo. The unpadded seats were sturdy but hard, and the elderly man didn't have much cushion on his spare frame.

"Don't apologize, son. It's better than walking to Smyrna." John took a few steps to stretch his legs. "Although I may have to rest for a week before I can even think about preaching." The twinkle in his still-clear eyes gave away the fact that he was exaggerating.

The old apostle was not nearly as frail as he looked, Antony had decided, and John approached life with tenacity. If nothing else, Antony had to admire him for hanging on to life for eighty-five years.

Marcellus motioned toward the army halt they had just passed. "I'm going to let the soldiers know we've pulled off the road and are stopping for the night. Otherwise, they might become suspicious. I don't want them to come snooping around." He marched off into the gray mist of twilight, and John went over to talk to the driver, who was tending to the horses.

Rebecca huddled under her cloak, her arms folded against her body to ward off the chill of the newly arrived cool front. "Where are we now?" she asked.

"Roughly two-thirds of the way to Smyrna," Antony said. "Depending on how early we leave in the morning, we should arrive there before noon."

Where they would go after that, he had no idea. He was beginning to second-guess his decision to follow Jacob to parts unknown. His first inclination in leaving immediately had simply been to find Jacob and stop him from doing anything rash; if there were any chance of negotiating with Naomi, he was likely to ruin it by impulsive action. Antony and Peter had hastily agreed, however, that with Damian taking the baby away from Ephesus, there might be no negotiations at all—and that meant Victor could be in great danger. Rescuing the child had become even more urgent, but how they were going to accomplish that was a question Antony didn't have an answer for; he didn't even know where to begin looking.

By the time Marcellus returned, a light rain had started to fall, and the passengers all climbed back into the carriage. This time the driver, a hefty stevedore Peter had conscripted for the assignment, squeezed in with them. Fortunately, Rebecca had had the foresight to fill a hamper with food, so they ate a light meal inside the cramped enclosure. She had also thought to bring blankets, which would make spending the night on the side of the road more tolerable.

After they ate, the driver went back outside to stand watch; Antony and Marcellus agreed to take turns with him later. Then Rebecca got John to telling stories about Jesus of Nazareth, whom he had followed for so long, and despite his natural skepticism, Antony found himself listening intently. An accomplished storyteller, John could quickly move his listeners from raucous laughter to quiet awe.

Antony became so caught up in the moment that he was actually disappointed when John's animation faded and he suddenly announced, "It's time to pray before we try to get some sleep."

Marcellus answered with a nod and a deep yawn. He'd been up all night the previous evening and had dozed off a couple of times during their trip, only to be jolted awake by a bump in the road.

In a hoarse but still strong voice, John began to implore God for Jacob's safety and for theirs. He also prayed that God would help them find Victor. "The secret things belong to You, O Lord. We ask You to reveal them to us now, in Jesus' name."

Within moments of pronouncing the amen, the old apostle was snoring lightly, and in spite of their uncomfortable positions, it wasn't long before Marcellus and Rebecca also fell asleep. Antony remained awake, and after a while he decided to go ahead and relieve the driver; he wanted the man rested when they resumed their journey.

Perched high on the driver's seat, wrapped in a warm woolen blanket, Antony watched the sky gradually begin to clear, the stars appearing intermittently through the clouds. He recalled John's prayer and wondered if the old preacher's God really could reveal secrets. Was it His unseen hand that now parted the clouds, revealing lights that had been completely invisible a moment earlier? Could He, would He, part the imperceptible veil that shrouded human knowledge?

Again, Antony began to think about Rebecca as part of his future. He had pieced her story together from things Jacob and Peter had said and from questions he had asked his mother. It had not been difficult to get Helena talking about Rebecca, so he now knew that she'd had a fiancé, who had apparently rejected her, although Antony couldn't imagine why. It didn't matter to Antony that Rebecca had a child. That was simply the way things were. If he wanted Rebecca in his life, which he did, then he wanted Victor as well.

As he gazed up at the stars and contemplated the future, Antony found himself uttering a prayer of his own—to what or whom, he wasn't sure. But the words were a prayer, nonetheless.

Please help me protect her. And please help me get her baby back.

✝

Early the next morning, Jacob woke the stable boy at the small inn on the outskirts of Smyrna and instructed him to groom the horse. Then Jacob went back inside the inn to warm himself by the fire. The sleeping quarters had been drafty and he'd slept poorly, lying on a thin mat on the hard floor, covered by a single threadbare blanket. Now he was groggy and chilled to the bone.

The innkeeper served him what passed for breakfast, and while Jacob ate, he listened to the innkeeper's wife berate her husband. They'd been bickering when Jacob had arrived the night before, and would no doubt still be at it when he left.

"Your sister is a cheap prostitute," the woman complained, her arms flapping as she furiously wielded a broom over the hearth.

"Tullia is not a prostitute," the innkeeper countered. The barrel-shaped man folded his arms across his broad chest and glowered. "She's a priestess of the fertility cult."

"Same difference."

"It is not—" The man stopped abruptly when he looked up and noticed Jacob, apparently deciding that in deference to his guest he should cease defending his sister from his wife's accusations, at least for the moment.

The woman, however, continued her harangue, sweeping around Jacob without ever looking up. "She sleeps with every man who comes around. You want to say that's part of her spiritual duties, Tarquinius, fine. I say she's a common whore."

The innkeeper listened to the tirade for a while, then abandoned his attempt to keep quiet. "I seem to remember you thought quite highly of Tullia that time she cast a spell on the butcher who cheated us."

The woman paused long enough to glare at her husband, then started scolding again. "She knows her magic, I'll grant you that, but it doesn't give her the right to lord it over everybody else. She comes in here last night, after I've already cleaned and closed down the kitchen, and wants a complete meal for her and that man. She knows I can't stand him."

This was apparently news to Tarquinius. "What man?"

The incident must have happened, Jacob surmised, while the innkeeper had been escorting him to the sleeping quarters. The man had wanted to engage him in conversation—Jacob could certainly understand how the man would want to talk to someone besides his wife—but Jacob had been too weary to do more than exchange a few polite words. Now he listened halfheartedly as the couple continued yelling back and forth. Jacob wished they would take their argument somewhere else; he was still too tired to think clearly, and he desperately needed a few minutes of peace and quiet to contemplate how to go about finding out where Damian might have taken Victor.

"You know the one I'm talking about," she said. "That little bantamweight bully she spent time with last year. He's back in town, and he was with her last night—just as surly as ever. I sent them away hungry, I'll have you know."

The light of comprehension dawned on the round man's face. "Ah, that man. The one who called you an old crow." Tarquinius quickly regretted speaking the memory aloud and tried to make amends. "I'm glad you sent them away, Severa," he said apologetically as the woman moved toward him, shaking the broom. "He's a bad sort, even if he is an officer."

"More than a 'bad sort,' I'd say. He's not only mean, he's married! Tullia had the audacity to ask for extra food for his family, while she's standing here, under my roof, with her arms draped around him. I tell you, she doesn't have a shred of decency, and I'm sick of her thinking she's better than the rest of us . . ."

Jacob stood up to leave. He couldn't take any more bickering. Fortunately, he had settled with the innkeeper in advance, so he slipped out quietly now, before they came to blows.

He mounted his horse and returned to the highway, uncertain

where to go. Should he continue on toward Pergamum, or should he stay and search in Smyrna? Jacob let the horse amble while he silently prayed for guidance. He allowed his mind to concentrate on the possibilities. He couldn't imagine Damian wanting to claim paternity, although he had sired the child; Jacob felt sure the kidnapping had been motivated strictly by Naomi's greed. If Naomi had wanted Damian to take the baby back to Rome for some reason, he would have left Ephesus by ship. And if Damian had simply wanted to remove the baby from Naomi's house and hide him somewhere else, he would have stayed around Ephesus. It was a huge city, a quarter of a million people, and there would be any number of places he could have hidden a small child.

No, Damian was taking the baby to a particular place, for a particular reason. Jacob just didn't know where or why.

With absolutely no clues to go on, Jacob made the decision to stay in Smyrna. He couldn't picture Damian traveling more than one day's journey from Ephesus with a young infant.

Once Jacob had determined to search Smyrna, he sought help from the one man in the city whom he knew personally. He'd only been to Polycarp's house once before, and then he'd entered the city from the harbor rather than the highway from Ephesus. But after a few wrong turns Jacob found himself in familiar surroundings, and a half-hour later he was knocking on Polycarp's door.

The young pastor greeted him enthusiastically. "Jacob, we'd gotten word you had been released, praise be to God!" Polycarp directed a young boy of ten or eleven, probably one of his disciples, to take care of Jacob's horse, then he asked, "Is John with you?"

"No, but he's planning to come soon," Jacob said. "He needed some time to recuperate, but he's ready to travel now. I would have brought him, but a situation came up and I had to leave suddenly."

The two men went inside the modest house, which could in no way compare to the familiar opulence of Jacob's family estate, but he felt comfortable and very much at home, as he had previously.

Thirteen months ago, Jacob had escorted John on a ministry trip to several churches in Asia, and while in Smyrna, John had appointed Polycarp bishop over the church there. Jacob had been privileged to preach for Polycarp's congregation, an experience he had both feared and relished. Shortly after that, while they were still traveling through Asia, Jacob and John had been arrested and brought back to Ephesus for the mandatory sacrifice.

Polycarp had not changed a bit in the year since Jacob had seen him. He still had the same serious, yet not stuffy, demeanor, still spoke in the same calm, compassionate voice. Even though he was quite young for the important position John had entrusted to him, Polycarp inspired confidence. He was also a sound teacher, a matter that had been important to John because some of the churches, even those well established in the faith, had fallen prey to false doctrine.

"John wrote that you have a plan to try and get the believers released from Devil's Island," Polycarp said. "Quite a few of our church members wound up there as a result of the persecution."

"I know." Jacob explained his intentions briefly, then gradually steered the conversation to the purpose of his visit. He told Polycarp about Rebecca and Victor, told him of John's prophecy over the child, and then he told how Damian had absconded with the baby.

Polycarp was uncharacteristically vehement in his reaction. "No snake ever crawled as low to the ground as Lucius Mallus Damianus."

"I take it you've encountered the man," Jacob said dryly.

"Not personally, thank the Lord, although he made several trips here last year, right after you and John were arrested. After he persecuted the believers here for a while, he went on to Pergamum and throughout the region. It's only by the grace of God that I avoided being caught in his snare."

"I have no idea where to look," Jacob said, "but I have a hunch that he may have brought Victor here to Smyrna." Jacob described the carriage in which Damian had been riding, the two black stallions that had pulled it, and the fact that a young woman had been traveling with him and the child. "Perhaps someone in your church has seen him or knows where he might be likely to hide in this area."

"I'll get the word out, and I assure you we'll do whatever we can to help. Above all, we will pray for God's will. Even a vile monster like Damian is not beyond God's reach; he cannot hold the child captive one minute longer than God allows."

Polycarp rose, saying, "I'll contact the deacons right away, and I'll ask them to spread the information."

Jacob nodded. "I appreciate your help."

Polycarp left to find a messenger, but Jacob suddenly called him back. Bits and pieces of the conversation he'd tried not to overhear that morning had been floating around in his mind, and now they seemed to come together all at once. The innkeeper's wife had referred to a bully who had paid attention to her uppity sister-in-law the previous year, a bully who had just returned. "He's a bad sort, even if he is an officer," Tarquinius had said.

An officer. Could it possibly have been Damian the innkeeper's wife had turned away at the inn?

"Polycarp, do you know a woman by the name of Tullia, a pagan priestess?" It was unlikely, Jacob told himself, unless Polycarp knew her by reputation. "She's a practitioner of the magical arts," he added.

Jacob knew it wasn't much to go on. If Smyrna were like Ephesus, that would describe four out of five people. Most of the population practiced some form of magic, whether it was wearing an amulet to ward off evil, or offering an incantation to beseech the spirits for assistance in some endeavor.

"Tullia? You think she has something to do with Damian bringing the baby here to Smyrna?"

"You know her?"

Polycarp sat back down, a most somber look on his face. "Tullia is a witch," he said. "The most wicked woman in this city."

8

AGATHA FOUGHT THE URGE to go back to sleep. Her head was throbbing but at least she had quit vomiting and she'd been able to nurse Aurora. That was the important thing, Agatha told herself. Nothing had happened to Aurora.

When the cook brought a bowl of thin gruel to her room, Agatha managed to sit up in bed. "What day is it?" she asked.

"Friday," the pudgy woman replied. She wore the proof of her skill in the kitchen around her waistline. "Steward has assigned another housemaid to your duties until you're up and about."

Agatha nodded and took another bite of the steaming hot gruel. It was bland but satisfying. "This is good," she said. "Thank you."

"Plain food is what you need when you're ailing. I'll bring you some more later."

When the cook left, Agatha slowly finished the meager but nourishing meal. The rumbling in her stomach settled down.

Friday, she thought. She'd been attacked two days ago, and most of the time since then was a complete blur. Marcellus had told her about the kidnapping when she first regained consciousness, but she'd been so sick and in so much pain that she had slept for long stretches of time. Now and then someone would wake her up to try and get her to eat a bite of food, or take care of her when she threw it back up. And during the night someone had brought Aurora to her to nurse. But Agatha couldn't straighten out the sequence of events in her mind.

After a few minutes, when she was sure the gruel was going to stay in her stomach, Agatha set the bowl aside and stood up. At first the room spun wildly, then she got a little steadier on her feet. She did not have to report for work, but she desperately needed to speak to her employer. If she hurried to the dining room, Peter might still be there.

She dressed as quickly as she could and started making her way to the main part of the house. Trembling and unsteady, Agatha had to stop and lean against the wall for support a few times. She closed her eyes and prayed silently. *Lord, please let me find favor in his eyes. He was kind to me before; please let him be kind again.*

Peter was the one who had found her that bitter, wintry day when she'd been huddled against the pier, her body wrapped protectively around Aurora, so tiny and frail and too weak to cry. They would have starved to death if Peter hadn't had mercy on them. He had taken Agatha in, given her a job, and allowed her and Aurora to live in this magnificent mansion. And he'd brought Agatha into the family of believers as well. She couldn't lose all that now; she just couldn't.

When she found Peter, he had finished breakfast and was preparing to leave for the harbor.

"Agatha! What are you doing out of bed?" Peter was startled by her sudden appearance in the dining room.

Trying not to sway, she reached out a hand and touched the sloping head of one of the dining sofas. "I needed to see you," she said, her voice fragile and breathy.

"Please, sit down." He walked over to Agatha and helped her sit down on the *triclinium* she was holding on to for support. "Now, what is it?"

After a few deep breaths, she looked up at him and said, "Are you going to send us away?"

He blinked and looked surprised. "No, of course not. Whatever gave you that idea?"

She covered her face in her hands as relief swept over her weakened body. Relief mixed with remorse. "I've brought such trouble on your house, and now Victor is gone. I should have stopped that man.

Like I told Marcellus, I didn't know who he was, but I should have done something."

Peter sat down beside her on the couch. "We know who took Victor. He's a very evil man, Agatha. You couldn't have done anything. I'm just glad you're alive. We thought he'd killed you at first."

"You know who did this?" Agatha asked. Her mind struggled to comprehend the implications of that.

"We think we do. This man . . . he hates our family and would stop at nothing to hurt us."

As Peter told her about the others leaving the previous day to find the kidnapper, Agatha felt guilty for being so relieved that they knew who had done this terrible thing. She'd been frantic with worry that the kidnapper had been after Aurora, although that didn't quite make sense. No one had wanted her to begin with, so why would they want her after all these months?

Aurora was *her* baby now, Agatha reminded herself, and no one was going to take her baby away. Not again.

By the time they neared Smyrna, Rebecca was miserable. Throughout the morning, she had barely spoken. The others probably thought it was because she was worried about Victor, and Rebecca did not bother to correct their assumption; it would be too embarrassing. She was worried about her son, of course, but that was not the cause of her silence.

The truth was that Rebecca was physically suffering. She had not nursed in almost two days. Now she was swollen, painfully tender, and growing increasingly upset about it. She didn't know how long she could go without nursing before her milk would dry up and she wouldn't be able to nurse Victor at all. Somehow that thought was almost as depressing as the fact that he'd been kidnapped.

The simple act of feeding her baby was one of the most precious things in her life. She'd been so traumatized by Victor's conception that she'd been afraid she wouldn't love him enough, and so isolated on Devil's Island at his birth that she feared she wouldn't know how to take care of him. How would she manage without her mother's guidance? she'd wondered. Or the guidance of any other woman, for that matter? But the first time Victor had latched on and started to suckle, Rebecca had felt not only a deep bond of love but a fiercely protective maternal instinct, and that instinct had kept her and her baby alive through the nightmare of exile on Patmos.

Even now she often thought about her own mother while nursing Victor. There were a thousand questions she'd love to ask about raising children, a thousand precious moments with Victor she'd love to share. She had always been close to her mother, and now that Rebecca was a mother herself, she missed Elizabeth more than ever. Rebecca knew she could always ask Helena whatever she needed to know, but it wasn't the same as having her mother nearby.

Rebecca also wished her father could have known Victor. She believed he would have been proud of his first grandchild, regardless of the circumstances of Victor's birth. It was only after she had returned to Ephesus that Rebecca learned her baby had been born on the day her father was executed in the Colosseum at Rome. She drew comfort from the convergence of the two events, realizing that at the very moment death had claimed her father, God was giving her a new life to cherish—giving her a new beginning, in a sense.

Two days ago that new life had been snatched from her, and now she was riding in a crowded coach with three men who were intent on helping her get Victor back. Rebecca tried to focus on their kindness now, but thinking about the loss of both her parents had compounded her physical misery, and her eyes began to fill with tears.

Antony noticed her distress. They were sitting so close that it would have been hard for him *not* to notice. He leaned over and reassured her. "We'll find Victor," he said. "And we'll get him back."

The carriage began to slow and Rebecca realized they must be entering the city. When they had stopped earlier, John had given the driver directions to Polycarp's house. Rebecca wondered now how much longer it would take them; she was more than ready to climb out of the coach and sit on a real chair, one that was cushioned and, above all, stationary.

She felt Antony's eyes on her and glanced to the side. He smiled, and it softened the hard lines of his sometimes-stern face. He wasn't really stern, she had learned; he was simply a man with many responsibilities, and he tended to carry the weight of those burdens in the lines of his face. She knew from what Helena had said that Antony's father had died seven years ago, when he was seventeen, and that he had taken quite seriously his new role as the head of the family, which also included a younger brother and sister. Helena's husband had not been a good money manager, and while far from destitute, the family had had to be careful with their finances. Helena was proud not only of the way Antony had assumed his new responsibilities, but of the fact that, over the next few years, Antony had worked hard to put them in a much better financial position.

Without reflecting on the reason for her thoughts, Rebecca began to compare Antony to Galen. The two men shared somewhat similar circumstances and ideals: each had lost his father at a relatively young age, each was a man of principle. However, they were very different in temperament and appearance. Antony was as quick thinking as Galen was deliberate; Antony was also as transparent and open as Galen was silent and private. Rebecca surmised that she would never have to wonder what was on Antony's mind; he would speak it directly and clearly, without any emotional upheaval.

The two were also very different physically. Galen's sculpted good looks and finely chiseled features gave the young artist the appearance of being a work of art himself. Antony was not nearly so striking, yet he had a very strong face, framed by a full head of dark hair with a slight natural wave. Unlike Galen, no long, straight shock of hair ever fell over Antony's forehead; he kept his hair trimmed fashionably short, and his clothes were meticulously groomed as well.

It's silly to make such comparisons, she told herself. Galen was part of her past, a past she wanted to forget. And it didn't matter that Antony was handsome; she wasn't attracted to him in that way. He was her family's lawyer, and now a friend. That's all. She told herself to be careful not to encourage him to think there could be anything more between them, if that's what was motivating his attention. Helena certainly seemed to be pushing them in that direction; however, Rebecca had no intention of being drawn into another intense relationship.

She closed her mind to such thoughts and tried to concentrate on enduring the final portion of what had seemed an almost interminable ride. Rebecca had sailed to Rome with her family before, but she had never been on such a long trip by carriage. She wondered what Smyrna was like. It was smaller than Ephesus, but still one of the leading cities in Asia, and another prominent seaport for the region.

As they exited the highway, the carriage suddenly lurched to one side. The driver reined in the horses and quickly stopped. The passengers were whipped from side to side, but no one was hurt, and Antony jumped out of the coach to see what had happened.

Moments later he stuck his head back through the door and said, "One of the fellies has worn through and partially slipped off the wheel. We'll have to find a wainwright to repair the rim before we can go any farther."

"What next?" Rebecca wondered aloud.

✝

Jacob mounted his horse and threaded his way back through the hills toward the southern suburbs of Smyrna. He had been stunned to learn that Tullia, the witch whom he suspected of harboring Damian, lived no more than a half-mile from her brother's inn, where Jacob had spent the night. It was mind-boggling to think he had possibly been that close to Victor without even knowing it. Jacob was furious with himself for not paying more attention, for somehow not figuring things out sooner.

But it wasn't certain, he warned himself. It was just a hunch, based on a few comments by a harping woman; still, the more Jacob thought about it, the more he became convinced it was true. He knew that Damian had spent time in Smyrna the previous year. In fact, when Jacob had been sentenced to serve on a Roman warship, he had been sent from Patmos to Smyrna, where he was transferred to the *Jupiter*. Damian had been on the same boat from Patmos, and Jacob recalled that the tribune had stayed in Smyrna after disembarking. Damian could easily have met the woman named Tullia then, and while he was in the area persecuting the Christians it would be just like Damian to take up with a woman who was either a prostitute or a pagan priestess, depending on your definition. Jacob was inclined to agree with the innkeeper's wife when it came to that assessment.

The horse picked its way carefully down a steep portion of the gravel road. When the road leveled out again, Jacob took a good look around. The inn was not much farther now; he was supposed to turn off on another road just before reaching it. Polycarp had given him the landmarks so he could find the way to Tullia's house.

Of course, Polycarp had also asked Jacob to wait until he returned with some of the deacons before going to Tullia's, and he had seemed quite adamant about it. The bishop had said he wanted to call the church leadership to prayer and to anoint Jacob with oil before he tried to find Damian and the baby.

But Jacob had grown impatient. If Damian had brought Victor specifically to this witch, then his intent could only be ominous, and the sooner Jacob found out what that intent was, the better. *I'll simply scout out the situation,* Jacob told himself, *then I'll go back to Polycarp's and get help. I just want to know if that's where Victor is.*

When he approached the inn, Jacob took the road Polycarp had indicated, and before long he spotted the small stone house he was looking for. The road went through a large thicket that lay between

the inn and Tullia's. While he was still a good distance away, Jacob dismounted and tied his horse to a tree, deciding to approach the house
on foot in order not to be so conspicuous. He could not exactly knock
on the door and inquire whether the household was sheltering a kidnapper with a young infant. But he could look to see if Damian's carriage was there, and listen for any signs that a baby was in the house.

Jacob entered the thicket and crept through the trees until he was
at the edge that ran along the side of the house. There was no sign of
a carriage there or at the front, which was the only side of the house
that opened into a clearing and was accessible from the road. He
moved further toward the back of the house; nothing there. Jacob
didn't think a carriage would be on the far side of the house; it didn't
appear there was enough room to maneuver a pair of horses and a
coach between the house and the woods. But he couldn't be sure, so
he decided to investigate.

It took Jacob almost a quarter-hour to move stealthily through the
woods until he had passed the back of the house and reached the other
side. *No carriage.* Perhaps Damian had left for a while, or perhaps
Jacob had drawn the wrong conclusion and Damian wasn't here at all.
Jacob began to slowly work his way behind the house again, keeping
well inside the thicket to lessen the chances of being seen.

He was about halfway back to his starting point when he heard
a door close and then heard footsteps. Jacob stopped suddenly, his
senses immediately alert.

9

ANTONY HELPED THE OTHER three passengers out of the carriage, now crippled by a bent wheel. He could see only a few buildings up ahead, which meant they were just at the edge of the city.

"How far are we from Polycarp's house?" Marcellus asked John. "Is it too far to walk?"

"Close to an hour on foot," John said. "It's uphill most of the way."

Antony looked at Rebecca, and she answered before he could ask the question. "I'll gladly walk." She turned to the Apostle. "But what about you? Could you make it that far?"

"Probably," he said. "But I might slow the rest of you down. Maybe I should wait here with the carriage."

"No need," Antony said. "We'll take one of the horses with us and leave one for the driver to use while he finds a wainwright. Later, Marcellus or I can bring the horse back."

It took both Marcellus and Antony to hoist John astride the powerful animal, but soon they were climbing through the hills of Smyrna at a steady pace. John had offered to share the ride with Rebecca, but she declined; her backside was sore enough from the long carriage ride, and she actually welcomed the long walk.

At midafternoon they finally arrived at Polycarp's house, only to discover that the bishop was not at home. John introduced himself to the young man who greeted them at the door and informed them that Polycarp was away.

"My name is Linus," the lad told them, "and I'm a student of

Polycarp." He stared openly at John. "It's a great honor to meet you, sir. A great honor."

John smiled broadly. "Would that honor extend to letting a weary apostle and his companions inside?"

"Of course. Forgive me, sir." The young student blushed in embarrassment and promptly showed them in. "It's just that I've heard so much about you."

"Is Polycarp away from the city?" John asked.

"No," Linus said. "He'll be back sometime this afternoon. At least I think he will. He left in a hurry because we had a bit of excitement here this morning."

It took only minimal prompting from John for Linus to expound on the excitement. "Polycarp has gone to find some of the deacons and bring them here for prayer. We had another unexpected visitor this morning. In fact, he was from Ephesus too. But he left a couple of hours ago, not long after Polycarp."

Rebecca exchanged a look with Antony, who asked Linus, "Was the visitor's name Jacob?"

"I didn't get his name," the lad said, "but I heard the man say that his nephew had been kidnapped, and they think a witch has him."

"A witch?" Tentacles of fear wrapped around Rebecca's heart. Damian, who was evil through and through, had stolen her baby and brought him to a witch?

†

Frozen in place, Jacob watched as a man and a woman came out of Tullia's house and walked toward his hiding place in the woods. The woman was carrying a baby—a crying baby—and Jacob immediately recognized the infant's wail. It was Victor!

Jacob crouched down behind a tree as the couple neared, and he noticed something he hadn't paid attention to the first time he'd crossed the thicket. A small area had been cleared at the center edge of the tree line behind the house. On the ground, in the center of the clearing, twelve large flat stones had been laid out in the form of a triangle, four to each side. Symbols had been painted on the stones, perhaps the signs of the zodiac; Jacob was not quite close enough to tell. In the center of the stone triangle stood a bronze bowl, also triangular in shape, perched on a tripod.

The man was definitely Damian. Jacob recognized his swagger even before he saw his face. But the woman was not the wet nurse who had left Ephesus with Damian; Jacob had gotten a good look at her then. This must be Tullia, he decided. The witch.

Jacob's mind reeled. *Dear God, help me,* he silently prayed. *What are they doing with my nephew?*

Tullia handed the baby to Damian, then kindled a fire under the odd-shaped bronze bowl. While she worked the sticks of wood into a small blaze, Jacob pondered the possibilities. Could he rush them and manage to take Victor? Damian was not wearing his sword—Jacob was; he had brought the abandoned weapon with him from Ephesus. But no doubt Damian would have a dagger stashed somewhere on his body. And Jacob couldn't attack Damian while he was holding Victor; it was simply too risky.

I should have waited for Polycarp and the others, Jacob belatedly realized. *I need help.*

The witch removed a small pouch from her cloak, poured its contents into the bowl, and watched as a plume of fragrant smoke arose. She held her hands toward the burning incense and spoke a few words in a language Jacob did not understand. Perhaps it was not even a language, Jacob thought, but just religious gibberish.

Then she turned to Damian and took the baby, lifting him high over the bowl of incense. Jacob clearly understood her next words, and they made his blood boil.

"I call upon Hekate, goddess of the underworld and guardian of the portals of death, to witness our prayers and protect us from evil. I call upon Artemis, Lord and Savior, Queen of the Cosmos. Display your power to us now, for we know that you govern all things, and that we possess great power through you.

"Give me your strength, enter into this fire, fill it with the divine light, and show me your might. I conjure you, holy light, holy brightness, breadth, depth, length, and height, by the holy names which I have spoken and am now going to speak."

The temperature in the thicket suddenly dropped, and the sounds of nature grew strangely quiet as Tullia began to pronounce the names of a string of gods and goddesses. The skin on the back of Jacob's neck crawled as he listened to the witch pronounce her "holy names." Some of them he recognized, like Helios, god of the sun; Selene, goddess of the moon; Tyche, goddess of fortune; and Ereschigal, a Babylonian goddess. The witch also called on Demeter and Dionysos, Serapis and Isis, and still others whose names Jacob did not recognize. He knew that the practitioners of magic ascribed great power to names, and that the supposed success of their incantations depended on being able to call on the right names and say the right words as they cast spells or invoked divine assistance from the spirits.

"Now, now! Quickly, quickly!" Tullia cried out. "Remain by me in the present hour until I achieve the ends I desire. This child is destined for greatness, and I pledge to train him for spiritual service to the Great Goddess. May every member of his family come to great harm, so that we may wield our influence on him unhindered, and may the wealth of his family be laid at our feet, now and forever."

Jacob wanted to move, tried to move, but his feet suddenly felt like lead and he couldn't quite lift them. He had to get out of there, had to go for help, yet he was unaccountably immobile. It seemed to require a monumental effort just to turn around, but he finally did. Jacob started to leave, sneaking through the thicket toward the spot where he had left the horse. He would ride like the wind back to Polycarp's, enlist some help, and return to rescue Victor from the evil that penetrated this forest.

He had only made it a dozen paces into the woods when he felt a crushing blow to the base of his skull. Jacob fell to the ground face first, tasting the moist earth as his open mouth bit into the dirt. He gagged and tried to get up, but couldn't get his arms under him to support his weight. He rose a few inches, collapsed again, then unseen hands rolled him over.

Jacob opened his eyes and looked up. All he could see were leaves and branches spinning and swirling above him. He could not move at all now, could not even blink his eyes.

"Is he dead?" It was a woman's voice Jacob heard. The witch's voice.

"If he's not, he will be soon." That was Damian speaking.

Jacob wanted to protest, wanted to scream, "I'm alive. Leave me alone!" But he was paralyzed. Not a single muscle would respond.

He felt a hand, a woman's hand, touch his face. Her fingers brushed over his eyebrows and downward, closing his eyes. He heard the witch uttering thanks to Artemis for answering her prayer so swiftly.

Then Jacob blacked out.

Sometime later, he came to briefly. He opened his eyes, but his vision was gray and blurry. He sensed rather than saw that the forest shadows had deepened, and he felt the damp earth all around him, closing in on him. He seemed to be in a shallow depression in the ground. He tried to move, but couldn't.

Then Jacob felt the first shovelful of dirt strike his face, and he knew his enemy was burying him alive.

10

WHILE THEY WAITED FOR POLYCARP to return, Antony watched Marcellus pace the floor of the small dining room. The medical officer had probably not stood sentry in over a decade, a fact that would not be readily discerned now: he maintained an upright and unyielding posture as he took six paces in one direction, then reversed direction for the corresponding six paces. The routine movement helped Marcellus concentrate, Antony supposed, although it had the opposite effect on him.

Distracted, Antony turned his attention to John, who was reclining on one of the sofas. During their trip Antony had learned that unless the old man was actually snoring, it was uncertain whether his closed eyes meant he was resting or praying. Given the news they'd received at their arrival, Antony guessed John was praying at the moment. He recalled the Apostle's prayer from the previous evening. John had said something to the effect that God would reveal "secret things." Perhaps they'd already seen an answer to that prayer, Antony admitted to himself; at least they now knew where to find Victor. How to get him back was another matter, however, and Antony wondered if God had a plan for that. It was strange to find himself thinking about a God who supposedly intervened in the affairs of men, a God who could right wrongs and reveal secrets. A few weeks ago the possibility would never have occurred to Antony.

At his request, Rebecca had gone to the kitchen with Linus to find something for them to eat. Antony hadn't wanted to tire her further, yet he had thought she needed something to do. His mother always responded to a crisis with a vigorous burst of cleaning or cooking, as if by tackling such mundane matters the things outside her control would somehow be straightened out in the process.

Before they'd reached Smyrna, Antony had been worried that Rebecca was becoming ill. Then after she'd heard the news about Damian taking Victor to some sort of pagan priestess, she had looked positively ashen. Perhaps he should go and check on her now, Antony decided. Rebecca was probably fine, but he needed an excuse to get away from Marcellus's focused pacing. And besides, Antony simply liked being in the same room with her.

He walked out of the dining room, intending to wander to the back of the house and find the kitchen, when he heard a loud knocking at the front door. Young Linus was in the back with Rebecca, so Antony went through the atrium to the courtyard at the entrance of the house to see who had arrived. It would likely be some of the church leaders whom Polycarp had gone to summon.

As he approached the door, Antony could hear two men arguing.

"I still say it was a mistake to let her in," one of them protested hotly. "She was only pretending to be a believer."

"We didn't know that at the time," the other man responded in a more patient tone. "Besides, what's done is done, and there's no way to—"

The voices broke off suddenly when Antony opened the door. The two men looked sheepish as they realized that a stranger had caught them disagreeing. Antony noted that the two bore a strong resemblance and shared the same short, compact build, with muscular arms that threatened to split the seams of their tunics.

For a moment Antony didn't know whether to invite them in. He figured the pair were part of Polycarp's church, but since the Christians met secretly, Antony wasn't sure how to broach the topic. Then he understood they would have a similar apprehension about him, so Antony introduced himself, saying he had come from Ephesus to see Polycarp.

"You must be the one whose baby was kidnapped. I'm Plautius, and this is my brother, Sergius." Antony recognized Plautius's voice as belonging to the more objective of the two speakers he'd heard outside. The man wiped a callused hand on his work apron and extended it to Antony, and his brother did the same.

"We closed our blacksmith shop and came as soon as we heard," Sergius said.

"Actually, I'm not the father," Antony said as he shook hands. "I brought the baby's mother here. Polycarp must have told you about her brother, Jacob, who tracked the kidnapper to Smyrna."

"Where is he?" Sergius asked. "We came to help him rescue the child—"

Plautius interrupted. "We came to pray with Polycarp and then determine what we should do next."

"We know what to do," Sergius insisted. "We need to get to Tullia's house as fast as we can."

Antony hadn't even moved the two men from the courtyard into the main part of the house, and they were already at it again.

"We shouldn't act hastily," Plautius said. "If she has the baby, she won't harm him, as long as we don't threaten her. You know Tullia loves children and has always wanted one of her own."

"That's what worries me. She's probably cast some demonic spell on him already. Just like my Cornelia. I hold you personally responsible . . ." Sergius's voice trailed off, leaving his accusation unfinished, and leaving Plautius with a pained look.

Antony sensed that Tullia, who must be the witch to whom Damian had brought Victor, was also the source of a longstanding point of contention between the two men. Taking advantage of the sudden lull in their conversation, Antony ushered them inside, but before he could get more information out of them, Polycarp showed up with two other deacons—whose names Antony promptly forgot as yet another man, this one named Verus, arrived.

The entire group crowded into the dining room with John and

Marcellus about the time Rebecca and Linus returned with a tray of food. Rebecca looked dismayed when she saw how many people had arrived and how little food they had prepared, but by that time Antony was not inclined to eat anyway.

"Thank you," he whispered to Rebecca. "We'll have to eat on the way. Marcellus and I are about to follow Jacob and see if we can find Victor."

Polycarp addressed the group that had gathered, expressing his concern that Jacob had already left. "I'm afraid he doesn't know what he's getting into," the bishop said. "I should have told him more about Tullia, but I never imagined he would rush off like that."

"He's very impulsive," John said, "and it gets him into trouble. Sometimes Jacob listens to his anger more than he listens to God."

"He's been gone a couple of hours," Antony said. "If the situation is as dangerous as you fear, then we need to leave *now*." He agreed with Sergius on that count. Antony had had a very uneasy feeling to begin with, and the brothers' discussion about Tullia had done nothing to alleviate his anxiety.

"We need to pray first," Polycarp said. "It's essential."

Antony didn't want to seem rude, but he was convinced that further delay could be ruinous. "We're running out of time," he objected.

"Which is exactly why we need to pray," John replied. "We're not battling flesh and blood, but powers and principalities, and we need God's guidance and His protection."

For the second time in as many days, Antony found himself in a group of praying Christians. However, the experience was different from the previous evening's bedtime prayer. This time Polycarp anointed Antony and Marcellus with olive oil as he prayed. Afterward, Antony's forehead felt hot where Polycarp had touched him, and that warmth began to suffuse throughout the rest of his body. The bishop also anointed Plautius and Sergius, who had agreed to accompany them to Tullia's house, and Verus, who also volunteered.

After that, John prayed boldly and eloquently, and although

Antony did not fully comprehend everything John said, he felt the power of the Apostle's prayer. John evidently believed that this Tullia woman was evil; in his prayer he rebuked the spirits of darkness that surrounded her and said something about opposing the spirit of witchcraft through the power of Jesus Christ.

When John concluded his prayer, the five men prepared to leave. Antony saddled the horse John had ridden from the highway. Plautius and Sergius had also arrived on horseback; now Marcellus and Verus doubled up with the two brothers. The animals would help them get to Tullia's house faster, even though they would not be able to reach a gallop traveling through the hills.

Just as they were leaving, Rebecca ran outside. "Don't leave without this," she said, reaching up to hand something to Antony. His eyes met hers as he bent down to accept the offering, and she blushed slightly as their hands touched. "You haven't eaten all day," she reminded him.

Rebecca quickly turned and handed the others a similar package: a cloth napkin with food enclosed. She must have wrapped the snacks while they were saddling the horses, and Antony appreciated the gesture. While they were praying, he'd forgotten how hungry he was.

As the horses ambled down the hillside, the riders nibbled on cold mutton and crusty bread. They also discussed their mission, and Antony pieced together the relationship between the two disputing brothers and Tullia, who turned out to be a relative of theirs—a second cousin, Antony surmised from the conversation.

Plautius described Tullia as a troubled soul who was always seeking spiritual sustenance. Sergius said she had never been anything but a troublemaker bent on mischief. While they disagreed on Tullia's motivation, they both admitted that she had caused a great deal of trouble for the church.

"Several years ago," Plautius said, "after I became a Christian, I shared my faith with Tullia. She was very interested and asked me many questions about it. She seemed so eager to learn about Jesus that

I finally suggested she come to our meetings. I vouched for her to the church leaders, and she was accepted as a catechumen."

He explained to Antony that a catechumen was a new convert who worshiped with the church while undergoing a period of instruction in the elemental principles of the faith before being baptized. Only those who were baptized could participate in the Eucharist, the sharing of bread and wine as a memorial to Christ. Antony did not want to get sidetracked into a doctrinal discussion, so he urged Plautius to continue with his story about Tullia.

"She attended for a while," Plautius said, "but she never went on to be baptized. She became disillusioned and left."

"And that's when serious trouble started." Sergius wiped the crumbs from his mouth and tucked his empty napkin under the edge of his saddle. "Tullia didn't get what she wanted, so she left the church and then tried to rob everyone else."

"She stole from the other Christians?" Marcellus asked.

"Not money," Sergius replied. "She stole hearts."

"The hearts and minds of people," Plautius explained. "She tried to draw others away from the faith, and she spread rumors that Christians practiced cannibalism and incest."

"Cannibalism?" Antony nearly choked on his last bite of mutton. He racked his brain, trying to think of anything his mother had ever said about her faith that would lead someone to think that Christians were cannibals. And incest? It was unthinkable. Peter and Jacob and Rebecca—they were some of the finest people Antony had ever met. At least, he had thought they were . . .

Of course, they were. Antony shook his head to clear the ridiculous thought from his mind. The few Christians he knew were kind, generous, and morally upright. Claims to the contrary must certainly stem from ignorance or prejudice.

"Whatever possessed Tullia to make such preposterous claims?" Marcellus asked. "Surely no one believed her."

"A few did." Verus, who was riding with Sergius, spoke for the first time. "My sister was one of them. She still won't have anything to do with me."

"But your own sister would know that you didn't practice incest," Antony observed.

"She didn't believe that part," Verus said. "She believed the part about being cannibals."

Plautius said, "We think what Tullia was referring to was the fact that we refer to each other as brother and sister. And in the Eucharist we say that the bread is the body of Christ and the wine is the blood He shed for the remission of our sins. She never took Communion with us, but she knew of the practice, and she distorted the symbols to mean something horrific."

"Why would she want to slander the believers in such a vile way?" Marcellus looked incredulous. "Why was she so bitter?"

"Because God didn't answer her prayers the way she thought He ought to," Sergius said. "So Tullia decided she hated Jesus and anybody who worshiped Him."

"She went back to her pagan religion," Plautius said, "and became steeped in witchcraft and sorcery. I didn't figure out until long after she'd left the church that manipulating spiritual forces was what Tullia had really been after, not a relationship with God."

He paused to direct Antony to turn left where two roads intersected just ahead of them. "Shortly after we became Christians," Plautius continued, "my wife was healed of a serious illness. I talked a lot about healing and praying in Jesus' name, and that's when Tullia became interested. She somehow thought Jesus was a divine talisman, that praying in His name was some kind of magic formula to guarantee that she would receive whatever she wanted."

"What she wanted," Sergius said bitterly, "was a baby."

His words caused a frisson of fear to ripple through Antony. Tullia had wanted a baby, and now she had Rebecca's. What did it mean?

"She'd been married seven years but hadn't conceived a child,"

Plautius explained. "She attended our meetings for almost a year, and for all those months she prayed fervently for a baby. But God did not answer her prayer. Not only that, Tullia's husband eventually divorced her because she couldn't produce the heir he wanted."

"Tell him what she did to Cornelia," Sergius said, his mouth a grim line that cut across his square face. For the first time Antony sensed that a profound sadness, not mere contrariness, lay behind the man's argumentative facade.

"After her departure from the church, Tullia did more than spread rumors," Plautius acknowledged. "She learned to cast spells, and she practiced on anyone she had a grudge against—most of them church members. About a year after she left the fellowship, Cornelia, Sergius's wife, became pregnant, and when Tullia found out, she went into a jealous rage. She put a curse on Cornelia." He shot an apologetic look at his brother. "We didn't know about the curse until later, though. All we knew at the time was that Cornelia became mysteriously ill. She kept getting worse, and eventually she lost the baby—"

"And her life." Sergius abruptly finished his brother's thought.

The men grew quiet then, and Antony was left to contemplate the fact that Sergius had lost his wife and unborn child because of a witch's curse. Was that really possible? Many people were superstitious and turned to sorcerers and mediums for all sorts of cures and remedies as well as predictions of the future. Antony had never consulted a magic practitioner and did not hold them in high regard, but he knew they could be found at all levels of society.

Marcellus finally spoke the question on Antony's mind. "Are you sure the curse killed her?" he asked Sergius. "Perhaps she fell ill from another cause and it was just a coincidence."

"She'd never been sick a day in her life," Sergius said.

"Several people claimed to have heard Tullia pronounce the curse," Plautius said. "They came forward after the funeral, and the news spread like wildfire." He paused to look at Sergius again, as if judging whether to continue. "I don't believe the curse killed Cornelia," he finally said, "but I can't explain why God healed my wife but not my brother's. I don't have an answer for it."

Antony certainly didn't have an answer for it either; he wasn't even sure where to begin asking questions when it came to matters of faith. After a moment he told Sergius, "I'm sorry for your loss."

Sergius responded with a solemn nod, then turned to his brother. "And I'm sorry for what I said earlier," he said to Plautius, "about holding you responsible."

"That was your grief talking," Plautius said sympathetically.

"I just got all stirred up again when I heard Tullia was making trouble. I don't want her hurting anybody else, and I don't want any more people becoming followers of hers."

Plautius related to the others how Tullia's reputation had risen after Cornelia's death. "A lot of people began to fear her, and to respect her magical abilities at the same time," he said. "Every time she casts a spell and it works, Tullia grows more powerful in the eyes of her neighbors."

"She doesn't grow more powerful in my eyes," Verus said. "More wicked."

"I'll grant you that," Plautius agreed. "And people seem to quickly forget the silly spells she casts that don't come to fruition."

Recalling something the brothers had said earlier, Antony asked, "Do you think Tullia has cast some kind of spell on Victor? Or put a curse on him?"

Plautius let the question hang in the air for a long moment, then he said, "It doesn't matter. God's power is far greater than any witch's curse."

"All we need to do," Verus said, "is get that baby away from there. God will assist us, just as we prayed."

"And we will trust Him that no harm will come to the child," Sergius said. He pointed to a building about a hundred yards ahead of them. "The road to Tullia's house is to the left, just before we get to that inn. Tullia's brother owns the place."

The group fell silent, and Antony brooded over their impending visit to the home of a witch. Was it possible she had access to a source of supernatural power? If so, was the Christian God truly more powerful, as his new friends believed? Antony suddenly wished he'd paid more attention to things his mother had tried to tell him about her faith over the years. And for the first time in his life, he wished he had the reassurance that he could rely on a power greater than his own.

✝

Marcellus saw the inn Sergius pointed out and reckoned they must have traveled back to the southern edge of the city. There were few houses now, and he could see the highway in the distance.

He also thought about what Plautius had said and knew in principle that it was true: Good and evil were not opposing but equal forces, and God's power was greater—infinitely greater—than that of the most accomplished sorcerer or medium or witch.

Yet in the few months Marcellus had been a Christian, he'd had no opportunity to put that knowledge to the test. And before his conversion he'd been a bona fide skeptic when it came to spiritual matters—like Antony, who now appeared disconcerted by the turn the discussion had taken.

As they turned on the road by the inn, the men discussed what to do when they reached their destination. Sergius wanted to demand that Tullia hand over the child, and to seize him by force if she didn't. Verus protested that they shouldn't use physical force unless absolutely necessary; and besides that, they had no weapons.

Antony and Marcellus admitted they had brought their daggers with them. "I've only had to use mine once," Antony said, "in self-defense." He turned in the saddle and smiled. "A client who wasn't too happy with the outcome of his case threatened to kill me."

Sergius did not return the smile. "Are you prepared to use your weapon now?" he asked.

"I'm prepared to do whatever it takes," Antony said slowly.

Plautius did not seem that concerned about a rescue strategy. "We'll know what to do when we get there," he said simply.

Marcellus noted Antony's determination and recalled his recent interactions with Rebecca. The lawyer had no legal obligation to help rescue her baby, and his willingness to get involved seemed to go beyond a simple desire to protect an innocent child. Antony was clearly developing feelings for Rebecca, and that both pleased and worried Marcellus. Antony was a fine man, and Rebecca needed someone like him in her life. But she also didn't need to be rushed into anything. Marcellus made up his mind to have a talk with Antony.

Marcellus had also been taken with Rebecca when he'd first met her, although his concern had been fatherly. His friendship with her and John had eventually led to important changes in Marcellus's life. For one thing, he had become a Christian through their influence, and he believed the same thing could happen to Antony— in fact, he prayed earnestly that it would happen.

Beyond leading to his conversion, Marcellus's relationship with Rebecca had renewed his concern for his own daughter, whom he had not seen in a dozen years. Before he left Devil's Island, Marcellus had promised God that he would try to find her and make things right. He'd never meant to abandon his daughter, but his military service had taken him away from home for months or years at a time. Unable to bear the long separations, Marcellus's wife had divorced him and remarried.

His mind drifted back to the last time he'd seen his little girl; she had just turned six, he remembered. She would be a grown woman now, a woman who probably had no memory of the father she'd barely known, and that realization pricked his heart like a needle.

Over the years Marcellus had buried the loss deep inside. When he'd met Rebecca, however, it brought the whole situation back to him. Rebecca was only a few years younger than his daughter, and Marcellus had been unable to resist trying to help the young prisoner survive the godforsaken island to which she'd been banished, even though it had entailed a substantial personal risk. All he could think of was how desperately he would want someone to help his own daughter if she were in such jeopardy.

For a moment Marcellus engaged in a bit of self-recrimination for not protecting Rebecca and Victor better. He wasn't sure he could have done anything to prevent the kidnapping, but he couldn't help feeling guilty that he had been the one to suggest she leave the baby with Agatha and start helping Helena a few hours every day. Perhaps if Rebecca had been at home with her son, this wouldn't have happened.

No, he thought, Damian would have found some other way to strike a blow to the family. Still, Marcellus was dismayed that it had come to this, and that they were now riding into an unknown, and quite likely dangerous, situation.

Suddenly a horse whinnied nearby and everyone's attention was once again riveted to the roadside. Marcellus did not see any other travelers, and he realized it had been a while since they had passed anyone on the road.

Verus was the first to spot the animal. He reined in his mount, and the others followed his lead. "Over there," he said, pointing to the left. The horse was tethered to a tree just inside the thicket, but no rider was in sight.

"This road doesn't get much traffic anymore," Plautius observed. "It only leads to Tullia's house and beyond that to an old abandoned mill. Not much cause for anyone to leave a horse tied up here."

Antony asked, "Do you think it could be Jacob's?"

"Perhaps," Sergius said thoughtfully. "He might have wanted to approach on foot—make it less likely for someone to spot him in advance. If you travel through these woods, you come up to the back of Tullia's house."

"See where the brush is disturbed? Could be a hunter," Verus pointed out. "I used to hunt deer in these parts all the time—before Tullia got so contrary, that is. I make it a point to avoid this area now."

The late afternoon sun beamed down on the gravel road, making it sparkle in spots, but the low angle of the rays cast deepening shadows inside the thicket. "Whoever owns the horse is going to have to come out of the woods soon," Marcellus said. "Another hour and it will be too dark to find the way out."

Sergius nodded. "And that means we need to conclude our business with Tullia quickly." He lifted the reins and prepared to ride again, but Antony held up a hand, signaling the others to remain still.

"Is it just me," Antony said, "or does anybody else sense it?" The usually articulate lawyer now struggled for words.

"Sense what?" Marcellus asked.

"That there's something ominous about that riderless horse," Antony said, looking torn. "I have a strong feeling it belongs to Jacob and that we ought to investigate, yet we can't do that *and* get to Tullia's house to rescue Victor before dark."

"We need discernment," Plautius said, "and we know where to find it." Before Antony or anyone else could object, Plautius bowed his head and prayed out loud. In three short sentences he petitioned heaven for the Holy Spirit's wisdom, asked God not only for guidance, but boldness, and thanked Him for a successful outcome.

As soon as the group echoed the amen, Verus suggested they split up. "You two should go to Tullia's," he said to Plautius and Sergius, "because you know her best." Offering a gap-toothed grin in Antony's direction, he said, "And a smooth-talking lawyer might help convince her to give up the child without coming to blows.

"Marcellus and I can follow the trail inside the forest. If it leads away from Tullia's house, we won't pursue it; that would mean it wasn't Jacob."

Plautius approved of the plan. "Check it out," he said as Verus and Marcellus climbed off the horses they were sharing with him and Sergius. "Then you can meet us at Tullia's in case we need your help."

The rescue party separated. Two men headed into the woods on foot while the other three proceeded on horseback.

11

ANTONY COULDN'T BELIEVE they were just going to stroll up to the front door and ask Tullia to hand over the baby, but that's exactly what Plautius intended to do. And for some reason, Antony did not argue with him. The stocky little blacksmith possessed a quiet confidence Antony could not fathom.

When they reached the stone house, they tied their horses in front. Antony hadn't known what to expect of the witch's house. It was small but neat, he noted, and would have appeared inviting in other circumstances. As they walked up to the door, Antony felt for the dagger under his cloak, satisfying himself that his weapon was still in place. He hoped he would not have to use it, but he had decided he would not leave this place without Victor, whatever it took.

Plautius rapped forcefully on the door, but there was no response. He knocked again; still no answer.

Sergius pushed on the door, but it didn't budge. Antony was sure it had been bolted from the inside. *So much for Plautius's idea,* he thought.

"Tullia," Sergius called in a loud voice. "Open up. We're not leaving until you do."

Antony looked around, wondering how else they could get inside. If there were windows along the side of the house, they would probably be shuttered; however, they would be easier to break down than the solid door. Before he could suggest it to the others, Antony heard footsteps approaching the entrance from the inside.

An attractive but disheveled woman opened the door. Her light-brown hair was unpinned and windblown, her clothes dirt-stained and in disarray. Oddly, though, her face and hands were clean and still damp, as if she had just washed. Her complexion was lighter than most of the local women, Antony noted, and her skin had a pinkish glow from the fresh scrubbing.

"Good day, Tullia." Plautius nodded politely.

"I'm not receiving visitors," she announced. "Especially not you two." Tullia did not invite them in, and she did not step over the threshold toward the unexpected guests. Keeping one hand on the open door, she glanced uneasily at her cousins, as if wary of their motives.

"We won't stay long," Plautius said. "We just came for the child."

"What are you talking about?" Tullia asked.

"You know exactly what we're talking about." Sergius was not as patient or as even-tempered as his brother. "We want the child Damian brought you for safekeeping."

Tullia's eyes widened, and she hesitated slightly before denying the accusation. "There's no child here," she said, "and I think you should leave now." She started to close the door, but Antony anticipated her movement and quickly wedged his foot inside.

"Where is Damian?" Antony asked, pushing the door open wide and forcing Tullia to take a step backward. "Is he here?"

"And just who are you?" Tullia demanded.

Antony stepped inside the atrium, and Plautius and Sergius quickly entered after him. "I'm the child's legal guardian," Antony said. He watched a flicker of alarm cross Tullia's face, and he took advantage of it to challenge her. "If you don't want to get in trouble with the authorities," he said, "I suggest you hand him over now."

He wasn't exactly Victor's guardian; that was stretching the truth. But Antony could legitimately be called the child's legal representative, and he was more than willing to use whatever leverage he might have to get Tullia to turn Victor over to them.

"You should be the ones worried about the authorities," she said. "You're trespassing."

Antony ignored the implied threat. Her defiance was a bluff, an attempt to distract them from the issue. "We know Damian is in Smyrna," he said, "and that he brought the baby he kidnapped here."

"Kidnapped? But—"

Antony watched Tullia's mouth clamp shut almost as quickly as the question escaped her lips. She had known about Victor, all right, but she hadn't known he'd been kidnapped. Even if she was telling the truth and Victor wasn't here at the moment, odds were that he had been. Antony's instincts told him that Tullia knew where the child was, and he pressed her for more information.

"If Damian is here," Antony said, a menacing tone in his voice, "you're harboring a criminal."

"Damian is not here," she said. "And he's not a criminal. He's a Roman tribune."

"He's a kidnapper," Antony countered.

"Taking your son away from an unfit mother is not the same as kidnapping," Tullia insisted. "That baby is Damian's own flesh and blood."

"I thought you didn't know anything about a child," Sergius said. "You never could tell the truth, could you, Tullia?"

"I never could abide *you*," Tullia snapped. "And I can't abide your presence in my house now."

Antony stepped between Sergius and Tullia. He didn't want their personal animosity to overshadow the attempt to find Victor. "So Damian did bring the child to you," Antony said to her. "Where is he now?"

Tullia glared at Sergius without responding to Antony's question.

"Tell me," the lawyer insisted. "I won't leave until I know where Victor is."

The witch turned to face Antony, fire flashing in her eyes. "The child is not here." She spoke slowly and with finality. "And you won't ever find him."

Antony moved his hand toward the dagger stashed in his belt. Something about the sound of her voice unsettled him, not to mention the eerie light in her eyes. He had the feeling he was looking into the beautiful face of evil, and it frightened him.

"I've cast a spell on the child's family," Tullia continued. "All of them will die or meet with grave injury." Her mouth twisted into a malevolent smile and the facade of beauty vanished in the blink of an eye.

"And it's working," she informed them. "One man is already dead, and you could be next." She pointed at Antony, and he felt a wave of pure malice radiating from her.

Antony did not pause to consider the implications of Tullia's spell on Rebecca and her family; he responded instinctively to the personal threat. In a flash he removed his weapon, and at the same time Sergius grabbed Tullia, pinning her arms behind her.

"Search the house," Sergius shouted. "Quickly!"

Plautius moved to help Sergius subdue the thrashing Tullia, who alternately screamed curses and invoked strange spirits.

Dagger in hand, Antony went looking for Victor. It took only a few minutes to go from room to room in the small house. There was no sign of the child, no sign of Damian.

He returned to the atrium and found the brothers holding Tullia. She was quieter now, but still furious.

"Did you find him?" Sergius asked. He had a mark beside his right eye, where Tullia had evidently managed to land a blow before Plautius had come to his assistance.

Antony shook his head. "No. Nothing," he said.

"I told you he wasn't here," Tullia said. "Now let me go."

Plautius stepped to one side, and Sergius reluctantly released his hold on Tullia. "You'll not prosper in this wickedness," he told her.

Tullia smiled again, and the sight sickened Antony. "You think not?" she asked. "Remember what happened to Cornelia, dear cousin. For your own sake, I suggest you leave me alone."

Antony heard a note of triumph in her voice, and it angered him. "We'll leave now," he said before Sergius could reply. "But we won't go back to Ephesus without Victor."

"We'll be watching you," Plautius said. "Watching and praying, Tullia."

The reference to prayer annoyed the witch. "Get out of my house this instant," she yelled. "In the name of Artemis, I command you to leave!"

Plautius responded, "In the name of Jesus Christ, and by His authority, I command you to leave this child and his family alone. The boy belongs to God, and you'll not harm him." He fixed an unflinching gaze on the nefarious woman as he spoke a word of prophecy: "Renounce your evil deeds," he said, "or all your curses will come back on you."

Tullia laughed, but it was a hollow sound. She appeared shaken as the three men left her house.

Outside, Antony sheathed his dagger and mounted his horse. He was relieved to be out of the place, but more concerned about Victor's whereabouts than ever. Where had Damian taken him? Tullia had said they would never find the baby. She knew where he was, Antony was certain; but how were they supposed to find the hiding place?

And what had happened to Marcellus and Verus? Antony suddenly realized they had never made it to Tullia's. He and Plautius and Sergius hadn't been inside the house for very long, yet it worried Antony that the others had not joined them. Were they still searching the woods?

Antony thought of the riderless horse at the edge of the thicket, and a new apprehension welled up in him. Not only had they not found Victor, they also had not run into Jacob—and Antony knew Jacob had left for Tullia's house a couple of hours before they had. Now Marcellus and Verus were unaccounted for as well. It was more than a little worrisome.

They rode about a quarter-mile, to the point where the cutoff to Tullia's house met the road they'd taken from the inn. Antony started to turn right and retrace their route, but Plautius called out for him to stop.

Antony pulled on the reins to turn his horse around. "What is it?"

Plautius looked thoughtful but didn't speak.

"Well?" Sergius prompted.

"Follow me," Plautius finally said. "I think I know where to find Victor."

Marcellus had taken only a few steps into the forest when he began to have the same eerie feeling Antony had tried to express—a feeling that some evil force lurked just ahead.

An experienced hunter, Verus took the lead. He could tell which direction the unknown man had taken by spotting broken twigs and trampled grass, and the trail was definitely leading toward the back of Tullia's house.

They had made it almost to the edge of the woods—Marcellus could see a house beyond the trees—when Verus suddenly stopped. "Look at that," he said.

Marcellus strained to see what Verus was talking about.

"Right here. The two ruts." Verus followed the closely spaced ruts for a few paces. "Looks like something—or somebody—has been dragged through here."

"Maybe somebody killed a deer . . ." Marcellus said tentatively.

Verus's voice was grim. "The ruts are too big for hooves. A bear, maybe. But the hunters have killed them all off. Haven't seen a bear in these woods since I was a kid."

If it wasn't an animal that had been hauled through the woods, Marcellus thought, then it must have been a man. He could picture a man's feet making the ruts as his body was dragged, and that image gave Marcellus a chill as he followed close behind Verus.

The trail led them into the clearing behind the house, and when the trail stopped, Marcellus's sense of foreboding mushroomed. A fresh mound of dirt lay in front of them. Any idea that someone had been dragging an animal through the forest vanished from Marcellus's mind. They wouldn't have buried an animal, and this looked exactly like a hastily prepared grave.

Verus reached the same conclusion. "The good news," he said, "is that it's much too big to be a child."

No, Marcellus agreed silently, the dirt mound was about the size of a six-foot man. A man the size of Jacob.

Marcellus squatted on his haunches and touched the damp earth. He wondered if his friend had been killed in the woods, then dragged back here and buried. Antony had had a strong feeling that the abandoned horse had belonged to Jacob. Was the lawyer right? Was it Jacob's body covered up here?

Verus touched Marcellus's shoulder. "Whoever it is," he said, "there's nothing we can do for him now."

Feeling helpless, Marcellus couldn't resist scooping a few handfuls of dirt off the top of the grave. He and Verus could dig out the body . . .

No, it would probably grow dark before they could finish the job, and what good would it do, anyway? It wouldn't bring Jacob back if he were indeed dead.

Marcellus thought about Rebecca and how she would take the news if Jacob had been killed trying to rescue Victor. It would be yet another staggering blow, and Marcellus couldn't bear the thought of having to tell her.

Maybe it's not even him, Marcellus reminded himself. But his gut told him it was.

He silently vowed to come back the next day and dig up the body; he had to know for sure. *If it's you, Jacob, I'll take you back to Ephesus. I promise.* Marcellus would make sure Jacob was buried in the family tomb with his parents. It was the least he could do for Rebecca.

Verus was right: There was nothing they could do here now; they'd better join the others. And they'd better do whatever it took to get Victor back. That was the one thing that would soften the blow to Rebecca if something terrible had happened to Jacob.

Marcellus was about to stand to his feet when the ground shifted slightly in front of him. It distracted him enough to look down. His first thought was that perhaps he had still been holding a handful of dirt and had dropped it without paying attention to what he was doing.

He abandoned that thought when five fingers suddenly burst through the ground and a man's hand reached for him.

✝

Antony and Sergius followed Plautius, who shielded his eyes against the late afternoon sun as he turned his horse to the left, heading away from the road they'd taken from town.

Sergius immediately hazarded a guess as to their destination. "You figure they're hiding the baby at the old mill."

"Makes sense, if you think about it," Plautius said. "It's close by, yet can't be seen from Tullia's if someone comes snooping around. And it's isolated. Few people travel this road, and they wouldn't stop at an abandoned mill if they did venture out this way."

It was isolated, all right, Antony thought. They hadn't ridden far when the road narrowed. Actually, *road* was an optimistic term for what was now an unpaved, overgrown path. But someone had been here recently: Antony could see the tracks of a wheeled vehicle in the hard-packed ground.

Sergius shook his head dismally. "Not a fit place for a child. The granary had all but crumbled to the ground last time I saw it, and that was several years ago."

The small milling operation had been abandoned almost two decades earlier, the brothers told Antony. In the larger cities, hardly anyone ground wheat for flour anymore; most people relied on large commercial bakeries for their bread. Those too poor to afford baked goods ate wheat porridge.

Decrepit was the word that came to Antony's mind when they reached the mill. The two round, flat millstones and the tall hourglass-shaped hoppers that sat on top of them were mostly intact, although badly cracked. The long wooden handles, which powered the mill when pushed by slaves or drawn by mules, now dangled uselessly from the sides of the stone hoppers. And as Sergius had said, the building where the grain had been stored was crumbling; one side of it, in fact, was nothing but rubble.

There was no sign of life as they approached the ruins. No sounds of life, either. The place appeared not only abandoned but uninhabit-able. Suddenly Antony caught a flutter of movement at the far edge of his vision. He turned in the saddle and stared at the half of the building that was still standing, and he saw it again. He couldn't see the animal, but the motion he'd seen was the quick flick of a horse's tail.

Gesturing for the others to follow, Antony slowly led his horse around the side of the building. There they found a horse grazing in the weeds, and beyond the horse was a carriage. The horse was unyoked but loosely tethered to the vehicle's axle.

From the description Marcellus had given, this could be the carriage Damian had taken when he left Ephesus. The large four-wheeled coach would have to be drawn by two horses, however, and Antony could see only the one horse. But the animal was solid black, like the pair of stallions that had driven Damian's carriage. And who else would park a fancy coach behind an abandoned mill? It had to be Damian.

Antony's heart began to pound as he realized they had found the hiding place, and his keen mind began to race. Was Victor inside the crumbling granary? Was Damian inside as well? Or had he ridden off on the second horse? Perhaps the other animal had gotten loose and was wandering nearby. Antony looked around but still did not see another horse.

He told the men who had accompanied him what he was thinking. "We have to go inside," Antony said quietly. "But we could be
ambushed."

Plautius nodded somberly. "God will go with us."

Antony hoped the blacksmith was right. "I'll go first," he said. "I
have a weapon." He dismounted and quickly removed his dagger. It
felt solidly reassuring in his hand, yet he knew that if Damian wielded
a sword, the three of them would have a hard time overpowering him.

The would-be rescuers stole back around to the front of the building and approached the entrance. The door had rotted off its hinges
years ago and lay broken on the ground, apparently kicked to one
side.

Antony felt an acid wave of fear rise up in him as he stepped
through the doorway into the darkened shell of a building. A single
shaft of light penetrated the ruins. It came from a small window near
the ceiling along the side wall to their left, the one complete wall that
was still standing.

He waited a long, breathless moment just inside the door, the two
brothers close behind him. Gradually their eyes adjusted to the dim
interior and they took a few steps forward, cautiously looking around.

Surely if Damian were there he would have attacked them by
now, Antony thought. It would have been the perfect opportunity
to catch them off guard, while they were still unable to see enough
to defend themselves adequately.

Their progress was slow. Antony couldn't see or hear anything that
would lead him to believe Victor was hidden here in the ruins. *But he
has to be here,* Antony's mind screamed. *We have to find him.*

"Over there," Sergius finally whispered. "Against the back wall."
He made a slight motion with his hand.

As Antony looked in that direction, he saw what appeared to be
a small heap of rags in the farthest corner of the building. He
approached with his dagger drawn and poised to strike. When he
crouched beside the rag pile, it moved.

"Please don't hurt me," a tremulous voice said. "Don't hurt the baby. Please—I'll do whatever you want."

"Victor!" Antony cried.

"We don't want to hurt you," Plautius reassured the petrified woman. "We just want the baby."

"Who are you?" she asked, clutching the child to her bosom.

"We're friends of the child's mother," Antony replied. "We're going to take him back to her."

"Take me with you," she begged. "Please." She looked imploringly at Sergius as he reached down and took the child from her arms. "He—he'll kill me if he comes back here and finds the baby gone."

"Damian?" Antony asked.

She nodded. "Yes."

"Where is he?" Antony instinctively pivoted and looked around him.

"He brought the baby back to me to nurse, then he left to get food for the horses."

Damian could be back any minute, Antony realized. They had to get out of there fast. "All right, we'll take you with us," he said. He reached out to help the woman to her feet, but she didn't move.

"I—I can't walk," she said. "My leg is fastened to the wall."

Antony swore. The barbaric tribune had chained the wet nurse who was keeping his own son alive. Antony knelt down and vigorously yanked on the large hook that fettered her ankle to the wall; nothing happened. The hook was firmly imbedded in the mortar and wouldn't budge.

He looked down at his dagger and wondered if he could pry open her shackles without slicing the woman.

Plautius realized what he was thinking and stopped him. "Even if it fits, the dagger might break," he said. "Use something else."

"But what?" Antony asked in frustration.

"We'll find something." Plautius looked around until he discovered some rusty implements. The blacksmith took a long, slender tool of some kind and placed it into the space between the woman's ankle and the circle of iron. The shackles had been designed for a large man, so there was space to work. He wedged a second tool in the circle and began to use the two iron implements as levers.

The woman grimaced but kept quiet as Plautius tried to pry the shackles open. The iron circle finally bent but did not break.

It's not going to work, Antony thought, *and Damian could be back any moment.* "Hurry," Antony urged the blacksmith, a note of desperation in his voice.

Sergius held out the baby. "Take him and leave," Sergius told Antony. "We'll follow as soon as we free the woman."

Antony hesitated, but not for long. As he reached for Victor, he offered his dagger to Sergius. "Take this," Antony said. "You may need it."

"You may need it more," Sergius said, refusing the weapon. "Go now."

Plautius said nothing but kept working intently on the iron fetters.

Antony hated to leave the others behind, but Sergius was right. Rescuing Victor came first.

Replacing the dagger in his belt, Antony took the child from Sergius and said, "God be with you." The benediction, which once would have sounded strange coming from the lawyer's lips, felt almost natural as he spoke it. The brothers would need divine aid if Damian returned and found the baby gone while they were still trying to help the woman escape.

As he turned to leave, Antony heard Plautius grunt. "Loosen, in Jesus' name," the blacksmith ordered.

Later, Antony would wonder what had prompted Plautius to issue a command to an inanimate object, but at that moment the only thing that struck Antony was the sound of the iron chain as it suddenly snapped open.

"Got it!" Plautius shouted.

Sergius helped the woman up, Plautius dropped the rusty tools to the floor, and before Antony knew what was happening, all of them were scrambling through the door and running toward the horses.

When they made it outside, Antony quickly handed the baby to the nurse, lifted her onto his horse, then jumped on behind her. He made sure she had a firm hold on Victor, then he goaded the horse into a run.

Plautius and Sergius caught up with them and the animals galloped, three abreast, toward the heart of the city.

As the road started to climb, they allowed the horses to slow a bit, then they merged into a single file in order to pass some travelers who were partially blocking the road ahead. Antony cautiously watched the roadside as they neared the scene. Surely it couldn't be Damian; he would be riding in the other direction. Besides, there were three travelers: two men were struggling to help a third man climb onto a horse.

As Antony and the others drew alongside, they heard the large man groan as the other two finally heaved him over the saddle.

Plautius, who was in the lead, suddenly reined in his mount. "Verus?" he asked.

Antony stopped, now close enough to get a good look at the travelers. It was indeed Verus who stood by the horse and rider, along with Marcellus. The horse was the one they'd seen tied at the edge of the thicket earlier; the rider, who was covered in dirt from head to toe, was unrecognizable. Yet there was something familiar about him . . .

"J-Jacob?" Antony finally stuttered. "Is that you?"

The man who was supposed to be dead grunted in acknowledgment, then slumped over the saddle.

12

PETER STOOD AND STRETCHED, then walked around the large desk he shared with Quintus and out onto the dock. He had been distracted ever since Antony and Rebecca had left the previous morning in pursuit of Jacob, who had followed Damian away from Ephesus. After their carriage departed, Peter had come to the harbor office as usual, but he had found it difficult to work.

This morning it was no easier. A small mountain of paperwork demanded his attention, but Peter couldn't seem to concentrate. He alternated between worrying about his kidnapped nephew and stewing over his sister's involvement. Why couldn't Naomi have conceded gracefully and gone back to Rome? Why did she have to do something so diabolical?

And why, Peter wondered, did he have to suffer from the physical limitations of a deformed ankle? For a few minutes he watched the boats in the harbor and indulged the wish that he could have joined the others in the attempt to rescue Victor. *I feel so useless sometimes,* Peter thought.

After a while he reminded himself that there was something useful he could do, and that was to take care of business. With a reluctant sigh, Peter turned and limped back to the office. There was plenty to do, even though commercial shipping had ceased for the winter. Just two days ago, one of their ships, the *Valeria,* had made harbor with its final load. Its cargo, along with what remained in their warehouse, would be delivered over land. Quintus would oversee the inventory, while Peter's primary job was to handle the year-end accounting. Judging from the preliminary figures, it appeared his father's business had enjoyed another prosperous year—an accomplishment Peter took pride in, although the credit for their success, he acknowledged, was due primarily to Quintus's careful stewardship.

An hour later Peter was still at the desk, matching shipping manifests with invoices and receipts, when Quintus interrupted him. "You have a visitor," Quintus announced in his deep voice, his tone customarily serious. But when Peter looked up, he saw Quintus trying to stifle a smile.

The visitor was Helena's youngest child. Peter was fond of the precocious eight-year-old and was glad to see her now. As she breezed into the room, Peter couldn't help thinking that Priscilla was the exact image of her mother, a fast-moving blur of dark honey-colored curls, with the same hazel eyes and heart-shaped face as Helena. But the little girl had also inherited a quick, logical mind, and in that, Peter now realized, she resembled her oldest brother, Antony. There was another brother in between the two, but he'd left home several years earlier and Peter had never met him.

"Where's your mother?" Peter asked. He looked around, expecting another flurry of activity to announce Helena's arrival, but Quintus left and no one else appeared in the doorway.

"She's at home," Priscilla said matter-of-factly. "She got sick yesterday, and she was still too sick to get out of bed today."

"You came all this way by yourself? Where's . . ." Peter paused to think for a moment. "What's her name? Your housekeeper."

"Calpurnia's daughter is having another baby, and Mama let her leave to help with the delivery." Priscilla sounded slightly insulted as she added, "And it's not all that far from our house to the harbor."

"Who's taking care of your mother while Calpurnia is gone?"

Priscilla looked puzzled. "I am. I always take care of her when she gets sick."

"I'm glad you came to tell me," Peter said. "I'll send someone to look after Helena right away."

"That's not why I came," she said. "It's just that with Rebecca gone, and now with Mama sick, there's no one to make their visits to the congregation. I'm worried some of the children will go hungry."

"I'll see about finding someone else to take care of the relief work for a while." Peter stopped to think who might be available to help, then he started to wonder what was wrong with Helena. "Is your mother very ill?" he asked.

Priscilla paused before answering. "She seems worse this time, I think."

"This time? Does she get sick often?" He could remember a few times Helena had missed attending church, but he didn't know whether she had been ill or if family duties had kept her away.

The little girl nodded soberly. "Not often, but it happens sometimes. Especially when it's cold."

Peter started to ask what was wrong with Helena but then decided it would be impolite to ask.

"I think Mama's working too hard," Priscilla continued. "She's been getting sick more often since she took over your mother's work last year. But this is the first time she's been in bed for more than one day."

"Has she consulted a doctor?" Peter asked. Abraham had not set much store by doctors, but Elizabeth had taken Peter to see one when he was younger. To her dismay, there had been nothing the doctor could do for her crippled child. But perhaps a doctor could help Helena. If Marcellus had been there, Peter would have sent him to see her, but the medical officer had gone with the others to find Victor.

Priscilla's curls bounced as she shook her head. "No, but she doesn't need to. Mama says God will heal her. We prayed again this morning."

Peter repressed a twinge of bitterness. At one time he had thought God would heal him too. The church regularly prayed for the sick, and Peter didn't know why others had been healed yet he was still lame. To be honest, it bothered him, and Peter's infirmity had led him to question God at one time. He had even felt ashamed; some church members had implied Peter hadn't been healed because he didn't have enough faith. Eventually he had come to terms with his disability, but occasionally he still wondered if, for some reason, God didn't love him very much.

"Peter, is it all right if I ask you for a favor? That's really why I wanted to see you today."

Priscilla's question brought Peter back to the present and he guiltily thought for a moment that the youngster knew exactly what he had been thinking. That was preposterous, of course. The eight-year-old was not a mind reader, although Priscilla did often amaze people with her astute observations.

"Of course," he said, suddenly intrigued by the notion that something besides getting help for her sick mother had prompted Priscilla to come see him.

"I want to use part of your warehouse," she said.

"My warehouse? Whatever for?" He would have laughed, except Priscilla looked completely serious. The little girl sitting across the desk—a child whose feet didn't even reach the floor—spoke as intently as if she were making an important business proposal.

"It would make Mama's work easier," she patiently explained.

Peter didn't see the connection but he said, "Go on."

"She and Rebecca spend a lot of time collecting things from other people to give to the poor, then they have to take it all to the families in need. So if we had a warehouse, all the church members could bring whatever they wanted to donate here, and you could store it. Then Mama and Rebecca wouldn't have to make so many trips across town. Right now they have to work almost every day, and they're still not able to get everything done.

"And not only that," Priscilla continued, "but we could keep big things here."

"Big things? Like . . ."

"Like furniture. You know the family in our church whose apart-
ment burned down?"

Peter nodded. The fire had occurred a few days earlier, when one
of the neighbor's children had overturned a burning oil lamp. Half of
the tenement had gone up in flames before the blaze was put out. If
the building hadn't been so close to the waterfront, the entire structure would probably have been lost.

"When they find another place to live," Priscilla said, "they won't
have any furniture at all."

Peter's amusement at Priscilla's proposal turned to amazement.
"Using the warehouse is an excellent idea," he said. "People always
have a table or chair or bed they're not using, and if they brought those
items here, then we would have whatever the family needs for their
new home, right in our warehouse."

"And the other families that lived there too," Priscilla said, beaming at his approval of her suggestion. "Even though they're not believers, shouldn't we try to help them?"

Out of the mouths of babes, Peter thought. He remembered something Helena had said once. She believed she'd been driven by
prophetic inspiration when she had decided to name her only
daughter after the woman who had been so influential in spreading
Christianity across Italy, Greece, and Asia. Over forty years earlier,
Priscilla and her husband, Aquila, had started the first church in
Ephesus in their home, working with the apostle Paul and his protégé, Timothy. A woman of considerable scholarly attainment,
Priscilla had expounded Scripture to some of the notable leaders of
the fledgling movement, including Apollos.

Peter didn't know if this Priscilla would rise to the same promi-
nence in the church, but she certainly had a wisdom beyond her
years and a heart for ministry. No matter how mature she was for her
age, however, an eight-year-old child had no business having sole
responsibility for her mother. With Calpurnia gone, and not know-

ing when Antony would return, Peter decided to make it his business. He would move Helena and Priscilla to the villa for the time being.

"We'll discuss your idea in detail later, but now you need to get back to your mother. How would you like to ride home in my litter?" All of their wagons were out making deliveries and Peter had sent the carriage with Antony and Rebecca, so the litter was the only means of transportation he could offer the sick woman at the moment.

Priscilla's eyes lit up, then she quickly turned serious again. "That's not necessary," she said. "I don't need it, but you can't get around without it, Peter."

"Neither can your mother right now, and I think it would be a good idea for the two of you to stay with us until your brother comes home. The litter can return to the harbor to fetch me after you and Helena are settled at the villa."

✝

When Helena woke the next morning, she wanted to cry from the pain but was too exhausted to make the effort. Her elbows and knees were red and swollen, and hot to the touch. Her shoulders and hips and feet ached unbearably. She hurt so much, she could not stand for anything to touch her; even the light pressure of the bedcovers seemed to sear her skin and seep into her bones.

The ride in the litter had been excruciating. Priscilla had piled cushions all around her, but being carried through the hills had jostled Helena's aching joints until they burned like fire. Now her pain was worse, and she didn't think she could move at all. With Priscilla's help, however, she made it out of bed to use the chamber pot. Then she hobbled back to bed, stopping a moment to hold her hands over the charcoal brazier, hoping the heat would relieve the cramping and unbend her frozen fingers.

"I'll go get you some breakfast," Priscilla said when she had resettled her mother, lightly spreading only the sheet over her.

"I can't eat," Helena said.

Priscilla patted her mother's hand. "It's all right. I'll feed you."

"I meant, I'm not hungry." She wasn't hungry, although if she had been, Priscilla would have needed to feed her. Helena didn't think she could lift a spoon to her mouth if she were starving.

"Maybe you will be in a little while. I'll go to the kitchen and ask the cook to prepare something for you."

When Priscilla left, Helena closed her eyes and tried to pray, but the pain made it too hard to concentrate on the words. This was the worst episode she had ever endured. The horrible pain and stiffness struck her from time to time, but it usually subsided after a day or two of bed rest.

Helena had overdone it the day Victor was kidnapped, going up and down the stairs all those times after walking completely across the city that afternoon. The next day she'd been unable to get out of bed. Two days later Helena had not improved, and she didn't know when she would be able to get up and resume her normal activities. It was disheartening, but at least she didn't have to worry about taking care of Priscilla now that Peter had moved them to the villa.

A few minutes later she had the opportunity to thank him personally when he knocked on the bedroom door. "I thought I'd come and check on you before I left for the harbor," he said when she had called out that it was all right to come in.

"I'll be fine," she said. "I have everything I need, thanks to your help, Peter."

"This room is tiny." Peter frowned as he surveyed the small room in the servants' quarters where Helena and Priscilla had spent the night. "Are you sure you wouldn't be more comfortable in Jacob's room?" he asked. "I can have someone carry you upstairs; it's no trouble."

"No, this is much more convenient, in case I need anything. Priscilla can watch out for me right here, and I'm sure I'll be back on my feet, and back in my own home, soon." The words were much more optimistic than she felt, but she told herself to trust God to raise her up quickly. He had always brought her through these sick spells before.

"Speaking of Priscilla, did she tell you about wanting to take over my warehouse? She has visionary ideas for it." Peter grinned as he spoke. "I was quite impressed, and she won Quintus over to the idea at dinner last night."

Helena listened as Peter began to outline the plans they had made to expand the relief efforts. "A small warehouse adjacent to ours is vacant," he said, "and Quintus and I had already been thinking about expanding into it. Last night we decided to go ahead and lease it, and we'll use it for the ministry. We won't really need any additional warehouse space for the shipping business until the spring, anyway. And I'm going to assign some of our dock workers to help with the project."

Peter's enthusiasm for the charitable work touched Helena. She was proud of her daughter's initiative, relieved that she would have more help, and yet a little disappointed that the ministry seemed to be growing beyond her ability to oversee it.

She also felt left out. Helena was used to being right in the middle of things, and she hated being helpless like this. If only she could get out of bed and do something . . .

At the moment, however, she hurt too much to even think about it. Perhaps tomorrow would bring relief to her aching body.

"Before I go," Peter said, "I have to tell you something else Priscilla said last night. I couldn't help laughing."

What has the child done now? Helena wondered, at once both curious and apprehensive. Priscilla could be far too outspoken around adults, and many people weren't used to it.

"When Quintus first joined us for dinner," Peter said, "he was even more reticent than usual. When he finally spoke up it was only to complain about something that had happened at the office. Priscilla let him finish, then she smiled sweetly and said, 'Quintus, what you need is a wife. It would improve your disposition considerably.'"

Helena was embarrassed but not surprised by her daughter's

impertinence. "Please apologize to Quintus for me," she told Peter. "Priscilla is too quick to speak her mind."

"He wasn't offended," Peter said. "Quintus actually smiled and told Priscilla she needed to grow up very fast, before he got too old to marry her.

"'I don't think you can wait around that long,' she told him. 'You'd better look elsewhere.'"

Helena smiled as she pictured her daughter engaging the dour Quintus in a bit of verbal repartee. To be fair, she thought, Quintus wasn't dour. He was serious-minded, and his long face sometimes gave the impression he was a stern man, but he was actually kind and considerate. She wondered why Quintus, who must be around forty, had never found a wife. He seemed to have been married to Abraham's business all these years.

As soon as Peter left, Priscilla returned, bringing Agatha with her. The maid set a breakfast tray by the bed, and Helena's mind began to spin with possibilities. She guessed that Agatha was about ten years younger than Quintus. A single woman with a small child, Agatha needed a husband as much as Quintus needed a wife.

Helena had the soul of a matchmaker, and that was something she could do even from her bed. She sighed and braced herself to move. "Help me sit up," she said to Priscilla. And to the other woman she said, "Agatha, dear, please stay and keep me company."

There was no chair in the small bedroom, so when Helena motioned for her to sit, Agatha perched on the edge of the bed. She felt a bit awkward; it did not seem appropriate for one of the servants to be treated as an equal. Yet this guest was staying in the servants' quarters, and this household did not seem to observe the usual class distinctions anyway.

"I'm so happy to see you recovering," Helena said. "I didn't think you would be back at work so soon."

"I'm not working yet. But I felt better this morning, so I went to the kitchen for breakfast. The cook asked me to bring this tray back to you."

"I could have carried it by myself," Priscilla said. She began to tear a small loaf of bread into pieces and feed them to her mother.

"My room is next door," Agatha said, "so I was coming this way."

In between bites of food, Helena said, "Tell me about yourself, Agatha. You haven't always been a housemaid, have you?"

"No, ma'am." Agatha hesitated. She was never sure what to tell people about her life before she started working for Peter and his family. "I once had a house of my own," she said tentatively.

"It must be difficult," Helena said, "being a widow with a small child. How old is Aurora now?"

"Almost ten months."

"She's a pretty baby," Priscilla said, her lovely curls bobbing as she turned from her mother to address Agatha. "Can I hold her sometime? I could keep her for you while you rest."

"That would be nice. She's asleep in my room right now."

Helena finished a few bites of fruit and resumed her questioning. "She was so tiny when you first came here. Was your husband still alive when Aurora was born?"

"Actually . . . I'm not a widow." It would be easier for Agatha to let people think that; it's what they usually assumed. She tried to avoid questions, but when someone asked her directly, she told the truth, as she did now. "My husband divorced me."

"That's a sin," Priscilla said. "I heard it in church."

"He's not a Christian," Agatha explained. "And neither was I at the time."

Helena shook her head sadly. "Imagine that—and you with such a young baby. How terrible for you!"

She couldn't know the half of it, Agatha thought. But all she said was, "My husband didn't want children." Well, he certainly hadn't wanted a daughter. She hoped Helena wouldn't ask too many more questions. Agatha was getting tired, and she was uncomfortable being the focus of attention.

"Have you given any thought to remarrying?" Helena asked, then she waggled her head when Priscilla offered her another bite. "That's all I want," she told her daughter.

The question surprised Agatha, and she didn't know how to respond. She really hadn't thought about it. At first she'd thought of nothing but survival. Lately all she'd thought about was work. She liked to keep busy so she wouldn't have too much time to be alone with her thoughts. The villa was huge, and she worked very hard; she wanted to do a good job so she and Aurora could continue to live there. She simply hadn't considered any possibilities beyond that.

Priscilla rushed to say, "Quintus needs a wife—you should marry him!"

Helena laughed and seemed to brush the comment aside. "I don't know where Priscilla comes up with these ideas."

"But he's really a nice man," the little girl said, "and not usually grumpy. He just works too hard. He has a lot of responsibility, you know." Like her mother, once Priscilla got going, she tended to keep on talking. "Have you ever been to the harbor to see Peter's office? That's where Quintus works too."

"Yes, I've been there," Agatha said. "And Quintus *is* a very nice man."

She thought back to the day she'd first met Quintus. When Peter had found her at the dock, he'd brought her inside his office. Quintus had gotten a blanket to wrap around her and had given her the food he had brought for his lunch that day. Then he'd held Aurora while Agatha, who'd had nothing but scraps from the garbage heap for two days, ate greedily.

Later she'd been embarrassed that Quintus had seen her like that, dirty and starving, even though he was gracious and never mentioned it. She had seen him at church almost every week since then, and he always spoke kindly to her but didn't say much beyond the usual greeting. Perhaps she'd never given him a chance to say anything else.

Helena leaned her head back on the pillow. "I'm sorry," she said. "Talking has exhausted me. I think I need a nap now."

"Can I go next door and see Aurora?" Priscilla asked her mother. "You can call if you need anything."

Helena nodded. "That would be nice—if Agatha doesn't mind, that is."

"I don't mind," Agatha said. "I feel like lying down too. You can watch Aurora for a while," she told Priscilla.

Agatha returned to her room, thinking about the possibility of getting married again someday but doubting that any man would want her, especially not a fine Christian man like Quintus. Divorce and remarriage were common in Ephesus, except among the Christians. And Agatha was not just another divorced woman with a child. She was a broken woman harboring an abandoned baby . . .

13

FROM THE MOMENT AGATHA had known she was pregnant again, she wore an amulet in the form of a copper cuff around her upper arm. Inscribed on the bracelet were the *Grammata*, six magical terms associated with the chief Ephesian deity, Artemis. More than a mere fertility goddess, Artemis was the all-powerful Queen of the Cosmos, and Agatha had desperately needed divine assistance.

So every morning and evening she stood in front of a small shrine in the atrium of her house and recited the *Grammata*, then beseeched the many-breasted image to bestow nourishing power on the child Agatha carried in her womb.

"I hope you're praying for a son," Falco had said when he first discovered his wife's daily ritual.

"I am," Agatha lied.

Her husband was determined that she produce a male heir, and he lost no opportunity to remind Agatha that was why he had married her. Part of his insistence on having a son was pride: Falco wanted a son to carry on the family name. And part of it was economic: A son would provide financial security during old age.

Falco operated a small fuller's shop and struggled to make ends meet. He envisioned having several sons to replace some of the slaves and freemen he hired to stand in huge vats of water and chemicals and tread the fine woolen fabrics to be cleaned and bleached, then sewn into rich men's clothes.

After three years of marriage, Agatha had given birth to the son Falco craved, but her firstborn had arrived weeks too early and had lived only a few hours. It had taken two more years for Agatha to conceive again, and now she didn't care whether the child she carried was a boy or a girl; she simply wanted a healthy baby, so her prayers to Artemis were gender specific only when Falco was nearby.

Agatha was not an avid practitioner of magic, but she chanted the *Grammata* with fervor, convinced she had found the right formula to guarantee the birth of a healthy baby. She had purchased the silver statue of Artemis with money she had saved out of their household expenses. At first Falco had been furious at what he perceived as extravagance, but he changed his attitude once he knew the purpose of his wife's worship of the goddess.

Falco had never been a particularly compassionate man, and since the death of their son, he had become increasingly cold and, on occasion, even cruel. He thawed somewhat during his wife's second pregnancy, and Agatha began to relax and enjoy the changes in her body. Even Nonius, their one household slave, was more deferential to Agatha as the pregnancy progressed.

As the time for her confinement neared, Falco contracted with a midwife to assist with the delivery because Agatha had no relatives, female or otherwise, in Ephesus. Hiring an *obstetrix* was one of the few expenses the frugal Falco did not find objectionable. The midwife he chose this time was named Alfidia, and she had a reputation as one of the best. Falco was immensely pleased to have secured her services.

Early one morning Agatha woke with a start. She'd had pain in her lower back for a couple of days; now it was suddenly sharp. She tried to go back to sleep but couldn't, and when the first labor pains began in earnest, she roused Falco.

"Go fetch the midwife," she said. "I'm having the baby."

Falco stumbled out of bed and threw his tunic over his head. He ran out of the room, his hair plastered to one side of his head and sticking straight up on the other.

When he returned with Alfidia, she immediately banned him

from the bedroom. The *obstetrix* examined Agatha and reassured her, "You're doing just fine."

Alfidia pulled the sheet up over her patient and allowed Falco back in the bedroom for only a moment. "It's going to take a while—several hours, probably," she said. "Go on to work. I'll send Nonius to notify you when the baby is born."

"I'm not leaving," Falco insisted. "Not until my son is born."

Alfidia shrugged her shoulders. "Stay or leave, it's fine with me. Just keep out of the bedroom. This is no place for a man."

When Falco left again, Alfidia removed some tools and supplies from her satchel. The tiny bedroom held only three pieces of furniture: the bed, a washstand, and a small storage chest. Alfidia spread her things on the washstand, then sat on the edge of the bed by Agatha. The midwife had sturdy, soothing hands, and she used them to massage Agatha's back while she writhed in agony.

In between the labor pains, the women talked about the many babies Alfidia had delivered, and the six children of her own.

"I would love to have that many children," Agatha said.

"Your husband seems to believe you're going to have a boy," Alfidia observed.

"That's what he's hoping for." Agatha clenched her teeth as another wave began to build.

"Will he be very disappointed if it's a girl?"

Alfidia looked troubled as she asked the question, but Agatha was too far into the contraction to wonder why. "Probably. But I won't be disappointed," she told the midwife. "I just want a healthy baby—and I want it soon!" She gave up and let the wave carry her into its depths.

Even though it was winter, Agatha was bathed in sweat as she groaned and travailed. Alfidia repeatedly ran a damp cloth over Agatha's face and murmured encouragement. Agatha sobbed and tried to chant her magic formula.

When Alfidia finally told her to bear down one more time, Agatha strained to push hard, and at last, she felt a welcome release as the baby dropped into the midwife's waiting hands.

With a sense of exhausted wonder, Agatha watched as Alfidia wiped out the baby's mouth, and then the new mother heard the most beautiful sound she'd ever heard—a loud wail.

"It's a girl," Alfidia said, laying the newborn at the foot of the bed.

"A healthy girl?" Agatha asked.

"Certainly appears that way." Alfidia grinned as she cut the umbilical cord. The baby continued to cry, her sobs now punctuated with tiny, trembling sighs.

Agatha reached out her arms. "Let me hold her."

"Be patient while I clean this little jewel," Alfidia said. "Then you can hold her until your arms drop."

The midwife washed away the slick, bloody mucous, then lightly rubbed the baby's skin with salt. Taking a large, clean swath of fabric, she began to swaddle the newborn from the waist down. While she worked, Alfidia said, "You can hold her while I go get your husband. Then we'll make the presentation."

As the *paterfamilias*, the head of the household, Falco would formally receive the child into the family. By Roman law, the father's power over his offspring was absolute.

Before Alfidia could finish wrapping the baby, the bedroom door burst open and Falco strode in, with Nonius on his heels.

"Well?" the new father demanded.

The midwife stiffened at the breach of etiquette. "If you had waited a few minutes, I would have brought the child to you. I always observe the proper customs."

"Let's dispense with the formalities," Falco said, walking toward the baby.

A sudden fear seized Agatha, turning the lingering residue of pain into a searing heat in her abdomen. "I haven't even held her yet," she protested weakly.

"Her?" Falco stopped, frozen in place. "Her?" he repeated.

Agatha cringed at her blunder. Before Alfidia could stop him, Falco yanked away the cloth to inspect the newborn, who screamed anew at the sudden jostling.

Instantly Falco's face contorted into a seething fury. "What happened to the son you promised me?" he raged at his wife.

Petrified, Agatha could not answer. She'd expected Falco to be disappointed, but she'd had no idea her husband would react so violently.

Falco turned his back on his wife and child and walked toward the door. "Take it away," he told Nonius.

The slave moved to pick up the baby, and Agatha gasped. "No! Falco, please," she pleaded. She managed to get to her feet and went after her husband. Grabbing the sleeve of his tunic, she begged, "Please don't take my baby away."

Falco removed her hand. "You can't do anything right, can you?" he said, not disguising his contempt.

Nonius walked out behind Falco, carrying the little girl, who was still wailing forlornly.

Agatha tried to follow, but Alfidia stopped her. "No," she said firmly but gently. "There's nothing you can do."

The midwife led Agatha back to the bed, then completed the birthing process. Alfidia removed the remains of the afterbirth and used saltwater to cleanse Agatha internally. She sobbed the entire time Alfidia performed her ministrations.

When it was over, Alfidia helped Agatha wash herself and put on a fresh tunic, then the midwife changed the bed linens and put Agatha back to bed.

"What will he do with my baby?" Agatha finally asked, her voice ragged from pain and weeping.

Alfidia skirted the question. "It's his decision, and his decision is law."

"Even though I was the one who gave birth, I don't have any say in my own baby's fate?" It wasn't really a question. Agatha knew the answer.

"No, even though you carried that child for nine months, you have no rights in the matter." With a sigh, Alfidia sat down beside Agatha.

"But I thought infanticide was illegal."

"It is," Alfidia said. "Has been for quite a while." She hesitated, then said, "But there are ways around it, if a man doesn't want a child."

"Tell me," Agatha implored. "I have to know." Her arms ached from the longing to hold her baby. She'd never even gotten to touch her daughter.

"He'll likely instruct Nonius to take the child somewhere outside the city and leave it to die of exposure. It's not really infanticide, see, because he won't have done the killing."

Agatha began to weep again, but with her strength depleted, the tears slid silently down her cheeks. Her heart was so grieved, she wished she could simply close her eyes and never wake up.

"Sometimes, though," Alfidia continued, "a stranger will have pity on an abandoned child and take her—it's usually a girl—in. Maybe that's what will happen to your baby." She patted Agatha's hand in a consoling gesture. "Maybe," she repeated softly.

Agatha thought briefly about praying for her newborn to be rescued, but her faith in Artemis had faltered.

†

For months afterward, Agatha wouldn't let Falco touch her. Barely able to tolerate being in the same room with him, she distanced herself physically as well as emotionally.

Frequently she was startled awake by nightmares of her baby girl lying in the rotting piles of garbage outside the city gates. Sometimes she saw the baby's face covered by maggots. Sometimes she saw vultures swooping from the sky to peck at the defenseless baby. And sometimes she dreamed that dogs devoured her daughter.

Life became intolerable. She couldn't exist like this. But what could she do? She could divorce Falco, she supposed, but where would she go? Agatha had no family nearby; her only relatives were still in

Miletus. Her father had been elderly when she was born; he had died while Agatha was still a young girl. A few years later her mother had succumbed to a protracted illness. Agatha's much older brother had been only too happy to see her married to Falco, a distant cousin who lived in Ephesus.

Feeling trapped and without options, Agatha suffered silently. She couldn't talk to Falco about her sorrow, and she had no close friends with whom she could unburden herself.

Finally, she made an effort to bridge the emotional estrangement from her husband. Agatha reasoned that she could not deny him conjugal rights forever; he was her husband. Besides, she still wanted a child, and there was only one way to create one.

All Falco said was, "I knew you'd come to your senses one of these days."

Several months later Agatha conceived again. Not trusting her husband's reaction, she hid her pregnancy for as long as possible. When she could hide it no longer, she told Falco.

Agatha prepared his favorite dinner and tried engaging her husband in conversation while they ate. Although he didn't say much, he at least made the pretense of having a dialogue. Business had picked up at the fuller's shop, so he was in a relatively good mood. The man dearly loved dirt—dirty clothes, that is. The more soiled garments his customers brought in, the happier Falco became.

After they finished the meal, Agatha refilled his wine goblet. She smiled and said, "I have some good news."

Rather than replying, Falco simply looked at her doubtfully, as if nothing she might have to say could be interesting enough to hold his attention.

Although stung by his arrogance, Agatha continued to smile. This news was too important to let her feelings interfere. "I'm going to have another baby," she said.

"Well, I hope you get it right this time." Falco drank the last sip of his wine, then pushed back from the table.

"Wait," Agatha said, her anger rising. "I have something to say."

Falco raised his heavy eyebrows at her show of emotion. "By all means," he said sarcastically, "let's hear what you have to say."

Agatha took a deep breath. "If it's a girl, we're keeping it this time. I know you want a son, and we'll keep trying until we have one. And I know that sometimes we're financially strapped," she said, "but we're not destitute, Falco. I'll work with you in the fuller's shop, to help cut expenses. I'm strong, I can do it—"

Falco erupted. "That's preposterous—a woman doing the work of a fuller. You'd make me a laughingstock." He rose from the table. "End of discussion, Agatha."

"But . . ." Agatha started to protest.

"Don't get any ideas. Just keep praying to your goddess that you have a boy this time. Because if it's another girl, I'll divorce you." Falco turned and walked out.

Agatha was stunned by his threat; she knew he meant it.

In the days that followed, she refused to let herself dwell on the possibilities. Instead, she renewed her daily rituals of prayer to Artemis, and this time Agatha prayed fervently for a boy. It was clear to her now: she had simply not prayed the right words the last time. Now she recited the *Grammata* and invented precise petitions, reworking her language until she thought there was no way Artemis could misunderstand her petitions or her devotion.

Alfidia attended the birth again, and Agatha was reassured by the kindly midwife's presence. But the delivery did not go well. The baby was too large, and no matter how hard Agatha tried, her body would not open wide enough.

She screamed from the horrendous pain, and periodically Alfidia soothed the worst of it with a bitter brew that contained mandrakes and poppies. Agatha's cries would diminish for a while, and once she even dozed fitfully. But the medication soon wore off, and the ferocious battle with pain would begin anew.

After an endless night of agony, Agatha was beyond exhaustion.

But she determined that if she died giving birth, so be it. She would give her own life in the process, but she *would* bring another life into the world.

Toward dawn, Agatha said weakly, "Promise me something."

"Shhhhh," the midwife replied. "Don't try to talk."

Agatha persisted, raising up on one elbow as she pleaded with Alfidia. "Please promise me that if it's a girl, you won't let Falco abandon her to die." With an urgency born of desperation in her voice, Agatha repeated, "Please."

Alfidia gently lowered Agatha to the bed, then looked away for a moment. Finally, she turned back. "I promise. Even if I have to raise her myself, I won't let him throw this baby away."

Her breathing shallow and her face contorted with pain, Agatha whispered her thanks. She lay quietly for a moment, then said, "I'm going to do this, Alfidia. I'm going to have this baby."

Holding the sides of the bed with both hands, Agatha summoned all her strength and gave a final, powerful push that wracked her body. But at the end of the movement, the baby's head emerged fully.

"It's coming," Alfidia said excitedly. Then she frowned in concentration as she twisted and pulled the child all the way out of the womb.

It didn't concern Agatha that the midwife did not speak again or that she had turned pale. It didn't occur to Agatha that the child was not crying. All Agatha could think was that she had done it; she had finally given birth. Numb from the pain and the narcotics, Agatha did not even realize that she had started hemorrhaging. When she passed out, she was smiling wanly.

Hours later, Agatha regained consciousness. She drifted in and out of a drug-induced haze for a few minutes, then finally woke up.

"Drink some more of this," Alfidia said, holding out a cup. "It will help you sleep."

Agatha didn't want to sleep anymore. She wanted to hold her child for a while first. "Where's my baby?" she asked hoarsely.

Alfidia placed the cup on the washstand without speaking.

"Was it a girl?" Agatha tried to sit up. "Did Falco take her away?" Alfidia had promised she wouldn't let him.

"No, it was a boy." The midwife spoke quietly and almost reverently.

"A boy?" Immensely relieved, Agatha lay back down. She'd had a boy. Artemis had answered her prayer. "Have you presented him to Falco yet?"

Alfidia came and sat on the side of the bed. She folded her hands in her lap before speaking. "The baby wasn't breathing when he was born. The cord was twisted around his neck, and he had been in the birth canal too long . . . there was nothing I could do."

Agatha's mind was still fuzzy, and the realization dawned slowly. "He's dead? My son is dead?"

"I'm sorry," Alfidia said helplessly. "So sorry."

She reached for the cup again and offered it to Agatha. "You bled some," the midwife said. "You need to rest."

This time Agatha took the cup and drank it all.

She woke just before daylight the next morning. Alfidia was gone, but she had cleaned up the bedroom. Falco was not there, and his side of the bed was undisturbed.

It was still early; he wouldn't be gone to the shop yet. The floors were cold, so she put on her slippers before she went looking for her husband. She found him in the dining room, reclining on the single *triclinium*; the room was too small for the traditional three sofas around the square table.

Falco did not look up when she entered. Agatha did not know what to say. She knew better than to expect comfort from her husband; he wasn't the type. But perhaps he would at least acknowledge their loss.

Instead, what he said was, "I'll give you a few days to recover. Then I want you to pack your things and leave."

"L-leave?"

He finally looked up at Agatha. "I'm going to divorce you and find a proper wife. One who can give me the one thing in life I want."

She was shocked. Falco had said that if it was a girl he would divorce Agatha, but it had been a boy. She had risked her life to give birth to their son—and it had all been in vain. Now her husband was through with her.

"Where will I go?" Agatha finally asked.

"That won't be any concern of mine once I file a bill of divorce." Falco calmly wiped his mouth, then stood up from the table. He left for work without another word.

Agatha did not look up as he left. The rejection was too great to fathom. He had never even liked her, let alone loved her. He'd wanted a wife to take care of his needs and to give him a son. She had tried her best but failed. Falco was correct; she couldn't do anything right.

Eventually Nonius brought her something to eat, but avoided looking at her as he served it. *Not even a slave can find anything worthy of respect in me,* she thought.

Falco had said he would give her a few days, but as Agatha ate her breakfast, she decided she couldn't bear to stay a moment longer. She didn't have much to pack—just a few tunics and some copper kitchen utensils that had been her mother's. The most valuable thing Agatha owned was the silver statue of Artemis. Surely she could sell it for enough money to travel to Miletus. Perhaps her brother would take her in.

But when Agatha went to the atrium, she found her shrine destroyed and the statue gone. Dismayed, she went to the bedroom, packed her few things in a threadbare valise, and left the house.

The day was cold and bleak, but that matched the way Agatha felt inside. Could she manage to walk to Miletus in the dead of winter? The journey would take a full two days, if Agatha had the strength for it. She wandered the narrow streets of the inner city, not quite sure of the route she should take but knowing that Miletus lay on the main road to the south.

Agatha was not too far out of the city gates when her nose informed her that she was close to the dump. She stopped in the road, put down her valise, and looked around.

This was where Nonius had left her daughter to die. Agatha wondered if Falco had ordered the slave to dispose of her son's body in the dump as well. No, her husband would have cremated the baby's body. Or should have. No telling what Falco had done—whatever entailed the least inconvenience and the least expense.

A cart drove through the city gates, and she heard the driver shouting. Startled out of her thoughts, Agatha picked up her bag and moved to the side of the road. She began walking toward the garbage heaps.

Dazed, she meandered around the path that circled the dump. It seemed that all her dreams had been consigned to these rotting piles of refuse. Agatha had always wanted a large family. In seven years of marriage she had been through three pregnancies, and still she had no children. The one healthy baby she'd delivered had been thrown out with the pottery shards and human waste and left to die.

The thought left her weak in the knees, and Agatha suddenly plopped down her valise and collapsed on top of it. Perhaps she would just lie down and die—right here, where her daughter had perished. Survival no longer mattered to Agatha. Who would mourn her passing? Would anyone care?

The tears that streaked Agatha's face felt icy. She hadn't realized she was crying until she reached up and wiped them away. A loud, keening sob arose from her chest then, and Agatha keeled forward. She stayed on her hands and knees, wailing brokenheartedly for a few minutes. Then, spent and depleted, she sat back down on the valise while her sobs subsided.

She stared into the garbage piled up near the path, willing herself to take off her cloak and lie down. She would die quicker without the warmth of the woolen outer garment.

When she first heard the tiny cry, Agatha thought it was her imagination. The poppies and mandrakes she had imbibed had played

tricks with her mind, and several times during the night she had awak-
ened briefly, thinking she heard her baby.

But Agatha not only heard the cry again, she saw movement just
at the edge of her vision. A man was walking away. He had dumped
some garbage a few yards from Agatha. Was that where she had heard
the baby cry? Agatha stood and walked toward the spot. Holding her
breath, she searched the debris littering the ground.

She had not imagined the sound. There, in between two heaps of
household refuse, was a baby. The child was carefully wrapped in a
blanket. Someone had wanted to give this little one a chance at survival. And she—was it a girl? Agatha did not remove the blanket to
find out, but she assumed the newborn was a baby girl, and she could
not have been there long; the child was not even cold.

As Agatha cradled the baby in her arms, she began to weep again.
She'd never had the opportunity to hold one of her own children—
not even her daughter. It felt so right holding this tiny life and croon-
ing to her.

With strength she hadn't felt a moment earlier, Agatha went and
picked up her valise, then she carried her bag and her new baby to the
opposite side of the path. Her back to the dump now, she sat down
beneath a tree and rested her back against its broad trunk.

Sheltering the newborn inside her cloak, Agatha unwrapped the
baby's blanket for a moment. She'd been right. It was a baby girl.

Agatha rewrapped the child, then rearranged her tunic to allow
the baby to nurse, drawing her cloak around them both. Time after
time she tried to feed the newborn, with no success. Agatha didn't
know if she had no milk, or if the child was simply too weak to
suckle.

Almost to the point of panic, Agatha finally leaned her head
against the tree and closed her eyes. She had to do something. She'd
been meant to find this baby; she had to be able to nurse her. Agatha
could not, would not let this baby die as her own daughter had.

The prayer rose from the depth of her being until the words burst from her mouth into the frigid air. "If any god can hear me," Agatha cried out, "please help me save this little girl."

Agatha's panic subsided, and she tried putting the child to her breast again. She stroked the little one's cheek as the tiny mouth searched for nourishment.

At last Agatha felt a determined tug . . . and this time the milk flowed from her breast.

✝

Aurora was still asleep on her pallet when Agatha returned to her room with Priscilla.

"I'll sit and watch her while you take a nap," Priscilla said.

"That's sweet of you to offer," Agatha replied as she stretched out on her bed, thankful to be off her feet. She was feeling better today, but being up still tired her quickly.

Priscilla smoothed the bed covers around Agatha, then got down on the pallet with the baby. Tending the sick seemed to come naturally to the young girl, Agatha thought. She hoped Aurora would one day be that kind and compassionate.

As Agatha closed her eyes, Priscilla softly said, "Do you think they'll find Victor? I've been praying for him."

Agatha looked at her sleeping daughter lying beside Priscilla, and her faith stirred. "God can find missing children. That's something I know for sure."

14

FOR THE THIRD TIME IN AS MANY DAYS, Rebecca rode in the bouncing carriage. This time, however, she barely felt the bumps. Polycarp had given her a plump pillow to sit on, but that was not what cushioned the ride. Rebecca's comfort came from holding her son in her arms and knowing that they were going home.

Antony had been terribly concerned that they leave Smyrna before Damian discovered where they were. So after a night of little sleep, they had departed before the sun had completely risen. It had been well after dark the night before when Antony and the others had returned with Victor, and they had all talked for several hours afterward.

Only one other passenger traveled with Antony and Rebecca in the newly repaired coach: the nurse Damian had mistreated so badly. The woman, whose name was Clara, had tried to take good care of Victor in spite of the difficult situation, and Rebecca was relieved that her son seemed to be fine. Victor dozed contentedly in her arms, unaware of the trauma he'd been through.

Marcellus had stayed in Smyrna with John. From there they would leave to deliver the copies of John's revelation to five other churches: Pergamum, Thyatira, Sardis, Philadelphia, and Laodicea. They planned to visit each congregation on the Lord's Day, so making the circuit would take them six weeks, counting the time they spent with Polycarp and his church.

Jacob had also stayed in Smyrna, too weak to travel yet, but strong enough to complain that the rest of them hadn't killed Damian when they'd rescued Victor.

"But Damian wasn't even there when we found Victor," Antony had protested.

"And thank God for that," Sergius said. One of his eyes was swollen almost shut, and he had a scratch down the side of his face. "Tullia was enough to handle."

A look from John had silenced Jacob—for the moment, anyway. "You don't need his blood on your hands," the Apostle had said.

Rebecca still couldn't believe her brother had been buried alive and survived. If Marcellus hadn't found Jacob when he did . . . well, she didn't want to think about that.

And if Antony hadn't found Victor . . . but he had. Praise God, he had. How thankful she was that Antony had been there to help. What would they have done without him?

She looked over at him now, and he smiled back at her. "Antony, thank you . . ." she said, wishing she could find words adequate to express her gratitude. Tears filled her eyes yet again. Rebecca had run the emotional gamut the last few days, having gone from profound fear to overwhelming relief, and her feelings were still fragile.

Antony shook his head. "You don't have to keep saying that," he said. "All the reward I need is seeing you and Victor together again."

Rebecca couldn't help remembering the reaction she'd had when Antony had returned with her son. Beyond her obvious relief, she'd been struck with the thought that Antony had looked completely natural when he walked carrying the baby.

"I've had lots of practice," he'd told her later when she commented on it. "Mother was sick off and on after Priscilla was born, and I helped take care of the new baby sometimes."

Now Rebecca turned away from Antony's gaze. She didn't know why she found his presence both reassuring and a bit unsettling at the same time. "Aren't we taking a different route out of the city?" she asked.

Antony confirmed the change in plan. "I asked Polycarp to direct us away from our original route. This will take us a bit out of the way, but we'll avoid the road that leads to Tullia's."

"I'm glad for that," Clara said. "I was scared when we passed that inn last night and saw Damian's horse." Her shoulders quivered in a slight shudder, then she added, "I don't ever want to see that man again."

"Tullia's brother owns the inn," Antony explained to Rebecca, "and Damian was probably there getting food for his horses. He had stabled them at the old mill where we found Victor."

"Either that or he was there getting drunk," Clara said. "He would start drinking around sunset every night. He was mean enough when he was sober, but when he was drunk . . ."

How like Damian, Rebecca thought. He'd been more concerned about indulging his appetites than feeding his horse—let alone caring for his son.

"Whatever the reason," Antony said, "it was our good fortune that he stayed gone long enough for us to make it out of there unseen."

Rebecca looked up at him for a moment. Antony often said things that reminded her that as nice as he was, he was not a believer. "It wasn't good fortune," she said. "It was divine providence."

"Perhaps so," he replied. "I suppose I wouldn't know anything about that."

He sounded a bit defensive and Rebecca was sorry that her words had implied disapproval. She hadn't intended to correct him; she spoke without thinking because she was firmly convinced that God—not some impersonal force or mere good fortune—had helped them rescue Victor.

Rebecca had been surrounded by believers for so long, she didn't really know how to interact with a man like Antony. How could she feel free to speak her mind and share her faith without sounding condescending? In the future she would have to be more considerate, she decided. She didn't want to offend him, for Helena's sake.

That was the only reason for being more friendly, Rebecca told herself. It had nothing to do with the way she felt inside when she caught Antony looking at her.

And the bumps in the road—that must explain why her pulse had quickened. That's all it was.

✝

After they had sung a hymn, Polycarp stood and addressed the believers who had gathered for worship early on Sunday morning. The young bishop introduced the elderly apostle and explained the purpose of John's visit. Then John began to tell the group about being a prisoner on Patmos, and how he had been "in the spirit on the Lord's Day" when he had received a vision.

Jacob listened halfheartedly. His head still throbbed from the blow he had received two days earlier. But his vision had cleared and he wasn't dizzy; he was grateful for that—grateful to be alive, actually.

He looked around at the people crammed into the dining room. Word had spread that the Apostle had returned with a special message for the church, and even though they met in one of the larger homes in the city, the place could not hold the crowd that had assembled for the occasion. The women and children sat on the floor, while the men lined up against the walls. Some stood in the doorway, and a few listened from the next room. Even the youngsters seemed to be spellbound as the Apostle recounted the story of his vision.

Having heard the account several times, Jacob let his mind wander. He felt oddly detached from his surroundings, as if he didn't belong. It wasn't just that he didn't know most of the people in the Smyrna church. Ever since he'd returned from exile he'd had a similar feeling whenever the church in Ephesus gathered at his family's villa for worship. Jacob knew the songs and knew the sermons—he had even preached some of them—yet he felt like an outsider now, and he wasn't sure why.

After a few minutes, John began to read from the lengthy scroll Rebecca had copied on Devil's Island. "To the angel of the church in Smyrna write: These are the words of him who is the First and the Last, who died and came to life again. I know your afflictions and your poverty—yet you are rich! I know the slander of those who say they are Jews and are not, but are a synagogue of Satan. Do not be afraid of what you are about to suffer. I tell you, the devil will put some of you in prison to test you, and you will suffer persecution for ten days. Be faithful, even to the point of death, and I will give you the crown of life."

Do not be afraid of what you are about to suffer. Jacob had heard the words before; they sounded hollow to him now. He wanted to stand up and contradict John. *Go ahead and be afraid,* Jacob imagined himself saying to the congregation, *because you can't even conceive just how bad things could turn out.*

He had been through the persecution, been imprisoned—and for a lot longer than ten days. Jacob knew that was a figurative number, but he could no longer suppress his resentment that things had turned out so horrendously and gone on for so long. For weeks he had been avoiding the thought, but now he admitted it to himself: Jacob felt as if God had turned His back on Abraham and Elizabeth and their entire family.

When they had arrived on Devil's Island, John had encouraged Jacob to be patient in suffering. *Patience* had never been a word in Jacob's vocabulary, but he had made a valiant attempt. Recently, John had even said that Jacob's patient endurance of life aboard the *Jupiter* was the reason God had sent someone to rescue him. Jacob didn't see it that way. He had saved the life of the highest-ranking admiral in the imperial navy; *that* was why Jacob had been given his freedom.

It wasn't that he wanted to reverse time and bring his parents back. That was impossible, and Jacob accepted it. And it wasn't that he expected God to undo all the damage that had been done. He *did* expect the suffering to come to an end, however, and it hadn't. Damian was still persecuting them.

Jacob was not convinced that it was God's will for Damian to torment them endlessly, and now more than ever, Jacob believed it was up to him to make the terror stop. If he killed Damian, there would be an end to his family's torment.

In Jacob's mind, it was that simple: no Damian, no terror.

Only one man was the source of their tribulation. The official persecution had ended, and politically things were settling down to the previous state of affairs—a sort of grudging toleration of those who denied the gods of Rome and worshiped only Christ. There was still hostility from certain quarters; in Smyrna it came especially from the Jewish population. "The synagogue of Satan," John had called them.

John was no racist. He was Jewish himself, and he loved the people through whom God had chosen to reveal Himself. John's accusation against them stemmed from their instigation of the persecution, in many cases. Jacob knew from Polycarp that even before Damian's troops had arrived in Smyrna, some of the Jews had been bringing charges against Christians to harass them. When the Tenth Legion had arrived, the harassers readily cooperated, helping the imperial troops target believers for the mandatory sacrifice.

John cleared his throat and Jacob looked up. The Apostle's voice— a voice Jacob had heard all his life—was not as strong as it once had been, but it was still as authoritative. John continued reading: "Then I saw in the right hand of him who sat on the throne a scroll with writing on both sides and sealed with seven seals. And I saw a mighty angel proclaiming in a loud voice, 'Who is worthy to break the seals and open the scroll?'"

Polycarp, who was seated to John's right on one of the few chairs in the room, leaned forward, a rapt expression on his face as the Apostle spoke. Jacob thought back to the time, just a year earlier, when he had sat at the front of the congregation with John and Polycarp. How proud he had been to be included in the inner circle, the young protégé of the last surviving member of the Twelve, the disciples who had left all to follow Jesus of Nazareth. The white-haired, wizened man with the raspy voice who now enthralled the listening throng with his revelation had been an eyewitness to the pivotal point of history: the crucifixion and resurrection. And not long ago Jacob had been an important part of John's ministry, with aspirations for a ministry of his own.

How could it be, Jacob wondered, that he now felt so alienated from it all? And why did that alienation not bother him more than it did?

John had confronted him about it the previous night. "You've left your first love," John had accused. "You've lost your zeal."

No, what I've lost, Jacob thought now, *is my family.* And all of it had happened at Damian's hand.

There was one other thing Jacob had lost, or was in danger of losing: his self-respect. He keenly felt that he was responsible for taking care of the family now, and part of that responsibility included stopping Damian from harming them further. Once Jacob had made sure of that, he could turn his attention back to the ministry, or whatever else he decided to do. Jacob wasn't sure now exactly what that would be; he simply knew that whatever it was, it couldn't start until Damian was out of the picture.

Jacob also knew John would be even more upset with him. The Apostle wanted Jacob to accompany him as he delivered the letters to the other churches. "We can finish the ministry tour we started last year," John had said. "You'll have more opportunities to preach."

But Marcellus would be traveling with John, so the Apostle would be in good hands. And Jacob could not see himself preaching again anytime soon. He had nothing to say to a congregation and didn't know if he ever would.

Jacob rubbed his throbbing temples, then turned his attention back to John. "When he opened the fifth seal," the Apostle read, "I saw under the altar the souls of those who had been slain because of the word of God and the testimony they had maintained. They called out in a loud voice, 'How long, Sovereign Lord, holy and true, until you judge the inhabitants of the earth and avenge our blood?'"

Avenge our blood. The phrase startled Jacob. *Avenger of blood* was the thought he kept coming back to.

It was the only way Damian would ever be brought to justice. The authorities would never bring charges against him. Damian was from a very prominent, very wealthy family; he could buy his own justice. As for the charge that he had raped Rebecca, there were no witnesses, so Damian would never be prosecuted. And on the charge that he had murdered Elizabeth, Damian could claim it was an unfortunate consequence of performing his duty: he was under imperial orders to enforce the mandatory sacrifice, and she had interfered.

The same thing could be said about his beating John with the whip: John was a prisoner who had not obeyed a direct order to carry a load of rocks. Damian had oversight of the prison camp, so he was acting within his responsibilities. Never mind the injustice of expecting an eighty-four-year-old man to lift a load of rocks that weighed almost as much as he did—and to do it over and over and over again.

Jacob wished he had killed Damian with the rock he'd thrown in the quarry that day. Of course, if he had, Jacob would have been executed on the spot, but he almost thought it would have been worth it. At least Rebecca would not have had to suffer as she had.

I won't miss another opportunity to take you down, Jacob silently vowed to his adversary. *I'm the closest male relative to my mother and my sister. I will be the avenger of blood, as the law of Moses decrees.*

When John finally concluded his reading, Polycarp led the congregation in prayer, then the attendees began to disperse. Plautius and Sergius, who had helped rescue Victor, spoke to Jacob as they donned their work aprons, then they left to open their blacksmith shop. Verus, who had helped Marcellus discover Jacob's would-be grave, also exchanged greetings with him, then quickly departed.

It was the first day of another week, and people had businesses to tend, jobs to perform. Everyone had someplace to go, something to do. Everyone else, that is.

Jacob watched the worshipers leave, feeling at loose ends, then he thought of Damian again. *I have something to do too,* Jacob told himself. *And the sooner I do it, the better.*

15

AT MIDDAY JACOB STOOD IN THE COURTYARD of Polycarp's house, debating whether to tell anyone that he was leaving. Once he had defined his mission, Jacob had seen no reason to linger at Polycarp's, and he'd had no lengthy preparations to make for his departure other than fetching his cloak and saddling his horse.

It would be rude to leave without saying good-bye to the bishop and thanking him, but Polycarp was not at home. He was off somewhere attending to church business, no doubt. Jacob also wanted to say good-bye to John, because it might be a long time before he saw the Apostle again. But after speaking in church that morning, John had been tired, and he was resting now. Jacob did not want to disturb him, and besides, Jacob did not want to hear any more arguments about vengeance. He was not out to seek revenge, he told himself; only justice. And justice had already been delayed too long.

No time for good-byes, he decided. Anyway, he might not be gone very long. In fact, it could all be over this afternoon, depending on how quickly he found Damian. It was possible that Damian had left Smyrna, yet Jacob had a feeling the murdering, raping, kidnapping brute was still in town. But if Damian had left, he had probably not returned to Ephesus; having been unable to complete their extortion attempt, he would not want to face Naomi anytime soon.

When Jacob walked outside, Marcellus was standing by the sorrel Jacob had ridden to Smyrna. The medical officer looked at the animal, which had been saddled and tied just outside the entrance, and then at Jacob. "Are you going back to Ephesus?" Marcellus asked.

Jacob met his gaze and knew there was something more behind the simple question. He didn't want to lie, but wasn't sure he wanted to tell Marcellus what he was about to do. Instead, he asked Marcellus to tell John good-bye. "Take good care of the crotchety old man," Jacob added with a smile. "I may not get to see him for a while."

"You didn't answer my question." Marcellus was unsmiling and resolute. "Are you going home?"

Again Jacob hedged. "Not right away," he said. "I have some business to take care of first."

Marcellus didn't say anything for a moment. "You don't need me giving you advice; you've had plenty of it." His voice had a gruff note in it, perhaps a fatherly note, Jacob thought. Two days ago the man had dug him out of a premature grave, and Jacob didn't know which of them had been more relieved. The austere military man had almost wept as he brushed the dirt off Jacob's face and helped him breathe normally.

"I suppose this is something you feel you have to do," Marcellus added.

Jacob knew that the other man had guessed the reason for his sudden departure. He offered no explanations or arguments but simply said, "I can't get on with my life until I deal with this."

After another long moment, Marcellus extended his hand. "Be careful, then. Your family needs you."

Jacob clasped the offered hand and nodded, a lump rising in his throat. He was grateful that at least one other person understood and accepted—or at least didn't try to restrain—his need to go after Damian.

His good-byes said, Jacob mounted his horse and rode to the center of the city. In the marketplace he bought a sword and a dagger. He also bought two tunics. The one he'd been wearing when Damian buried him had later been washed and mended, but it still looked ready for the rag pile, which is where it was now destined. Jacob changed into one of the new tunics and left his old clothes with the shopkeeper.

Because he had left Ephesus in such a hurry, Jacob had arrived in Smyrna without provisions, and he'd used what coins he'd had on him that first night at the inn. But Antony had arrived with quite a bit of money for Jacob to use in finding Victor, so now Jacob was well funded.

When he left the marketplace, Jacob headed for the southern edge of the city. There were only two places he knew where he might find information on Damian's whereabouts: Tullia's house or the inn her brother, Tarquinius, owned. The thought of going back to the witch's place was daunting, so Jacob decided to make a few inquiries at the inn first. Then he remembered Antony telling about the abandoned mill where they'd found Victor. So he rode past the inn and past the entrance to Tullia's, and kept following the road when it narrowed, just as Antony had described it.

At the mill Jacob found the coach and only one horse, which meant Damian was probably at Tullia's, or at least that he wasn't too far away. It also meant that he would be coming back. All Jacob had to do was wait. Eventually Damian would show up.

Jacob let the horse amble back to the spot where the road narrowed. If Damian were in town, he would have to come down this road to reach Tullia's house or the mill. Or if he happened to be at Tullia's now, he would have to come this way when he left. Jacob purposed to be lying in wait whenever that happened.

He dismounted and walked his horse into the brush at the side of the road. It wasn't as wooded here as the thicket behind Tullia's house, but he could still watch the road from this vantage point without being too visible.

As the hours passed, Jacob had plenty of time to think about what had happened the last few days. He didn't want to go back to the witch's house. It wasn't so much that he was afraid, even though what had happened to him there had been frightening beyond his experience. But Jacob wanted to face Damian alone, in a place where his enemy could not call on anyone—or any power—for assistance.

Jacob had encountered evil in the forest behind Tullia's house. She had tapped into some kind of supernatural force, and it had momentarily paralyzed Jacob, keeping him immobile just long enough for Damian to reach him and deliver the blow that felled him. Thinking about the attack now, Jacob touched the spot at the base of his skull where Damian had struck him. The knot had gone down, but the place was still painful.

Afterward, when Jacob had told the others about his experience, Rebecca had been distraught. "She put a curse on the whole family?" his sister had asked. "Does that mean we're doomed?" Her voice wavered and her eyes grew large.

John had dismissed her worries emphatically. "Absolutely not," he said. "The witch's curse will not have any effect on a true child of God."

"But look what happened to Jacob," Rebecca had protested.

"Yes, look what happened," John replied. "Jacob is alive because God sent Marcellus and Verus to find him at the appointed moment. Tullia's curse could not kill Jacob—God didn't allow it."

To prove his point, the apostle quoted one of the proverbs of Solomon: "Like a fluttering sparrow or a darting swallow, an undeserved curse does not come to rest." Then he had launched into an impromptu sermon on Balaam, whom the ancient Moabites had hired to pronounce a curse on the new nation of Israel. "The Lord would not listen to Balaam," John said, "and He turned the curse into a blessing."

A witch might manage to harness a measure of demonic power, John had gone on to explain, but whatever power she possessed was subject to the sovereignty of God. As the Lord had demonstrated through the life of Job, Tullia could not harm a hair on their heads without God's permission.

The conversation had calmed any lingering fears Jacob had had. Still, he now thought it prudent to avoid Tullia's house, if possible. No sense in giving her any opportunity to invoke her spirit companions.

Jacob waited so long, he began to think he might have to spend the night by the roadside. Colder weather had arrived the day he'd ridden into Smyrna, and sitting on the ground, his back against a tree, Jacob was getting chilled and damp. He removed his cloak, took the other new tunic from his saddlebag, and put it on over the first one. The extra layer would give him added warmth if he had to sleep outdoors.

The sorrel snorted and stamped, as if signaling her impatience. Jacob had brushed and fed the horse this morning, but he would have to find food and water for the animal before long.

Twilight was falling when Jacob finally heard hoofbeats coming from the direction of Tullia's house. He scrambled to his feet and untied his mount, but stayed out of sight. In a moment, Damian turned onto the road and passed Jacob's hiding spot at an easy lope. He was riding in the direction of the city, not the old mill, Jacob noted as he climbed in the saddle and started to follow. He had hoped Damian would go to the abandoned mill first; it would be an ideal place to ambush an adversary. And it was so isolated, Jacob could bury the body and it was quite likely that no one would ever find it.

Maintaining a good distance between them, Jacob followed Damian, wondering where he was headed. Probably not very far, if he intended to return to Tullia's before dark, yet he didn't seem to be in a hurry. Jacob was, however. He'd been waiting far longer than the hours he had spent watching the road today; he had waited for more than a year.

Time for justice, he decided now. *Past time.*

Jacob dug his heels into the sorrel's side, and she broke into a trot. The quicker gait began to close the gap between him and Damian, and as the horse's hooves struck the ground Jacob silently repeated the ancient legal decree: "The avenger of blood himself shall put the murderer to death."

But Jacob had waited too long to pick up speed, and before he could overtake his foe, Damian turned off the road. Jacob continued on for a few paces, then reined in his mount and turned around. He hadn't realized they were already that close to the inn; the rundown place wasn't as visible from the back road as it was from the highway.

Jacob nudged the horse into the yard of the inn in time to see Damian slip through the door.

What's my next step? Jacob asked himself. If Damian were simply stopping for supplies, he would return shortly. Perhaps Damian would ride back to the mill to tend the other horse; that would be a boon to Jacob. But if Damian went back to Tullia's, that was a different story.

Waylaying him on the road before he reached the cutoff to Tullia's seemed to be the best option. Jacob pictured himself killing Damian and dragging his body back to the mill to bury him. Or perhaps he would leave Damian's sorry carcass on the side of the road and pray that wild animals would devour the remains before they could be identified. Jacob intended to be back in Ephesus before anyone knew what had happened to Damian.

Any minute now, Damian would reappear. Jacob did not let his eyes stray from the door of the inn, and he kept a hand near the dagger secured in his belt. He was ready to carry out the scriptural death sentence.

I am the avenger of blood.

Damian did not return promptly, however. When it was almost dark, Jacob decided to go inside. He was mentally prepared to confront his enemy, and could not bear to prolong the inevitable.

After he tied his horse by the watering trough, he stepped inside and surveyed the dim room. Damian was sitting at the far end of one of the long wooden benches placed on either side of a battered trestle table. He had placed himself near the hearth, where an inviting fire blazed. A blackened, dented pot hanging over the flame simmered with a pungent-smelling concoction.

The innkeeper was admonishing his sole patron. "If you stay and drink yourself into a stupor by the fire, I'm not rousing you this time. You can sleep on the cold floor, for all I care."

"The only thing you should care about, Tarquinius, is keeping my goblet filled." Without looking at the man, Damian extended a tall earthenware drinking vessel toward him.

The innkeeper upended a terra-cotta amphora and refilled the goblet, then walked away, muttering.

Jacob stepped out of the shadow and walked toward the hearth. When he reached the bench opposite Damian, Jacob hauled one long leg and then the other over the plank and sat down.

Damian looked up, a startled expression wrenching his face. He plunked the freshly filled goblet on the table and the wine sloshed over the rim. "You!" Damian choked out. "By the gods . . ."

16

"YOU LOOK LIKE YOU'VE JUST SEEN A GHOST," Jacob said.

Damian had blanched when he discovered Jacob sitting across from him, and now he quickly glanced around the inn, as if seeking confirmation that Jacob was real and not an apparition. Jacob relished the confusion he had created.

While Damian was still composing himself, the innkeeper spotted Jacob and came over to the table. "Welcome back," he said. "What can I get for you?"

Upon hearing the question, a bit of color returned to Damian's face. He was evidently relieved not to be hallucinating; someone else had seen Jacob.

Jacob shook his head. "Nothing, thank you. I have some personal business with your patron here. *Very* personal."

Tarquinius shot Jacob a wary look and moved away, but he remained within hearing distance.

"I thought you were dead," Damian finally said.

His eyelids fluttered, and Jacob wondered if the reaction were mere disbelief or perhaps a flicker of fear. He hoped the latter. "Didn't you notice that the grave you tossed me in had been disturbed?"

"I figured some animal had been scavenging your flesh. Or that perhaps your friends had taken your body to give you a proper Christian burial." Damian's upper lip curled in a sneer. "You people are devoted to your peculiar traditions."

"My friends dug me up all right," Jacob said. "But as you can see, I'm very much alive."

Damian lifted the goblet and gulped. Jacob wondered if the bully's courage had always been found at the bottom of a wine cup. He leaned forward, subtly threatening his adversary by moving close to Damian's face. "You didn't kill me after all," Jacob taunted.

"I can finish the job." Damian drained the last of his wine and leaned forward to meet Jacob's gaze.

"Try it. *Please*, try it." Jacob's words were edged with a steely resolve.

Their open animosity created a tension that curled over the room like tendrils of fog. Tarquinius approached the table, his beefy arms folded across his chest. "Look here, I don't want any trouble—"

"Don't worry," Jacob interrupted. He addressed the innkeeper but kept his eyes focused on Damian while he spoke. "I won't shed his blood in here. We'll settle our disagreement outside."

"What disagreement?" Damian snapped. "You got your sister's bastard child back—what more do you want?"

Jacob slammed his fist on the table. "I want to break every bone in your body. I should have killed you on Devil's Island—"

"You'd better leave now." Tarquinius placed a thick, callused hand on Jacob's shoulder.

Damian suddenly bolted from the table and ran for the door. Jacob shook off the innkeeper's hand and sprinted after Damian.

While Damian was smaller and faster, the wine had slowed his reflexes; anticipation and anger had only whetted Jacob's. Before Damian could reach his horse, Jacob lunged for him. He grabbed Damian's arm and yanked him around, lifting him off the ground for an instant. Then, holding onto his opponent so he couldn't run, Jacob rammed his fist into Damian's jaw. The impact of the blow resounded with a cracking noise that gave Jacob immense satisfaction.

Jacob let go, and Damian staggered backward briefly. Then he came back at Jacob, swinging with alcohol-fueled arrogance and demonic rage. Jacob dodged the punch to his face, but the second one caught him in the abdomen. He absorbed the blow, bending forward slightly, then raised up and slammed his much heavier body into Damian before he could launch another swing.

The motion knocked Damian to the ground, and Jacob landed on top of him. They scuffled in the dirt, and Damian managed to get his hands around Jacob's neck, trying to choke him. But Jacob had his hands on either side of Damian's head, and when he pressed his thumbs into Damian's eyes, Damian released his grip. The two men rolled, pushing, clawing, and grabbing hair.

Tarquinius and the stable boy stood in the yard, watching the fracas, but neither one dared to intervene.

With a powerful shove, Jacob finally pushed Damian off and got to his knees. But before Jacob could stand, Damian pulled a dagger and rolled toward him, lightly nicking the outside of Jacob's calf. He fell to his side and kicked furiously. It was a blind kick, but his foot happened to land squarely in Damian's groin, and a wounded roar immediately filled the air.

Taking advantage of his opponent's vulnerability, Jacob wrested the dagger from Damian's hand. By the time Damian's scream had died, Jacob had pinned him facedown and placed the dagger at the back of his neck.

Jacob's breath was coming in quick gasps as he looked down at the one who had unleashed so much devastation on his family. The moment had arrived. One plunge of the dagger would bring the fight to an end. The blade was long enough to rupture Damian's heart, if Jacob struck in the right spot.

Yet he hesitated. Stabbing an opponent in the back seemed cowardly, and Jacob was not a coward. He had no compunction about killing Damian; Jacob had settled that matter in his mind. But stabbing his enemy in the back was not the way he'd intended to do it.

There were also the witnesses to consider. Jacob knew the innkeeper didn't like or trust Damian, but what would he tell the authorities? If Tarquinius told the truth, it would be that Jacob was the one who started the fight. The prospect of being sent to prison for murder was not a strong enough deterrent to stop him from killing Damian. Bringing the murderer to justice would be worth the risk, although Jacob certainly preferred to do it without witnesses.

But there was yet another reason Jacob did not seize the opportunity to thrust his weapon into his opponent: Damian had not suffered enough, and Jacob suddenly wanted this barbarian posing as a tribune to endure at least a fraction of the suffering he had caused.

With his knee pressed into Damian's back, and his hand yanking Damian's head back, Jacob placed the point of the dagger in the hollow behind Damian's ear. Slowly he traced a line from the earlobe along the underside of Damian's jaw toward his chin. Jacob watched the thin stripe of crimson appear where he had lightly pierced the skin, then he leaned down and spoke in Damian's ear. "I'm going to kill you. But not here . . . not now."

Jacob rocked back on his heels, then stood. "Get up," he growled at Damian. Jacob kept the dagger in his hand, ready to strike, as Damian got to his feet. Unarmed now, Damian stood with his arms spread in a mocking plea for mercy. Jacob walked slowly to his horse, still clutching the blood-tinged dagger.

Damian straightened and called out, "Coward."

"No," Jacob barked. "Avenger."

The two men stared at each other for a long moment, then Jacob motioned with the dagger he had taken from Damian. "Now get on your horse," Jacob instructed.

Damian took a few steps backward, keeping a cautious eye on Jacob. When he reached the animal, he turned and sprang into the saddle.

The stable boy was suddenly at Jacob's side, holding the sorrel's reins, and as Damian spurred his stallion into motion, Jacob mounted his horse and grabbed the reins.

Damian raced away from the inn, with Jacob following in hot pursuit. They were heading for the open road, Jacob realized, not Tullia's.

By the time they reached the highway, the last rays of twilight had disappeared. A gibbous moon faintly illuminated the road, making nighttime travel possible, though still treacherous.

At the intersection, Damian turned in the opposite direction from

Ephesus. Jacob had no idea where Damian was going. Not that it mattered. Right now, Jacob would follow his enemy if he were headed straight into hell.

As they raced into the night, Jacob considered whether he should overtake Damian on the road. Jacob still had Damian's dagger in addition to his own. But a telltale glint of metal in the shadows ahead indicated that Damian's sword was fastened to his saddle. Jacob had a sword as well, but a sword fight while riding at a full gallop in the moonlight was too risky. Jacob could get himself or his horse killed, and neither prospect was acceptable.

So for the moment, Jacob settled for attempting to inspire fear in Damian. He'd seen Damian toy with his victims before he attacked, and Jacob wanted to give Damian a taste of the same kind of torment. He wanted Damian to welcome death when it finally came.

Jacob urged his horse forward, catching up with Damian but staying far enough to the side to be out of reach. Damian looked up in surprise.

"I can catch you anytime," Jacob yelled. "And when I'm ready, I'm going to kill you."

Damian leaned forward in the saddle, his head close to the horse's neck, and drove the animal faster.

Jacob suddenly eased up and let Damian pull a couple of lengths ahead of him, then after a minute he urged his horse forward, again catching up with his prey. When Damian looked over at him this time, Jacob threw back his head and laughed, his breath bursting into the cold air in visible puffs.

Yes, Jacob thought, he could catch Damian and kill him anytime he wanted. In the meantime, he was content to chase Damian—to the ends of the earth if need be.

Wherever Damian looked, the avenger of blood would be right behind him, and there would be no refuge.

17

December, A.D. 96

REBECCA WATCHED ANTONY pop a candied orange slice in his mouth. The dried-fruit treats made her nostalgic; they had been her mother's favorite way to satisfy a craving for sweets. "Don't you have something you need to be doing?" Rebecca asked, forcing a smile as she turned and scanned the row of small bottles and jars on the highest shelf in the kitchen.

Antony chewed slowly and finished the bite before answering. "Why? Are you trying to get rid of me?"

"No, of course not." A flush spread across Rebecca's cheeks. Getting rid of him was exactly what she had in mind, and she was annoyed that he had seen through her. For two weeks now Helena had been at the villa, and Antony had been underfoot the entire time. Every time Rebecca turned around, he appeared at her side. Just now, she'd thought he was working in the library; he had moved some of his scrolls and documents there days ago, but he never managed to stay behind the desk more than a few minutes at a time.

Rebecca positioned a small stool under the shelf and stepped up. Before she could reach for the containers of spices and ointments, Antony was beside her. "Let me get it," he said. "Which one do you want?"

"I can do it myself . . ." Rebecca's voice trailed off as she turned toward him. Standing on the stool put her directly at eye level with Antony, and she was close enough now to count every eyelash. *He must have his father's eyes,* she suddenly thought. Helena and Priscilla had hazel eyes, light brown flecked with green, but Antony's eyes were dark, the color of burnt almonds.

He had placed a hand on Rebecca's arm to steady her, and his touch stirred feelings in Rebecca that she didn't want to consider. She quickly jumped off the stool. "The small jar on the end," she said. The words came out a bit more roughly than she had intended.

Antony retrieved the container and handed it to Rebecca. She nodded her thanks, not trusting her voice to cooperate, then opened the alabaster jar and carefully measured a portion of frankincense into the sesame oil and honey mixture she had already prepared. Next she added small amounts of myrrh and oil of cinnamon.

"What is this fragrant concoction you're blending?" Antony asked.

"A poultice for your mother. It seems to ease her pain." Rebecca spoke without looking up.

"Does my being in the kitchen make you uncomfortable? Is that why you were trying to shoo me out of here?"

"That is *not* what I was doing," she said, knowing she didn't sound the least bit convincing, but unwilling to admit the truth. "It's just that you've had to spend so much time here since Helena has been ill, I figured you must have clients you've neglected and business to tend to."

"Your safety *is* my business," he said.

Rebecca stopped mixing and glanced up. "I thought Victor's safety was the primary concern."

"And yours." Antony leveled another gaze at her that made her uncomfortable. "I don't want anything to happen to you," he said.

Rebecca turned back to her preparation, carefully placing the pot of thick liquid over a small brazier. The balm released a pungent but pleasant aroma. "Nothing's going to happen to me," she grumbled. "Peter hired a bodyguard, remember?"

Even before Peter had hired the man, Rebecca couldn't take a breath without someone checking on her. And as often as not, that someone was Antony. She was immensely grateful for his help in rescuing Victor, but lately Antony's interest in her had become entirely too proprietary, and she was beginning to feel stifled.

Rebecca was also angry with herself for not having had the talk with Helena she'd vowed to have on their return from Smyrna. The woman's none-too-subtle matchmaking had gone on long enough. As sick as she was, Helena persistently contrived to put Rebecca and Antony together, thinking up errands for them to do, or sending one of them to fetch the other. Rebecca supposed she could say something directly to Antony, but what if she had misinterpreted his intentions? It could be that he was merely demonstrating a brotherly concern for a friend and client. If that were the case, she would be embarrassed and even more uncomfortable around him. Silently, she chided herself for not being able to figure these things out.

"The bodyguard is for Victor," Antony said, "not you. And his instructions are to stay in the same room as the baby at all times. Except for nighttime, when he's supposed to sleep right outside your bedroom."

"The man certainly follows instructions; he definitely sleeps. All night long I listen to him snoring on the other side of the door—it sounds like thunder."

Antony raised his voice in anger. "That's not acceptable. Why didn't you say something before? I'll tell Peter to have him replaced immediately."

"No! That's not what I meant." Rebecca hadn't wanted the bodyguard in the first place, but she didn't want to get him fired. "The guard has to sleep sometime," she said, "and I'm sure he would wake up if someone came upstairs and tried to enter the bedroom. It's just that I'm a light sleeper, always listening for Victor. I'll get used to the snoring. At least I know the guard is there if I need him."

"And I'm there too," Antony said. "Just down the hall." Antony had been occupying Jacob's bedroom. Helena was in too much pain to be moved, and because Antony had been worried about Rebecca and

Victor as well as his mother, he had decided to stay at the villa for the time being.

For the first few days Rebecca had been very grateful for the extra precautions, but now they seemed unnecessary. Nothing had happened in the two weeks since they'd brought Victor home. There had been no sign of Damian, even though they'd had someone watching Naomi's house around the clock. Yet Peter worried that Damian might come back to Ephesus without trying to contact Naomi; the two of them might have had a falling out since the kidnapping–extortion scheme did not work out as planned. Or Naomi could be planning some other devious move without Damian's help.

In some ways Rebecca felt imprisoned all over again. She needed time to herself. She longed to go for a walk in the hills, but Antony would insist on coming with her—as he had insisted on accompanying her on visits to the church families she was helping. Rebecca decided she would try to slip outside this afternoon, as soon as she tended to Helena.

Rebecca dipped a finger into the pot to test the temperature, and she was relieved to find the mixture had heated adequately. "I have to apply the poultice while it's warm." she informed him.

"Do you want me—"

"No, I don't need any help." Rebecca lifted the pot and turned to leave. She didn't want to need his help, didn't want to grow dependent on Antony, because that would only make it worse when he wasn't around anymore. Rebecca had learned that you shouldn't take it for granted that people, even the ones who were supposed to love you and take care of you, would be there when you needed them.

Antony briefly looked offended, then he smiled, as if slightly amused. "I'm sorry my presence makes you so jumpy."

He didn't look very sorry to Rebecca. He looked pleased with himself, in fact. And handsome—devilishly handsome—when he smiled like that. For some reason, that irritated her even more.

"Anyway," he continued, "I was going to ask if you wanted me to go with you to the warehouse later. So much has been collected that Quintus suggested we make an inventory."

"If it's not too late when I'm through," she said. So much for her walk in the woods. She did want to go to the warehouse, though. Coordinating the relief efforts was a source of satisfaction for Rebecca, and she had been excited at the ways in which the ministry was expanding.

A few minutes later, when Rebecca told Helena that the warehouse space allocated for their ministry was overflowing, she was excited too. "Now we can help some of the people from the other congregations in the city as well," Helena said.

Rebecca perched on the edge of the bed and applied the fragrant poultice to Helena's red, swollen fingers. Then she covered her friend's painful hands with warm cloths, to help the medication penetrate below the skin. Helena closed her eyes and sighed in relief. Rebecca repeated the procedure on Helena's knees and ankles.

Usually Helena drifted off to sleep as the pain subsided, but today she remained talkative. Rebecca knew she had to find the courage to talk to Helena about Antony; she couldn't keep putting it off, and now was as good a time as any. Helena provided an opening when she began talking about Quintus.

"I don't understand why he has never married," Helena said. "He's a good man, even if he's a little on the staid side."

"Perhaps Quintus prefers to be alone," Rebecca said.

"It is not good for man to be alone," Helena objected. "The Bible says exactly that."

"I won't argue Scripture with you," Rebecca said, "but there may be times when it's not God's will for a person to be married." She took a quick breath and continued before Helena could contradict her. "In fact, I believe that's God's will for *me*."

On the verge of speaking, Helena suddenly closed her mouth and looked at Rebecca for a moment. "Where did you come up with that idea?" Helena finally asked.

"I've been praying about it for a while," Rebecca said, "and I'm convinced that's what God wants for me." She removed the cloths from Helena's hands and warmed the cotton strips over the brazier by the bedside.

"But you need a husband to provide for you." Helena's tone of voice matched her look of disbelief.

"I have my family, and money will never be a problem. I'll be well provided for."

"But a husband does more than just provide financially. A husband loves you and protects you."

"My brothers love me," Rebecca said, "and they can protect me." Rebecca kept her voice lighthearted as she added, "Look how seriously Peter has taken that responsibility—he's even hired a guard."

Helena did not respond with a smile. "Your family can't meet all your needs," she said. "You need the companionship of a husband, Rebecca."

"I don't need that kind of companionship." Rebecca reapplied the heated cloths to Helena's hands. *That's not for me,* Rebecca reminded herself. She had been dishonored—she wasn't marriageable material, and that was the painful truth. Rebecca was determined to accept it and go on with her life.

"You may not think so, but you do." Helena lifted a wrapped hand and placed it over Rebecca's. She waited until Rebecca looked up, then she added, "You also need more children."

Rebecca felt a sudden pang. She had to admit that she wanted more children. She'd always planned on having four children, maybe more, and it would be nice for Victor to have a younger brother or sister. Long-cherished dreams of a husband and a house full of children tugged at Rebecca's heart. As her mother had, Rebecca thought the happiest time of day was when everyone gathered in the *triclinium* for dinner. Now she was mistress of the house and presided over family meals, but it still wasn't the same as having a husband and family of her own. Or a house of her own.

Quickly, Rebecca stood and brushed the folds of her skirt, dismissing the painful memories as if she were brushing off bread crumbs after dinner. "It's not meant to be, Helena. I'm never going to marry."

"Don't cut yourself off from happiness, dear girl. Don't say 'never.'"

Rebecca decided she would have to be more direct with Helena. "If—and this is a very big if—I were ever to marry," Rebecca said, "it would not be to an unbeliever. My husband would have to be a Christian, someone as devoted to God as he was to me."

"Someone like Galen?"

The reminder of her broken engagement wounded Rebecca, but before she could react, Helena pressed on. "Maybe that was cruel, but just because someone is a believer doesn't mean he's the right person for you or that he won't hurt you." Helena softened her voice as she reached toward Rebecca. "And just because Antony is an unbeliever doesn't mean he wouldn't be good to you. I think you're trying to convince yourself that being alone the rest of your life is God's will just because you've been hurt and you're afraid."

Rebecca wanted to defend herself, but she was struck by the fact that Helena's charge contained a kernel of truth. She had been hurt, and she had been afraid. Perhaps it was easier to be alone, more comfortable to push people away, to not let anyone get too close—especially Antony. Right now, however, it was all more than she wanted to think about.

Helena persisted in extolling the virtues of her son. "Antony has many fine qualities and would make a wonderful husband. He loves children and is very devoted to his family. In fact, he's been devoted to Priscilla and me to the exclusion of his own happiness. But now it's time for my son to have a family of his own. He wants that—he deserves it."

"Yes, he deserves a family of his own," Rebecca said. "He does not deserve to be saddled with another man's child."

"You know Victor is not an issue with Antony. He loves the boy and would raise him as his own."

But Victor *was* the issue, and he would always be the issue. Rebecca knew she would never outlive her past. It was an obstacle that would always stand between her and a husband.

"He's said as much to me," Helena continued. "Antony cares about you, Rebecca."

Enough, Rebecca thought. She steeled herself to end the discussion and put a stop to Helena's maneuverings. "Tell Antony I'm flattered, but I'm not the one for him."

"No." Helena struggled to sit up, the effort leaving her winded but not speechless. "Tell him yourself. *You'll* have to be the one to tell my son he's not good enough for you."

"That is not what I said." Rebecca felt her cheeks flush in anger.

"It's what you meant, though. My son is one of the finest men you'll ever meet, but he's not good enough for you because he's not a believer."

"Helena—"

"Would you be so kind as to call Priscilla for me?"

"I'll help you," Rebecca said, figuring Helena needed to relieve herself.

"I'd rather have my daughter," Helena said, her voice as stiff as her limbs. Her face was bright with exertion, or perhaps fever.

Helena's rejection of her help stung Rebecca, even though she was angry with her friend for meddling. "I'll get Priscilla for you," she said.

What do I do now? Rebecca wondered as she left the room. She had hurt Helena's feelings. Evidently she was going to have to hurt Antony's too. Yet it had to be done. Rebecca now knew he definitely had more than a brotherly concern for her, and she couldn't go on letting him think the two of them might have some kind of future together.

18

THE NEXT MORNING ANTONY AND REBECCA visited the new warehouse. He offered to arrange for a carriage to take them; however, Rebecca insisted on walking, and since she seemed to have her mind made up about the matter, he didn't argue.

A fine day for walking, Antony thought as they left the villa. There was an early December chill to the air, but the day was clear and sunny. Traveling on foot would give him more time alone with Rebecca, and he certainly didn't mind that. He wanted to discuss several things with her, one of which was the troubling conversation he'd had with his mother the previous evening.

It had been too late to make the trip to the warehouse yesterday, so Antony had spent some time visiting with Helena, who seemed to have taken a turn for the worse. Not only had her pain increased in recent days, but it had been accompanied by a growing despondency that worried him. His mother was normally so animated that it was hard to keep pace with her. He'd expected the illness to slow her down; now it was destroying her spark of liveliness as well.

He asked Rebecca about it and she agreed that Helena was more subdued. "But then she's been hurting more each day, and the fever rises more frequently. She doesn't complain much about it, but I can tell it's wearing her down."

"She wants to go home. Today. I've tried to talk her out of it, but she won't listen."

Rebecca immediately protested. "Helena can't stay by herself. And it's too much to expect Priscilla to take care of her."

"I agree, and Mother understands all that. But Calpurnia has returned from taking care of her daughter and the new baby, so Mother wouldn't be alone. And she's dead set on going home."

Antony offered a hand to Rebecca as they navigated an uneven portion of the steep Marble Way that led to the heart of the city. In addition to her cloak, Rebecca had worn a head covering, and he couldn't help noticing how the light-blue fabric contrasted with the few strands of glossy, dark hair that had escaped. He also couldn't help wondering what it would be like to loosen the pins and let the thick locks fall through his fingers. Rebecca wore her hair pinned up when she went out—proper decorum for a young matron—but at home she often wore it long and natural. He much preferred it that way. Antony pushed the image out of his mind and refocused on his mother's stubborn demand. "I would still feel more comfortable if she remained with you. If that's all right," he added.

"Of course it is. There are plenty of people to look after her at our home. I've told Helena she can stay as long as she needs to." Rebecca looked at him briefly before glancing away. "Did she say why she wanted to leave?"

Rebecca had been avoiding looking at him, he realized, and now that she had, he was unable to read the expression on her face. Embarrassment, perhaps? He couldn't imagine why. Guilt? Perhaps she didn't really want Helena there. Antony didn't think that was the case. Rebecca and his mother had always enjoyed each other's company. Still, enjoying the company of a close friend wasn't the same as having that person under the same roof day and night— especially when that friend had become an invalid. Both Rebecca and Peter had indicated that they welcomed the imposition, but were they merely performing what they perceived as their Christian duty?

"Well?" Rebecca prompted.

Antony repeated his mother's words. "She said she wanted to die in her own bed." He swallowed hard, seeing in his mind the pale, pinched face as she'd spoken, the words escaping with a slight gasp through clenched teeth.

Rebecca stopped and turned to face him. She started to put a hand on his arm, then dropped it awkwardly to her side. She continued to be nervous around him, and he'd been hoping it was because she felt attracted to him but didn't know what to do about it—which was the other thing he wanted to talk to her about. It was time to tell Rebecca how he felt.

"Is it really that bad?" Rebecca asked. "Did the doctors offer no hope for her recovery?"

Antony chided himself for selfish thoughts of marriage when his mother might be dying. He recounted for Rebecca his dealings with the two doctors he had brought in for consultations. "They made contradictory recommendations," he said. "Special diets, one of which included disgusting animal parts and strange roots. Mother turned up her nose at that. The other doctor said to eat nothing but fresh fruits and vegetables. Hard to get at this time of year, though.

"One doctor said fresh air and moderate exercise; the other called for bed rest in a dim room. She's had two weeks of that and has only gotten worse, so I don't put much stock in that opinion. I'd encourage her to try the other treatment, but how can she get any exercise when it's all she can do to get out of bed and walk a few paces?"

He frowned as he recalled his lengthy conversations with the two men. "For all their words," he said, "neither doctor could tell me exactly what is wrong with Mother, and their hemming and hawing suggested that neither one was entirely convinced of the treatment he recommended. 'Let the sickness run its course' seemed to be the crux of their advice—'she'll either get better, or she won't.'

"So much for highly esteemed medical experts." He laughed ruefully, then sobered. "I even thought of sending for a doctor from Alexandria. I've always heard the Egyptian physicians are the best. But sailing is impossible now, and besides, Mother simply refuses to see any more doctors."

"I'm so sorry," Rebecca said. A worried look creased her fine forehead, and Antony regretted burdening her with all this. But whom else could he talk to about it?

"Helena has never expressed any fears that she was dying before," Rebecca said. "Most of the time she won't even acknowledge how bad the pain is. I only know she's suffering because she gets very quiet." She paused for a moment, as if hesitating to say what was on her mind. Then she said, "I pray every day with her, and I have to believe she'll get better, Antony. I believe God will heal her."

Antony knew Rebecca was sincere in her belief, and he sincerely hoped she was right. "I told myself she was exaggerating," he said, "that she isn't really going to die from this illness, whatever it is. But who knows?" Antony sighed his frustration. "And now she wants to go home. But you know what Mother's like—she needs to be around people. Would you talk to her, Rebecca? Ask her to stay a while longer?"

"I don't think . . ." Rebecca's voice trailed off. She definitely looked embarrassed this time, Antony thought as a faint blush colored her cheeks. She took a quick breath and continued, "I'm not sure she'll listen to me. We had quite a disagreement yesterday."

A disagreement? Antony wondered what the two of them could have possibly found to disagree about. Neither woman was prone to contrariness, although his mother could be a meddler at times. She was usually so obvious and cheerful about it, though, that people rarely found it annoying.

The pair walked in silence for a moment. They had almost reached the harbor, and Antony could see Quintus up ahead. He was standing on the street side of the wooden pier, watching two men unload a wagon. As Rebecca and Antony approached the steps to the pier, he stopped. "If you'd rather I took Mother home . . ." he said.

"It's not that," she said quickly, returning a wave to Quintus. "Let's talk about it later, all right?"

Antony brooded about Rebecca's disagreement with his mother

while they inspected the new warehouse, but he couldn't stay sullen long in the presence of Rebecca's enthusiasm.

"Quintus, that's ingenious," she said when he explained the new procedure he and Peter had implemented for redirecting lost or damaged shipments to the relief effort.

"Usually we don't have too much left at the end of a season," Quintus said, "but it still takes up valuable space. Your father was the kind to cut his losses and clear the warehouse to make room for new inventory. Now that we've rented the additional space, we can salvage more items and store them for distribution to the needy. And we hired a man—one who lost his job and hasn't been able to find work because he's a Christian—to repair goods that were damaged but can be made serviceable."

"A wonderful idea," Rebecca said. She surveyed the new addition to the warehouse with obvious delight, commenting occasionally as Quintus pointed out various items in the process of being rescued and repaired. Practical items such as iron implements, wooden utensils, copper and tin pots. Cracked and chipped pottery, and terra-cotta containers that were still usable. And even a few pieces of damaged-but-functional furniture and several water-damaged carpets.

"Isn't it perfect?" she asked Antony when Quintus finished showing them around and went back to work. "Things destined for the scrap heap will take on new life here—and bring new hope to families who have so little."

Antony couldn't help smiling at the faraway gleam in her eyes. Rebecca had walked into a nondescript warehouse, looked around her at an odd assortment of discards waiting to be repaired, and had seen lives being reclaimed. This charitable work was important to her, he realized, and it was something she would want to continue even after they were married. That was perfectly acceptable to Antony. It would occupy much of her days, but she would find it fulfilling, and there was no reason it had to interfere with their private time together.

He was doing it again—letting his mind run ahead to the future.

And a pleasant future it would be, he thought. But first he had to talk to Rebecca. They were alone again, but this wasn't the right place for the conversation; he did not want to declare his feelings for her here, in the middle of a warehouse. And besides, he needed to settle the matter of moving his mother first.

"Rebecca, what we talked about earlier . . ." He watched her excitement fade and a wary look return. He hated to make her uncomfortable, but he needed to know what to do. "About Mother."

"Our disagreement is not important," Rebecca said. "I'll talk to her and ask her to stay. I just hope she'll listen."

"I don't mean to pry, but is the disagreement something I could help with? Maybe smooth things over?"

Rebecca shook her head emphatically. "No." She dropped her gaze, then squared her shoulders and looked him directly in the eyes. "But it's something you should know about."

Her demeanor was so determined, it put Antony on his guard. He thought she might be trying to intimidate him, for a change. He never intentionally tried to intimidate Rebecca, of course; he just seemed to have that effect on her.

"We should have a clear understanding," she added, "since you'll continue to spend a lot of time at the villa with Helena."

Not "with us," but "with Helena." There was something odd in the way Rebecca phrased that, as if he would be seeing only his mother when he visited. Just where would Rebecca be?

"By all means," he said. "We shouldn't have any misunderstandings."

Antony looked around for a chair or stool, but there were no such amenities in the warehouse. It was a workspace, not an office. And it certainly wasn't home. Not a comfortable place for conversation, but if they were going to have a talk now in order to reach whatever "understanding" Rebecca had in mind, then they might as well make themselves comfortable. He patted the top of an unopened barrel and started to help her up.

She brushed aside the offer to sit. "This won't take long."

"Go ahead, then."

"Your mother thinks I'm wrong about a decision I've made, but I'm very firm about it." Rebecca appeared to choose her words carefully. "Helena took it personally because she had, I believe, some aspirations in that regard."

"And what is this decision that upset her?"

"I've decided that I will never marry." Her chin gave a slight lift as she made the announcement. "*Never,*" she emphasized when his startled movement tipped over a broken table that had been propped against the wall. "It's God's will for me." She offered the statement with great finality, as if she had clarified the matter once and for all and decreed it off limits for discussion.

Antony was so stunned, he didn't know how to respond. *What kind of idiotic deity requires a young woman to remain single?* he wanted to ask. Especially a beautiful young woman who loved children and already had one of her own. He'd pictured Rebecca with a house full of children—his children. And Victor, of course. That was taken for granted. Surely she didn't intend to raise the boy by herself. It didn't make sense.

His mind was still reeling with unanswered questions when Quintus poked his head back into the room. "Good, you two are still here. Peter wants to see you before you leave. He said it's important."

"Tell him we'll be right there," Rebecca said.

"We'll finish this discussion later," Antony told her. He didn't know where she'd come up with this idea, but he was already thinking of ways to talk her out of it.

"There's nothing to discuss," she insisted. "I simply wanted you to know my decision so you'll . . . so we'll have a clear understanding."

Rebecca turned and started toward Peter's office next door, and Antony followed. If she thought the topic was closed, she was sadly mistaken. Here he'd gone and fallen in love with her, and now she was vowing to never get married? There would be *plenty* of discussion about that, Antony decided.

They found Peter sitting at one of the harbor office's twin desks, his expression somber. He dispensed with the formalities and got right to the point. "I received a letter," he said, "from Marcellus."

"Is it John?" Rebecca asked. "Is he all right?"

"John is fine. Overdoing it but enjoying himself thoroughly, according to Marcellus."

"Then what is it?" Rebecca took the chair across from Peter and Antony leaned against the floor-to-ceiling cabinet that housed the company's financial records in its myriad of pigeonholes.

Peter picked up the letter and scanned it. He found the passage he was looking for and began to read:

> "I thought you should know that we haven't seen Jacob since the day after Rebecca and the others left for home. I talked to him briefly that day, as he was leaving to find Damian. It's something he feels he has to do, and I realized it was futile to try and stop him.
>
> "I waited several days before writing you, thinking Jacob might return to Polycarp's house at any time, but now we're ready to leave for Pergamum so I'm sending this on to you. I don't know if Jacob is still in Smyrna, or if perhaps Damian has left and Jacob has gone after him. I've asked around, with little success. Tullia's brother said the two of them scuffled outside his inn that same night. Then they rode off, and he hasn't seen either one of them since.
>
> "John is very concerned, of course, and we pray for Jacob's safety daily. If Jacob has returned to Ephesus, perhaps you could get word to us through one of the churches."

Peter let the letter roll closed and placed it to one side. For a moment, no one spoke.

"When Jacob didn't come back right away," Antony finally said, "I thought he must have decided to travel with John and Marcellus. They wanted him to go with them."

"We all thought that," Peter said.

"We all *wanted* to think that." Rebecca looked crestfallen, and she twisted her hands in her lap. "But from the moment we left Devil's Island, I knew he might do something like this."

Antony instinctively moved toward Rebecca and put a hand on her shoulder. She sent him a frosty look, which he ignored. But he settled for a quick squeeze of her shoulder, then let his hand rest at the back of her chair.

After all his family had been through, why would Jacob do this? Antony wondered. "Something he feels he has to do," Marcellus had said in his letter. Antony knew that Jacob carried a heavy load of guilt for not protecting his sister from Damian.

Looking down at Rebecca now, Antony thought about someone trying to hurt her and suddenly wondered if he would be tempted to take the law into his own hands to get justice? Probably. He would certainly want to.

He silently vowed that no one would ever hurt the woman he was going to marry—and he *would* marry her, no matter what she said.

19

JACOB SCRATCHED HIS SCRAGGLY CHIN as the horse plodded along the mountain road toward Caesarea Mazaca, the capital of Cappadocia. The fact that he might have lost Damian's trail nagged at him even more than the itching stubble of his beard.

When Jacob had chased him out of Smyrna two weeks ago, Damian had headed east, into the interior of Anatolia. They traveled toward Cappadocia, with Jacob following Damian closely, playing a cat-and-mouse game, periodically closing the distance between them and then falling back. Jacob could tell the game irritated Damian, and that had made it even more satisfying.

He stopped only when Damian did. In Sardis Damian had bought supplies; Jacob did likewise, selecting dried fruits and nuts, a leather wine flagon, which he filled with water, and two extra blankets to use as a bedroll and cover. At sunset each evening, when Damian had made camp, so did Jacob. He tried to keep a bit of distance between them yet remain within eyesight. And, knowing his voice would carry in the still night air, Jacob sang. He lay on his bedroll and serenaded Damian with improvised songs about an avenger of blood pursuing and killing his enemy.

For the first time in ages, Jacob had felt free and unhindered. *He* was in control; there was no one to tell him what to do. No family members with conflicting opinions. No prison guards with whips and chains. No warship captains or oarsmasters. He was his own man, and he was a man with a mission.

Now that mission was in jeopardy, and he had no one to blame but himself. Yesterday afternoon Jacob had let Damian get too far ahead of him, and before he could catch up, a flock of sheep had crossed the road, delaying him even further. Jacob had yelled at the shepherd in frustration, but to no avail. The herd of woolly animals bleated as they slowly ambled across the road under the watchful eye of the shepherd, who was either unwilling or unable to hurry the process along. When the path was finally clear, Jacob had lost sight of Damian. By nightfall Jacob still hadn't found him.

Jacob had been riding all morning and hadn't caught up with his enemy yet, and it worried him. He'd come to no major cross-roads; however, Damian must still be traveling toward Caesarea. There was a large military outpost there, which was probably why Damian had headed in that direction in the first place.

A light snow had fallen overnight and fresh powder dusted the road. It wasn't enough to seriously hinder travel, but a few heavy snowfalls would render these mountain roads impassable. Jacob real-ized he would be spending the winter somewhere besides home, and that thought made him still angrier with himself.

Why hadn't he killed Damian when he'd had the opportunity? Jacob repeadedly asked himself that question as he meandered through the surreal scenery of Cappadocia. Everywhere he looked, huge cone-shaped formations of multicolored tufa, a soft volcanic rock, jutted from the ground—towering obelisks of terra-cotta pink, mustard yellow, sandy beige, and eggshell white. Some of the unusual formations were topped with heavy basalt pillows that appeared ready to tumble from their lofty heights but had perched there for centuries as the wind and water had sculpted the rocky wonderland.

Some of the larger towers and cones had a series of windowlike openings, and from a distance they looked like giant pigeon cotes. It finally dawned on Jacob that these were troglodyte homes: many of the people here were cave dwellers. For centuries they had carved their living spaces out of the soft volcanic rock.

The more Jacob looked at the strange shapes, the more it appeared as if an audience had lined either side of the road. Some of the smaller tufa structures looked like animals or people. One outcropping looked like a man with his arms raised to the sky. Jacob had the strange sensation that the rocks were mocking him, deriding him for his failure: "Avenger of blood? Hah haaaaah!"

As he topped a hill Jacob realized that the sound he thought he'd imagined from the rocks was actually a camel braying. There were three camels, in fact, and the heavily laden animals, along with a couple of donkeys and a handful of men, were completely blocking the road ahead of Jacob.

He wasn't surprised to encounter a trade caravan. Asia and Anatolia formed a land bridge between the Roman Empire and the East, and there was active trade along the so-called Silk Route. The emperors had long imported exquisite fabrics and jewels from the farthest reaches of the world, and caravans from India and China crossed through this region on their way to the Mediterranean.

But he was surprised to encounter a trade caravan stopped in the middle of the road. Usually they set up shop on the side of a road just outside a large town. Why had they stopped in the road itself? And why here, in the middle of nowhere?

Not exactly nowhere, Jacob realized as he glanced up. A decent-sized city loomed in the background. Could it be Caesarea already? It must be. The region was sparsely populated, and a city of that size had to be the capital. Jacob had traveled farther than he'd thought, and he rejoiced to be so close to his destination—his enemy's destination.

So close . . . and yet he couldn't move.

Jacob studied the scene. One of the humpbacked beasts had sat down, squarely in the middle of the road, and did not appear to be interested in moving anytime soon. A wiry man in a striped broadcloth coat leaned leisurely against the seated camel while three other traders kept a wary eye on the other camels and the pair of donkeys.

The caravan itself blocked the road, but the main event was transpiring off to the side. Apparently a couple of locals had flagged the traders down en route. Two men appeared to be arguing with one of the sellers. The shorter of the two locals was an older man with a shock of silvery-gray hair that fell below his cap. The other was younger, perhaps an apprentice. Tall and slender, the lad kept his hands tucked inside the sleeves of his coat.

It had been several hundred years since the Persians had ruled here; then the region had come under the dominion of Greece and finally Rome. But the local people had yet to adopt modern dress or customs, and the two men now arguing with the traders wore the traditional Persian costume: trousers under their tunics, coats with long sleeves, and felt hats.

And it did appear to be more than typical haggling. From the yelling and gesturing going on, a deal had gone sour and the two customers were very unhappy. More than once Jacob heard the word *worthless* emanating from the heated discussion as the men shouted in a mixture of heavily accented Greek and Latin.

So far no one had noticed him. He was afraid to get off the road and try to go around the caravan. With the fresh snowfall it was not easy to see where the ground slipped away, and Jacob was afraid his horse might stumble.

Jacob watched the dispute progress for a minute, then dismounted. He intended to ask one of the men to move the camels enough to allow him to pass through. Jacob figured he might have to buy something, but perhaps the traders had some inexpensive trinket that would catch Rebecca's eye.

The wiry man in the striped coat noticed Jacob approaching and straightened up, then he moved to stand between Jacob and the merchandise. The trader looked as if he had slept with the camels, with bits of straw still clinging to his clothes. Jacob started to speak when, just to his right, the quarrel erupted again between the locals and the chief trader. The two men had started to walk away, then the younger man whirled around, evidently demanding the last word.

Jacob was suddenly worried that the men were about to come to blows, and he did not want to get in the middle of a full-fledged fight. The older man put out a hand to restrain the younger, who was gesturing wildly and shouting, "You're a thief! It was everything I had in the world, and you robbed me!"

The voice and gestures were a bit effeminate, and Jacob felt sorry for the gangly lad, who had been fleeced out of what little he had by an unscrupulous trader. Jacob knew what it was like to feel helpless and cheated out of something precious, and perhaps that empathy with the unknown young man was what determined his next move.

With a final cry of "Thief!" the apprentice flung a small pouch to the ground. The older man had tried to stop him, so the toss went astray. The pouch landed between the chief trader and Jacob, and without really thinking, Jacob moved to reach down for it. So did the chief trader, and the two of them collided; but when he righted himself, Jacob had the pouch in his hand.

He intended to hand it back to the apprentice; perhaps it was not as worthless as the boy had implied with the gesture of defiance. The traders had not refunded his money, so the distraught young man was walking away with nothing. But before he could move, Jacob suddenly realized that while he had been distracted, he had dropped the reins. Jacob looked up to see the unkempt trader in the striped coat mount Jacob's horse and ride off.

"Stop!" Jacob yelled. "That's my horse!" He started to run after the wiry man who'd stolen his horse, but the chief trader was coming after Jacob with a furious gleam in his eye.

"You won't get away with this!" the man shouted as he tried to grab Jacob.

Get away with what? What had he done? Jacob was thoroughly confused with no time to figure it out. One trader had stolen his horse, the man who was apparently their chief was fighting him, and the three remaining traders were running toward the disturbance. *They must intend to rob me,* Jacob thought. *These men aren't just unscrupulous traders but outright thieves.*

Jacob still had a considerable amount of money stashed on him, and he wasn't about to lose it. With a swift movement he deposited the apprentice's pouch in his belt and drew out his dagger. The threat of a weapon made the new attackers hesitate just long enough for Jacob to move. He used the opportunity to sidestep the chief trader and flee.

He ran hard, quickly catching up with the two locals, who had headed back toward town. When they saw the chief trader chasing Jacob, they began running too, their long coats billowing around them. The three of them sprinted down the road, their arms pumping as fast as their legs. Fortunately, the old trader was overweight and out of shape, and they were able to outpace their pursuer.

After a couple of minutes, the apprentice veered off the road. The older man followed, and not knowing what else to do, Jacob did as well. Straight ahead he could see one of the huge tufa towers, a ladder propped against its side. The apprentice scrambled up the ladder and disappeared into an opening in the mountain.

Jacob did not wait for an invitation. As soon as the second man was halfway up the ladder, Jacob started to climb. When he reached the top, the two locals yanked him inside.

"Pull the ladder up behind you," the apprentice ordered Jacob.

The lad's felt cap had skewed to the side during the chase, and now he reached up with a slender hand to remove it. A tumble of thick, chin-length raven hair fell out. All Jacob could do was stare open-mouthed. The apprentice was not a young man, as Jacob had assumed from the costume, but a young woman. A woman with deeply bronzed, velvety skin, and lovely black eyes. Eyes that flashed in anger.

"I said, pull up the ladder. Now! Do you want to get us killed?"

Looking below, Jacob saw that the trader had almost reached the ladder. Jacob quickly pulled it inside, then he looked back at the intriguing woman. His frustration at the prospect of spending the winter in Cappadocia instantly vanished.

If I'm lucky, he thought, *spring will be late this year.*

20

WHEN THE MAN HAD CAUGHT HIS BREATH, he propped the ladder against the interior wall of the cave house and unrolled a heavy drapery that had been fastened above the opening. As the curtain fell, Jacob got a final glimpse of the chief trader, hands on his hips, yelling something in a language Jacob didn't recognize. The trader had used a mixture of Greek and Latin to conduct business, but he had evidently slipped back to his native tongue to send a stream of curses their way.

The heavy drapery cast a shadow across the entry chamber, but an overhead ventilation shaft allowed light into the room. Jacob noticed stairs off to the left; straight ahead and to the right were arched passageways leading, Jacob presumed, to the main rooms of the house.

After a moment the trader's voice receded and the local man lifted the edge of the curtain to peek outside. "He's leaving," the man announced.

The woman was clearly furious. She looked at Jacob with undisguised hostility, then turned on her companion. "What are we going to do with our uninvited guest?" she demanded with a jerk of her arm toward Jacob.

"What we always do with guests," the man said patiently. "Offer hospitality." After a reproving glance at the woman, he turned to Jacob to offer an apology. "My niece is still angry about being cheated—"

"I have every right to be!"

"Yes, but what's done is done," the man told her, "and you can't let it eat away at you." He extended a hand to Jacob. "My name is Gregory. This is my niece, Livia, who is not usually so ill-mannered."

After he introduced himself, Jacob said, "I'm sorry to invade your home like this. I followed you by instinct—I didn't know what else to do."

She eyed him suspiciously. "Why was that trader chasing you?"

Jacob shrugged. "To rob me, I suppose. You said yourself they were thieves. They'd already made off with my horse."

That set Livia off again. "Thieves of the worst kind," she grumbled. She couldn't seem to stand still for very long, Jacob noticed. He watched her pace around the room with a long stride. Livia was taller than her uncle; in fact, she almost matched Jacob's height of six feet. He'd never met a woman that tall, and he'd also never met one who wore her hair that short. It wasn't cut so short as to look masculine, but it only fell a couple of inches below her ears. The ends cupped under and swung toward her chin as she walked back and forth, and Jacob found himself mesmerized by the sight. This Livia appeared to be a remarkable woman, and even though she'd shown him nothing but antagonism, he was intrigued.

Gregory ushered them through the long passageway directly across from the entrance. "You'll join us for a bit of refreshment," he said to Jacob.

The spacious room to which Gregory led them was sparsely but well furnished, and surprisingly light and airy. Two windows had been carved into the far wall, and there was a ventilation shaft overhead. It didn't feel like a cave at all, Jacob thought. Certainly not like the caves on Devil's Island. If he hadn't had to climb up a ladder propped against a rocky surface to enter the home, he would not have believed they were inside one of the tufa cones jutting out from the earth.

They sat on cushions around a low table, and over a cup of something hot and spicy to drink—Jacob thought it best not to inquire as to the contents—Gregory recounted the story of how the traders had swindled his niece. "Livia is a metalworker," he said, "a very good one, and she also works with enamel. We sell her decorative objects—jew-elry, trinket boxes, mirrors, and the like—both locally and to importers. Lately she's done quite a bit of custom work for the Roman soldiers stationed here. The officers want engraving or inlaid work on their swords and armor."

"And horse trappings," Livia added. "They take great pride in their horses and think nothing of spending a month's wages for some bit of ornamentation."

She smiled for the first time, and the effect on Jacob was startling. She wasn't beautiful in the conventional sense, but then this woman seemed to be unconventional in every way. Livia's large eyes domi-nated her rather long face, but her mouth was wide and full, and when she smiled it balanced her features. Jacob briefly thought of his older sister and how jealous she would be. Naomi spent hours applying kohl and other cosmetics to try to get her eyes and lips to look as large and full as Livia's were naturally.

"But their horses are magnificent animals," Livia said. "The best—and the breeders also make good clients."

The Romans maintained stud farms in the region to breed horses for their army, Gregory explained. "*Katpatuka* is the old Hittite name for Cappadocia. It means 'land of the beautiful horses.'"

Jacob filed that bit of information away; he would have to buy another horse now, and Livia's association with the breeders might be helpful in negotiating a fair price.

As Gregory went on to tell how Livia had recently started work-ing with semi-precious stones, the smile vanished from her face. "It makes my work more costly to produce," she said, "but fetches a much higher price, of course. For three years I've been using a small portion of my profits to buy stones, while I continued to perfect my technique. This summer I decided I was ready to make a major invest-ment, but we had few caravans come through Caesarea with the kind of stones I was looking for. Until today."

Frowning, Livia set her cup down and commenced pacing again.

"I was afraid to pass up the opportunity. With the snows arriving, I knew I wouldn't have the chance to make a similar purchase for months. So I took the small inheritance my father left me as well as the profits I'd managed to save . . . and I bought stones."

Her eyes narrowed and she spat out her words. "That crafty old trader had exactly what I wanted. Carnelian, obsidian, nephrite, jasper—even amber and lapis. He spread the stones out for me on a velvet cloth, and I carefully picked the ones I wanted. Took my sweet time about it, too, because I was investing everything I had. Then Gregory haggled with the man until we settled on a price."

"Livia's actually a better negotiator than I am," Gregory said, "but a lot of the foreign traders won't conduct business with a woman. That's why she dresses the way she does when we're dealing with a caravan."

"The locals don't like it much either," Livia said, a trace of bitterness in her voice, "but my work speaks for itself. They get used to doing business with a woman after a while."

"So what happened to the stones?" Jacob asked. "Were they really worthless, after all?" He was confused. She said she had inspected them carefully, but *worthless* was the word she had kept throwing at the trader when Jacob had encountered them in the road.

"Oh, no. The ones I saw were high quality—quite valuable. After we settled on a price, the trader collected all the stones I'd chosen and put them in a leather pouch. I watched him closely. But somehow when the money changed hands, he must have switched pouches on me. He must be very practiced at the swindle because I never saw the switch. But when I got home later and opened the pouch, the good stones weren't in there. Just some cheap, inferior stones and a few glass beads."

"We went back to find the caravan," Gregory said, "and discovered they had already left. We were able to track them down just outside of town, but the trader would not give us the stones we'd paid for, and he refused to refund the money."

Livia quit pacing and dropped to a cushion, her anger spent at least for the moment. "I feel so stupid. So very, very stupid. How could I have let myself be cheated like that?"

"If it's any consolation," Jacob said, "I'm sure you weren't his first victim, and you won't be his last. The swarthy old man was a professional swindler . . . And I feel a little stupid myself." Jacob removed the leather pouch from his belt and placed it on the table between them. "When you flung this in my direction, I risked my neck to recover it. I wanted to return the pouch you threw away, thinking you might have been acting hastily and would regret it later. But before I could give it to you, the trader started chasing me."

Livia left the pouch untouched on the table. "That was kind of you," she said after an awkward pause. "But the contents are worthless. Compared to the jewels I paid for, anyway."

She tucked a strand of swinging hair behind her ear and Jacob noticed that her chin quivered. She was a strong woman, one who had just been cheated out of almost everything she had, but she was determined not to break down.

"Something doesn't make sense," Jacob said. "Why would the trader want to fight me for some cheap stones and glass beads?"

He recalled the scene and the startled look on the trader's face when Jacob had picked up the pouch they'd both been scrambling for. "You won't get away with this," the man had said as he'd started to chase Jacob.

Jacob opened the pouch now and spilled its contents onto the table. Livia gasped and her eyes grew huge at the sight. *They really are amazing eyes,* Jacob thought.

"No wonder he was chasing you," she cried. "Those are the stones I bought!" She scattered them across the table in excitement. "Look, Gregory. The amber—I told you it was the best I'd seen. The jasper, carnelian . . . it's all here."

Gregory patted her hand delightedly, then turned to Jacob. "But how did this happen? How did you recover the stones?"

"I'm not sure," Jacob admitted. He thought for a moment. "I collided with the trader when we both reached for the pouch Livia had thrown. He must have had an identical pouch with the genuine stones inside his belt, and it probably fell out when we hit the ground. I must have managed to pick up *that* pouch and not the substitute he had pawned off on Livia. And when the trader realized that, he came after me."

"This calls for a celebration," Gregory said. "And you must stay and join us, Jacob."

"I can't believe it," Livia said over and over. "How can I ever thank you?"

Jacob resisted the urge to tell her that the radiant light in her beautiful black eyes was all the thanks he needed.

Antony sat by his mother's bedside, his knees on his elbows, head in his hands. He was tired, worried, and disappointed. Tomorrow he would probably be angry as well, but for the moment he couldn't get beyond simple frustration.

Helena's eyes fluttered open for a moment. "Go to bed, Antony." Her voice was not much more than a whisper and her eyes closed as soon as she'd spoken.

Antony stayed where he was. It wasn't bedtime—it wasn't even dark yet—and he needed the reassurance of her presence, even though she was too ill to offer advice or comfort. His mother was sicker than he had realized. Helena was the source of his worry, but Rebecca had caused his disappointment, and Antony reflected on both as he sat in the companionable silence of his mother's room.

Peter had wanted to discuss a legal matter while they were in his office, and Rebecca had not waited in the warehouse as Antony had asked her to do. She had walked home by herself, which upset Antony; he did not want her walking across town unescorted.

Then, when he returned to the villa, he found that Helena had sent for a carriage and Priscilla had packed their things. His first instinct had been to dismiss the carriage, and he wished now he had followed through with that. But Helena had been adamant, Rebecca had been grim faced and uncommunicative, and Priscilla had whined about wanting to go home. Antony had catered to his mother's wishes and carried her outside.

To take her mind off the painful carriage ride, Antony had tried to keep her talking. Helena loved to relay the household gossip, and she told him that Quintus had started spending time with Agatha. Antony surmised that his mother might have had something to do with that.

He decided to ask about her disagreement with Rebecca then. But when he started to tell her about talking to Rebecca earlier, Helena had surprised him by starting to cry. "I'm so sorry," his mother said. "I wanted to come home anyway, and I just couldn't stay there anymore, knowing she thought my son wasn't good enough for her."

By the time they arrived home, Antony had pieced together the gist of his mother's conversation with Rebecca. It hadn't been easy, because Helena was crying from physical and emotional distress, her fever was rising, and she never had been able to express her thoughts in a logical progression.

Not good enough. That's what Rebecca thought of him.

Antony raised his head and looked over at his mother. She looked frail and feeble, and even while asleep her features were not peaceful. The light blanket covering her rose and fell with each labored breath. She was not resting comfortably, and he feared the pain would wake her soon; she never managed to sleep very long at a stretch.

Not good enough. The woman he wanted to marry thought he wasn't good enough.

It was true that his family did not share the same social status as Rebecca's, but few did, and why should that make a difference, anyway? It didn't with the rest of her family: Peter and Jacob had treated him as an equal from the beginning. And it wasn't as if Antony were poor. True, he would never be able to provide a palatial home like her father's villa, but Antony had done well for himself and lived comfortably.

The anger he had thought would not arrive until tomorrow took up early residence. Rebecca was wrong. He *was* worthy of her. If she thought otherwise, then she ought to have the gumption to say it to his face. And he intended to give her the opportunity to say it, right now.

He went to find Calpurnia and asked her to stay by Helena's bedside for a while, then he departed for Rebecca's. Antony was a proud man. He would not beg. But he would speak his mind to Rebecca, then insist that she look him in the eye and tell him straight out what she felt. No more blushing and changing the subject or leaving the room. No more skirting the question with an "I'm never going to get married" answer.

When he arrived at the villa, the steward told him that Rebecca was in the dining room, entertaining a visitor. "I'm sure she would want you to join them," he said, leading the way across the atrium courtyard and into the main part of the house.

Antony took one look at Rebecca's visitor and knew who it was, even though he had never met the man. The tender look on her face as she reached up and pushed back a lock of his hair gave it away.

It was Galen. The former fiancé. Only he didn't look so "former" at the moment, and a knot twisted in Antony's gut as he took in the picture.

21

LIVIA'S EXCITEMENT AT RECOVERING her investment was contagious, and for the first time in weeks Jacob relaxed and enjoyed himself. He also enjoyed two bowls of Gregory's hearty mutton stew, while listening intently as Livia described her plans to use the semi-precious stones in her work.

Jacob didn't quite follow her detailed explanation of hammering and casting and enameling, but he certainly admired the end results when Gregory proudly showed off a piece of her jewelry. It was an intricate design of beaten copper overlaid with gold and brilliantly colored enamel. The necklace was bold and delicate at the same time, as contradictory and unusual, Jacob thought, as its designer.

Livia not only created works of art, he learned, but she had also helped Gregory build the cave home. "The tufa is soft and easy to carve," he told Jacob. "It took us about six weeks to excavate this room and my sleeping quarters. Later we carved out a room for Livia and also a workshop. The rooms are on several levels, all joined by passages and stairways."

Once they had moved away from the drafty opening, Jacob discovered the cave home was warm and cozy. He couldn't quite say what it was that appealed to him about it, but he found the place inviting. Perhaps he simply found the young woman who lived here appealing, and that attraction rubbed off on the surroundings.

She had an unconscious habit of tucking her hair behind her ears, he noticed. When she caught Jacob watching her, she explained her hairstyle. "I keep it short so it doesn't fall over my face when I'm working. Even at this length, though, I'm constantly fiddling with it. I'd cut it off as short as a man's if it wouldn't scandalize Gregory."

"Well, it would," her uncle said with a huff. "I make too many allowances for you as it is."

"You love indulging me," she said, breaking into another broad smile, "and you know it."

Jacob relished the lively conversation as much as the food, and when they finished the meal, he realized that he hadn't thought of Damian even once since he'd been in their home. He couldn't avoid it, though, when the topic of conversation turned from Livia's work to Jacob's unexpected arrival.

"What brought you all the way from Ephesus to Cappadocia?" Gregory asked. "Do you have business here?"

Jacob paused before answering; he wasn't sure what to tell them. "I guess you could call it business—the same kind that sent you chasing after that trade caravan. Someone cheated me, and I followed him here. I lost him yesterday, but I think he was heading for the army post at Caesarea."

"It's only a few miles from here," Livia said. "It was a soldier who cheated you?"

Jacob nodded. "A tribune. Or, he was. He's not in favor with the new emperor, and I don't think he actually has an administrative assignment at the moment."

"How did he cheat you?" she asked. "If you don't mind my asking," she added when Gregory cleared his throat.

Jacob shook his head. "I don't mind," he said. But he didn't answer right away.

Livia's curiosity got the better of her and she broke the silence. "He must have taken something very valuable from you, if you've followed him such a great distance."

"The most valuable thing of all. He took my family."

The answer confused Livia. "You mean, he actually took your family away somewhere? Or he . . . eliminated them?"

"Both," Jacob replied, leaving it at that. He did not want to go into a detailed explanation. Gregory had listened to the exchange without comment, but the stony expression on his face made Jacob uncomfortable. Perhaps it was time to leave.

"My bedroll and equipment were stolen with my horse," Jacob said to the older man. "Perhaps you could direct me to a nearby inn where I can spend the night."

"You'll stay with us," Gregory replied.

"No, I've appreciated your hospitality, but I don't want to impose—"

"Please. It's the least we can do," Livia said. "You saved me from financial disaster."

Jacob did not require much persuading, and when he agreed to stay, Gregory rose and started to clear the table. "Good, then. I'll prepare a bed for you in my quarters," he said, his voice cordial, his posture relaxed.

Then the impassive look returned to Gregory's face, and he stood completely still, dirty dishes in each hand, looking at Jacob for a long moment. Jacob felt exposed, laid open, and his skin began to crawl.

Finally Gregory spoke, and although his voice was still normal, there was a different quality to it. Jacob knew that quality, that intangible, authoritative quality, and he knew its source was beyond the natural realm.

"Your mission will not succeed," Gregory told him. "If you will let it go, your enemy will destroy himself. But if you continue your pursuit, you will fail. And you will find that the real enemy is inside you."

With that, Gregory turned and left the room. Jacob was shaken. He hadn't said anything about being on a mission, although Gregory could have surmised that from what Jacob had said. Still, the word *mission* had startled Jacob because it was the way he had justified his pursuit of Damian.

He looked over at Livia, who was studying his reaction intently. "Is your uncle some kind of prophet?" Jacob asked.

"Gregory has been known to utter prophecies on occasion," she said.

"Accurate prophecies?"

She nodded yes. "Are you a religious man, Jacob?"

"I used to be," he said slowly. "Very religious."

"And now?"

"Now I'm not so sure." For some reason, Jacob was comfortable admitting his doubts to this woman he'd just met. A woman whose religious background, if any, was a mystery to him. For all he knew, Livia and her uncle could be worshipers of Cybele, the Mother Goddess. Jacob knew the cult was strong in the eastern part of the Empire.

"Gregory is a religious man," she said, "but he doesn't worship the traditional gods of Rome or Asia. He's what you would call a Christian, if you know what that is." She hesitated only a moment, then plunged ahead with her confession. "And so am I."

Jacob couldn't help it. He shook his head and started to laugh, and once he started, he couldn't stop. Livia looked alarmed, and he tried to get control of himself so he could reassure her that he was laughing at himself, not her. She probably thought he was some sort of deranged maniac.

But how could he explain the irony? Jacob had left the spiritual naysayers behind—those who had begged him to leave Damian in God's hands—and traveled several hundred miles, only to land in the home of a Christian prophet who, within two hours of meeting Jacob, had delivered the very same message.

"Antony!" Rebecca looked up from the sloped couch in the dining room, where she was sitting with Galen. How many surprises did this evening have in store? First Galen had shown up unexpectedly, and now Antony.

She quickly rose, feeling a bit guilty, although she had no reason to be ashamed. There was ample reason to feel awkward, however, with the two men staring at each other. Galen looked disappointed at the interruption, and Antony appeared grim, as if he had just received some very bad news. She hoped it didn't concern Helena.

"Is everything all right?" Rebecca asked Antony.

He quit staring at Galen and turned his attention to Rebecca. "Fine," he said. "I didn't know you were entertaining tonight. I had hoped to talk to you."

Rebecca was glad she had an excuse; she had wanted to avoid another conversation with Antony today. "Perhaps another time would be better," she suggested.

Antony appeared not to have heard. He walked over to Galen and said, "I don't believe we've met."

Flustered by her lapse in observing the social proprieties, Rebecca rushed to make a formal introduction. Galen stood to shake Antony's hand, and she watched as the two men sized each other up.

Rebecca was at a momentary loss for what to say or do. Galen said, "I should be leaving anyway. I have to be up early tomorrow to finish an order for a client."

Antony smiled slightly, as if he'd won a small victory, and Rebecca tried to stifle a surge of irritation at his unannounced appearance as well as apprehension about the reason for his visit. She'd said what she had to say to him earlier—what else was there to discuss? "I'll just see Galen out," she told Antony, "and I'll be right back. If you wouldn't mind waiting here."

"I'll wait," he said.

Rebecca walked with Galen through the atrium to the main entrance, wishing she could erase the look of misery from his face. She had rebuffed his attempt at a reconciliation and she'd known it would leave him feeling dejected, but Antony's arrival had made things even worse. However, she would let Galen sort out his own feelings and not try to draw him out. Now was not the time for that. Actually, there would never be a time for that again, she realized with a slight twinge of regret mixed with relief.

When they got to the door, however, Galen surprised her by deciding to say exactly what he felt, and by doing it with an uncharacteristic display of anger. "Just a few minutes ago," he said, "you told me you had decided to remain unmarried." A dark lock of hair had fallen over his forehead again, but he did not brush it back absent-mindedly this time. Instead, he stood with his arms folded across his chest. Both his tone and his look were accusatory. "Did you mean that?"

"Yes," she said slowly, wondering where this was going. "I did."

"I've never known you to be a liar before, Rebecca. It doesn't suit you."

She was so taken aback, she was tongue-tied for a moment, and then she was indignant. "I'm not a liar. Why would you even think that?"

"Because I saw the way Antony looked at you just now, and I also saw the effect it had on you."

Rebecca blushed, and the realization that she was blushing made her even angrier, adding still more color to her cheeks.

She didn't respond, so he continued. "The two of you have been keeping company quite a lot, haven't you?"

"His mother," she said defensively, "is quite ill. She's been staying with us, so Antony has been here a lot as well."

"Is that all it is? Nothing more?"

"Yes. I mean no, there's nothing more. That's all it is." Galen's sudden jealousy exasperated her. Their engagement was over—had been over for quite a while. His half-hearted attempt to patch things up tonight had been a result of loneliness, not love, and she'd seen it for what it was even if he hadn't. Galen had a right to be disappointed, even hurt, but not jealous.

"You don't have feelings for him?"

"No," she insisted. And that, Rebecca finally admitted to herself, was not true. She *did* have feelings for Antony. Perhaps it had taken seeing him and Galen together to realize that. Yet as strong as those feelings were, she was not going to act on them, so it didn't make any difference that she hadn't answered truthfully.

"I think you should leave now, Galen."

He stepped through the door, then turned around. "If you ever change your mind about not getting married—"

"*Please*, Galen."

"All right, I'll go." He reached up and brushed her cheek with his hand in a sad, sentimental gesture. "Good-bye, Rebecca."

When he left, she bolted the door and leaned back against it. She had just shut the door—again—on a chapter of her life. She still cared for Galen, but it was not the same love she had once felt for him. That was gone, and even though it had left a void in her life, she would not try to rekindle it.

And yes, she acknowledged again, *I have feelings for Antony now.* That's why she did not want another conversation with him, but since he was waiting inside for her at this very moment, she supposed it was inescapable.

Steeling herself for the confrontation, Rebecca went back to the dining room. Antony had poured himself a glass of wine, but it did not appear to have lightened his mood.

"I was about to think you'd left with your fiancé."

"He's not my fiancé."

"No?"

"Not anymore."

For a moment Antony contemplated the pattern on the silver wine goblet in his hand, then he placed it on the table and sat down on one of the *triclinia*. "Let's talk, Rebecca. Sit." He patted the sofa beside him. "Please," he added when she hesitated.

She thought it was somehow dangerous to be that close to him, but she joined him on the sofa anyway.

"It's time to be completely honest," he said. "Both of us. This afternoon you made a big show of telling me you were never going to marry. Then I came here tonight and found you and your *former*"—he was careful to emphasize the word—"fiancé in an intimate moment."

"That's not what it was."

"That's what it looked like." She didn't respond, so he finally asked her, "Are you still in love with him?"

"No," she replied, able to look Antony directly in the eye because it was the truth. "I loved him very much once, but that's in the past."

"Galen is still in love with you, though."

Rebecca acknowledged the observation with a nod, then said, "He thinks he is. But he's really in love with the *idea* of being in love with me. He's in love with a woman who doesn't exist anymore." It was a little odd, she thought, but she did not feel that uncomfortable talking to Antony about Galen. She had needed to talk to someone about it, and Antony was a good listener, even now, when he was upset with her.

"And he still wants to marry you."

"That's what he said. But I told Galen the same thing I told you, that I—"

"I know," he interrupted. "You said, 'I'm not ever going to marry.'" He smiled at her then, and even though the words and the smile were laced with irony, she couldn't help smiling back.

"Do you really believe that, Rebecca? Would your God actually deny you the pleasure of marriage? Or are you using that as an excuse so you don't have to deal with an area of your life that can be fraught with difficulty as well as happiness?"

Not knowing how to answer, Rebecca looked down at her hands. He was asking the questions she'd been asking herself.

Antony let her remain quiet for a moment, then he picked up her hand and placed it in his. "Look at me, Rebecca. I want to tell you something."

She wanted to resist, but his gentle voice was like a magnet that drew her head up in spite of her reluctance. When his eyes locked onto hers, she was powerless to look away. And what she saw in his eyes was as riveting as the words he spoke.

"Rebecca, I've never hidden my feelings for you. I haven't spoken of them directly, but I haven't hidden the fact that I've been attracted to you from the moment we met. And I believe—no, I know—you have feelings for me too, whether you'll acknowledge them or not."

She did not admit her feelings, but she did not deny them either, so he continued. "That's why it hurt so much when I found out you think I'm not good enough to marry you. Rebecca, does it really make such a difference to you that I'm not wealthy? I have a good law practice with a good income, and I would provide for you and—"

"You found out *what?*" His words finally penetrated her emotional fog. "I think you're 'not good enough' because you're not wealthy?"

Antony looked puzzled. "Isn't that what you told my mother?"

"That's not what I said." Rebecca stood and moved away, saddened by the memory of her disagreement with Helena, and saddened by the reason she couldn't marry Antony even though she cared for him: he was not a believer. It was Helena who had responded to Rebecca's decision by saying, "You'll have to be the one to tell my son he's not good enough for you." But that wasn't what Rebecca had meant at all. It wasn't a matter of money; the issue was faith.

Antony stood and walked up behind her. She didn't turn around when he placed his hands on her shoulders, but she didn't move away. He leaned close and softly asked, "Then what is it? Rebecca, I love you so much. Can't that be enough for you?"

She trembled slightly and couldn't quite catch her breath. He loved her. Until that moment she hadn't realized how much she had wanted to hear him say that—how much she had *needed* to hear it. The words sounded so good that she fought back a powerful desire to ask him to repeat them.

Antony slipped his arms around her, pulling her close. "Marry me, Rebecca," he whispered. "Marry me."

She closed her eyes and leaned against him. It felt . . . right. But it was wrong . . . wasn't it? Her heart was pounding, and a struggle warred between her emotions and her will.

Finally she pulled away. "Antony, I can't." She had to swallow hard before she could get the words out. "I'm sorry, but I just can't marry you."

"Why not?"

She couldn't bear the look in his eyes. This was so cruel, so unfair, both for him and for her. *Why* did it have to be this way? But it did, even though he loved her, and she loved him. She knew that now; she was in love with him. But she could not be unequally yoked, and that's what marriage with Antony would be.

Rebecca took a deep breath. "Because you're not a Christian," she said. "So in spite of the fact that I . . . have feelings for you, I can't marry you . . . Please don't ask me again, Antony."

He stared at her for the longest time, and she watched a silent display of emotional fireworks cross his face: longing, hurt, rejection, anger. Finally, he said, "Very well, I won't ask again."

When he turned and left, she dropped her head to her hands. She'd made the right decision, she reminded herself as the tears started to fall. But wasn't there supposed to be joy in following God's will?

22

January, A.D. 97

ON THE FIRST SUNDAY OF THE NEW YEAR, Rebecca sat on a cushion on the dining-room floor while John addressed the church that met at the villa. It was too cold to meet outdoors in the peristyle garden, so they had rearranged the *triclinia* in the dining room to accommodate the worshipers. Word had spread that the Apostle had returned to Ephesus, so the service was well attended in spite of the bitter weather and the early-morning hour before the workday began.

"I bring you greetings from your sister churches in Asia," John said. "They gladly heard the word of the Lord, which I received on Patmos." John gestured toward Rebecca. "And thanks to the assistance of my faithful scribe, each congregation now has a scroll containing the full Revelation."

It pleased Rebecca to be recognized for her contribution, but she was not pleased to see that John was weaker after the six-week trip. He seemed to be more stooped than ever, and he had developed a tremor. His voice was not as strong as it had been, and sometimes it faded out in midsyllable. She noticed he tried to compensate by speaking more loudly than usual.

"Each of the churches has suffered during the recent persecution," John reported, "although none as much as the church here in Ephesus." One by one, he named the pastors of the other churches, beginning with Polycarp, and said a few words about the struggles of each congregation as well as the victories they had experienced. "The kingdom of God is being advanced through our adversity, and I give praise and glory to Jesus Christ, our risen Lord, with whom I walked

the shores of Galilee, and whom I have served with joy and great glad-
ness for close to seven decades."

Although spoken in a weakened voice, John's words still carried
the imprint of apostolic authority. He began to describe the office of
pastor, "the one who stands as a representative of the Great Shepherd
before His sheep," and then called for Theodorus to come forward.
A long-time elder in the church, Theodorus was on the short side but
still quite muscular for a man approaching forty. He had the appearance of an athlete, not a scholar, yet he was both. Before becoming a
Christian, Theodorus had won prizes for both boxing and Latin
poetry when Domitian, early in his reign, had introduced Greek-style
games to the Empire. The Roman populace, however, was enthralled
with chariot races and the gladiatorial events at the magnificent new
Colosseum. The more serious athletic and cultural events of the
emperor's Greek-style games had never managed to rival the blood
sport of the arena in popularity.

As Theodorus moved to take his place beside John, Rebecca
looked at the congregation around her. She noticed Agatha blushing
when Quintus looked her way. He smiled and then looked off.

Galen was not there this morning, Rebecca saw, and she couldn't
help being glad for that. She'd felt sorry for Galen after she had
rejected his attempt at reconciliation, but the following Sunday he had
done something that had infuriated her. During the worship service,
he had given out an emphatic message in tongues. Rebecca had felt
uneasy during the message; she sensed something wasn't quite right.
Immediately afterward Galen gave the interpretation, and it was full
of admonitions to "shun the very appearance of evil." He rambled on,
saying that righteousness has no part with unrighteousness, and that
believers were not to be unequally yoked with unbelievers. Everything
he had said was true and it all sounded very spiritual. Yet Rebecca
knew that Galen had intended the public message to be a private
warning to her.

Evidently Theodorus, who had been in charge of the service, had sensed something inappropriate as well. Rebecca saw him speaking sternly to Galen afterward, and since then, Galen had not uttered a word in church.

Rebecca refocused her attention on John as the elders of the church also came forward and joined him in laying hands on Theodorus. John anointed him with oil and prayed a prayer of dedication over Theodorus as the new pastor of the church. The elders had all taken turns serving in that capacity since John had first been banished to Devil's Island, and now he was elevating Theodorus to the position on a permanent basis.

After John dismissed the congregation, he stood and greeted the members as they filed out to leave. Marcellus stayed by his side, looking concerned and trying to get the Apostle to sit down. But John thrived on being with the people of God, and as long as anyone stayed to talk, he would not ignore them.

Finally, when everyone had left, Marcellus and Rebecca helped John to the library. Peter was coughing and felt terrible, so he excused himself and went to his room to rest before lunch. Rebecca fetched a blanket for John, who stretched out on the long settee for a nap.

Rebecca expected John to go right to sleep; he looked exhausted. Instead he said, "This was a disappointing day for me, and for the church."

"Why is that?" Rebecca asked. "I would think you would be happy to know the church has been blessed with strong leadership. Theodorus is a good man, very solid."

"Aye," John said, "he is. Solid of build and solid of mind. Theodorus teaches sound doctrine, and he'll do right by the people." He raised up on one bony elbow and looked at Rebecca. "But I had hoped to anoint your brother as pastor of this congregation someday. Instead . . ." John paused as his voice faded momentarily, then he continued, "Jacob walked away from the call of God to pursue a fool's errand. Now I don't even know if I'll live long enough to see him again. That boy is a bitter disappointment."

John lay back down on the settee and was asleep almost as soon as he closed his eyes. Rebecca and Marcellus conversed softly while the disappointed preacher dozed.

"He's not doing well," Marcellus told Rebecca.

"I noticed the tremor," she said.

"And his eyesight has dimmed. You can see the cloudiness if you look closely."

"That explains why I thought he might be having trouble recognizing people this morning. He usually greets the church members as 'dear brother' or 'dear sister' if he can't recall someone's name right away, but today he kept saying, 'It's so good to see you, dear child of God.'"

Marcellus grinned. "John is so good at compensating for his physical limitations that few people notice the extent of his frailty."

"I wish we could get him to move in with us," Rebecca said. "I worry about him so much."

"He needs the independence of living in his own house; he just doesn't need to be alone. I've lined up someone to stay with him at all times . . ."

"So, will you be leaving us, now that you've helped John deliver the letters to the churches?" Rebecca knew that Marcellus had never planned to stay long-term. His return to Ephesus with them had always been a temporary thing, a transition from his many years of military service into civilian life, and a favor to the man who had led him to the Lord.

"I had intended to," Marcellus said. "Now I'm not sure what God would have me do. I want so much to try and find my daughter, but I can't help thinking that perhaps I'm supposed to stay with John. His spirit is still so strong, but his body is wearing out. He could live several more years, or he could be gone in a matter of months. Weeks, maybe."

The thought of losing John sobered Rebecca, but so did the prospect of Marcellus's departure. John had always been a fixture in her life, and for almost a year the Apostle and the medical officer had been the only people she had seen. She would miss Marcellus terribly when he left; selfishly, she wished he wouldn't. After a long pause she asked, "Do you know where your daughter is?"

"When she was born," he said, "I was stationed almost at the eastern edge of the Empire. My wife's family was from that area, so that's where I would start looking. Even if my wife and daughter are not there anymore, surely there would be some relatives who would know what happened to them."

Marcellus talked about his daughter for a few minutes, then he said, "I still have a few weeks to decide what to do. The winters in the East are severe, so I couldn't begin to travel until it warms up. I'll see how John is faring when spring arrives."

He turned the conversation toward Rebecca. She hadn't intended to say anything about it, but she found herself talking about Galen's attempt to get back together and Antony's proposal, which had occurred the same evening. Marcellus listened with keen interest, offering a reassuring word now and then as she told him what had transpired. It was like talking to her father, Rebecca thought, and she felt better when she had poured her heart out.

"I just want so much to do the right thing," she said. "But it's so difficult. Antony is a good person even though he's not a believer. Sometimes I wonder, would it really be so bad to marry him? His mother's a good Christian . . ."

Marcellus reached over and gave her hand a paternal squeeze. "I can't tell you what to do, Rebecca—"

"I can." The voice coming from the settee was surprisingly strong. John grumbled as he struggled to sit up. There were no arms on the settee for him to grasp, so Marcellus quickly moved to help him.

"We thought you were sleeping," Rebecca said.

"I was," the Apostle replied with a wan smile when he was upright again. "But I sleep lightly. And the Spirit always seems to wake me when I need to hear something important."

John's eyes were indeed cloudy now, Rebecca noticed, yet they still possessed a liveliness that belied his advanced age. "So what should I do?" she asked.

Without hesitation John said, "Be faithful to God. He has someone for you, Rebecca—a godly man. You must be patient and let God work."

Rebecca pondered the Apostle's words while he turned to address Marcellus. She wanted to believe that what John said was true, that God did have someone special for her. At the moment she couldn't get beyond the thought that she wanted that someone to be Antony, and she was afraid God might have other plans. How long would she have to be patient?

"God has something special in store for you too," John told Marcellus. "He will reward your faithful service to this most ancient servant of His—me—by bringing your daughter back. You will not have to search far and wide to find her. *She* will come to *you*."

He said it with such emphasis that Rebecca wondered if the statement were actually a prophecy. She hoped so. That would mean Marcellus would not have to leave her, or John. And that would please her immensely.

Even if the utterance *had* been prophetic, John's spiritual statement quickly turned into a physical complaint. "Surely that cook has had time to prepare lunch by now," John said. "Why doesn't somebody go find out?"

Rebecca rose, suppressing a laugh. "I'll see what the delay is," she said. There was no delay, of course. It was barely past midmorning. But John was always hungry when he woke up from a nap, and she would see to it that he got something to eat now.

As she left the library Rebecca heard John mumbling, "The wealthiest home in town, but an old person could starve to death around here."

23

LIVIA STOPPED HAMMERING the thin sheet of copper and glared at Jacob. "You're doing it *again!*"

"What?" He stepped back, startled.

"Standing in my light." She tucked her hair behind her ears and leaned back over the workbench, which was positioned to take advantage of the morning light streaming through the window carved into the tufa.

"I'm sorry," he said, moving away. "I got caught up watching you work."

Every morning for the past six weeks the stranger her uncle had taken in had visited her workshop. Most of the time Livia didn't mind, as long as he kept quiet and didn't get in her way. Sometimes she even put him to work; yesterday he had ground cakes of enamel into fine powder with a pestle and mortar while she dipped thin sheets of metal into an acid-and-water bath. When they dried, the metal sheets would be ready for the application of the colored enamel paste. Jacob had saved her a half-day's work by pulverizing the hard enamel.

Today, however, Jacob's presence irritated Livia. She wasn't sure why, and she didn't want to stop to puzzle through it. She just wanted to work. "Go bother Gregory for a while," she snapped.

Jacob folded his arms across his chest. "Gregory has gone into town," he said stubbornly.

"Then why don't you go chase that evil man you're after and leave me alone?" She knew *that* would make Jacob mad. They'd had many discussions about his "mission," as he called it; when Jacob wasn't loitering around her workshop, he was in Caesarea scouting around the army post for any sign of Damian. So far Jacob had been unsuccessful at gaining entrance to the camp—he had no legitimate business to conduct there—and he had never seen Damian leave the premises, even though Jacob had managed to verify that the tribune was indeed there.

Livia knew a couple of people with access to the post, but she wasn't going to tell Jacob. Even after Gregory's prophecy, Jacob had not given up pursuing his enemy; she wanted no part of it, however.

As expected, Jacob's good humor completely vanished at the reference to Damian. "Fine. I'll be happy to leave you alone." He squared his shoulders, then turned and marched out of the room.

Livia went back to hammering the copper while she listened to Jacob go down the stairs to the main part of the house. But her concentration had been shattered, and her enthusiasm for the piece was now lost. She sighed and dropped her tools, then stood up and walked over to the window just in time to see Jacob reach the bottom of the ladder outside the entrance below. He was wearing the fur-lined coat and high felt hat she had helped him purchase at the marketplace in Caesarea.

With a long, angry stride Jacob started walking toward the city, and Livia chided herself for managing to spread her nasty mood to him. He didn't deserve that kind of treatment. The only thing Jacob had done was to be himself. And that, Livia thought, was what had her stewing.

She enjoyed his company, at least when she wasn't working. Because she was rarely around people her own age, his friendship was especially satisfying. He was easy to talk to—and easy to look at too. Sometimes she wished she were a sculptor so she could capture in stone the square set of his stubborn jaw and the warm humor in his eyes. But her attraction to Jacob involved more than that. He was intelligent, well mannered, and well traveled. He had been places—the kind of places she had only dreamed about.

For the first time in her life, Livia longed to be more like other women. She'd always been different, and most of the time it didn't bother her. Lately it had.

She knew she didn't look very feminine. It's not that she was unattractive; her features were pleasant enough, she supposed. But not only was she taller than most men, she also earned her own living and cherished her independence. Not a very womanly thing to do, but something Livia did not want to relinquish.

In two months she would be twenty-four years old, long past the age to be married. She'd had one serious marriage proposal—well, not directly; it had come through Gregory. Her uncle had told Livia about the widower with four children who had asked to marry her. A month shy of eighteen, she had talked Gregory out of it. Her parents had been dead for two years by then, and Gregory was worried about her future; but Livia could not imagine becoming an instant mother to four children and wife to a man she barely knew, a man more than twice her age. She didn't regret her decision even though she had come to realize it might be the only proposal she ever received.

Livia sighed again and returned to the workbench; she couldn't afford to waste the sunlight. She was just different, that's all there was to it. What made her hope that Jacob would find her attractive? And even if by some miracle he did, he wouldn't be around for very long. He was terribly restless, and when spring came, he would probably return to Ephesus. Either that, or the fool would get himself killed trying to catch Damian.

Gregory had tried talking to Jacob about it once or twice since they'd taken him in, but Jacob remained fixated on his pursuit of vengeance. "You can't change a man's mind for him," Gregory had told Livia. "Just leave him be, and pray that God will change his heart."

She *had* prayed, but she still couldn't quite leave it alone. Talking to Jacob about his "mission," however, was like arguing with a fence post. So they had gradually reached a tacit agreement not to discuss it. Instead, they talked about other things, especially their families. Livia understood Jacob's loss. Both her parents had died during an epidemic that had killed a quarter of the population in the surrounding area. Gregory, who was her mother's brother, had also lost his wife and their two children to the plague. Livia missed them all. Her cousin Marcia, just two years younger than Livia, had been her closest friend. How she wished for a confidante like Marcia now. Marcia would know exactly how to get Jacob's attention.

Recently Gregory had told Livia that God had brought Jacob to them for a purpose, and Livia believed that. She thought the purpose was to persuade him to abandon his quest for revenge; she couldn't dare to hope God's purpose would involve something more personal between her and Jacob. Could she?

✝

Rebecca smiled as she watched Quintus coo and make faces at the two babies. She'd forgotten he could be so lighthearted and unbusinesslike, and she was glad she had asked Agatha to accompany her to the warehouse today. They'd brought Victor and Aurora, escorted by the ever-present bodyguard; after two months of constant supervision, Rebecca was finally getting used to having a guard around.

"I didn't know you enjoyed babies so much, Quintus." Rebecca couldn't resist teasing him just a bit.

"Then you have a short memory," he replied.

"Oh?" Rebecca looked up from the bolt of cloth she and Agatha were unrolling and inspecting. Most of it was ruined, but whatever remnants of the woolen fabric could be salvaged would be cut and sewn into tunics and cloaks for several members of the congregation who had inadequate clothing for the winter.

"When you were a wee thing and your father brought you with him to the harbor, the moment you saw me you would raise your hands and say, 'Ride, Quintus, ride!'"

"And you would hoist me on your back and run up and down the wharf."

"As I recall," he said, "you wouldn't let me stop. Whenever I slowed down, you threatened to tell your father that I wasn't doing my job."

The memory made Rebecca laugh. "I suppose I thought you were my personal pony in those days."

Quintus extracted a long finger from the clutches of Victor's chubby little hand. "And I imagine this one will think the same thing in a couple of years. The difference is that I won't be running up and down the wharf quite so fast." He stood and held the long wooden spindle while the two women removed the last of the cloth.

"I wish I had ten times this much wool," Rebecca said with a sigh.

Agatha hurried to offer consolation. "I'm sure it will be more than enough for what we need. And it will be very much appreciated."

Quintus dragged his gaze away from Agatha for a moment. "What would you do with more cloth?" he asked Rebecca.

Her reply was immediate and forceful. "Make blankets and ship them to Devil's Island." She closed her eyes against a sudden memory, then explained in a soft voice, "It's so cold in the caves this time of year. I could never get warm. It's something I won't ever forget."

Quintus thought for a moment. "We could seek permission to send a ship to Patmos this spring, if we had the goods to send, that is."

"I'll find the goods," Rebecca vowed, suddenly filled with determination to be bold in asking for donations. She told Agatha how Peter and Quintus had gotten permission from the military authorities to send a shipload of food and used clothing to the prisoners on Devil's Island the previous spring.

"You can't imagine what it was like when Marcellus showed up at our cave with extra blankets and clothing," Rebecca said. "I had worn the same tunic until it was rotten, not just threadbare. John, too. It's a miracle we didn't die of exposure."

And the irony, she thought, was that it had been Naomi's expensive clothes Peter had gathered up to send. Rebecca had recognized some of them. In fact, she had been wearing her sister's brilliant peacock-blue tunic the day Jacob had arrived to bring them home, and from a distance he had thought Naomi was there on Devil's Island.

Rebecca smiled at the memory of Jacob's confusion, but her amusement vanished as she thought about her brother. They hadn't heard a word from Jacob in two months. She was worried about him and angry with him, all at the same time.

A look of affection passed between Quintus and Agatha as they spread the fabric on the warehouse floor. It pleased Rebecca that the two of them seemed destined for happiness together. It pleased her, yet it also made her a bit envious. Rebecca had tried putting Antony out of her mind, but she missed him more than she wanted to admit. Now she wondered why she had found his attention so smothering before. Probably because she'd been trying to deny her feelings for him.

Whenever she thought about Antony, she prayed for him; afterward, she usually felt guilty for praying selfishly. Did she pray for his salvation only because it would then be permissible for her to marry him? Rebecca tried telling herself that wasn't the reason, yet she knew it was a large part of it. Once she had recognized that she'd fallen in love with Antony, her feelings had been overwhelming.

Most of the time Rebecca was fine. She had thrown herself into charitable work, and that filled up her days. But at night, when the house was finally quiet, she had trouble falling asleep. No matter how much she told herself not to, she thought of Antony and longed for him.

She knew she'd done the right thing, but at times she wondered if the hurt would ever go away. With time, she supposed it would.

In the last six weeks she had seen Antony only once, when she was visiting Helena. Rebecca had been to see her several times. On her good days, Helena was desperate for company and cherished having someone to talk to. On her bad days, she needed comfort, not con-versation. And massage. "No one has the same touch as you," Helena told her. "You always do it exactly right."

One day Antony had arrived during Rebecca's visit. It had been awkward for all of them. Rebecca had caught her breath when she looked up to see him standing in the doorway. He was staring at her, and Rebecca thought for a moment that she had seen affection in his eyes; then his face clouded over and she couldn't read his expression. But she knew from the way he clenched his jaw that he was not happy to have found her there. He spoke a curt greeting, exchanged a few words with his mother, then quickly left the room.

Rebecca had fought not to stare at him, and when he left, she had felt abandoned as well as relieved. She had been back to see Helena only once since then; Rebecca didn't want to risk running into Antony again. It was simply too painful. And too tempting to give up her principles.

When she heard Quintus rise and greet a visitor, Rebecca shook off her thoughts of lost love and prepared to be sociable. She was stunned to see that it was Antony and Priscilla who had arrived at the warehouse. One look at the tense, haggard expression on his face, and Rebecca knew his mother had taken a turn for the worse.

"I didn't know what else to do," he said simply. "Would you come?"

"Of course." Rebecca stood and started to collect her things.

"Don't worry about Victor," Agatha said. "Quintus and I will watch him until you get back."

Rebecca nodded her acknowledgment as she fastened her cloak. She was worried about Helena and nervous about being with Antony.

"Where's Peter?" Priscilla asked.

"He's not here," Rebecca said. "He's at home today."

"Peter must come too," the little girl insisted. "If Peter prays for Mother, she will be healed. I *know* it."

Antony drew Priscilla back to his side, reining her in. "We were up all night," he said, exhaustion evident in his posture and his hoarse voice. "I don't think Mother can make it through another one . . ."

Quintus asked, "Do you want me to go get Peter and bring him to your house?"

Antony shook his head no. "I brought a carriage. We'll go to the villa first, then home."

Rebecca started to object but didn't know what to say. She didn't know if Peter could or would come with them. He hadn't been feeling well himself the last few days, and the cold weather made it difficult for him to get around. She also didn't know how he would react to Priscilla's request that he pray for Helena. He wasn't good in situations like this, and she hated putting her brother in such an awkward position.

If Peter wouldn't come, though, Rebecca knew someone else who could offer medical advice as well as prayer. "Perhaps you could find Marcellus and send him," she told Quintus. "He left the house early this morning to visit John."

In the carriage, Priscilla sat next to Rebecca and held her hand. Rebecca didn't know whether the child needed comfort or was offering it to her, but she was glad Priscilla was there as a buffer between her and Antony. She couldn't help thinking of the last time they'd ridden in a carriage together, when they had returned from Smyrna with Victor. That was the first time she had felt attracted to Antony; so much had happened since then.

Antony's eyes closed several times during the ride. He was not just exhausted, Rebecca thought, he was already grieving the loss of his mother. He must have held on to some hope, though; he'd asked them to come and pray. But perhaps that had been simply to appease Priscilla, who had been so adamant about it.

Rebecca wanted to reassure Antony that Helena would be all right, that God would indeed heal her. But would He? She had prayed for Helena at every visit. Other people from the church had prayed for Helena, anointing her with oil. Would this time be any different?

When they arrived at the villa, Priscilla scampered off to find Peter before Rebecca and Antony were even out of the carriage. By the time they caught up with her, she had cornered Peter in the library and was saying, "Please, you *have* to come. *You* have to be the one to pray for Mother, so she will be healed."

Rebecca had no idea where Priscilla's sudden faith in Peter's ability to pray had come from. It was unprecedented. Only recently had her brother even prayed aloud in public for the first time. Was it a childish whim, this feeling of Priscilla's that if Peter prayed, Helena would be healed? Or was it spiritual insight?

Peter looked up at Rebecca, and she felt her brother's unspoken reservation. Her heart went out to him, but she kept silent. She would not try to persuade him one way or the other; it had to be his choice.

"All right," he finally told Priscilla. "But I want to get something first."

Peter slowly walked from the library into the adjoining bedroom and returned a few minutes later, a small bundle under his arm. "I'm ready," he said. "Let's go."

24

AN HOUR LATER THEY WERE WAITING OUTSIDE Helena's bedroom while Marcellus, who had arrived about the same time, examined her. When the medical officer opened the door and motioned for the others to enter, Rebecca was shaken by the grave look on his face. "I'm sorry," he said to Antony. "There's nothing I can do for your mother."

Antony nodded grimly. "Thank you for coming," he said.

Rebecca struggled to keep her composure when she saw Helena. Her condition, which had been progressive, had worsened dramatically in the two weeks since Rebecca's last visit. Now her friend clung to life with a fragile hold. Helena's hands were clamped shut, her fingers curled together like tight claws, and her limbs were rigid. The dark-honey-colored curls hung limply around her sunken face. Her breathing was shallow, and Rebecca noted there were slight pauses between breaths. As she stood by the bedside, she found herself willing the other woman to breathe.

Priscilla took Peter by the hand and led him forward. "Please pray," she said in a small voice. "Please."

Peter sat down on the edge of Helena's bed and Priscilla climbed up beside him. Calpurnia, the family's housekeeper, was on the opposite side. Marcellus was at the foot of the bed, and Rebecca stood between him and Antony, who kept patting his mother's clamped hand. "Don't leave us, Mother," he said, his voice choked with emotion. "Your friends are here to see you."

"And pray for you," Priscilla added.

Rebecca's heart ached for Antony and Priscilla. And for Peter. He looked both sad and frightened. She knew he was wondering what he would tell Priscilla if he prayed for her dying mother and she was not healed.

After a moment Peter cleared his throat. "Would you bring some oil for anointing?" he asked Calpurnia. She nodded and left the room, returning quickly with a small container of olive oil.

Peter unwrapped the bundle he had brought with him from home, drawing out a long piece of white fabric with a blue stripe running along the border. It had fringe along the edges and tassels at the corners.

"It's a *tallit,*" he told Antony. "A prayer shawl. It belonged to my father."

Rebecca was surprised. Her father had kept some of the Jewish feast days, and he loved to read the Scriptures in Hebrew, but she had never seen him in the prayer shawl.

"He wore this sometimes when I was a child," Peter said. "But he was so hurt by the local synagogue's rejection of Jewish followers of Christ, he eventually gave up the practice. Anyway, after Father died, I found the *tallit* in his things and kept it."

In just a few words, Peter explained that the fringes on the prayer shawl represented the 613 commandments of the Mosaic Law, and that the tassels spelled out the Hebrew name for God, Y-H-W-H, in the number and sequence of the knots. "So it's a symbol of the authority and power of God's name," he said. Peter paused slightly, then added, "I brought the *tallit* to help us remember that healing is released by our faith in God's power."

Rebecca felt a surge of tenderness toward Peter and a bit of sisterly pride in his willingness to be the one to pray for Helena's healing when prayers for his own healing had not been answered. "Many times," Rebecca told the group, "I've heard John tell stories of how Jesus healed everyone who touched the tassels of his prayer shawl. He would have worn a *tallit* just like this."

"John often talks about Jesus as the Great Physician," Marcellus said. "'You're a good doctor' he'll tell me. 'But Jesus is the true Healer.'"

Antony's look was a combination of skepticism and desperate hope as Peter carefully spread the prayer shawl across Helena's body. Antony's mother was close to death, and the situation did look hopeless. Rebecca knew, however, that nothing was ever completely hopeless with God. She longed to reach out a hand and reassure Antony, but she held back, worried that her touch might offend him.

Peter glanced up briefly at Rebecca, and she nodded, offering silent encouragement. He took the container of oil from Calpurnia and dipped his finger in it. Then he touched Helena's forehead, transferring the oil.

"Put your hands up here," he told Priscilla, "on your mother."

The little girl placed her hands on her mother's body, then Peter placed his hands over Priscilla's and began to pray out loud.

It was a simple prayer, and later Rebecca would not be able to recall a single word of it, but she would never forget the impact.

After everyone joined Peter in pronouncing the amen, they fell quiet. But the silence around them seemed to hum and vibrate, and the room seemed to grow smaller. A presence—an immensely powerful, peaceful presence—filled the room and overflowed Rebecca's heart until she thought she would burst. The presence was as sweet and tender as it was powerful, and the beauty of it made her cry.

She looked around, wondering if the others felt it too. Yes, she decided. Marcellus's ramrod military bearing was gone; he held on to the foot of the bed with one trembling hand, and with the other he wiped his eyes. Peter's eyes were closed, but Rebecca had never seen such a glow on his face. Antony had crumpled over the edge of the bed, unable to stand as the divine presence permeated the room and vanquished the specter of impending death.

Rebecca saw Antony reach for his mother's hand, then watched as Helena's fingers slowly relaxd and uncurled. When she squeezed her son's hand and opened her eyes, Antony began to weep.

In a fraction of a moment, Helena's rigid limbs returned to normal. Rebecca noticed there was no swelling or redness. She'd never seen Helena's hands look so beautiful, so young. Even the knots on her knuckles were gone. How often Rebecca had gently massaged those painfully sore and tender hands. Now they were whole.

"I knew it!" Priscilla cried. "I knew Jesus would heal Mother if you prayed." She threw her arms around Peter's neck, and he broke down and cried then.

Calpurnia uttered, "Thank you, Jesus!" over and over. Then she raised her hands and started singing a hymn of praise. The others joined the singing, except for Antony, who didn't know the words. But in a moment, when Helena's faint voice began to echo the words to the song, he jumped to his feet, raised his hands, and cried, "Thank you, Jesus!"

Everyone was crying and laughing and rejoicing all at the same time. Antony grabbed Rebecca and hugged her, lifting her off the ground. Then he stepped back, looking embarrassed, and started to apologize.

"It's all right," she said before he could get the words out. She knew it was just an expression of enormous relief. But Antony's touch had sent her heart soaring and she secretly wished he would hug her again.

"Calpurnia!" The strength of Helena's voice got their attention. Everyone turned around, and somehow Rebecca was not surprised to see Helena sitting up in bed.

"Yes, ma'am." Calpurnia tried to regain a proper decorum as she answered her employer, but she could not stifle her smile at the sight of Helena sitting upright.

"Get to the kitchen," Helena said. "I'm as hungry as a bear."

"I'll get you something to eat right away," the housekeeper said, then she hurried out of the room.

Priscilla plumped several pillows against Helena's back. "You won't need me to feed you this time, will you?"

"No, but you can do something else for me, baby."

"What is it? Anything, I'll do anything." Priscilla bounced off the bed and stood beside her mother.

"I want you to brush my hair and help me put on a clean tunic."

Helena waved a thin arm at the others. "Now, the rest of you get out of here so I can get dressed. Wait for me in the dining room," she said. "I want to eat a real meal around a real table."

"I'll wait outside," Antony said. "I'll carry you to the dining room when you're ready."

"Oh no, you won't. I don't need your help."

Antony blinked in surprise at his mother's quick rebuke. Rebecca couldn't help smiling. Helena's color had not only returned, but so had her attitude.

Helena announced, "God has healed me, and I'll be able to get to the dining room on my own two feet."

A half-hour later she did just that, and while the thrown-together meal was meager, those in attendance considered it a great celebration.

25

February, A.D. 97

JACOB WAS SICK OF SNOW. Before he'd arrived in Cappadocia he'd only seen it once or twice. As a novelty, snow held a certain fascination. And even now, as he looked out the window of the room he shared with Gregory, Jacob could admire the pristine beauty of the white-blanketed landscape. Trudging through the snow to work was a different matter, however, and it was time to leave.

Jacob dressed in the trousers and boots he'd added to his meager wardrobe. Even with his heavy coat and hat, it would be a cold walk. Having lived all his life on the sunny seacoast, he was not acclimated to the more frigid mountain temperatures.

A month ago he had taken a job in order to finance the purchase of a horse to replace the one that had been stolen. He had ample funds for living, since he'd been furnished a place to stay, but buying a horse would have depleted his purse. Livia had seemed reluctant to intervene on his behalf, so Jacob had finally asked Gregory to introduce him to one of the reputable breeders who supplied the army.

Pomponius had asked an exorbitant amount for the horse Jacob wanted, and as skillfully as Gregory had wrangled with him, the breeder had ceded little on the price. He knew Jacob was stranded and, therefore, knew how much Jacob needed what he had for sale.

The horses were, as Livia had said, the most magnificent animals Jacob had ever seen, and he made up his mind that he just had to have the chestnut filly with the white blaze on her forehead. After an entire afternoon of bargaining, however, Gregory had wanted to call a halt to the proceedings. Still, Jacob hesitated, and before they could leave,

Pomponius's two young boys had run through the stable. Once he had corralled them, Pomponius explained that he had not been able to locate a suitable replacement for their schoolmaster, who had recently quit. Within minutes Jacob had sealed a bargain to tutor Pomponius's sons as part of the purchase price.

Since then he'd walked the two miles to Pomponius's house six days a week. Jacob was teaching the boys, who were seven and nine, languages, history, geography, and math. His father's wealth had provided him with an outstanding education, so Jacob was well prepared to tutor. The lads were progressing nicely with their studies, and as a reward for behaving themselves, Jacob took them riding when the weather permitted.

Each afternoon when the lessons were finished, Jacob returned to Gregory's and spent the remaining daylight hours building an enclosure for his new horse; until it was ready, the filly would remain stabled at Pomponius's. In the evenings, Jacob enjoyed talking to Livia, and then he fell into bed, exhausted. It was a quiet life.

A rather pleasant life, he thought as he tramped along the icy road this morning. Pleasant, yet unfulfilled. Jacob was no closer to apprehending Damian than he'd been when he arrived in Caesarea over two months ago. The army post was impenetrable, he'd discovered. And besides, he couldn't exactly try to bring Damian to justice inside a camp full of soldiers.

Eventually, Jacob had given up his daily visits to the past. There was no way he could watch it continuously, and he didn't think Damian would try to leave Caesarea until the roads cleared in the spring, so Jacob had figured he might as well make the most of his time.

He would rather spend more of his time with Livia. He enjoyed being around her, and especially enjoyed watching her work—although the pleasure was not mutual. Sometimes Jacob thought she didn't even like him, and at other times she seemed enchanted by his company. The woman was a complete conundrum, which only made her more challenging, and therefore more attractive, in Jacob's eyes.

He also liked being around Gregory. After his initial prophecy about Jacob's purpose for being in Caesarea, the older man had not lectured Jacob. Instead, Gregory had been a gracious host, insisting that Jacob stay with them as long as he wanted. Over the weeks the two of them had had many occasions to talk, and Jacob found himself telling Gregory all about his family, especially his father. Gradually the deep hurt was diminishing, and a lot of Jacob's anger as well.

But Jacob could not—would not—return home a failure, no matter how homesick he was. He had to accomplish what he'd set out to do. He had to figure out how to get close to Damian.

That thought was fresh on his mind when he arrived at Pomponius's and learned the boys were too sick for lessons. They were both feverish and coughing, and their father had given permission for them to forego schoolwork for the day.

"I couldn't get word to you. But perhaps the day won't be a total loss," Pomponius said with a hearty slap to Jacob's back. "You can spend some time with that filly who's stolen your heart."

For a moment Jacob was confused and thought Pomponius was referring to Livia, and he wondered what had given Pomponius that ridiculous idea. Then Jacob noticed his employer gesturing toward the stable, and he smiled. "That filly has stolen my heart indeed. And you knew it the moment you introduced us."

Pomponius's weathered face split into a wide grin. "You're a good horseman, and I knew you'd appreciate the best of my stable."

The two men spent an agreeable hour in the stables. Jacob groomed the chestnut, while Pomponius checked on the other animals. He employed several groomers and handlers, but supervised their work closely.

"Would you like to do some riding with me?" Pomponius asked.

"I'm always ready to ride," Jacob replied, thinking Pomponius intended to exercise some of the horses in the paddock next to the stables.

"I have some business at the army post," Pomponius said, "and the

road into town should be clear enough to travel; we haven't had any
fresh snow in a few days. You'll have a chance to see how that filly
takes to the road, not just the track."

Jacob nodded his agreement, but he hadn't really heard anything
past the statement that Pomponius had business at the army post.
Finally! Jacob thought. He had finally found a way inside the camp!

Barely able to contain his excitement, Jacob spread a saddle blanket over the filly's flanks, then cinched the bridle and harness in place.
She seemed to catch his enthusiasm and whinnied in anticipation.
"Yes, girl," Jacob said with a pat to her muzzle. "We're going for a
ride." *A very important ride,* he added silently.

Trousers were not just warmer, Jacob decided as he mounted, they
were much more comfortable for riding than the tunic and heavy toga
he had previously been accustomed to wearing. He was glad he had
adopted the unusual garb, and glad to see how well the filly performed
on the road. The animal was sure-footed and strong, and although
spirited, she readily obeyed Jacob's commands.

Pomponius and Jacob said little as they rode. When they did
speak, their words formed puffs of frost in the air. It was so cold that
inhaling deeply was like breathing in tiny daggers. Fortunately, the
army post was only a short ride away—two miles at the most.

When they arrived at the camp and were cleared by the sentry,
who immediately recognized Pomponius, Jacob was elated. He
couldn't help thinking of all the days he had scouted the place and the
time he had tried to talk his way past the guards. It hadn't worked
then, but now, thanks to his new employer, he was inside.

They tied their horses outside the main building. A guard ushered them into the commander's office, which was spacious but
spartan, and Pomponius introduced Jacob.

Regulus, the commander, was an affable sort for an army officer,
but he definitely had the authoritative bearing of a man in power.
And he had no tolerance for breaches of discipline, as Jacob soon
found out.

After a few minutes in which the three men talked idly of the weather, comparing it to the temperate Aegean coast around Ephesus, which Regulus had once visited, the commander and the breeder got down to business. Jacob paid scant attention as they talked about foals and feed. He imagined himself slipping through the camp and scouring the long rows of barracks for the man he'd hated for so many months.

Suddenly he heard loud voices in the outer office, and the hair on the back of his neck stood up. Was it Damian's voice, or was Jacob imagining things?

He did not have long to wonder. The door burst open and Damian pushed his way past the soldier who tried to stop him. "I won't abide this, I tell you." Damian swaggered into the room, yelling. He pointed a finger at Regulus and said, "The lack of respect around here is outrageous. Completely unacceptable! Do you hear me?"

It had been three months since Jacob had gotten a good look at Damian, and the signs of dissipation were evident. His face was bloated, his eyes bloodshot. His words ran together, and his gait was unsteady. It was all Jacob could do not to jump out of his chair and grab Damian. To be so close after all this time . . .

Regulus stood up, glowering. "How dare you burst in here uninvited! I have guests."

Damian blinked and looked around him, as if suddenly aware of his surroundings. He glanced directly at Jacob, but did not appear to recognize him. Perhaps it was the local costume Jacob wore. Or perhaps it was the fact that Damian was dead drunk, and it was not yet noon.

Damian mumbled something Jacob couldn't make out. *I could take him so easily,* Jacob thought. *Right here, right now.* His heart was pumping so fast, the blood thundered in his head.

"Out! Now!" Regulus ordered. "Or I'll have you court martialed. There will be no second warning."

Damian started to protest but reconsidered. He turned and

walked to the door, then twisted around and addressed Regulus. "I'll have your commission." Damian spoke slowly and deliberately this time, making an effort not to slur his speech. "When I get back to Rome and report to the emperor, I'll see that you're replaced."

When he left, Regulus spoke to the soldier Damian had shoved out of the way. "Confine him to quarters," the commander said, "and don't let him leave. If he gives you any trouble, tell him it's at my direct order. Station a guard outside his door. I will not tolerate another one of his outbursts."

There was a moment of awkward silence when the guard left, then Regulus said, "I apologize for the intrusion."

"Appears you've got a bit of a discipline problem on your hands," Pomponius said.

"Not among the enlisted men. This troublemaker is not stationed here, thank the gods, and he'll soon be gone, I hope."

"A drunkard is always trouble, and it sounds like this one has a grudge against you." Pomponius, apparently worried about Regulus being replaced, asked, "Can he make good on his threat?"

"I doubt it." Regulus retook his seat, looking concerned in spite of his disclaimer. "I would have sent him packing already, but he is a tribune of some importance, and I thought it best not to antagonize him. He was an assistant commander here several years ago—before my time—and he was not well liked, apparently."

Jacob spoke for the first time. "He's not well liked in Rome, either."

The commander leaned forward, his brows furrowed. "You know this man?" he asked Jacob.

"If his name is Damian, I do."

Regulus nodded. "It is."

"I haven't seen him in a while," Jacob said, "but I thought that was him. I'd heard he might be in the area." He spoke casually, but his mind was racing as he tried to decide how much to tell the commander about his involvement with Damian.

"How do you know this tribune from Rome?" Pomponius was

studying his new schoolmaster with a keen interest and perhaps a new appreciation.

"His father, who happens to be married to my older sister, is a powerful senator." Jacob turned to Regulus. "Damian poses no political threat to your command. He was Domitian's flunky, but Emperor Nerva has no use for the tribune, in spite of the senator's influence."

Regulus brightened and relaxed in his chair. "So his threats are idle bluster."

"Yes." Jacob hesitated before continuing. "However, I wouldn't say he means you no harm. He has a reputation for ruthlessness—a well-deserved reputation—toward anyone who gets in his way. I've seen it firsthand."

Jacob briefly recounted how he'd seen Damian flog an elderly man and stab a defenseless woman under the guise of enforcing the law. Jacob omitted the fact that the woman was his mother or that he'd been a prisoner on Devil's Island when he'd watched Damian whip the apostle John.

"I'd hoped the rumors of violence were just that—rumors," Regulus said.

"No, I'm afraid they're true. I'd watch my back, if I were you. He's a very violent man." Jacob thought of what he would do to that violent man when he caught him, and his pulse raced even faster. *The avenger of blood has found you, Damian.*

"Thank you for the information," Regulus said. "I'll keep him under house arrest for a few weeks, and as soon as the mountain passes thaw, I'll give him the boot."

Jacob nodded as if acknowledging that as a sensible solution. Then he said, "When Damian leaves, would you let me know as soon as possible? I will try to get word to my family, to alert them. They fear him greatly, with good reason."

To Jacob's delight, Regulus agreed. The commander and the breeder went back to their business discussion, but Jacob's mind was fixed on one thought: The pursuit of his enemy was about to resume.

26

PETER DESPISED CONDUCTING BUSINESS AT THE BANK; he was uncomfortable outside the familiar environment of the harbor office. He was also uncomfortable flaunting his wealth, but he did use it to his advantage occasionally, and summoning Nicasius to his office rather than visiting the bank in person was one of them. Nicasius, who had handled financial matters for the shipping business for many years, was quite happy to oblige his establishment's largest depositor.

The occasion of Nicasius's visit to the harbor was an auspicious one. The long months of legal wrangling over Abraham's will were finally over and Peter, older than his absent twin brother by a few fortuitous moments, was now head of the household and in charge of managing the estate.

Peter enjoyed assembling the small group in his office to transact a transfer of funds. Antony was there as the legal representative for the estate. Nicasius, resplendent in his white woolen toga and gold jewelry, looked officious and prosperous, as befitted his position. After Quintus ushered the banker into the office, he nodded respectfully toward the others and turned to leave.

"Quintus," Peter said, "please stay. This meeting actually concerns you."

"Me?" Quintus looked flustered for a moment and stood awkwardly by the door.

Antony rose. "Take my chair," he said. Quintus tried to protest but Antony insisted. "I think you should sit," he said with a broad smile. When Quintus took the offered chair, Antony leaned back against the long cabinet built into the wall.

"You know Father's will has been upheld by the court," Peter said to Quintus. "Nicasius is here to handle some financial matters related to the will. And that's why we need you here as well."

Peter informed them of the will's bequest regarding Quintus, and when he announced the amount, Nicasius arched an eyebrow. While the sum slightly surprised the banker, it floored the recipient. Quintus, who customarily showed little reaction, blinked and dropped his jaw, lengthening his elongated face to almost comic proportions. "I expected Abraham to remember me in his will," he said after a moment of stunned silence. "But that is beyond generous."

Peter simply nodded and smiled at Quintus, then exchanged a look with Antony. He had asked the lawyer not to disclose the fact that he and Rebecca had doubled the amount of Quintus's share of the estate. Peter reasoned that if he could somehow have had the opportunity to discuss it with his father, Abraham would have readily agreed.

Quintus had worked for the shipping company since its inception, had run it in Abraham's absence, and had taught Peter everything he knew about the business. Without Quintus, the operation would have ceased at Abraham's death. He was far more than an employee; Quintus had been like a member of the family before Peter was ever born.

Nicasius asked a few pertinent questions and acquired the information he would need to effect the transfer of funds to Quintus. Their business concluded, the four men continued to talk about commerce in general and shipping in particular. With sea traffic about to open in a few weeks, life was already getting hectic for Peter and Quintus—a prospect that also pleased Nicasius, since it would mean extra revenue flowing through his hands.

While they were chatting, the subject of Naomi came up. "I suppose you heard the news about Senator Mallus," Nicasius said. "It was in the *Acta Diurna.*" The handwritten journal of important social and political news was posted daily on white boards in prominent places around the capital city and distributed in the provinces. It took a while, but copies eventually made their way across the Empire.

"With the shipping season about to start," Peter said, "I've been too busy to catch up on the news from Rome." Naomi's husband was a powerful senator, so it did not surprise Peter that he would be mentioned in the *Acta.*

"It seems he's had a stroke and has been unable to attend the Senate for several months. He's in financial trouble, as well." Nicasius went on to tell them what he'd heard from business associates in Rome—that the senator had made a number of risky investments in the last few years, and now they had gone sour, draining his resources. Maintaining power and prestige in Rome was an expensive enterprise, and the once fabulously wealthy senator was, for all practical purposes, bankrupt.

"The creditors are circling like vultures," Nicasius said, "and all of Mallus's property will have to be sold to pay his debts." The bejeweled banker loved to gossip, and he gestured expansively as he chattered on about the political and financial repercussions of the senator's demise. "I doubt he'll live much longer. In fact, he's likely to be gone by the time your sister gets back to Rome to see if she can salvage anything from his estate. There's probably not much she can do, but that's no concern of yours anymore—not after what she tried to do to your family."

That's putting it mildly, Peter thought.

"I had to refuse to extend her any more credit," the banker said. "Naomi was boiling mad, I can tell you that. But what else could I do? She had already borrowed quite a bit against her husband's name, and I'll never see a *denarius* of it now. Well, that's just the cost of doing business, I suppose."

When Nicasius finally emptied the last arrow from his quiver of gossip, he left for the bank. Quintus went back to work, considerably wealthier than when he had arrived that morning. Antony continued to lounge against the cabinet, while Peter remained lost in thought.

After a while Antony sat in the chair across from Peter. He did not have to be told what had Peter looking so somber. "There's nothing Naomi can do," he said. "Not legally, anyway."

Peter nodded slowly. "I'll take your word for that. But I'm not worried about further legal maneuvers from Naomi. I'm worried because I don't know what she's capable of doing when she's desperate. And if Mallus is as broke as Nicasius says he is . . ."

"She'll be leaving Ephesus soon. She'll have to go back to Rome to take care of her husband's estate, or what's left of it. And once she's gone, there's nothing she can do to you or your family."

"I'm sure you're right," Peter said. "Naomi will be gone, and that will be the end of it." What Antony said made sense, but it did not completely allay the apprehension resting in the pit of Peter's stomach. That would finally leave, he supposed, when his nefarious sister did.

†

The next morning, just before dawn, Rebecca willed herself awake. She lit an oil lamp and dressed quietly, then tiptoed out of the room. The guard outside the door had nodded off, so she gently tapped him on the shoulder. Instantly he was on his feet. "What's wrong?" he asked.

"Nothing," Rebecca assured him in a soft voice. "I have something to do downstairs, but I didn't want to wake the baby yet. If he cries before I return, please bring him to me."

"Yes, ma'am." The guard nodded, and in the glow of the lamp, Rebecca saw a relieved smile lift his round face. "Don't you worry," he said.

Victor would probably sleep for at least another hour, Rebecca thought on her way downstairs. And by then she should have found out what she needed to know. The immense house was eerily quiet, and the lamp cast strange shadows on the tile floors as she walked past the servants' quarters and exited onto the short corridor that ran from the main house to the detached kitchen. The cook would be up soon, but at the moment the kitchen was empty and the fire had not been lit. Rebecca shivered in the darkness and used her lamp to light several more.

She wasn't sure this was the right place to wait, but if Agatha had been sneaking out as accused, she would not likely use the main entrance to the house. That left the corridor between the kitchen and the main house as the spot to watch.

Most of the time Rebecca enjoyed managing the household, but this was the kind of problem she hated having to deal with. Yesterday the steward had approached Rebecca about the matter, saying that Agatha occasionally left the house in the dead of night, then returned just after dawn. He seemed reluctant to make the report and was quick to assure Rebecca that Agatha's work was oustanding in every way. It was just that her behavior was so strange, and he was worried that the staff would start to talk—and worried about Agatha too, he'd said.

Rebecca was certainly worried. What could Agatha be up to, prowling around in the darkness? It was not only suspicious, but it was also dangerous. *If it's true,* Rebecca reminded herself. She hoped the steward was wrong, but she'd found him to be reliable and trustworthy and couldn't imagine what motive he would have for accusing Agatha if he didn't have some evidence.

As she waited, Rebecca periodically unlatched the shutter and peeked out the kitchen window, then closed it quickly to keep out the cold air. By now the sky had lightened to a dull pewter but she'd seen no sign of Agatha. The household would be stirring soon and Rebecca was beginning to feel silly. For all she knew, Agatha could be asleep in her bed right now.

Rebecca asked herself what her mother would have done in the situation and decided that Elizabeth would give Agatha the benefit of the doubt and would ask her quite directly, but without accusing her of wrongdoing, for an explanation. With that thought in mind, Rebecca snuffed out the lamps and left the kitchen to go back upstairs.

As soon as she stepped onto the corridor, she saw two figures approaching the house. One was a woman wearing a hooded cloak. The other was quite tall and thin, and could only be—Quintus! Rebecca was shocked. Agatha was sneaking out at night with Quintus?

Too stunned to move, Rebecca was still standing on the flagstone walkway when the two of them reached the corridor.

Quintus nodded as if nothing were out of the ordinary. "Good morning, Rebecca."

She responded to his greeting and turned to say something to Agatha, who shifted from one foot to the other, looking embarrassed. Agatha spoke first. "I'd better see to Aurora before starting my duties." She glanced briefly at Quintus, then darted through the door into the main house.

Quintus moved toward the kitchen door. "Let's go inside and talk," he said to Rebecca.

She followed him inside and watched silently while he got a fire started in the hearth. As she warmed her hands in front of the blaze, he said, "It's not what you think, Rebecca."

"Then what is it?"

Quintus stared into the fire for a moment, thinking. "Agatha has had a lot of pain in her life," he said, "but I don't imagine she's said anything to you about that."

"No, she doesn't say much about what her life was like before she came here. And I haven't pried." Rebecca didn't want to pry now, but she sure wanted to know—she had a right to know—what her house-maid was doing out all night with Quintus. "You haven't answered my question," she said.

"I'm getting there." Quintus stepped away from the fire and sat on the wooden bench in front of the table. Rebecca turned to face him, standing with her back to the hearth. She had gotten chilled earlier and needed the warmth.

"You've known me all your life," he said. "Have you ever known me to lie to you?"

"No." That was one thing you could say about Quintus: he was scrupulously honest. Rebecca's father had trusted him implicitly, and in all the years they had worked together, Quintus had never once done anything to destroy that trust.

"I can't tell you where Agatha goes or what she does; that would betray a confidence. But trust me when I say that it involves nothing immoral. I know it must appear odd, her slipping out of the house in the wee hours of the morning, but it's something that's very important to her—and to me too, now that I know about it."

"Quintus this is very strange behavior . . ." Rebecca was more puzzled than ever by his answer, if you could call it an answer.

"I know. But I can't tell you any more than that."

"The servants are talking. Yesterday the steward mentioned to me that Agatha had been seen several times coming home just after dawn. He didn't mention you being with her, though."

"I worry about her walking through the hills alone in the dark, so when I found out about it, I asked her to let me accompany her. This is only my third time . . ." Quintus paused, evidently worried that he was disclosing too much. "I'll talk to her again, but in the meantime I'd appreciate it if you wouldn't say anything to her."

"I'll have to say something to the steward. He likes Agatha, but he thinks she should be reprimanded. It sets a bad example for the staff if we don't deal with it. And what about Agatha's reputation? I believe you when you tell me that this sneaking around does not involve anything immoral, but you know how people talk."

"In just a couple of weeks it won't be a problem for the staff or for her reputation," he said. Then he grinned sheepishly. "I've asked Agatha to marry me."

Quintus was practically blushing, and Rebecca almost laughed at the sight, but the lump rising in her throat stopped the sound. "I'm happy for you, Quintus," she finally said. Then her eyes widened in surprise. "In a couple of weeks? . . ."

"Well, I'm forty-two years old. I didn't want a long engagement." He did blush this time. "And the shipping season starts in a few weeks. You know how busy it's going to be. So we were thinking that we would get married at the next *agape* feast. The church will already be gathered here for a meal, and we could also make it a wedding celebration—if it's all right with you, of course."

"Certainly it's all right with me. It just doesn't give us time to plan much of a celebration."

"Now, I don't want you to make a big fuss over it. We'll just—"

Rebecca shook her head. Honestly, men could be so dense. "Quintus, it's time for *you* to trust *me*. We're going to make a fuss."

27

March, A.D. 97

REBECCA WISHED SHE'D HAD MORE TIME TO PLAN, but by the end of the second week in March, she and the household staff had put together a proper wedding supper. It was still too early for flowers, so she couldn't make a garland for Agatha's hair, but they had taken one of the elaborate tunics Naomi had left behind and fashioned it into a wedding garment.

Quintus had been a fixture in the Christian community since he was a teenager, so believers from all over the city wanted to join the celebration, and the crowd was much larger than the usual attendance at their monthly agape feast. The weather had turned milder, so tables had been set up along the colonnade around the peristyle garden in addition to the dining room.

Antony was there. Rebecca had hoped he would be. He'd been coming to church with Helena the last few weeks, but Rebecca hadn't had the opportunity to say much more than a few words to him. The day after his mother had been healed, he had sought out Peter and Marcellus and professed his faith in Christ. Two weeks later, Antony had even been baptized.

She noticed now that Helena had cornered Burrus, a deacon from one of the other churches, and was regaling him with the story of her dramatic healing. She would tell the story to anyone who would listen. And if she didn't, Priscilla would. Rebecca didn't know why the little girl had had so much faith at the exact moment it was needed, but she had. If anyone had any doubts that Jesus was the Healer, they had only to look at Helena.

She was beaming today. Of course, Helena took credit for bringing the happy couple together—another story she delighted in telling.
Quintus and Agatha seemed blissfully serene in the midst of the hub-
bub around them. But when Rebecca had managed to speak to them
earlier, Quintus had hugged her and said, "Thank you for making a
fuss."

The only thing that could have made the event perfect, as far as
Rebecca was concerned, would have been for Antony to not be so distant toward her. In the last two months he had not been to the villa,
except for church, and had been at the warehouse only long enough
to drop Helena off, once she had regained enough strength to help a
few days a week.

Rebecca didn't try to avoid Antony, but she didn't seek him out,
either. She didn't know what to say to him. It was not as if she could
go up to him and blurt out, "Now that you're a Christian, I want to
marry you," even though that's what was in her heart. Antony must
still be very angry at her for rejecting him. He was cordial when he saw
her at church, but their short conversations were nothing more than
polite social interchanges between strangers. Seeing him now, laughing and enjoying himself at a wedding celebration, put Rebecca in a
melancholy mood.

Her mood must have been noticeable, because Marcellus came up
to her and asked, "Would you like a bit of fatherly advice?" He nodded in Antony's direction to indicate he knew what she was thinking.
"I could talk to him, if you want me to."

Rebecca was embarrassed that she'd been caught staring at Antony,
yet grateful for Marcellus's concern. "N-no," she stammered.

"Then I'll tell you what I would tell my own daughter."

Rebecca noticed the way his face softened when Marcellus spoke
about his daughter. She recalled John's prophecy, if that's what it truly
was, that God would reunite Marcellus and the daughter he hadn't
seen since she was a child.

"What would you tell her?" Rebecca asked.

"That when there is a distance between two people, one of them has to be willing to take the first step toward bridging the gap. Perhaps that person is you this time."

"I don't know what to say to Antony," she admitted.

Marcellus reached out and squeezed her arm lightly. "The words will come," he said, "when you make the attempt to speak them."

The steward interrupted them then, and for a few minutes Rebecca was preoccupied with giving instructions for the servants. When she finished, she decided to follow Marcellus's advice and seek Antony out. For once, she would *make* him pay attention to her.

Antony smiled when she approached, and she took that as a good sign. She said hello and then asked, "Could we talk for a minute?"

"I'd like that," he said, "but it's awfully noisy with this crowd."

Rebecca was not dissuaded. "We can find some place a little more private," she said. Her heart pounded as she led Antony to the library, which seemed to be the only public room the guests had not invaded. She was glad the room was empty. Rebecca was comfortable here, among her father's scrolls and parchments and maps. When they sat down on the long striped settee, both of them spoke at once.

"Antony—"

"Rebecca—"

"You go first," he said with a grin, but when Rebecca was momentarily tongue-tied, he changed his mind. "No, I'll go first. And the first thing I have to do is to ask your forgiveness."

That surprised Rebecca. "My forgiveness?" She hadn't been prepared for an apology, and wasn't sure he had done anything to require one.

"I've been very angry with you, and I need you to forgive me for that. That kind of anger is a sin, you know." Antony grinned so broadly that Rebecca couldn't help smiling back. "Did you ever think you'd hear me say that?"

Before she could answer he said softly, "Besides, I love you too much to stay angry with you."

For a moment Rebecca thought that her heart had stopped, but she seemed to be breathing. Her tongue seemed to be working as well, so she asked, "You still love me?"

He nodded. "I've never stopped loving you for a moment, Rebecca."

"But you haven't said three words to me in all these weeks."

"Then I suppose I should apologize for that as well." Antony paused for a moment. "My pride was wounded when you refused me. I understand better now why you did, but I was very, very hurt at the time. And even when I would have set aside my pride, I didn't say anything to you because I didn't want you to think I had become a Christian just so you would marry me. I wanted you to have time to see that I've truly changed."

Rebecca's mind was reeling at the revelation that he still loved her, and she longed to speak of her love as well, but he didn't seem to be through with his speech yet.

"I'm not sure when I would have gotten around to saying something to you," he admitted, "but Marcellus just gave me a bit of fatherly advice, as he called it."

"Oh, he did?" Rebecca tried to keep a serious tone in her voice, but amusement at the doctor's double dose of "fatherly advice" bubbled up to the surface in a chuckle.

"He said that one of us had to take the first step toward patching things up, and that I ought to be man enough to do it." Antony reached for her hand. "How about it, Rebecca? Will you forgive me for being so angry?"

She didn't think she could get enough of looking into his eyes. Tonight the love was plain to see, and it was a balm to her bruised heart. "Yes," she said. "I forgive you."

Antony's face relaxed into a relieved smile and he squeezed her hand. "I almost forgot," he said. "What was it you wanted to talk to me about?"

"I think I was going to demand to know why you were avoiding me." Rebecca smiled briefly, then turned serious again as she looked straight into his eyes and said, "And I was going to tell you that my feelings for you haven't changed. I love you too, Antony."

"I've wanted to hear you say that so much." With his free hand he reached up and touched her face. For a few moments neither one spoke, letting sight and touch convey what words could not. Finally Antony said, "There's another question I want to ask you, Rebecca. I asked it before, but I'm hoping I'll get a better answer this time."

Rebecca suddenly seemed to have lost her ability to speak, so she nodded for him to continue.

"Will you marry me?"

She released the breath she had been holding with a long whoosh and found her voice. "Yes, Antony, I will marry you."

He completely closed the distance between them then with a kiss. It was a wondrous sensation, a feeling of incredible lightness, as if she could soar, and she was quite certain that she had never been this happy before.

They were still sitting on the settee, Antony's arm draped around her shoulders, talking about plans for their own wedding, when Peter walked in. Rebecca jumped and sat up straight. She had no idea how long she and Antony had been in the library. She had completely forgotten about Quintus and Agatha and all their guests. What must they be thinking?

"I'm sorry," Peter said, surprised and a bit embarrassed at interrupting them. "I didn't know anyone was in here."

"Is it bedtime already? Are you not feeling well?" Rebecca tried to stop herself from babbling self-consciously. Peter's bedroom opened onto the library; she hadn't thought of that when she had brought Antony here so they could talk privately.

"No, I'm fine," Peter said. "And the guests are still here. I just wanted to put this up." He lifted the small parchment he was holding. "A messenger just brought it."

"A messenger?" Rebecca thought it must be important business if it had been delivered to the house on a Sunday evening.

"I need to send a reply in the morning. Perhaps you could help me with it then," he said to Antony.

"I'll be glad to," Antony said.

He seemed completely unperturbed by the fact that Peter had interrupted their intimate conversation. At least, Rebecca thought, Peter hadn't walked in while Antony was kissing her. She would have been mortified.

Peter started to leave, then stopped. "Actually, I'd like you to read it now, if you don't mind. I'm rather upset by the news."

Rebecca stood up. "I'll leave you two alone," she said. "I should see to our guests."

Peter motioned for her to sit back down. "Please stay. It concerns you too. The message is from Naomi."

Antony took the scroll from Peter and read the contents aloud. Rebecca was dismayed. What could Naomi possibly want now?

†

Peter waited two days before replying to Naomi. She hadn't specified when she was leaving for Rome, and he liked the idea of leaving her dangling for a while. His initial reaction had been to ignore Naomi's message altogether. They had no business dealings, and he certainly wanted no personal dealings with his estranged sister. Based on what he'd learned from Nicasius, Peter had a good idea why Naomi wanted to see him: She needed money. But just what did she intend to do to get it? he wondered.

Curiosity finally got the better of him. Curiosity, and an intuition that perhaps *he* needed to meet with Naomi. He needed to see her face to face one last time, if for no other reason than to prove to himself that he was strong enough to do it. Peter was the head of the family now, and he was finally beginning to grow into the position.

He scheduled the meeting for early morning, knowing Naomi hated leaving the house before noon. He intended to hear Naomi out and then send her on her way, hoping that she would soon be back in Rome and out of their lives forever.

Antony, who had been invited to lend moral support and legal advice, if needed, arrived at the harbor early for the meeting and, much to Peter's surprise, so did Naomi. She had lost weight in the six months since Peter had seen her. Now she looked gaunt, and the heavily applied cosmetics did not hide the dark circles under her eyes. Peter thought of the vivacious beauty who'd had dreams of conquering Roman society and wondered if she now thought the price had been worth it. Naomi must truly be desperate for money if it meant being here at this hour, looking haggard and considerably subdued.

As soon as Antony ushered her into a chair, Naomi got right to the point. "I won't insult you by pretending this is a social call," she said to Peter. "I have a request to make. But first, I would like to clear something up. I want you to know that I had nothing to do with taking Rebecca's baby. Damian surprised me with that ploy, and before I could do anything about it, Jacob showed up and got me angry." She paused for a wry smile, and for a moment Peter caught a glimpse of the old Naomi, not the shell of a woman who sat across from him now.

"Jacob always did have a knack for that," she said.

That was certainly true, Peter thought. The headstrong brother and sister had frequently clashed, with Peter or Rebecca often caught in the middle. It had been a continual source of friction in their household.

"Anyway, I hope the child is all right. And Rebecca."

"They're both fine," Peter said. It wasn't exactly an apology, but it was the closest he'd ever heard Naomi come to one. He wondered if she had experienced genuine remorse or if she merely wanted to soften his attitude toward her. He surprised himself by brusquely responding, "State your request, Naomi. My time is limited this morning."

"Very well," she said. "I need to leave for Rome immediately. Lucius has been taken ill and needs me. He had planned on joining me here this spring, but of course that's out of the question now. I had no way of getting home until the seas opened again, and now that they have, I've been unable to make travel arrangements . . ."

She paused, and Peter thought he saw her hand shaking, but she quickly covered it by clasping her hands tightly in her lap. "Go on," he prompted.

"I'm short of funds and the bank won't extend any credit. Which is ridiculous, given my husband's position."

He exchanged a look with Antony. Not so ridiculous, Peter thought, considering what they now knew about the senator's dire situation. "What do you want from me?" he asked.

Naomi took a deep breath and quickly said, "I want to hire the *Mercury* for the voyage. I'll pay the crew as soon as we arrive in Rome and then send the *Mercury* back to you immediately, along with a generous fee for the use of the ship."

"And why should I do that for you, Naomi?" Even if she could have paid him a small fortune—which he knew full well she couldn't—Peter would never have let Naomi use his father's private cutter.

This time her chin quivered, and there was no mistaking the tremble in her voice. "Please don't make me beg, Peter."

Her manner, as well as the statement, was so uncharacteristic that Peter couldn't speak for a moment. Naomi looked completely unwell, and she was not faking it this time. Not only unwell, but undone.

The loathing he had felt for his supremely selfish sister began to meld into something akin to pity. For a long time Peter stared at her across the desk, his chin propped in the palm of his hand, the index finger tapping his cheek. She was pathetic. Truly pathetic.

Finally he leaned forward. "The *Mercury* is not available. But we have a cargo ship leaving for Rome in two days. I'll make sure the captain has room for you—no charge. But no shenanigans, either. No histrionics. No ordering the crew around. You'll keep to your quarters and do whatever the captain says. That's the offer. Take it or leave it."

Her eyes briefly flashed and her nostrils flared, but Naomi was far too desperate to allow herself the luxury of expressing outrage or any other emotion. She swallowed hard and nodded her head. "I'll take it."

Peter stood to signal that their meeting was over. "I'll make the arrangements," he said.

As Naomi rose from her chair, the struggle to maintain her composure was obvious. Peter was actually a bit embarrassed for her.

She paused at the door. "Thank you, Peter," she said softly.

He suddenly couldn't speak again, so he simply nodded, and she went out the door. Peter sat back down. He heard Naomi's footsteps echoing on the dock, heard the gulls screeching as they swooped to the shore for crumbs, and it all seemed anticlimactic. *It's over,* Peter thought. *Finally over.*

He supposed he should feel gleeful over the fact that Naomi was headed for utter humiliation when she arrived in Rome. In all likelihood, she would wind up destitute. And after all the misery she had caused, she would deserve whatever she got.

Peter did feel a certain relief, but it brought him no joy. Instead, he felt a deep sorrow. It was tragic to see someone you had once loved self-destruct.

Antony allowed Peter to sit in silence and collect his thoughts for a while, then asked, "Are you all right?"

"Fine," Peter said. "I think I'm going to be just fine." He smiled slowly, then stood and stretched. "As a matter of fact, I think I'm ready to do something I've put off for a long time."

Antony raised an eyebrow as he looked up at Peter. "What's that?"

"How would you like to go for a sail?" Peter asked. "A short trip on the *Mercury*?"

"Where are we going?"

"Nowhere in particular," Peter said. "Just up and down the river. Kaeso has had the *Mercury* ready for travel for a few days, but he hasn't had her out on the water yet. I thought you might like to help me do the honors."

Antony brightened. "I'd love to. I've always wanted to see your father's famous ship firsthand."

Peter didn't tell Antony that he'd never been on board the *Mercury* either. He had simply decided he wasn't afraid of sailing anymore.

28

LIVIA HELD THE SMALL BOX UP TO THE SUNLIGHT, checking for minute imperfections. Not a single visible flaw; she took pride in that. The four sides of the wooden box had been covered with thin sheets of copper and polished to a brilliant sheen. The box lid had first been covered in copper, then overlaid with tiny strands of gold to form channels for the different colors of enamel. She had spent many hours forming the delicate gold wires into a series of undulating shapes, carefully hammering the heated gold to the surface, then filling the channels with various shades of blue enamel, each shade a bit paler than the previous, until they almost faded to white. The effect was like clouds hanging over the water. The work had been painstaking, but she was pleased with the results.

Several months' worth of work lined the shelves in the workshop. Livia had finished dozens of items she would sell at the market in Caesarea and to the caravans that would soon be passing through. Necklaces, bracelets, anklets, earrings, and rings for fingers and toes. Decorative housewares. Even a matched pair of jeweled daggers. But the piece she was holding now was special: the box was for Jacob.

Livia didn't know when she would give it to him, but it would be soon. She'd always known he would leave when spring arrived. It was March now, and while it was still cold, winter was all but over. Recently she'd heard Jacob asking Gregory when he thought the mountain roads would be clear enough to travel. That could only mean one thing: Jacob would be leaving soon. She planned to give him the box as a parting gift.

His departure would leave a void in her life, and just thinking about it put Livia in a melancholy mood. They had spent many companionable hours talking, laughing, and sharing their lives. They'd also argued over his obsession with Damian.

The last time he'd mentioned anything about Damian was a couple of weeks ago, after Pomponius had taken Jacob to meet Regulus. Evidently seeing Damian at the army post had whetted Jacob's appetite to fulfill his so-called mission. Since then he'd been preoccupied, as if he were already distancing himself from her and Gregory.

Still, there were times when she and Jacob talked that she thought he was on the verge of telling her something important, perhaps revealing something he'd never shared before. He would lean toward Livia, an earnest look on his face, and then suddenly look away. Once he had even touched her arm and started to say something. For some reason she'd thought he was about to speak of his personal feelings for her. But perhaps she had just imagined that.

She couldn't blame Jacob, though, for the inability to speak his deepest feelings; she'd experienced it for the first time herself. Livia had never had trouble speaking her mind. In fact, she usually had the opposite problem and spoke before she thought. But now, when it seemed to matter more than at any time in her life, she could not verbalize her feelings for Jacob. Not unless he said something about it first. And it was *his* place to speak of such things, wasn't it?

That's why the keepsake box was so important to Livia. She had put what she wanted to say to Jacob into the box—and if she had the courage to give it to him, then he would know how she felt.

Livia placed the box back in its hiding place. It was midafternoon, and she didn't feel like starting another project. Jacob would be home soon, and perhaps she would help him work on the improvised horse barn he was building. She wanted to spend as much time with him as possible before he was gone and out of her life.

As she walked downstairs, Livia heard the sound of a horse

approaching the tufa cone. They didn't get many visitors on horse-back, so she ran to the anteroom and peeked out. She saw Jacob gallop to a halt and dismount, and her heart rose in her throat. Why was he bringing the chestnut home? The barn wasn't finished . . .

Her fingers fumbled as she unfastened the heavy drapery covering the opening in the tufa. By the time she rolled up the curtain and fastened it, Jacob had scrambled up the ladder and stepped inside.

"You're home early," she said. "And you brought the filly. She's beautiful."

Jacob didn't reply for a moment, but he seemed excited. He took a deep breath and said, "I have good—I have some news."

Livia's practical streak asserted itself. "Then come in out of the wind and tell us about it." She refastened the entry curtain and they walked into the dining area, where Gregory joined them around the low table.

"I got word from Regulus today," Jacob said. "He's sending Damian away tomorrow."

"And you're going after him," Gregory said.

"Yes, I *have* to—"

Gregory held up a hand to stifle Jacob's defensive reaction. "You won't get an argument from me," the older man said. He glanced briefly at Livia, who was struggling to keep an impassive expression on her face, and added, "You know how we both feel, but it's your decision. I had hoped you would have thought things through by now and changed your mind, but so be it. We will wish you Godspeed."

Jacob merely nodded, his stubborn jaw set in an unyielding line.

"You'll have a good meal first," Gregory said. "And then we'll say our good-byes." He stood and went to the cooking area to heat some stew and flat bread.

Jacob looked at Livia for a long time. His face softened, but he didn't speak. Neither did she. Even if she'd known what to say, she wouldn't have trusted her voice.

Finally Jacob rose and said, "I'll pack my things." He smiled briefly. "It won't take long, seeing I have so few possessions these days."

Livia watched him leave the room, then she slipped off to her workshop, where she stayed until Gregory called up the stairs that dinner was ready. She retrieved the box she'd made for Jacob and placed it in a leather pouch. *Too soon,* she thought. *It's too soon for him to leave.*

She deposited the pouch in a niche in the anteroom and joined the men around the dining table. They made an attempt at normal conversation while they ate, but it required more effort than Livia was able to muster. When she did speak, she knew her voice sounded too bright, too false. When she tried to smile, her face felt heavy. But not nearly as heavy as her heart.

When they finished the meal Gregory cleared the table, and his absence deepened the silence between Livia and Jacob, who finally said, "I should be going. I want to be at the army post before dark. I'll camp outside the gate so I'll be there when—so I'll be ready."

As they got up from the table, Gregory came back with a small parcel. "I packed you a few things to eat later," he told Jacob.

As Gregory said his farewell to Jacob, Livia quietly left the room. She wanted to say good-bye privately.

Gregory had lit the wall lamps in the anteroom, she noticed. The room was still somewhat dim, with only a faint stream of fading light spilling in through the ventilation shaft. Livia unlatched the curtain but let it hang loose after she extended the ladder. The wind had died down some, so the draft was not too bad in the anteroom.

She thought back to the first time she'd seen Jacob, the day they'd run from the trader who had tried to cheat her. Livia could never have imagined that the stranger who had climbed this ladder uninvited would become such an important part of her life.

And now he was leaving. Jacob had been with them for three months, and she couldn't imagine living three days without him now.

She looked up as she heard Jacob enter. He paused by the far wall, the lamplight limning his rugged features. *This is the way I'll always remember him,* she thought. She wanted to memorize the way he looked, the way he stood, the way he filled up a room just by walking through the door.

"I will miss you, Jacob," she finally said. "And I wish you success, whatever that means for you."

"Thank you," he said as he moved toward her. "I will miss you too."

"And I will pray for your safety." They stood at almost exactly the same height, so it was easy to search his eyes, but impossible to read what was in his heart.

He nodded. "I will appreciate your prayers."

"Go with God, then." She allowed herself one last, long look into his eyes, then she turned to raise the curtain.

Jacob reached for her hand and stopped her. "Livia, come with me," he blurted out.

She turned around in astonishment both at his words and the feel of her hand in his. "I don't want to leave you. Come with me," he repeated.

"I . . . I can't do that." The idea was preposterous. As much as she wanted to be with Jacob, it would be completely inappropriate for her to travel with him, and there was no way she was going to stand by and watch while he killed his enemy.

The expression on Jacob's face told her that he realized the foolishness of the notion as soon as he'd spoken it. "You're right," he said. "But I'll come back for you. After I find Damian, I'll come back."

"No, you won't." Her voice was soft, but Livia surprised herself by being able to say it so matter-of-factly. "You'll forget about me." She knew Jacob meant what he said—for the moment. But she also knew that his obsession with hunting down Damian would crowd out any intention of returning to Cappadocia.

"I could never forget you." He brought her hand up, pressing her fingertips against his lips. "Never," he murmured into her hand.

Livia's heart swelled and she couldn't stop the words that rose in her throat. "Don't go, Jacob. Stay here . . . Stay with me."

He gave her fingers a final kiss, then looked away. He squeezed her hand as he lowered it. "I can't," he said, meeting her glance again. "As much as I want to . . . I can't."

She slowly untwined her fingers from his. "No, not *can't*. You *won't*. There's a difference."

"Livia . . ." His voice trailed off. There was nothing left to say, and they both knew it.

"Go, then." She raised the curtain and latched it above the opening, then moved to one side.

Jacob took a step toward the door. "Wait," she said suddenly. "I have something for you."

With a purposeful step, Livia moved to the niche below the wall lamp and returned with the leather pouch.

"What is it?" Jacob asked.

She took a deep breath and handed it to him before she could change her mind. "Something to remember me by."

He looked down at the gift, then up at her. "This is the same . . ."

"Yes," she nodded, her heart pounding. She knew he would recognize the leather pouch he had rescued, and that was why she had chosen it to protect her offering.

Jacob loosened the string and pulled out the box. "It's beautiful," he said reverently. "And you made it for me."

"It's a keepsake box," Livia said. "You know, to store little things you want to save." She couldn't stop chattering nervously as he stared at the box she had designed especially for him. "Silly, sentimental things . . . memories . . ."

"Thank you," he said softly. "I'll treasure it."

She didn't know what she would do or say if he opened the box. At first she was scared he would, then scared he wouldn't, and finally, disappointed that he didn't.

Without looking inside, Jacob slipped the box back into the

pouch and tightened the drawstring, then placed her gift inside the parcel from Gregory. "Good-bye, Livia."

She managed to choke out a good-bye, then watched Jacob climb down the ladder and ride away. She stared until his retreating form was no longer visible, until she could no longer hear the hoofbeats of his horse, and even then she kept staring into the twilight.

After a while Gregory slipped up behind her and put his arm around her. "He's gone?"

Unable to speak, Livia merely nodded.

"If it's meant to be," her uncle said, "he'll return. And if not . . . well . . ." He cleared his throat.

Sweet Gregory. He was at a loss for words, but she knew how much he cared. "Thank you for understanding," she said.

He leaned up and kissed her cheek, then said good night.

For a long time Livia stood in the doorway, watching the darkness descend, wondering how it happened that she had given her heart to a man who didn't want it, wondering where Jacob would be when he finally opened the box, and wondering what he would think of the things she had placed inside. Perhaps she shouldn't have done it—no, she would allow herself no regrets. But she did hope that tomorrow she wouldn't feel quite as foolish and desperate as she did now.

Jacob made camp outside the army post, selecting a spot that was a good ways from the road but close enough to watch the gate. Before it was completely dark, he gathered plenty of wood for a fire. Some of the branches were still slightly damp from melted snow, so the wood popped and hissed as it caught, but before long he had a nice blaze going.

He was grateful for the fur-lined coat. The wind had died down, but it would still be a cold night, and the heavy coat would be much warmer for sleeping than the two light woolen blankets Jacob had had for his original journey to Caesarea.

Between the farewells with Gregory and Livia and the effort at getting a fire started, some of Jacob's excitement had diminished. He tried to focus on the satisfaction he would feel when he had delivered justice to Damian, but Jacob's thoughts kept wandering from his enemy to the friends he had just left. He was beginning to realize just how much he would miss them.

Jacob had not prayed very often in the last few months; he had little to say to God and didn't think he wanted to hear what, if anything, God had to say to him. It had seemed safer to keep his distance from the Almighty. At the moment, however, Jacob wanted to pray. He wanted to ask God to watch over Gregory and Livia, to bless them for the hospitality they had shown him, and to protect and prosper them. But Jacob felt too guilty to form his thoughts into a prayer. He supposed God knew what was in his heart, anyway.

What *was* in his heart? Jacob wondered. He didn't know anymore. He recalled Gregory's prophecy the night they met, the prophecy that Jacob's mission would not succeed. Gregory had said, "If you will let it go, your enemy will destroy himself. But if you continue your pursuit, you will fail. And you will find that the real enemy is inside you."

At first the prophecy had rattled Jacob, but as the days went by, he had shaken it off. Now, as he stared into the fire and waited for the chance to pursue his enemy again, Jacob couldn't get the prophecy out of his mind. Was the real enemy inside his own heart?

Jacob's thoughts drifted to home, and he had trouble imagining himself back in Ephesus. Everything had changed for Jacob. He no longer had a desire to be in the ministry, and no idea what to do with his life after he dispensed with Damian and returned home. He couldn't see himself running the family business. He couldn't even see himself living in the huge villa again, with every luxury imaginable and servants to take care of his every need. He'd grown quite comfortable living in the cozy cave house, with Gregory taking care of the household chores and Livia running him out of her workshop, then staying up late so the two of them could talk.

Livia. His thoughts always came back to her. She hadn't believed Jacob when he'd said he would come back for her . . . but he would. As soon as he finished what he'd set out to do, he would come back for her.

Jacob remembered the gift she'd made for him and pulled it out of the parcel where he'd stashed it. The small box was unlike any of her other designs—even more intricate and detailed. And very inventive. The pattern she'd created with the blue enamel reminded him of waves. Livia knew how much he loved the water; he'd told her it was one of the things he'd missed most about home.

A "keepsake box," she'd called it. As he moved the box, he felt something shift inside, so he opened the lid. She'd said it was a place for him to store things; he hadn't thought about her putting something inside for him.

A glimmer of reflected light coming from the box caught his eye, and Jacob reached for it. The stone he pulled out was a cabochon— polished smooth, without facets—and it was amber, her favorite. He was sure it was one of the stones she had purchased from the trader and Jacob had recovered.

He wrapped his fingers around the stone, warming it in his palm, and recalled the day they had spread the stones out on her workbench and Livia had begun planning how to incorporate them into her designs.

She had first separated the stones by size and color. "I just think they're beautiful," she said. "But some people attach special significance to them."

Jacob told her about a sailor he'd known, who treasured a small stone of amethyst, believing it would bring him to a safe harbor. "It's a common superstition," Jacob had said, "although some sailors think it's emeralds that will protect you on a voyage."

"I like amethyst because it's the color of new wine," she said.

They'd discussed all the different stones she'd purchased, but she had declared that amber was her favorite, because it reminded her of sunrises and sunsets.

"Do you know what the Egyptians say about amber?" Jacob had asked.

When she shook her head no, he said, "They believe that when the setting sun strikes the water, the rays of light become solid, and the ocean waves carry them to shore in the form of amber."

"What a lovely thought," Livia had said with a laugh. "Pure nonsense, of course, but a delightful idea. No wonder amber strikes my fancy."

That she had made a parting gift of one her favorite stones touched Jacob deeply. As he placed the amber back in the box, he noticed something else— a lock of hair, fastened by a tiny gold wire wrapped around the ends.

"Something to remember me by," Livia had told him. A lump rose in Jacob's throat as he picked up the lock of hair. How could he possibly forget the way she continually tucked that lovely raven hair behind her ears? He recalled the gesture with a smile that quickly faded when he thought how much he would miss seeing her do that.

He had been surprised to discover that Livia thought herself plain. So many times he'd started to tell her just how beautiful she was, but something had kept him back. He wasn't sure what it was. It didn't bother him that Livia was older than he was. It didn't bother him that she cropped her hair short or dressed in men's clothing to sell her own designs on her own terms.

Jacob didn't know why he couldn't tell her the truth: that he'd fallen in love with her when he crashed to the floor of the cave house and she'd yelled at him to pull the ladder up behind him. He had looked up into those huge dark eyes and something had grabbed hold of him and had never let go.

For a long time Jacob fingered the lock of hair. She was right, he thought. He probably wouldn't come back for her. Oh, he wouldn't forget Livia. That would be impossible. But how could he come back for her when there was nothing inside him worth giving to anyone?

The real enemy is inside you. The thought taunted Jacob, and it wouldn't go away. A wild animal cried out in the darkness, and it sounded like laughter to him. Laughter that mocked his emptiness.

Finally, he put the precious lock of hair back in the keepsake box, and when he did, his hand struck a piece of metal lying against the velvet lining. It was a small sheet of copper, the kind Livia used for overlays, and it was engraved with writing.

He took a stick and poked the fire, causing it to blaze brighter, then held the copper sheet toward the light so he could read the words.

> LET ME BE A SEAL UPON YOUR HEART,
> LIKE THE SEAL UPON YOUR HAND.
> FOR LOVE IS AS FIERCE AS DEATH,
> PASSION AS UNYIELDING AS THE GRAVE;
> IT BURNS LIKE DARTS OF FIRE,
> LIKE A BLAZING FLAME.
> MANY WATERS CANNOT QUENCH LOVE;
> RIVERS CANNOT WASH IT AWAY.

The words of Solomon's beloved in the Song of Songs. Jacob's eyes stung with unshed tears as he reread the words.

Livia loved him. He did not understand it, and knew he did not deserve it—and never would. But she loved him, and she had asked him to stay with her. And what had he done? He had walked out on her.

The fire eventually died, but Jacob did not lie down and try to sleep. All night long, he sat and thought about Livia and searched his heart. How could he be worthy of her love?

He thought of Damian and murder and justice and vengeance, of persecution and bloodshed and martyrdom. Why did God allow it to happen?

When the deep black of night turned to gray, Jacob was still thinking. He heard a rooster crow, announcing daybreak, and not long after that he heard a horse whinny. The huge wooden gate of the camp swung open, and a rider on horseback emerged into the faint light of dawn.

Even from a distance Jacob could tell it was Damian. There was an unmistakable arrogance about the way the rider sat astride the black stallion.

Damian rode within twenty paces of him, but Jacob made no move to saddle his horse and follow. He let Damian pass and then said, "You'll get what you deserve, Damian—whatever it is. But it won't be at my hand."

For the first time in months, Jacob felt a quiet peace. And then, at last, he began to pray.

29

LIVIA SNEEZED AS SHE DUSTED THE storeroom shelves. Obviously it had been a while since she had gotten around to cleaning in here. Gregory was meticulous about his kitchen, but the rest of the house was a hit-or-miss proposition. Theoretically, they shared cleaning duties, but Livia was often preoccupied with her work and Gregory wound up doing her chores as well. At times like this, when she was not designing, she tried to make up for her lackadaisical attitude toward housekeeping with a flurry of activity. And today of all days she needed something to occupy her mind and keep her body moving.

After Jacob had ridden away last night she had stayed awake for hours, and when she had finally gone to bed, she slept fitfully. Yet she woke at the usual time. Livia was an early riser, never wanting to waste the natural light, which was best for working.

Once she finished in the storeroom, she swept the entire house. And when that was done, she decided to air the bed linens. She stripped her bed and then went to Gregory's room, but her burst of energy suddenly waned at the sight of the bed where Jacob had slept. The reality of his absence settled over her like the blankets covering the bed, and Livia finally gave way to the tears she had denied herself since he had walked out the previous evening. Bereft, she sat on the bed and sobbed.

He truly was gone, and he wasn't coming back. She loved Jacob fiercely, but it hadn't been enough for him. *She* hadn't been enough for him, and the realization was overwhelming. She was fundamentally flawed, with some character defect that prevented her from being loved.

Rarely one for emotional displays, Livia was surprised at the depth of her grief. Eventually the flood of tears subsided, and while she felt drained, she also felt strangely calmer. She dried her face, gathered the bed covers, and took them outside.

Gregory was tilling a garden. He always planted a few vegetables in the spring, as well as the herbs and spices he used for cooking and medicines. When he saw Livia carrying a huge load of linens, he left the garden and helped her drape the bed covers across a rope Jacob had strung from the side of the house to the shed he had been building for his horse. The unfinished shed was another sight that tore at Livia.

If her uncle noticed she had been crying, he didn't comment on it. "I forgot to check the water supply this morning," he said. "I'll have to tend to that when I finish tilling." No wonder Gregory had forgotten; hauling water was a chore Jacob had been taking care of for the last few months. He'd even purchased a small hand cart so he could haul several large jugs at one time, cutting down the number of daily trips they made to the communal well not far from the house.

Well, fine, Livia thought as she picked up a beater and swung it furiously against the defenseless bed covers, stirring up a small whirlwind of dirt. *We managed to get along before you got here, Jacob of Ephesus, and we'll get along just fine now that you're gone.* The ache in her heart gave lie to her thoughts, but she pushed that aside and pummeled the laundry until her grief and anger were spent, at least for the moment.

Satisfied that she had beaten the blankets into submission, she left them to soak up the fresh air and sunshine and finished straightening up the house. After lunch, Gregory took a nap, and Livia dozed for a while as well—something else she rarely did.

She woke up feeling groggy, not rested, which did nothing to improve her mood. For a few minutes she stood and stared out the window aimlessly, then she went outside to bring in the bed covers. She couldn't help thinking that this time yesterday Jacob had come home from work early, galloping up on the chestnut, only to leave again—for good, this time—turning her whole life upside down.

Lost in her thoughts, Livia did not at first hear the sound of hoof-beats, and when she did, she assumed it was because she had been thinking about Jacob's return the previous day. It was not until the rider came into full view that she realized someone was actually approaching. She stood rooted to the spot, not trusting her eyes, when Jacob rode into the yard and dismounted.

He stared at her for so long without speaking that she wasn't quite sure whether he was really there or not. Finally she asked, "What are you doing back here?"

Jacob took a step closer. "I'd like to stay . . . if it's all right."

"What about Damian?" Could Jacob have dispensed with his enemy already? Why else would he be back so soon?

"He's gone," Jacob said. "I let him go."

Something was different about him, Livia thought. Jacob looked tired and haggard and spent, but he also looked peaceful. Her heart pounding in her chest, she said, "Don't just stand there. Help me get these inside."

She shoved an armful of bed covers at him, then removed the remaining blanket from the rope. When she turned back around, Jacob was standing there, draped in laundry, a broad smile creasing his rugged face.

"Is this your way of saying, 'Welcome home'?" he asked.

Livia blushed and almost stammered a reply. "I suppose it is."

While Jacob helped Gregory remake their beds, Livia went to her room and dropped the covers on her bed. She would tend to that later. Right now she wanted to wash her face and change into a fresh tunic. It suddenly mattered that she look her best.

He came back! The thought reverberated in her head and her heart like a joyous refrain. *He came back!* And he hadn't killed Damian.

A few minutes later Livia sailed into the kitchen, where Gregory had poured Jacob something to drink and was plying him with food. She plumped a cushion and joined them around the low table.

"I've already eaten," Jacob told Gregory. "I had lunch with Pomponius and the boys after our lessons. And then we went for a ride—it was a perfect day for it."

"You went to work today?" Livia asked, incredulous. Jacob talked as if this were just another ordinary day, as if he had gotten up this morning and gone to work and returned home as usual. But nothing was ordinary about this day. The three of them were sitting around the same table, having the same kind of conversation they always did, yet everything was different. *Jacob had come back for her.* He'd said he would, and she hadn't believed him.

"Yes," Jacob said in answer to her question. "I went to work, and Pomponius was quite relieved that he would not have to find another schoolmaster."

Livia's insides lurched when Jacob looked intently at her. Slowly, he smiled. He had opened the keepsake box; she could see it in his eyes. Jacob knew how she felt now. Warmth flowed into her cheeks and she forced herself to breathe deeply as he continued gazing into her eyes.

When he finally broke eye contact with her, Jacob told them about his long night of introspection and his decision to abandon his pursuit of Damian. "I suppose I've always been a champion of truth and justice," Jacob said. "Even when I was young lad, I was always quick to take up a cause when someone was wronged. I'm like my father in that sense. He was constantly trying to fix things, working to make everything right, and eventually it cost him his life. Father's appeal to Caesar on my behalf not only failed to bring justice, but it culminated in his own death sentence."

Jacob paused for a moment, probably picturing his father's brutal death in the Colosseum. Then he swallowed hard and continued. "Last night I realized I cannot right every wrong, not even the ones that affect me the most. One day God will bring every wrongdoer to justice. In the meantime, life is not fair, and cruel men sometimes get away with horrific evil."

Livia recalled saying almost the exact same words to Jacob months ago. He hadn't been ready to hear them then, but praise God, he had heard them last night.

"Christ is our Avenger of Blood now, not me," Jacob said with a sheepish grin. "He is our Kinsman-Redeemer. It may not happen as quickly or decisively as we want, but His justice will ultimately prevail."

"Amen to that," Gregory said softly.

Jacob continued recounting the conclusions that had led him to relinquish his self-appointed mission, and finished by quoting the words of Christ. "'In this world you *will* have tribulation,' Jesus promised. But He also said, 'Be of good cheer, for I have overcome the world.' I have to learn to start living as if Jesus really has overcome the world."

Livia was too filled with emotion to speak, and Gregory was blinking rapidly, as if he had something in his eye.

Jacob cleared his throat. "Beyond that," he said, "I learned something else about myself last night." He paused and fixed another riveting glance on Livia. "I discovered that what I wanted most in life was right under my nose, and I had been too blind to see it."

Livia thought she would melt under the heat of his stare. She reached up and tucked her hair behind her ears. "Are you asking me to marry you?" she blurted out, and immediately bit her tongue. Why, *why* had she said that? It's what she was thinking, but she shouldn't have divulged it so readily.

"Well . . . I . . . ." Jacob appeared flustered by the direct question. "I intended to speak to Gregory about it first, of course."

In a flash Livia went from embarrassment to anger. She couldn't stop herself from asking, "Why? So you could negotiate a price for me like I was some piece of merchandise for sale in the marketplace?"

Jacob raised his voice in frustration. "That's just the way we do it where I come from—at least the Christians do!"

"And we still do it that way here too," Gregory said, quickly shooting an apologetic glance at Jacob and then a sympathetic one at Livia. He tried smoothing things over by saying, "Livia is a little over-wrought by all that's happened."

Livia uncrossed her long legs and stood up from the table. "I'll wait outside while you . . . you *men* sit here and decide my future for me."

Before either of them could say a word, she bolted from the room and climbed down the ladder. Outside, she gulped in the fresh air and tried to let it soothe her frazzled nerves. When she heard the chestnut whinny, Livia walked over to the shed where Jacob had tied the animal.

"I just don't know how it's done," Livia told the horse as she stroked its muzzle. "I don't know anything about being in love, or about marriage, or—or why men think they rule the world."

Jacob's horse neighed sympathetically, and Livia chuckled. "They do rule the world, of course. It doesn't mean we have to like it, though."

In a few minutes Jacob came outside to the shed. He stood on the opposite side of the chestnut and let the animal nibble the bite of food he offered in his hand.

"So, how much did I bring?" Livia asked, keeping her voice light.

"I'm sorry," Jacob said. "I seem to have made a mess of things, and I really wanted to do this right."

"No, *I've* made a mess of things." Livia attempted to smile but wasn't sure if she succeeded. "I'm not very good at social proprieties, as you've noticed."

"You're good at knowing what you want and speaking your mind. That's one of the things I love about you, actually. And I *do* love you, Livia."

She blinked back tears at his words. "I love you too," she said. "But you already know that."

"Yes, I know." He stretched his arm across the horse and found Livia's hand. "Your love was what finally reached through all my anger."

She clasped his hand tightly, so grateful that she had found the courage to wrap her feelings in a tiny box and give it to him. How very different things might have been if she hadn't.

The chestnut lowered her head and Jacob lifted Livia's hand up high and walked around the horse, their fingers still twined together, until he stood in front of Livia. "I know that bride-prices and dowries and such are old-fashioned, almost a thing of the past," he said, "but my family still follows the tradition where a prospective husband approaches a girl's father, or her closest relative—"

"Closest *male* relative," Livia muttered with a smile.

Jacob returned the smile and continued, "—and requests permission to ask for a woman's hand in marriage. He demonstrates his worthiness and makes all kinds of promises to take care of his bride and to provide for her and . . . well, all the usual things a man is supposed to do."

"I see. And what is the woman's role in all this?"

Jacob shook his head in mock dismay. "If she loves the man, she's supposed to be patient and let him work out all the details."

Hand in hand, they walked out of the shed and stood in the late afternoon sunlight, their silhouettes casting long shadows on the exterior of the house carved out of the towering tufa cone.

"By chance did you just have such a conversation with my 'closest male relative'?" Livia asked.

"No," Jacob said, grinning at the impatient look that crossed her face. "I tried," he quickly added, "but Gregory told me not to even mention it until I had talked things over with you."

Livia burst out laughing. *Bless Gregory's heart,* she thought. He knew her so well, and loved her in spite of all her idiosyncrasies. As did Jacob.

"I'm not the patient kind," she told him. "And as you know, I'm not accustomed to doing things the proper way. So . . ." She looked down at their clasped hands and then back at that handsome face she loved so much. "So let me ask you a question, Jacob of Ephesus. Will you marry me?"

His answer was written in his eyes before he opened his mouth to speak. "It would be my great honor to marry you, Livia of Caesarea."

She sighed and leaned forward slightly, pressing her forehead against his cheek. Jacob released her hand and slipped his arms around her. He started to kiss her then, but she pulled back, suddenly realizing that Gregory could see them from the window if he had a mind to keep an eye on them. Her uncle may have been tolerant of her unconventional ways, but Livia did not want to seem *too* improper.

"Not now," she said. She took Jacob's hand again and they strolled toward the house. When they reached the base of the ladder, she turned and said, "So, how does Sunday sound to you?"

"For what?" Jacob asked, a puzzled look on his face.

"For getting married."

This time it was Jacob's turn to burst out laughing. "Now that," he said, "is something we should talk over with Gregory."

†

Antony and Rebecca stood on a level spot on Mount Koressos about a quarter of a mile below the villa. They could not see the harbor from here, but the location offered a pleasant view of the rolling hillside and the southern district of Ephesus, which lay another half-mile or so below them. It was the first truly mild spring day, and Antony was grateful that the brisk March winds had decided to take a respite.

A lot had happened in the ten days since Rebecca had accepted his second marriage proposal. He intended to tell her everything but wanted to do it in a logical fashion, and he had chosen this spot to make his case.

Rebecca looked around, obviously puzzled. "I don't see whatever it is you brought me here to see. There's nothing here, and the city looks the same as it always does."

"There's nothing here *now*. But there could be."

"What are you talking about?"

"A house," he said, noting with pleasure how the idea lit up her face.

"A house—for us?" Excitement raised the pitch of her voice and Antony couldn't help smiling in spite of his qualms.

He nodded. "A big house, with plenty of room for children . . . and for Mother and Priscilla. I need to provide a home for them too, and I can't maintain two households." He couldn't afford to build the kind of house he was talking about, either—not without help. But that had already been offered.

"Of course. Oh, Antony, it would be perfect." She extended her arms and twirled around. "My very own house!"

Peter had been right, Antony thought, when he'd said that Rebecca should have a house of her own and had offered this land, which was part of the estate, as a wedding present. Antony really preferred to wait a few years, until he could afford to build a small villa for them. In the meantime they would be comfortable enough in his family home, which was spacious by city standards, although nothing on the scale of her family's villa. Seeing her reaction, however, Antony knew he should reconsider his hesitation to accept Peter's offer, not just of the land, but of the money to build. He had urged Antony to use part of Rebecca's inheritance, an idea which did not set well with Antony.

"It's very important to you, having a house of your own?" he asked.

Rebecca noted his somber look and made a visible effort to temper her enthusiasm. "I do dream about it," she said.

The excitement had faded from her voice, but he could see the spark of that dream still alive in her eyes.

Rebecca placed her hand in his. "But I'll be happy living anywhere, as long as it's with you."

"I want you to have your dream house," Antony said. "It's just that we would have to use part of your inheritance to build it, unless we waited a few years. My law practice is mushrooming, and I've saved quite a bit, but not enough for the kind of house you're thinking about."

"Ah," Rebecca said, comprehension dawning, "and you'd rather not use *my* money to build a home for *us*."

It sounded so lame when she put it that way. "Well . . ."

"So in your mind the marriage vows only work in one direction. I expected much better of you, Antony."

He bristled. "What do you mean by that?"

"I'm just playing the lawyer here." She grinned up at him. "Marriage is a covenant, right? And in a covenant, what belongs to one party becomes the property of the other party, and vice versa."

"But I'm not marrying you for your money."

"Of course not. But you can't get around the fact that I *do* have money. And when you marry me, then that money is yours too. All of it."

Antony didn't reply immediately. Stubborn masculine pride was holding him back from using her inheritance, and he knew it.

"If we didn't have the resources," she said, "it would be different. I don't have to have a big house to be happy, but I do want a house of my own, whatever size it is." She hesitated a moment, her soft-brown eyes appealing for his understanding. "It's hard to explain why it's so important to me."

"You've done a good job of making your case so far. Try to enlighten me." He issued the challenge in a gentler voice.

"There's more than enough room for us to live at the villa. Helena and Priscilla too. And Peter wouldn't mind, I'm sure of it."

Antony agreed. "He's already told me that."

"We could live in your family home too. I'm sure your mother would welcome us there."

"She loves the idea, of course."

"It's just that your house will always be Helena's, the same way the villa will always be my mother's, even though she's gone now. I want a home of my own, one that is mine from the beginning, one where I can leave my own imprint."

Her smile weakened his resistance even further. They were setting a precedent here, Antony knew. For the rest of his life, he was going to find it difficult to deny Rebecca anything she wanted.

"It's silly, I suppose, wanting my own space so much."

"No, it's not silly. It's normal for you to want that, and normal for me to want to be able to provide it for you. If you don't mind using your inheritance to build it, then I'll swallow my pride."

She threw her arms around him. "Oh, thank you, Antony."

Her happiness was palpable, and as he hugged her close Antony thought he would gladly have sacrificed the last vestige of his self-dignity to build her Caesar's palace, if that's what she wanted.

After a moment, he released the embrace. "Let's find a place to sit down," he said. "There's another decision we need to make today." And this one would be more difficult, he thought.

They found a smooth rock large enough to sit on, and Antony brushed off the surface dirt to clear a place for them. After they sat down, he took a moment to gather his thoughts.

"I have an opportunity to take on some interesting legal work," he said. "Not very lucrative work, I'm afraid, but the kind of work that really matters."

"It sounds exciting," Rebecca said.

"It is, but there are some drawbacks. And I want you to fully support the decision before I agree to take it on. If you have any reservations, I won't make the commitment."

"What kind of drawbacks?"

"For one thing, it would mean spending a lot of time in Smyrna. And that would mean spending time away from you—not something I look forward to." The timing could not have been worse, Antony thought. Here he had asked Rebecca to marry him, and before they could even set a wedding date he was considering a temporary move to Smyrna, a full day's journey away from his fiancée.

"In Smyrna? You've never had clients there before, have you?"

"No, and it's not the kind of legal work I've done before either." Most of Antony's work had been the sort of services he had rendered to Rebecca's family in the probate of their father's contested will. He wasn't sure what all the new cases would entail, but they would be vastly different—and a lot grittier.

"So what would you be doing?"

"I don't know exactly, but a few days ago I received another letter from Polycarp—"

"The bishop? He's been writing you letters?" The look on her face was one of pleasant surprise.

Antony figured he'd better start at the beginning. "Back in January I sent a letter to Polycarp. I wanted him to know that I had become a Christian. I told him all about my mother's healing, and I told him what an impact being in his home last fall had made on me. I closed by saying that if there was ever anything I could do for him, to let me know.

"I sincerely meant that offer to help, of course, but I didn't really expect there would ever be anything I could do for the bishop. In a recent letter, however, he implored my help. Polycarp remembered that I'm a lawyer, and he wrote that quite a few people in his congregation desperately need the advice of an attorney. They've been plagued with lawsuits and various legal harassments.

"Do you remember Plautius and Sergius?" he asked. "The two brothers who helped us find Victor?"

"How could I forget? I recall every detail of that harrowing time."

"The authorities are trying to close their blacksmith shop—something about operating without a permit. They *had* a permit, of course. Only now it's been deemed invalid for some flimsy reason, and the officials refuse to issue a new one. Another church member is in danger of losing his property over a baseless boundary dispute. Another man is facing a criminal trial on a trumped-up charge. And those are just a few examples.

"Polycarp says it's like the persecution has never ended, only the arena has now shifted to the courtroom."

"That's terrible." A look of genuine concern lined her face as she asked, "Can you help them?"

"I think so. I'd have to know more about the cases, of course. But there's bound to be something I can do. I can certainly provide some legal research, anyway."

"Then you should do it."

"There's more." Antony hesitated to tell her the next part, but he wanted no secrets between them, and she had a right to know. He took a deep breath before speaking. "They suspect that Tullia is behind all this."

"The witch?"

Antony recognized the fear in Rebecca's voice, and it worried him. "Yes, she's been stirring up trouble again. She publicly put a curse on her cousins, Plautius and Sergius. What Tullia predicted didn't happen, but a few weeks later the question of the business permit arose. And then the other members of the congregation started having legal woes as well. Polycarp suspects that when she couldn't achieve the results she wanted with her curses, Tullia started trying to manipulate the courts—same intent to injure, different method of retaliation.

"The church is fasting and praying for relief, but they need legal representation as well. And it goes without saying that most of them can't afford it—not with their livelihoods and property being threatened . . ." He trailed off, realizing he should stop and give Rebecca time to think it over.

For a while she simply stared at the city in the distance, then she finally said, "This is very important to you, isn't it?"

"In a way I suppose it's as important for me to do this as it is for you to have your own house."

She shook her head sadly. "No, Antony. This is much more important than a house. This is about people. Persecuted people."

He had tried to keep his feelings neutral as he told her about the situation, but now he leaned toward Rebecca and spoke earnestly. "It's my chance to do something for God by helping His people. I'm a new Christian, and I still have a great deal to learn. I can't preach or teach, I don't even know that much about prayer. But this is something I can do, something that will make a difference."

Antony paused to rein in his emotions. He wasn't trying to persuade a jury; he was seeking the support of the woman who was about to become his wife, and he shouldn't try to unduly influence her. "I won't go to Smyrna at all if you're not comfortable with the idea, Rebecca. You're far more important to me than my desire to help."

She was quiet, but Antony read the uncertainty in her face and her posture. "You're upset about this, aren't you?" he finally asked.

"It's not the money," she said. "We don't have to worry about the lack of income if you take on new clients who can't pay."

"That's right," he said with a smile. "*We* have all the money we need."

Her face relaxed enough to return the smile. "And don't you forget it."

He leaned down and kissed the top of her head but didn't respond. She was still thinking it through, and he wanted her to have the time she needed.

"As much as I'd miss you," she said, "it's not the separation that concerns me. It just worries me, your being in Smyrna . . . going against Tullia . . ."

That was the thing that concerned Antony too, more than he wanted to admit. The legal aspects, while unfamiliar, were not daunting. But the spiritual aspects of the situation would be uncharted territory for him.

Rebecca let out a long sigh. "But who will help them if you don't?"

"I don't know," he said. "And I don't like to think about the consequences of not doing whatever I can."

"Then you must help." Her decision made, she straightened and turned to face him. "How long will you be gone?"

"I can't really say. It depends on how complicated the cases are, how congested the courts are . . . But Smyrna is only a day's journey. I can spend time here too."

He rose and held out a hand to pull Rebecca up. When she stood, she looked around her for a moment, and he knew she was thinking of the house he'd promised her.

"We'll start building right away," he said. "Peter will help me oversee the construction. One of the church members is a stone mason, you know. Peter says his work is excellent. If we have a mild spring, we can probably complete the house this summer, and by that time my work in Smyrna should be finished. I know it means waiting a while, which I really don't like, but it will be worth it. And as soon as the house is ready, we can get married—"

Rebecca put a hand to his chest to stop the torrent of speech. "You've made your argument, counselor, and the jury is convinced."

He smiled sheepishly as she looked up at him tenderly and said, "I'm content to wait for you, Antony, as long as it takes. Go to Smyrna and do what you have to do."

30

IT WAS A SMALL TRIUMPH, Jacob decided, getting Livia to wait an additional week to be married. He wasn't sure why he insisted—perhaps just to prove he could be as stubborn and strong-willed as his bride. Or perhaps to give her an opportunity to reconsider; Jacob still found it difficult to believe she could love him as much as she did.

But Livia never wavered in her decision, not even for a moment, and on the last Sunday morning in March the two of them stood before a handful of fellow Christians and exchanged their vows. The believers in Cappadocia were not as well organized as the ones in Ephesus, and the church groups were much smaller. Even so, Jacob could recall the names of only one or two people at the wedding; he had seldom attended worship with Gregory and Livia in the months he had been living with them—a lapse he now regretted and intended to rectify.

As he stood with Livia in front of the congregation, his heart swelled with love and pride. She had never looked more beautiful. The elaborately embroidered tunic she wore fell just below her knees. "It was my mother's," she had told him, "and she was a lot shorter than I am." For the sake of modesty, Livia wore a pair of thin, flowing trousers under the tunic. The ensemble would probably have looked ridiculous on another woman, but on Livia it was somehow appropriate and elegant.

She had swept her ink-black hair away from her high forehead with a gleaming braid of copper and gold strands—something she had designed herself, no doubt—and it emphasized her large, expressive eyes. She had fashioned the earrings as well. The long dangles of amber swung whenever she turned her head. Standing close to her now, Jacob could see the delicate fuzz along the soft lobes of her ears. She smelled of sandalwood and cassia, a spicy–sweet blend, and he found the familiar fragrance suddenly intoxicating. Afterward Jacob would not be able to recall any details about the short ceremony, but he would long remember that his senses were so overwhelmed, he had trouble catching his breath.

That afternoon Gregory left to visit a cousin of sorts who lived on the other side of Caesarea. Jacob was grateful for the opportunity to enjoy a few days of privacy with his bride, yet relieved when Gregory returned on Thursday, before the newlyweds could starve to death. Livia's cooking skills were rudimentary, to put it charitably.

Life quickly settled into a comfortable routine. Jacob left for work early each morning and returned by midafternoon. He had finished paying off the horse several weeks earlier, and now that he had completed the shed, he rode the chestnut to and from Pomponius's.

Gregory tended to the house and worked in his garden, while Livia occupied herself with her designs. On market days they took some of Livia's work into Caesarea and sold it. Jacob was happy and content and surprised at how much pleasure he took in this simple, quiet life. He enjoyed being married to this outspoken, unconventional beauty who had declared her love when he'd been unable to sort out his own feelings.

Jacob also enjoyed not worrying about where Damian was or what he was doing. It occurred to Jacob that he finally felt liberated, as if his imprisonment had at long last come to an end, even though he had officially been set free eighteen months ago. For most of that time, however, Jacob knew he had locked himself in a prison of his own making.

In spite of his happiness now, something lurked in the back of Jacob's mind. He felt guilty that his family didn't know where he was. They would be worried about him, and angry with him, and Jacob certainly couldn't blame them. But he had no way to get a letter to his family without hiring a private carrier, and he no longer had the resources for luxuries like that.

If it had been mere homesickness or worry about his family, Jacob would have put it out of his mind. But what truly nagged at him was the thought that he was not providing for Livia. He brought a modest amount of income into the family from his tutoring, but her designs brought in much more money. He was comfortable in the cave house, and she was too—Livia had never once said a word about wanting anything more than what she had. Yet it was within Jacob's power to give her more—much, much more—and he longed to do so.

That would mean going back to Ephesus. How could he uproot Livia from the only home she had ever known? And he certainly couldn't take her away from Gregory, her only living relative. Jacob could ask Livia's uncle to go with them, of course, but would Gregory leave everything he owned and move halfway across the Empire?

For several weeks Jacob prayed about this without saying anything to his wife or her uncle. Before Jacob could decide which one of them he should approach first, the idea of moving to Ephesus came up without his mentioning it.

It happened one mild spring afternoon when Jacob escaped the confines of the cave house to spend some time outdoors. He would not have admitted it if questioned, but his primary motivation was to escape the daily cooking lesson. Livia had decided she lacked the requisite domestic skills to be a suitable wife and had been badgering Gregory to teach her to cook. So far the results had been abysmal. Livia, for all her innate intelligence and artistic talent, had no natural ability in the kitchen, and Gregory, who cooked by instinct and inspiration, evidently lacked the patience to impart his years of experience.

Jacob spent some time grooming the chestnut, and when he came out of the shed, he heard voices drifting out of the window above him. The first voice belonged to Gregory, who was shouting, "How can you cook a proper stew if you don't even know the difference between cumin and coriander!"

Livia shouted back, "How am I supposed to know the difference if no one ever told me?"

"I told you yesterday!"

"Well, tell me again. I'm new at this . . ."

Listening to the yelling, Jacob winced. He wondered how long the two of them would keep at it before they realized this experiment was doomed to failure. Perhaps he should encourage Livia to get back to her work and leave the kitchen to Gregory.

In a few minutes, Gregory scuttled down the ladder and stalked off to his garden. Jacob let the older man work some of his frustration off, then he went over to him.

"I'd offer to help, but I'm not sure I can tell the herbs from the weeds," he said.

"And I'm not of a mind to show you," Gregory replied curtly. Then he rocked back on his heels, still holding a fistful of weeds, and looked up at Jacob. "Sorry," he said, "I'm just dismayed to discover that I'm not much of a teacher."

"Perhaps your pupil simply doesn't have an aptitude for the subject."

"My niece has drive and determination, I'll give her that. But when it comes to the kitchen, she's as lost as a goose in a snowstorm." Gregory shook the clumps of soil from his hands, then stood to his feet. "I should have taught her to cook years ago. I failed her in that."

"You taught her other things," Jacob said. "And you gave her the freedom to develop her true talent. I wouldn't call that failure." Jacob shaded his eyes against the late-afternoon sun and looked up at the house. "Perhaps I should have a talk with her, let her know she doesn't have to learn to cook just to please me—if that's what she's doing. I don't expect that—it's not like I married Livia for her cooking."

"It's a good thing, too." Gregory sat down on the rough wooden bench at the edge of the garden and motioned for Jacob to join him. "You'd waste away to nothing if you had to live on what she's able to cook."

Gregory quickly turned his head to cough. He'd been doing more of that lately, Jacob realized. During the winter Gregory had been sick with a cough and fever; he had recovered after a few days, but the cough had lingered for a while longer. Gregory had finally cured it with some kind of aromatic brew of dried herbs. He was known as a healer, and some of the townspeople sought his advice about herbal medicines for various ailments.

The last few nights, though, after they had gone to bed, Jacob had heard Gregory wheezing in the other room. Jacob had even asked Livia if they should go check on him.

"He'll be fine," Livia had said. "He gets spells like this at night sometimes, but they always pass. And he'll just get angry if you make a fuss over him."

Jacob looked at Gregory now and wondered if it was time to make a fuss anyway. "Your cough is back," Jacob said.

"We had a late spring." Gregory tilted his head toward the garden. "In a few weeks, I'll have a fresh supply of medicine." He talked for a while about the various herbs he'd planted and their uses. "Fennel and sage are good for failing eyesight. Anise or mint will get rid of indigestion. And I'm sure you're familiar with the benefits of a mustard plaster."

Jacob laughed. "I'm familiar with the smell and the awful heat; I never was convinced of the benefits."

Gregory laughed too, and it caused him to cough again. As the spasm subsided, he drew out a handkerchief to wipe his mouth, and Jacob was shocked to see a spot of bright red on the cloth.

"I want to talk to you about something," Gregory said.

Jacob did not reply. He was still too stunned by the realization that Gregory was coughing up blood.

"Jacob?" Gregory asked.

Jacob forced himself to quit staring at the handkerchief and answer. "Sorry. What did you want to tell me?"

As casually as if he'd been talking about the weather, Gregory said, "I've been thinking that you should take Livia to Ephesus. To live, I mean."

"You do?" Jacob could not have been more surprised. He had never expected that Gregory or Livia would suggest moving to Ephesus. But he'd never suspected that Gregory could be seriously ill, either.

"Now that you're married, her place is with you."

"Are you saying we're not welcome here any longer?"

"No, no. Not at all." Gregory looked off in the distance, watching a bird circle overhead. When it landed at the top of a tufa cone, he spoke again. "It's just that Livia's been alone too much of her life. She needs family."

"She has you. You're family."

Gregory turned toward Jacob again. "You're her family now," he said softly.

Jacob met his gaze, and if he hadn't already been sitting, the impact would have brought him to his knees. "Are you that sick, Gregory?"

"Promise me you'll take her to Ephesus. Promise me."

"I won't promise any such thing. Not unless you answer my question."

Gregory's look pleaded as eloquently as his voice. "Livia has already lost too many people in her life; I don't want her to watch me die. Please, Jacob."

"And because she's lost so many people, she would never agree to leave here without you—and I wouldn't either." Jacob put a hand on Gregory's shoulder and swallowed hard before continuing. "So if you're not well enough to make the journey with us, then this discussion is over."

Gregory blinked and couldn't seem to find his voice for a moment.

"If you'll promise to take Livia to your family, then I'll *get* well enough to travel."

Jacob nodded soberly, realizing that his plan to go home to Ephesus would be suspended indefinitely, and accepting it without question. "You have to promise *me* something, though," he said.

Gregory hesitated again. "What is that?"

"Promise that you'll get well enough to do the cooking."

Antony yawned and rubbed his eyes. He couldn't go to sleep yet. It was the first chance he'd had all week to write a letter to Rebecca. But every time he looked down at the parchment, his eyes blurred and the words he'd scrawled swam together. Fatigue swept over him, and he fought the urge to lay his head on the writing desk. If he did that, he'd be there come morning.

The lamp flickered and sputtered, and Antony suddenly remembered he had no more oil in his room. He rose, took the lamp to the kitchen, and replenished the oil. He also filled another lamp and brought it back with him, just in case. Polycarp's house was completely quiet, a testament to the lateness of the hour. During the day, the place was a beehive of activity.

When he returned to his bedroom, Antony opened the window. He had shuttered it earlier to keep out the noise of the revelers. Nature worshipers welcoming the summer solstice, he imagined. Hard to believe he had been in Smyrna almost three months, and in all that time he had only squeezed in one visit home. He had been inundated with work and so gripped by the urgency of some of the cases that it had been impossible to tear himself away again.

He could not have borne the separation from Rebecca if it hadn't been for their frequent correspondence. Peter had arranged for a courier to travel from Ephesus to Smyrna each week, carrying their letters back and forth. The courier also brought a stipend from Peter to cover all of Antony's expenses. He had never asked Peter for help, but was grateful for his friend's generosity. The income allowed Antony to reimburse Polycarp for his room and board and to have the finances necessary to carry out investigations and legal research.

From daybreak until early evening, Antony met with clients, interviewed witnesses, and made court appearances. A few times he'd been able to sit in on a class Polycarp held for his disciples. Antony had been enthralled by the bishop's teaching and wished he could spend more time in the classroom. But he was learning quite a bit about the faith just from staying in Polycarp's home.

For a few minutes Antony stood in front of the window, letting the cool summer breeze relieve the worst of his fatigue. The revelers had all gone home; the only noise drifting in now was the monotonous drone of insects. Before the sound could lull him to sleep, Antony went back to his desk and sat down.

He picked up Rebecca's last letter and reread it. It was an interesting epistle, full of news about Victor, who would be a year old in only six weeks, and reports on Priscilla and Helena, who could read and write reasonably well but was not the kind to sit still long enough to pen a letter of her own. Rebecca, however, was quite articulate, and her long letters more than made up for the lack of communication from his mother.

His fiancée went on to describe the progress of their new house and how thrilled she was with it. Peter had hired someone to oversee the construction and usually sent a short weekly report to Antony as well.

Rebecca had also written about Quintus and Agatha, the shipping business, the church, and the relief work. But one paragraph in particular held Antony's attention tonight:

> In all these months, seven of them now, we have had no word from Jacob. I grieve for him, Antony. What has happened to my brother? Where could he be? Why hasn't he returned? I cannot believe he would turn his back on his family forever. Some evil has

befallen him, I fear, and I have no way of knowing. I'm sure if
Polycarp had received any word of Jacob, you would have told me.

Antony was equally worried that some unspeakable evil had befallen
Jacob, especially in light of what he had learned just yesterday from
Plautius and Sergius.

The brothers had relayed two bits of news when Antony had met
with them. The first was the fact Tullia was gleefully announcing to
anyone who would listen that she was carrying a child.

"Actually, she doesn't even have to say anything," Plautius had
said. "It's quite obvious that she's expecting."

Sergius snorted his disapproval. "Doesn't have the decency to stay
at home but parades around in public, proudly patting her swollen
belly. I tell you, it's scandalous." He paused for a moment and stroked
his chin. "Maybe she's wearing a pillow under her tunic; you suppose
she's delusional?"

"We'll know in two months," Plautius had remarked calmly.
"That's when she says she's due."

Antony wasn't sure why Tullia's being pregnant should worry
him, but it did. Perhaps it was just the fact that Tullia worried him
in general. He was certain that she had either bribed or blackmailed
the public official who had denied business permits for the brothers'
blacksmith shop and several other Christian businesses, but he
couldn't prove it. Corruption was a serious offense, and under the
Lex Calpurnia, a magistrate could be heavily fined and prohibited
from ever holding public office if the crime were proved. Antony
had been able to get the permits reinstated for his clients but had not
brought charges against the official in question. Not yet, anyway.

Every time Antony interviewed a witness, he had the feeling that
Tullia had been there ahead of him. Some of them refused to talk at
all. A couple of them had made veiled references to a witch's curse if
they spoke to him, confirming Antony's suspicions.

As he listened to the drone of insects outside his window, Antony wondered if Tullia's pregnancy had any implications for his clients. He doubted it. But the other news Plautius and Sergius had delivered was replete with significance for Antony personally: Damian had returned to Smyrna.

"He's been back for a couple of months," Plautius had said. "Long enough, anyway, that our cousin banned him from the tavern several weeks ago."

"Evidently Damian spends all his time drinking and brawling," Sergius added. "Guess that's why we haven't seen him before now."

Antony rolled up Rebecca's letter and set it aside, then picked up his pen. A moment later he put it back down. There was no way he could write a letter to her now, not with all this weighing so heavily on his mind.

Damian was back. Jacob wasn't. And any inference Antony could draw from the juxtaposition of those two facts was ominous.

31

July, A.D. 97

"WHAT DO WE REALLY HAVE to keep us here?" Gregory asked. "A piece of rock?" He gestured toward the house tucked into the tufa.

Livia drew herself up to her full height and looked down at her uncle, hands defiantly on her hips. "I helped carve this 'piece of rock,' I'll have you know."

"And you feel pride of ownership. I do too. But when you get right down to it, it's still just a hunk of rock. *Home,*" he said, "will be wherever we make it."

Livia changed tactics. "It's not fair, you and Jacob ganging up on me like this. It's all so sudden." Yesterday was the first time her husband had mentioned the possibility of moving to Ephesus, but she quickly pried out of him the fact that he had already discussed it with Gregory, who had agreed to the plan. But leaving everything she'd ever known did not sound like a good idea to Livia.

"The idea may seem sudden, but the move would not be." Gregory sat down on the garden bench. "We wouldn't leave until fall. No one in their right mind would travel in this blasted heat." He removed the damp towel draped around his neck and wiped his forehead.

He looked tired, Livia thought. At least he'd gotten stronger the last couple of months. The winter had been hard on Gregory, and all during the spring he hadn't quite been himself. He seemed much better now, in spite of the heat, and she was glad.

"Besides, I wouldn't want to leave until I've harvested all my herbs and dried them for the winter."

Livia dropped to the ground with a sigh and leaned back against the bench where her uncle sat. The thought of traveling excited her, yet the thought of leaving home scared her, and she couldn't exactly put into words why. She'd never lived anywhere except Caesarea or its outskirts. And while she loved the house she and Gregory had carved out of the tufa, it was just a house, as he'd said; she refused to think of it as a "piece of rock," however.

There was also her workshop, which she loved; but tools and equipment could be picked up and moved. Jacob had promised to build her another workshop, with more windows and more light, in Ephesus. If Gregory went with them, there truly would be nothing to keep her here. Her parents had been dead for eight years now, and Livia had no other relatives. Perhaps that's what made her reluctant to consider cutting all ties to her place of birth.

She spoke her thought aloud. "It would be like leaving them behind."

"Who?"

"My mother and father."

Gregory reached over and stroked her hair. "But that's just it, Livia. They're gone. Now you have a new family, Jacob's family, and they're in Ephesus."

"But I don't even know them." She couldn't help sounding petulant.

"You won't ever know them if you don't go to meet them. And if we travel all that distance, we might as well stay." He reached down and turned her face up toward his. "It's where Jacob's roots are, child. Where you can put down roots with him."

"I'll think about it," she said grudgingly.

†

Someone handed Antony a blanket and he went to work with the others, beating out the flying sparks the moment they touched the ground. He looked up briefly, watching helplessly as brilliant flames danced across the roof of the blacksmith shop and leaped into the night, then he resumed the watch for falling embers.

The building was engulfed now; all they could do was try to

keep the fire from spreading. More volunteers kept arriving to combat the blaze. They soaked the ground around the building with as much water as they could haul, and they beat the ground with their blankets. Fortunately, the shop was detached from the brothers' two houses, which were set back a good sixty paces, and there was no wind to drive the flames. The homes where Plautius and Sergius lived would probably be spared. That was Antony's prayer, anyway.

The older of the two brothers, ordinarily so placid, was distraught. "It's gone! We've lost it all," Plautius cried. Two horses, a new wagon, all their tools and equipment—their entire livelihood.

Twin flames of fatigue and fury ignited the acid in Antony's stomach until he thought he would be sick. He had solved the brothers' legal problems, but he couldn't save their business. His anger stoking his energy, Antony stomped sparks and flailed his blanket against the flying embers.

The volunteers, a few neighbors and a good number of fellow Christians, toiled through the night. At dawn, plumes of black smoke still poured from the building, but the fire had been contained. When he finally deemed it safe to stop working, exhaustion melted Antony's bones and he sank to the ground. The smoke had burned his eyes so bad, they kept tearing up. Rivulets of sweat streaked down his face, and he wiped them away with a grimy hand.

Sergius, his face black with soot, walked over to where Antony was sitting and dropped down beside him. "This one wasn't an accident," the blacksmith said.

In spite of the intense heat that still radiated from the smoldering structure, Antony felt a chill at Sergius's pronouncement. But the lawyer was too tired to question the statement; besides, he was as skeptical as Sergius. Antony had had the same suspicion.

Sergius was the second client to lose his business to a fire this month, and Antony didn't think it was a coincidence. And if it wasn't a coincidence, then somehow Tullia was behind this. Tullia, and perhaps Damian.

In a moment Sergius began to elaborate on his allegation of arson. "The bakery fire might have been an accident, although I doubt it. But I know for a fact this fire was deliberately started."

The owner of the bakery was another church member for whom Antony had gotten a business permit reinstated. Speculation was that a cooking fire had not been extinguished properly and something had fallen into the oven, causing a blaze. The owner vehemently denied it, but he had no other explanation for the fire.

"How do you know it was deliberate?" Antony asked.

"Because I saw someone throw a torch into the building."

Antony snapped his head around to look at Sergius. "Did you see who it was?"

Sergius gave a quick, despondent shrug. "No, I was too far away. I'd just stepped outside to go next door and ask Plautius something. It was a man, though, I could tell that." Sergius paused to cough violently. Inhaling so much smoke had obviously irritated his lungs. "I ran straight for the shop," he said when the coughing spell passed, "but the torch thrower must have soaked the perimeter in oil first. It was blazing out of control by the time I got there."

Antony thought back to his arrival. He hadn't noticed anyone leaving the scene; he must have arrived just moments after the arsonist had left. "If only I'd gotten here earlier," he mumbled.

"You got here awfully fast as it was," Sergius said. "Were you coming to see us for something?"

"No, I was on my way back to Polycarp's when I passed by and saw the blaze. Young Linus was with me, so I sent him to get help. I just wish we could have done something else."

"We saved the houses; that's the most important thing. No one was injured. Praise God, we're alive and we still have a roof over our heads. After a few hours' sleep, I imagine my brother and I will begin figuring out how to start over."

For a few moments, the two men sat in silence as they watched the crowd disperse one by one. Antony saw Polycarp place an arm around Plautius and walk him back to the house.

"One question keeps haunting me," Sergius finally said, "and I wish I had an answer for it."

When he didn't go on to state his question, Antony prompted him. "An answer to what?"

"Who's going to be next?"

Sergius rose and walked wearily home, leaving Antony to ponder the question.

In the days following the fire, the question continued to nag at him. First the bakery, then the blacksmith shop. *Who's next?* More than a month would pass before Antony had an answer.

†

Antony's weekly letters to Rebecca became shorter and sketchier. He told her about the fire, saying that it had been intentionally started, but he did not share his suspicions regarding who was behind it. Part of his hesitation was a well-honed lawyerly caution against jumping to conclusions not supported by the evidence, and part of it was due to a protective instinct.

When he stopped long enough to think about it, doubt and fear assailed him. Should he warn Rebecca, or at least Peter, that Damian had returned? Yet, it would only add to their worries that Jacob had met a horrible fate and renew fears for Victor's safety. Antony rationalized that no one had actually seen Damian yet; Sergius and Plautius had merely heard that he was back in town. Was their cousin, Tarquinius, a reliable witness? Antony didn't know.

Should he go to Ephesus for a while, just to make sure Rebecca and the baby were safe? The thought that Damian might do something to harm them preyed on Antony's mind, and several times he dreamed of the abandoned mill where they had found Victor. In a letter to Peter, Antony urged him to retain the bodyguards.

At times Antony was tempted to leave Smyrna, marry Rebecca, and get on with his life. He had even tried to talk to Polycarp about it, but when he had finally managed a few minutes alone with the bishop, Polycarp embraced Antony and thanked him yet again for his "invaluable service to the kingdom of God." Antony couldn't bring himself to disappoint Polycarp by reneging on his pledge to help, and Antony certainly didn't want to disappoint God. So he kept rising at dawn and working until he fell asleep at his desk late at night.

Antony was pulled in every direction at once—working with city officials to secure business permits, defending two men who had been falsely accused of crimes, resolving a boundary dispute in order to forestall a lawsuit, and drafting wills for worried church members who wanted to protect their families in the event of a catastrophe.

The summer heat was oppressive, and the disciples who gathered daily at Polycarp's to study the Scriptures began praying earnestly for rain. Most of the congregation was also fasting two days a week for relief from the legal harassment and for the protection of their property.

For several weeks after the bakery and the blacksmith shop burned there were no additional fires, but other disturbances gave cause for alarm. Several local businesses were burglarized, some of them belonging to Christians, and a man who was not a member of the congregation was robbed and severely beaten. It was possible, Antony supposed, that the latest crimes were unrelated to the arson of the church members' property, but he had a hunch they were connected in some way. And when slaughtered animals began appearing on the doorsteps of those who had been targets of legal persecution, Antony *knew* there was a connection. There had to be. The perpetrator might have switched from arson to butchery, but the intent was the same: intimidation and wanton destruction.

At the end of August, there was another fire, but the victim this time came as a surprise. Plautius and Sergius delivered the news early one morning.

Polycarp was at prayer with his students and Antony was in the dining room when the brothers arrived, covered in soot, their soggy clothes smelling of smoke. Immediately Antony shoved aside his breakfast and rose, fearing the worst.

"There's been another arson—" Sergius began.

"But not one of the church members," Plautius interjected. He waved Antony back to his seat.

"Whose property?" Antony asked.

"Our cousin, Tarquinius." Plautius started to sit, then noticed his filthy clothes and remained standing.

"The one who runs the inn?" Antony asked.

Sergius nodded. "His wife died in the fire." He paused to wipe a grimy hand across his forehead. "She was a shrew, and I never liked her. But to die like that . . ."

Antony set down his spoon, sobered by the news. No one had died in the previous two fires; now a woman had perished. "It was arson?" he asked.

"Just like our place," Plautius said. "The stable and lodging rooms are gone. The fire would have spread to the tavern too, except for the sudden downpour. The rain put out the fire."

"Downpour?" Antony hadn't heard it rain, and he slept with the window open. Certainly, if it had rained, he would have noticed water in his room when he got up.

"Came out of nowhere," Plautius said, "and left as suddenly as it came. Looks like it didn't even reach this part of town."

"It rained just long enough to put the fire out," Sergius added. "I sure wish it would have done that the night our place burned."

"The Bible says it rains on the just and the unjust," Plautius said. "Maybe God had a purpose in sending the rain to spare Tarquinius's tavern. It doesn't make sense to me, but I guess it doesn't have to."

Finished with his meal, Antony wiped the crumbs from his mouth. He thought of all the prayers for rain that had been offered; perhaps God had answered them in a way no one could have foreseen.

He rose from the table and walked outside with the two brothers, who looked as if they could drop from exhaustion.

"Something else doesn't make sense," Sergius said. "All along we've figured that Tullia was behind all the legal problems we've had, and that she had probably paid or persuaded someone to start the fires. But burning her own brother's place? She and Tarquinius always had a good relationship."

"Maybe they had a falling out," Plautius said.

"We would have heard about it." Sergius shook his head doubtfully. "I just don't see the connection. The previous fires were intended to destroy the property of Christians."

Antony saw a possible connection, and it disturbed him greatly. "What about Damian?" he asked. "A few weeks ago you said that Tarquinius had banned him from the tavern for brawling. Perhaps Damian acted on a grudge against your cousin."

Plautius considered the statement while Sergius coughed and spat on the ground. His lungs cleared, Sergius said, "He's kept a low profile since his return. But you're right—he did have a run-in with Tarquinius."

"I would have thought Damian would have gone back to Rome by now," Plautius said. "I wonder what's keeping him here."

"He has no reason to go back to Rome, and may not have the resources," Antony said. And that, he thought, could explain the recent rash of burglaries. Damian was the type who would easily resort to robbery to finance a long journey, or simply to purchase enough alcohol to fuel his drinking binges.

Antony told the brothers about Senator Mallus's illness and bankruptcy. "Damian's father died not long after I arrived in Smyrna. I read the account in the *Acta Diurna*."

"So if Damian has amassed no independent wealth of his own . . ." Plautius trailed off, thinking of the implications.

"I doubt that he has," Antony said. "Damian strikes me as a man content to live off someone else's hard work."

After the two brothers left, Antony continued to think about the fire, and early the next morning, he decided to do something. He visited Tarquinius at the inn—or what was left of it.

Antony found the innkeeper raking through the rubble of his establishment. If the stocky hulk of a man had been a gracious host at one time, there was no sign of it now.

"Who might you be?" Tarquinius demanded.

Antony introduced himself as a lawyer from Ephesus and a friend of Plautius and Sergius.

"A lawyer, huh?" Tarquinius propped his shovel against the remains of a burned-out wall, then looked down at his feet as he spoke. "Might be needing one of them myself."

"You have some legal problems?" Antony's interest was piqued. Perhaps that could be a way to gain the innkeeper's cooperation.

"The authorities say the fire was deliberately started . . ."

"Arson," Antony prompted when Tarquinius hesitated.

"Right. And because my wife was killed in the fire . . . well, they're saying that I might be charged with murder." He looked up, becoming agitated. "But I didn't set the fire, I didn't!"

"Do you know who did?"

Tarquinius studied Antony for a moment, as if sizing up his trustworthiness before speaking. "I got a suspicion."

"So do I, and that's what I wanted to talk to you about."

For the first time since Antony's arrival, Tarquinius visibly relaxed. "Would you like to come inside?"

They entered the tavern, which was heavily smoke damaged, but still standing. It wouldn't take much work to get this part of the business reopened, Antony noted. But if Tarquinius ever hosted overnight guests again, it would mean completely rebuilding the rest of the inn.

Tarquinius ushered Antony to a seat on one of the long wooden benches and even offered his guest something to drink. Antony declined.

The innkeeper seemed reluctant to speak, so Antony asked a

leading question. "You said you have an idea who might have wanted to burn down your place. Who?"

"You go first," Tarquinius said. "Who do you suspect?"

"I think it was a man named Damian."

Tarquinius's eyes widened slightly but he showed no other expression. "And I think you're right."

"Tell me how it happened," Antony said, "and why you suspect Damian."

"I'm not sure where to start." Tarquinius splayed his wide fingers on the table and looked down while he gathered his thoughts. "I guess you know he's been living with my sister, Tullia." The innkeeper looked across the table for confirmation.

Antony said, "I know who she is." He wondered if Tarquinius knew of Tullia's involvement in hiding Rebecca's baby. Thinking about his fiancée now needled Antony's conscience, so he put Rebecca out of his mind and nodded for Tarquinius to continue.

"Tullia recently gave birth to Damian's son. Severa, that's my wife, wouldn't have anything to do with Tullia, but I paid my sister a visit to make sure she was all right after the baby was born. A sickly looking child, but Tullia seemed not to notice. All she could talk about was how proud she was of her baby's noble heritage." Tarquinius gave a disgusted snort. "Noble, my eye. Damian may have a wealthy father, but he's a common drunk—and a mean drunk, at that."

"I understand you barred him from coming into your tavern."

"Arrogant little rooster was always picking a fight with the customers. I finally had my fill of it. Told him not to set foot on my property again. As you can imagine, Damian didn't like it one bit. But I didn't give him any choice; just picked him up and tossed him outside. 'Good riddance,' I told myself."

Antony could clearly picture the innkeeper's broad shoulders and beefy arms physically ejecting Damian from the tavern. "Only he came back," Antony said.

"Not for a long time. But then a few nights ago he returned.

Damian was all charm, said he was sorry about the misunderstanding we had had. Misunderstanding . . ." Tarquinius rolled his eyes and swore. "He asked very nicely if he could have a room for the night. Said he couldn't get any sleep at home with the baby crying all the time. I don't know why, but I relented and let him stay.

"He drank quite a bit that night, but he was on his best behavior. Didn't cause any trouble. Finally, he went to his room to sleep it off. When Damian woke up the next morning, he had a roaring hangover. He was surly and rude to Severa, and when I asked him to settle his bill, he was angry.

"'I don't have any money with me,' he said, 'but you know I'm good for it.' And that made *me* angry. I didn't bother to argue with him, I just threw him out, shouting a few choice words after him." Tarquinius paused, then said with a sad sigh, "That night my inn went up in flames . . . and my wife too." He looked around the large room, as if half expecting to see Severa there.

"I'm sorry for your loss," Antony said. He allowed the innkeeper a moment of silent grief before asking, "Where were you when the fire started?"

Tarquinius cleared his throat. "There's a mangy old dog that hung around here. Severa was always chasing him off with a broom, but I felt sorry for the mutt. Sometimes after supper I would sneak scraps out to him. That's what I did that night. I went outside and whistled for the dog, but he didn't come. So I walked away from the tavern a bit, and then I found him . . ."

The innkeeper swore again. "Someone had cut the animal's throat. The blood was still fresh. It turned my stomach to smell it, but all of a sudden I noticed another smell. Smoke. I knew the cooking fire had been extinguished, and the smoke was not coming from the tavern anyway. It was on the other side. I ran around to the front of the property, and by the time I got to the courtyard, the whole downstairs of the inn was in flames.

"I pushed down the door, but I couldn't find Severa. We didn't have guests that night, and she was doing some cleaning. I didn't know what room she had been in. I called and searched, but within a few minutes the blaze became too intense to keep looking. I was nearly overcome by the smoke, but I made it out alive. My wife didn't."

Trembling with emotion, Tarquinius paused in his narration. "I *know* that fire was deliberately set," he concluded. "If it had been a lamp that tipped over and broke, the flames would not have spread that fast. Sergius told me about seeing a man throw a torch into the blacksmith shop the night it burned down. I think the same thing happened to me, but I don't know how to prove it."

Antony quizzed Tarquinius about why the authorities thought he might have set the fire himself.

"People in the tavern often heard me arguing with Severa, but that was just our way. We didn't mean anything by it, and I always gave up and let her win after a few minutes. Now they're saying that I carried a grudge against her all these years. It's not true, but even if it was, I wouldn't burn down my own business to get back at my wife."

"But what if they don't believe me?" Tarquinius asked. "I . . . I could be in a lot of trouble."

"I can help you," Antony said.

Tarquinius looked skeptical. "I don't have any way to pay a lawyer."

"I don't want your money. If the authorities charge you with murder, I'll defend you for free."

"Nothing is ever free." Tarquinius shook his head. "If you don't want money, you want something else."

The astute observation pleased Antony. The man may have been uneducated, but he was smart enough, and that could come in handy. "I want your help to pin the crime on the real culprit," Antony said. "Help me catch Damian."

For a moment the innkeeper simply stared, then he extended a meaty hand toward Antony. "I'll do whatever it takes."

So will I, Antony thought as they shook hands. *So will I.*

32

LIVIA AND GREGORY STOOD TO ONE SIDE and watched in amusement as Jacob negotiated a price for the necklace with a chirpy-voiced woman wearing a green tunic with a blue *stola*. Her cheeks and lips were stained deep red, and the combination of the colorful cosmetics and apparel reminded Livia of a parrot. The woman would never get lost among the crowd conducting business in the marketplace in the center of Pisidian Antioch.

The necklace was the last remaining piece of the dozens of jewelry items Livia had made over the summer. She'd worn it several times and had thought about keeping it for herself, simply because Jacob had said he loved the way it looked on her, and Livia thrived on his attention. He actually thought she was beautiful, and just knowing that had made her start to *feel* beautiful. But the necklace was not one of her favorites, so she was not that sad about parting with it.

"Not every woman can wear this type of necklace," Jacob told his customer. "But you have—if you'll forgive me for saying something so personal—a very thin, elegant neck that sets off a fine piece of jewelry like this."

A scrawny neck was more like it, Livia thought as Jacob handed the woman a bronze mirror. She checked her reflection and fiddled with the long beaded strands dangling from the choker.

"I don't know . . ." The woman turned her head back and forth. "Do you have anything else?"

"I wish you had been here earlier," Jacob said with a sigh. "This is our last item. My wife is a very talented designer and her jewelry is in much demand." With a conspiratorial wink he added, "We're going to sell her work in Rome next year, you know."

"Shameless," Gregory whispered with a jerk of his head toward Jacob.

"Yes," Livia replied, suppressing a chuckle, "he is. Shameless but successful." She was proud of her husband. And even though she'd been married for over six months now, it still thrilled Livia to hear Jacob refer to her as "my wife."

It hadn't taken very long for Gregory to convince Livia that moving to Ephesus was the right thing to do. "You belong with Jacob," her uncle had said repeatedly, "and Jacob belongs in Ephesus." Jacob had said he would be perfectly content to stay in Cappadocia if that's what Livia wanted. But the more she had thought about it, the more she realized Gregory was right—not only about Jacob belonging in Ephesus but that there really was nothing to hold them in Caesarea.

They hadn't wanted to travel during the worst months of the heat, so they'd waited until early September before leaving. A month later they were over halfway there, yet it was still another two hundred miles to Ephesus, and in spite of the fact that she was having the time of her life, Livia was road weary. They had indeed talked about going to Rome, as Jacob was telling his customer, but right now all Livia wanted to do was to meet Jacob's family and then stay put for a while.

Jacob concluded the sale with the parrotlike lady, who reached a decision to buy as soon as he mentioned that this particular style of necklace was favored by Roman women of note. After he bid her farewell and deposited the coins in the leather wallet on his belt, Jacob rejoined the others.

"So, what shall we do for the rest of this fine fall day?" he asked. Energized by the transaction, Jacob walked with a bounce in his step. "We should celebrate Livia's success. We've sold every last bit of merchandise."

"And at higher prices than we've ever gotten before," Gregory said.

"I have to hand it to you, Jacob. You're far better at this than I ever was."

"You always did fine by me," Livia said in defense of her uncle.

"Aye, we did all right." Gregory picked up his hat from the cart and positioned it atop his silver-streaked hair. "But your young man here has a real flair for it."

Jacob winked at Livia. "That's because my wife produces the best handcrafted jewelry in the world. Quality commands the highest price. I couldn't sell inferior baubles with this much enthusiasm."

While Gregory reattached the small cart to the harness of the donkey they'd bought for the trip, they discussed their plans.

Jacob said, "We could go back to the inn and spend another night in Antioch, if you like."

"It's barely noon. I'd rather start traveling again." Livia looked at her uncle. "Unless you're too tired." Even though Gregory had been well the entire time they had been traveling, Livia still fretted that it was too much for him. Once or twice she had heard him cough during the night, but the cough wasn't nearly as bad as it had been last winter.

"Me? I'm fine," Gregory said. "As far as I'm concerned, we might as well get on the road."

They'd sold the last of the inventory, so there was little to load in the cart—just the mirror and the display cloths. Livia's tools and supplies and the few household items they'd brought with them were stashed in the bottom of the cart. Jacob put the other things on top, then saddled the donkey for Gregory.

This will be our last market. It was a poignant thought for Livia. She had never traveled so far from home before, and she had enjoyed the experience of seeing so many new places and the excitement of the public marketplaces. From Cappadocia they had traveled south through Lycaonia, stopping for days at a time to sell her jewelry and housewares at the markets in Derbe, Lystra, and Iconium.

Gregory had eagerly pointed out that they were following the route taken by the apostle Paul on his second missionary journey.

Her uncle had sought out Christians in every city, and it amazed Livia, the way he managed to encounter fellow believers wherever they went. It wasn't as if they wore unique clothing or special signs that identified them, but somehow Gregory's instincts always led him to start a conversation with a person who turned out to be a believer. And before long Gregory, Livia, and Jacob would be sharing a meal or even accommodations with a new Christian friend.

After Jacob mounted the chestnut, he reached down and helped Livia climb on behind him. They both were wearing trousers, but Livia wore them for comfort in riding, now, not for a disguise. They left Antioch and headed southwest, toward Phrygia. When she asked, Jacob said it would take another ten days before they reached Ephesus.

Ten more days to worry about what his family would think of her. "They'll love you," Jacob always said when she brought it up. Livia wished she could truly believe that. She didn't know how they would react to Jacob being married, let alone married to someone who wasn't at all like them. She had started letting her hair grow out—over Jacob's objection; he had said he liked it short. In a month it would grow out enough to pin up and then she wouldn't look quite so odd; they would be in Ephesus long before then, however.

At twilight they stopped and made camp. Gregory cooked some flat bread in a skillet over an open fire and threw some fresh vegetables he'd bought at the market into a pot with some of his dried herbs. Jacob usually tried to stop for the evening at a town, where they would find an inn, but when the weather was nice, Livia actually preferred sleeping outdoors. Lying next to Jacob and gazing up at the stars was a great way to fall asleep.

As they ate their meal, she studied Jacob's face across the firelight. His square jaw still had that stubborn set to it, but there were no harsh lines around his mouth. He was quicker to laugh, and there was a lightness about him that Livia had glimpsed only briefly during the first months she had known him.

The amber she had given Jacob adorned his hand; she admired its gleam in the glow of the fire. She had set the stone in a ring for him, and he never took it off. The lock of her hair and the copper engraving from the Song of Songs still resided in the keepsake box. It pleased her that it was Jacob's most treasured possession.

The evening was clear and a bit cool, as it was now October, but a far cry from the cold to which Livia was accustomed. She wondered what winter would be like in a warmer climate. When they were snuggled together under their blanket, she said to Jacob, "Tell me about the ocean."

"You're forever wanting to know about the ocean," he said. Livia couldn't see his face, but she knew he was smiling. He always smiled when he talked about the water. That was one of the reasons she loved to ask him about it.

"I've never seen the ocean," she said, "and I'm glad that when I see it for the first time it will be with you."

Jacob talked about sailing over rough water and smooth seas. He talked about his father's ships and the cargoes they carried to the far reaches of the Empire. Livia had heard it all before, but it still fascinated her. After a few minutes, Jacob fell quiet and she thought for a moment that he'd fallen asleep. Then he said quietly, "I don't know what's waiting for me at home, Livia."

"What do you mean?"

"I don't know if my family will be glad to see me or not. It's been almost a year, and I left without even saying good-bye. Except for Marcellus," he added.

Livia remembered that he was the medical officer Jacob had met on Patmos and that he had come to Ephesus to live with the family. She knew about Jacob's twin brother, Peter, and their sister, Rebecca. Livia had been concerned about how they would receive her and Gregory; she hadn't even considered that Jacob's family might not be overjoyed at his return.

"I feel a bit like the prodigal son returning home after a long sojourn in the far country," Jacob said.

Livia shoved her own worries to the back of her mind. "They'll welcome you with open arms and kill the fatted calf, so to speak. I certainly hope so, anyway. It would be a welcome addition to one of Gregory's stews."

Jacob laughed. "At least we haven't gone hungry, and we haven't had to spend too much of the money we've earned. Or you've earned, I should say."

She noted the subtle change in his voice. "Does it bother you, Jacob? My working, I mean?"

"No," he said after a moment. "I'm proud of your ability and your independence. It was one of the things that attracted me to you. I suppose I'm chagrined by the fact that I haven't contributed anything to our expenses lately."

"But you have," she protested. "You've done almost all the selling, and before we left Caesarea, you used the last of your finances to buy the donkey for Gregory."

"I should be taking better care of you," he insisted. "And I will, when we get to Ephesus. Assuming I still have an inheritance waiting for me, I will build you a huge house in the hills, complete with a workshop. It will overlook the ocean, so you can see it from your window every day. And if I don't get my inheritance for some reason, then I'll work my fingers to the bone and build that house for you anyway."

"Oh, Jacob." Livia rolled to her side and draped her arm across his chest. "You already take better care of me than you could ever imagine. I don't need a big house. Your love is all the shelter I need."

He wrapped his arms around her and hugged her tightly. "Is that so?"

"Absolutely so."

"Well, if it turns cloudy and rains tonight," he said, "I don't want to hear a word of complaint."

Livia rejoiced in his embrace, thinking she would not complain if the skies opened up and drenched them to the skin. She was happier sleeping outside on the hard ground with Jacob than she had ever been in her life.

"'Many waters cannot quench love,'" she whispered into the night, then finished with a yawn, "'Rivers cannot wash it away.'"

✝

Rebecca paced the floor of the library. She was supposed to be writing a letter to Antony but didn't know what to say. After a few minutes of walking back and forth, she returned to the desk and picked up the most recent note from him. Barely more than a half dozen lines, it most certainly could not be called a letter. She quickly scanned it, then tossed it aside angrily and continued pacing.

Evidently Antony was no better at writing his mother. Rebecca had talked to Helena about it, and both women commiserated at his lack of communication. Helena had, of course, come to her son's defense. She had told Rebecca, "He's engrossed in his work, dear. That's all."

Well, Antony had been engrossed in his work for over six months now, and Rebecca was out of patience. At first she had written him three or four letters a week, and while his letters had never been as numerous, they had been long and overflowing with love. They had also been full of news about what was happening in Smyrna. But lately he had written only one letter a week, and it was always vague and short. So short, she pictured Antony dashing it off while the courier waited.

"I love you . . . I miss you . . . I'll be home as soon as I can." As brief as they were, Antony's letters always said the right things. But there was a distance there, and Rebecca couldn't seem to break through it. It puzzled her, saddened her, and angered her.

The courier would be there first thing in the morning to pick up her letter. It would take him all day to travel to Smyrna. He would spend the night at Polycarp's house, then return to Ephesus the following day with Antony's letter to her. Rebecca was weary of the routine, and weary of waiting for Antony.

She sat down at the desk, picked up the quill, and dipped it into the ink. But before she placed the pen to the parchment, she put it back down. What she had to say could not be put in a letter. And even if she managed to express her feelings in writing, what kind of a reply would she get from her fiancé? Three or four lines that said nothing meaningful?

With a sigh, Rebecca abandoned the attempt to write a letter and went upstairs to bed.

✝

"No letter?" Incredulous, Antony stared at the courier, who had just arrived from Ephesus.

"No, sir," the young man with the illustrious name of Cato replied. "No letter."

"But Rebecca always writes a letter."

"Not this time, sir." Cato shifted nervously from foot to foot.

"Did you speak with her this morning?"

"Yes, and when I asked her about it, she said, 'Just tell him there is no letter this week.'"

Antony was speechless.

"I offered to wait while she wrote something," Cato added, "like I always do for you, I said."

"And what did she say to that?"

Cato looked uneasy, but he did not avoid the question. "It seemed to make her mad. She sent me on my way."

Antony dismissed Cato, so the courier could enjoy a meal and get some rest before making the round trip the next morning.

Alone in his bedroom, Antony pondered the significance of Rebecca's refusal to write. Was she simply too busy? Had she been sick? he wondered. Cato had not said anything about that, and from what he *had* said, Antony could only conclude that Rebecca was very, very angry with him.

But not to write at all . . . that was uncalled for. Antony knew he should have been better at communicating with his fiancée, but the work he was doing was vitally important—it was God's work—and it consumed his waking hours, and sometimes invaded his sleep.

The more Antony thought about it, the more his vague sense of guilt turned to righteous indignation. When he finally sat down at the desk, he wrote well into the night.

✝

Rebecca unrolled the parchment for the hundredth time since Cato had delivered it a few hours earlier. She knew she should just go to bed and worry about answering Antony's letter in the morning. But she was too stirred up to sleep, so she sat at her father's desk in the library and poured out her frustration in a letter.

In her agitation, she dripped ink on the parchment. It didn't matter. She could copy the letter over at her leisure; Cato wouldn't deliver it until next week.

Much as she imagined Antony would approach a legal case, Rebecca set out to rebut each point in his lengthy letter. "I thought you would be more understanding," he had written, "and a little more patient."

She replied . . .

I *have* been understanding. I know the work you're doing is important, very important, but so am I. Our future is important; at least it is to me.

And I *have* been patient—for seven long months. When you first went to Smyrna, you promised you would come home as often as possible. You have been home once, Antony. One short visit. You originally said that by the time our house was built, your work there would be done, and then we would be married. Now the house is ready, sitting here empty, and you have not even seen it. You left the entire construction project up to my brother. Peter did not mind doing it, but he shouldn't have had to; it was your responsibility.

Rebecca consulted Antony's letter again. For the first time in several months, he had written in detail about the kinds of cases he was working on. As angry as she was, she couldn't help feeling proud of him. The Christians in Smyrna had been hit from every angle, and the legal assistance Antony provided was, without a doubt, crucial.

Still, he could not stay there forever. Some other lawyer would have to take over the work, that's all there was to it. Antony's place was here, with her, with his family.

What was it with the men in her life? Rebecca wondered. Why couldn't they seem to stay around? Galen had run away from her emotionally. Jacob had gone chasing after Damian and had not been heard from since. And now Antony had abandoned her in favor of his own personal ministry. She was sick of it.

Rebecca continued writing . . .

> I know you have a trial coming up, and that you can't leave until it's finished. But as soon as the trial is over, I want you home. I'm tired of our future being suspended indefinitely. I want to get married. I want to move into our house. I want to have a life.

Over the next few days she read her letter over several times. Rebecca knew it sounded selfish and at times whining, but she didn't change a word of it. She didn't even copy it over; she sent the letter as it was, ink stains and all.

†

Antony stared at Rebecca's letter in disbelief. An ultimatum. She'd written him an ultimatum! There was no "or else" spelled out, but it was certainly implied.

He had even gotten a letter from his mother, who had let him know, in her peculiarly roundabout way, just how upset his fiancée was—as if he couldn't figure that out from Rebecca's letter. Helena had written a rambling non sequitur, jumping from topic to topic, yet she managed to clearly establish her point: Rebecca was terribly unhappy with his prolonged absence, and so was his mother.

Putting the two letters aside, Antony stretched out on the bed and stared at the ceiling. What was he going to do? He was not worried about the upcoming trial; he was well prepared. What had him worried was the one thing he had not told Rebecca about: Damian. Even if the trial were over tomorrow, Antony couldn't just pick up and leave. Not with Damian out there waging a campaign of hate and destruction.

Antony had wanted to catch Damian and turn him over to the authorities before saying anything to Rebecca or her family. And Antony had not gone to the authorities because he knew they wouldn't do anything unless he could present solid proof that Damian was the arsonist.

As he did every night, Antony lay in bed and prayed that God would deliver Damian into his hand. He also prayed for the safety of his fellow believers in Smyrna and in Ephesus, and particularly for his loved ones. He prayed that he could somehow make things right with Rebecca. Antony would have wearied God all night with his petitions, but fatigue overcame him. Soon he was asleep.

Early the next morning Linus roused him from bed. "You have a visitor," the young disciple told Antony. "His name is Tarquinius and he says it's very urgent."

Antony groaned and sat up. It must be important if Tarquinius had arrived at this hour. "Show him to my room," Antony said.

He got out of bed, then quickly washed his face and ran his fingers through his hair. He seldom got a full night's sleep, and as usual his stomach felt uneasy. But the thought of food did not appeal to him this early in the morning.

Tarquinius was red faced and slightly out of breath when he entered the bedroom. He did not apologize for waking Antony. "I found out something important," he said, "and I had to come tell you before you got off somewhere today."

Antony pulled out a chair for Tarquinius, then unshuttered the window and perched on the sill. The sun was just coming up, but he was too tired to enjoy the beautiful sight.

"I've been keeping an eye on Tullia," Tarquinius said, "just like we talked about, and checking up on Damian too. I've been to her house several times, and she seemed grateful for the visits. She's lonely, you know, just her and the baby. She thinks he's a special child, by the way. Sebastian, she named him. Says he's a . . . a 'spiritual being' and has some great destiny. Started naming off a list of her goddesses . . ."

Tarquinius grinned and shook his head. "I never know what Tullia is talking about half the time. I just let her ramble, hoping she'll say something we need to know about Damian. Anyway, she finally did. She said she had made him leave because he was drinking too much and she was scared to let him stay around the baby. She is terribly afraid something is going to happen to her special child."

"So where is Damian?" Antony hoped Tarquinius would get to the point soon.

"Tullia said she didn't know where he'd been staying, and she didn't care. But I'd seen tracks leaving her place. There's an abandoned mill down the road—"

"I know where it is," Antony interrupted.

Tarquinius looked surprised, but he continued his narrative. "So when I left Tullia's late yesterday afternoon, I decided to snoop around the old mill. Before I even got there, though, I saw Damian coming from that direction. I followed him, and he went to Tullia's. That surprised me, because she said she had kicked him out.

"Evidently it surprised Tullia too, because I heard them yelling when I got close to the house. I crouched under the window and listened."

Wide awake now, Antony leaned forward. "What did they argue about?"

"Damian begged her to let him come back and promised to

behave himself. She didn't believe him. Then he said he loved her and wanted to prove it to her. I nearly guffawed when I heard that. He wanted a decent roof over his head, that's what he wanted—and he would've said just about anything to get it.

"They went round and round for a while, until Tullia finally said he could prove his love for her and for his son by getting rid of the enemies that would hinder Sebastian from reaching his destiny. I figured out that the enemies she was talking about were you Christians.

"'You want me to kill them or just destroy their property?' Damian asked her.

"She told him the fires weren't working. 'I want you to kill them,' she said, 'but just one. Get rid of their leader, Polycarp, and the rest of them will be powerless.'"

Tarquinius paused while Antony absorbed the news. Tullia had been behind the persecution, as they had suspected all along, and Damian was definitely the arsonist. Now they were plotting murder, and the bishop was their target.

Antony stood and grabbed Tarquinius by the arm. "We have to stop them. Will you go to the authorities with me?"

The innkeeper straightened, a sober look on his square face, then he nodded. "I said I'd do whatever it takes to catch Damian. I won't back down now."

33

WALKING THROUGH THE HILLS WITH MARCELLUS, Rebecca paid scant attention to the fact that it was a beautiful, sunny day or that the fall foliage was spectacular. She was too preoccupied with thoughts of Antony to enjoy the time outdoors. It would be almost a week before she had Antony's reply to her letter, and Rebecca didn't think she could wait that long.

Marcellus, always sensitive to her moods, let her walk a while in silence, then said, "You have that little line around your mouth that means something is on your mind today. Do you want to talk about it?"

They reached the spot along the path where the city of Ephesus came into view below them and Rebecca stopped. "You know me too well," she said. "Something *is* troubling me."

She told him about her letter to Antony. "I was just wishing I could go to Smyrna to see him, since he doesn't seem inclined to come home to see me. I've made the trip before . . . but it's just not practical."

"It would be very taxing with a fourteen-month-old."

"Yes, and I couldn't leave Victor here; I'd be away too long." She started up the path again. "At times like these, I really wish Jacob were here. I'd ask *him* to go to Smyrna and find out what's going on with Antony. That would be a good job for a brother. I can't ask Peter, though; a trip like that would be more than he could manage.

"And I'm not asking you to go," she added. "I know you'll offer, but you can't leave John for something as trivial as finding out why my fiancé can't find the time to write."

Marcellus smiled. "You know me well too. I was going to say that I could try to find someone to stay with John."

"You wouldn't be able to find anyone who could take care of him the way you do."

Why couldn't Antony be more like Marcellus? Rebecca wondered as they neared the new house. There was a man who understood commitment. Even though the doctor had important things he wanted to do, taking care of John was his number-one priority. The venerable apostle was declining, and he had missed a Sunday service recently— something Rebecca could never remember happening before.

"It's such a nice location for a house," Marcellus said when they arrived. "You'll love living here."

"If I ever get to," Rebecca complained.

"You will. Just be patient."

"That's what Antony said." It didn't rankle her quite so much, however, when it came from Marcellus.

They spent a pleasant half-hour walking through the new house, making plans for what would go where. They had visited the construction site almost daily, and Rebecca had loved watching the spacious stone house go up.

It was really three separate buildings joined by a common area, a large two-story atrium with a louvered skylight that could be opened to let in the sunshine or closed to keep out the rain. The atrium was so lofty and airy, it gave the impression of being a much larger space than it actually was.

The rooms off the atrium to the left, the side that overlooked the city, would be for Antony and Rebecca. There was one large bedroom downstairs, plus a study for Antony, with smaller bedrooms upstairs for Victor and their future children. The kitchen and dining room were in the building at the back of the atrium, directly across from the courtyard entrance. And to the right of atrium was a small one-story dwelling for Helena and Priscilla. A stairway led from the atrium up to what would have been the second story of this section. For now, it would be a long balcony overlooking the hills, but the area could be walled off and converted to rooms later on, if needed.

Peter had hired a double crew of masons in order to get the project completed by the end of summer. The tile workers had spent another six weeks laying the flagstone floors. There were no intricate mosaics or expensive patterned marble, so the installation had gone quickly. The trimmers were still there, finishing a few details on the inside, but the supervisor came up to Rebecca and told her she could move in whenever she was ready.

She was more than ready. The home was by no means fancy, but it suited her tastes, and Rebecca couldn't wait to make it truly hers.

When they returned to the villa, Marcellus went off to the library and Rebecca went to find Agatha and the children. Agatha visited frequently, and she often helped out with the relief work, which Helena was once again taking an active part in, freeing Rebecca to spend some time at the new house. Since her healing, Helena especially loved to visit the sick and pray for them. Rebecca and Agatha took care of distributing food and clothing.

Agatha had looked downcast when she'd arrived that morning, and as Rebecca went upstairs now, she thought about what Quintus had once said, that Agatha had had a lot of pain in her life. She and Quintus seemed very happy together, but every now and then Rebecca noticed that Agatha would slip back into—not sadness, exactly, but a kind of mild melancholy. And Rebecca still didn't know where they went or what they did in the predawn hours, but several times she'd seen Quintus and Agatha walking home across the hills just after sunup. As she'd promised, Rebecca had never said anything. But now she resolved to ask Quintus about it. Perhaps those early-morning sojourns had something to do with Agatha's melancholy moods.

Rebecca grinned at the sight of Victor and Aurora toddling all over her bedroom, chasing and reaching for each other, then falling down on their little bottoms, jabbering happily the whole time. She was not as happy to see Agatha with a dust cloth in her hand.

"How many times do I have to remind you that you are no longer a servant?" Rebecca asked gently.

"I was just sprucing up the room a bit," Agatha said, blushing at being caught working again.

"You're a friend, not an employee, and I don't want you ever to feel obligated to work when you're here."

"I don't," Agatha said quickly, "I don't. It's just that your family has been very good to me, and I love to do things for you. Besides, I never was one for sitting around. I always have to be up doing something. You know that."

Rebecca smiled. "And you couldn't help noticing that the new housemaid is not up to your standards."

"Well, it's a huge house. I remember how I never could seem to stay on top of it at first, even though I was only responsible for the upstairs rooms."

Slightly tired after the long walk, Rebecca sat down on the long chaise in front of the window and invited Agatha to join her. The two women talked for a few minutes while their babies laughed and squealed.

"They're so precious," Rebecca said as she watched the children play. "And growing so fast. It makes me want to have another baby soon."

Agatha observed her with a miserable expression, but quickly turned away when Rebecca looked up.

"Why are you so downhearted sometimes?" Rebecca leaned forward and appealed to her friend. "I shouldn't pry, I suppose, but I can't help noticing and wondering what's wrong."

"It's . . . it's nothing," Agatha said, trying to smile but failing.

"You mean it's none of my concern?"

"No, I didn't mean that. I just . . ." Agatha closed her eyes momentarily and bit her lip, then looked down at her lap.

Rebecca waited, silently praying that the other woman would speak again. *When the time is right, she'll tell you,* Quintus had said, but Agatha didn't respond.

Finally, acting on an internal prompting, Rebecca asked, "Are you wanting to have another baby too?"

Agatha looked up, lines of grief etched in her face. "It's been almost two years," she said softly. "Two years."

Rebecca thought for a moment. "Since you had Aurora?" she asked. Agatha's little girl would be two in a couple of months, Rebecca calculated.

"I really wanted another baby before Aurora was weaned. I've searched and prayed so hard," Agatha said. "Almost two years . . ."

Rebecca was puzzled. Why was it so important for Agatha to have another child before Aurora was weaned? And why had she been praying for two years? She and Quintus had only been married seven months.

"You can still have a baby," Rebecca said. "It will happen—just give it time."

Agatha continued as if she hadn't heard Rebecca. "Aurora still nurses, but it won't be much longer before she's fully weaned. And then what will I do if there's not another baby?" The distress was evident in her voice, and she was on the verge of tears.

Rebecca reached out a hand to offer comfort. Before she could think of something to say, the new housemaid came scurrying into the room. The girl was so flighty, it drove Rebecca to distraction, and her timing was completely inappropriate; she was always interrupting conversations. Rebecca had spoken to the steward about it. Evidently he had said something to the housemaid because she suddenly slowed down and with a slight bow said, "Begging your pardon, ma'am, but we have visitors."

"Who is it?" Rebecca asked. She wasn't expecting anyone, and whoever it was couldn't have come at a worse time—just when Agatha was about to open up and talk about what was troubling her.

"Foreigners," the girl said, "wearing strange-looking clothes. One of them says he's your brother."

"My brother?"

Rebecca jumped to her feet and Agatha shooed her out with a wave of her hand. "I'll bring the babies," she said. She swooped Victor up, grabbed Aurora by the hand, and followed Rebecca, who was already flying down the stairs.

Rebecca would hardly have recognized Jacob if she hadn't heard that her brother had arrived. He was indeed wearing foreign clothes—some kind of long coat with trousers, and a funny-looking hat. An older man with streaks of silver in his dark hair wore the same kind of outfit as Jacob, and with them was a very tall, very exotic-looking woman with short black hair and beautiful olive skin.

"Jacob!" Rebecca ran to her brother and embraced him. When he squeezed her tightly, she couldn't help crying. For the second time, her brother had returned when she had all but given him up for dead.

"I didn't know if you would be happy to see me," he finally said.

"Of course, I'm happy!" she cried into his shoulder. "How could I not be?" She drew back for a good look at Jacob. "We've been so worried about you. Almost a year, and we didn't even know where you were." Rebecca reached up and wiped her eyes. "I wasn't even sure you were alive."

"I'm sorry," he said. "I had no way to get word to you."

"And just look at you!" Rebecca almost laughed at the unusual garb her brother wore. "Where have you been?"

Agatha arrived in the atrium with the two children, and Marcellus came in from the library, holding a partially unrolled scroll.

"Someone should go to the harbor and get Peter and Quintus," Rebecca said. She turned to ask Marcellus but he was transfixed by the arrival of the foreign visitors as well, and Jacob was starting to answer her question.

"I've been in Cappadocia," Jacob said. He took the arm of the tall woman and brought her forward, presenting her to Rebecca. "This is my wife, Livia."

"Your wife . . ." Rebecca could scarcely believe it. Jacob had not only come home, but he'd brought a wife with him. Rebecca started to extend her hand to the woman, then opened her arms and hugged Livia instead. "Welcome, sister," she said.

Livia seemed overcome by the affectionate greeting and Rebecca thought for a moment that she had stepped outside the bounds of propriety. Perhaps where Livia came from such behavior was too demonstrative. But Rebecca was so overjoyed at Jacob's return that she couldn't help herself.

"This is Gregory," Jacob said, "Livia's uncle."

Rebecca greeted the older man, then Jacob waved Marcellus over to introduce him, but the retired soldier stood motionless. All the color had drained from his face.

After a long, awkward pause, Gregory stepped forward and held out his hand. "Hello, Marcellus. It's good to see you after all these years."

†

The scroll fell from Marcellus's hand, the wooden spindles clattering on the tile floor as the parchment rolled out to its full length. Marcellus made no move to retrieve it; all he could do was stare at his daughter.

He had always wondered whether he would recognize Livia if he ever saw her again. He needn't have worried. Except for her height, Livia was the image of her mother. Looking at his daughter now was like being transported back in time. Twenty-five years ago Claudia had had the same high cheekbones, the same glossy-black hair, the same large, luminous eyes—eyes so expressive and deep that looking into them was like falling down a mine shaft. When Marcellus had met Claudia, he'd tumbled down that shaft and couldn't climb out.

So in spite of the incompatibility of family life and an army career, Marcellus had married her, and they had produced a wonderful daughter. He had feared that daughter was lost to him forever, but here she was.

Marcellus turned his gaze away from Livia long enough to shake hands with his former brother-in-law. Gregory clasped his arm firmly for a moment, then the two men embraced.

"I don't understand," Livia said. "You two know each other? How is that possible?"

Flustered by the question, Gregory stammered, "Your . . . Marcellus was . . ." He gave his niece a confused look. "I guess you could call him a student of mine. I taught him all about herbs."

"I've never forgotten what you taught me," Marcellus said. "The knowledge was very helpful over the years—I even became a doctor."

He turned to Livia. "You don't remember me, I'm sure. I believe you had just turned six the last time I saw you."

Marcellus couldn't help being disappointed that Livia did not recognize him, even though he'd known that would be the case. After all, he had been away on a military campaign when she had been born, and had probably spent more time apart from his young daughter than with her.

His eyes threatening to fill and his voice full of emotion, Marcellus said, "John told me you would come, but somehow I couldn't quite believe it."

Perplexed, Livia turned to her husband. "John?"

"The Apostle," Jacob said. "I've told you all about him."

"I know who John is. But how did he know who I am? Or that we were coming?"

"I've been praying for you . . ." Marcellus began to explain. Then he noticed Gregory shaking his head, pleading silently for Marcellus to keep quiet. What was the problem? Marcellus wondered. Of course, Livia was bound to be shocked at being reunited with a father she didn't recognize after all these years. He understood that, and he didn't want to upset Livia. But why should it upset Gregory if Marcellus let Livia know who he was?

"It's a long story," Marcellus finished lamely.

"And we'll hear it later," Rebecca said, putting a reassuring hand on Marcellus's arm. She told Livia, "I'm sure you're probably tired after such a long journey."

Rebecca stepped toward Jacob and linked arms with her brother. "How long have you been traveling?"

"Almost six weeks," he answered. "We took our time."

Marcellus watched helplessly as Rebecca took the awkward situation in hand. She turned to him and asked, "Would you mind going to the harbor to get Peter and Quintus? I'll show our guests upstairs so they can rest a bit. Then we'll have a big family dinner and catch up on all the news."

As Rebecca led the travelers upstairs, with Agatha and the babies in tow, Marcellus bent down and picked up the scroll. He carefully rolled the parchment back onto the spindles, wishing he could roll back time, wishing he had never been separated from his only child.

Thank You for bringing her home, he prayed silently. *Please help me explain why I wasn't there when she was growing up. And please, please let her understand.*

✝

Livia was astonished at the enormity of the place—both the overall size of the villa and its individual rooms. Marcellus was now occupying the bedroom that had been Jacob's, Rebecca told them, so she had put Livia and Jacob in the master bedroom. Never had Livia seen a room of any kind, let alone a bedroom, so large. Most of the cave house in Cappadocia would fit inside this one room.

And the furnishings went beyond anything she could have imagined. Plush, patterned carpets covered the marble floor. There were few pieces of furniture, but they were all exquisite. Livia ran her slender fingers over the carved headboard of the massive teak bed, feeling completely overwhelmed.

Jacob sprawled across the bed and reached a hand toward her. "Let's take a nap," he said.

"I'm too excited to sleep," Livia said. "Too excited, and too worried."

"What are you worried about now? You saw how Rebecca greeted you. She even called you 'sister.'"

"She was very sweet. But . . ." Livia sat down on the bed next to Jacob, looking around her at the opulent room. "I don't know what to say to your family. And I don't have the proper clothes; all my tunics are so plain and drab."

"But *you're* not plain and drab." Jacob pulled her down beside him, settling her in the crook of his arm. "So don't give it another thought. I'll have some new clothes made for you. In the meantime, you can always borrow a tunic from Rebecca."

Livia couldn't quite picture herself asking her new sister-in-law to borrow clothes. Not yet, anyway. Perhaps Livia would let Jacob buy her a new wardrobe; she didn't want to embarrass her husband by looking like a poor country girl.

She asked Jacob about something else that had puzzled her. "How do you suppose John knew we were coming?"

"I have no idea," Jacob said with a yawn. "We'll go see him tomorrow and ask him."

What would that be like, she wondered, *meeting someone who had actually known Jesus?* She started to ask Jacob about it, but he had already closed his eyes. Livia did not think she could fall asleep, yet she dozed off almost immediately.

When she awoke two hours later, she felt refreshed. She used water from the hammered bronze basin on the washstand to clean up, then decided to dress in the nicest thing she owned—the embroidered tunic of her mother's, which Livia had worn for her wedding. She slipped it over the silk trousers and turned to Jacob for his approval.

"Do you think it's too different, too . . . foreign?"

"Relax," he told her. "They will think you're the most beautiful foreigner they've ever seen. I certainly do."

When they joined the family in the dining room, Livia met Peter.

He was as gracious and friendly as Rebecca had been earlier. Quintus and Agatha were there, and of course, Marcellus. The retired army doctor was rather peculiar, Livia thought. She didn't know what to make of him. When she first walked into the room, he turned pale again. Then he cleared his throat and told her, "You look lovely tonight, Livia."

Rebecca directed them to their places around the table. She and Peter occupied the center *triclinium;* Quintus, Agatha, and Marcellus took the left-hand couch; and Jacob, Livia, and Gregory reclined to Rebecca's right. Livia had never dined in the Roman way before, and at first it was very strange to be lounging on a wide, sloping sofa rather than sitting cross-legged on a cushion on the floor. But the conversation was lively, and everyone made her feel at ease.

She had once joked with Jacob that at his return his family would kill the fatted calf. She'd been wrong about that, but the meal was a feast nonetheless. There was a wonderful dish of roast mutton and two kinds of fish. Livia had never tasted fresh seafood, and she found it very tender and tasty. Gregory was enthralled with the seasonings and sauces on the various meat and vegetable dishes, and Livia knew he was itching to explore the kitchen.

Jacob entertained them by telling how he had chased Damian all the way to Cappadocia, how he'd come to live with Gregory and Livia, and how he'd made his living as a schoolmaster. He also bragged on Livia's skills as an artisan, which pleased but also embarrassed her. Marcellus was fascinated by the subject of Livia's work, while Rebecca was visibly relieved to hear Jacob say he had relinquished his pursuit of Damian.

"I have a feeling *you* had something to do with that," Rebecca said, nodding toward Livia.

"Jacob knew how I felt about it," Livia said. "Not that he paid much attention to what I said. At least not for a long time."

Rebecca laughed. "That's my hard-headed brother."

"The important thing," Jacob said, "is that I finally did listen."

Quintus and Agatha left right after dinner, but the others lingered in the dining room. Rebecca dismissed the servants as soon as they had served the *mulsum*. Livia found the warm, honeyed wine with spices too sweet for her tastes.

Jacob was telling about the horses Pomponius raised when a memory that had been stirring in Livia's mind finally broke loose and bubbled to the surface.

"I do remember you," she told Marcellus. "You gave me a little wooden horse on wheels. It was my favorite toy for a long time."

Marcellus immediately brightened. "You loved to go riding with me, but your mother never approved. That's why I bought the toy horse for you, and brought it all the way from Carthage. You named it Hippolyte after—"

"The queen of the Amazons," they said in unison.

"I used to tell you that you would grow up to be tall and strong, like the mythical women of Cappadocia."

"I don't know about strong," Livia said, "but you certainly got the tall part right." She laughed, but the sound quickly died as another memory rose, and she frowned.

"Is something wrong?" Marcellus asked.

"No . . . It's just that Mother must not have liked you for some reason. I remember how she would avoid saying your name, and she made me refer to you as 'Gregory's friend.'" The memory wasn't quite clear, and it troubled Livia, but when she saw the stricken look on Marcellus's face, she rushed to say, "I'm sorry. I shouldn't have said that. I have a bad habit of thinking out loud."

Gregory quickly changed the subject, but Livia did not follow the conversation for a minute. She couldn't help thinking how strange it was that she had been reluctant to leave Cappadocia because it would be like leaving the memory of her mother and father behind. Now here she was, halfway across the Empire, having a conversation with someone who had known her parents. She wondered why her mother had not liked Marcellus and whether her father had felt the same way.

"Did you know my father?" she asked Marcellus.

He started to answer, then looked at Gregory's stony expression and hesitated before saying, "I only met him once. He seemed like a nice man." Marcellus paused and blinked a few times. "I moved away right after that."

"Papa was a wonderful man," Livia said. "You would have liked him."

"He was a good father to you?" Marcellus asked softly.

"Oh, yes. The best. He died eight years ago, and I still miss him."

Jacob told the others about the plague that had killed Livia's parents and Gregory's wife and children. It did not usually bother Gregory to talk about his family, but Livia noticed that her uncle was unusually quiet now. Come to think of it, he had been acting odd ever since they'd arrived. Perhaps he wasn't feeling well.

Marcellus suddenly excused himself, and shortly after that Peter declared he was ready to retire. When Rebecca started to leave as well, Gregory implored, "Please stay a moment. My niece needs a friend. A sister." He turned to Livia, his demeanor uncertain and perhaps apprehensive. "Especially now . . ."

He stopped speaking while a cough wracked his body. Then he took a deep breath and said, "I have something important to tell Livia. Something I should have said a long time ago."

Rebecca hesitated. "Are you sure you want me to stay?"

"Yes," Gregory said.

"Livia? Jacob?" Rebecca waited until they both nodded, then she took her place on the sofa again.

No one spoke for a moment, and Livia suddenly felt numb. She had a premonition that her uncle was about to deliver bad news, the kind of news that would change her life.

"It's time I told you about your father," Gregory finally said. "I hope you won't hate me for this . . ."

Livia closed her eyes, steeling her mind against the assault. She did not want to hear a negative word against her father.

"I made a promise to your mother," Gregory said, "a promise I came to regret. She convinced me it was for the best, and I thought so at the time. But later . . ." He cleared his throat and took another sip of *mulsum.* "After Claudia died, I no longer felt bound by the promise, but I thought it would be cruel to tell you about your father then. It would have served no purpose."

"Just say it, Gregory." Livia felt anger rising. The sooner he said whatever he had to say, the sooner she could dismiss it.

Gregory took another deep breath. "The man you called Papa was not your father. He adored you, and you adored him—"

"What are you talking about—not my father?"

"Not by birth, but he raised you as his own from the time you were five." Gregory reached for her hand, but she yanked it back. He continued, "That's when your mother married him, after she divorced your father . . . the man she made you call 'Gregory's friend.'"

Rebecca's jaw dropped and Jacob spilled his wine. Realization swept over Livia then, and she could barely breathe. "Marcellus? You're saying that Marcellus is my *father?*"

"Yes, and I should've told you a long time ago. I'm sorry, sorrier than I can say. But I never thought we would see Marcellus again."

"I don't believe you." Livia nudged Jacob, wanting him to move aside so she could get up from the *triclinium;* she desperately wanted to escape. But her thickheaded hulk of a husband did not get the hint, and she remained trapped on the wide sofa between him and her uncle.

"It's true," Gregory said. "Why do you think Marcellus looked like he had seen a ghost the moment he laid eyes on you? He had to imagine he was looking at his former wife; you resemble Claudia a great deal."

"You're lying," Livia cried, near tears. She wanted it to be a lie.

"Why would I lie to you now, child?"

"Evidently you've been lying to me my whole life!" In an ungraceful move, Livia wiggled off the end of the sofa and fled the room.

34

"YOU CAN'T HIDE IN THE BEDROOM avoiding your uncle the rest of your life," Jacob told his wife when he returned from breakfast. Livia had not come downstairs because she was still angry with Gregory for what he'd said the previous evening. Jacob understood that she'd received quite a shock and had a right to be upset. But he thought she was behaving childishly.

Livia stared out the window, searching the horizon. The sky was overcast, and the harbor was barely visible." I don't want to talk to him right now," she said. "I may not talk to him for a long time."

"He was only doing what he thought was right. You know Gregory would never hurt you intentionally."

"He should have told me the truth," she insisted.

"And what good would that have done? You were too young to understand such a complex situation." Gregory and Marcellus had talked about it that morning, and Jacob now understood that both men had made difficult choices when it came to Livia.

"Then he should have told me later, when I was old enough to understand."

Jacob was relieved that her voice was steadier now. She finally turned away from the window and came to stand beside him. Just when he thought Livia had calmed down, however, she quit blaming her uncle and lit into Jacob.

"Why didn't *you* tell me Marcellus was my father?"

"What? . . . I didn't know anything about it."

"You knew he had a daughter he hadn't seen since she was a little girl—"

"Yes, but—"

"And you knew he was stationed in Caesarea years ago."

"He's been stationed all over the Empire. If Marcellus ever told me about being posted to Caesarea, I forgot it. And I didn't know his daughter's name, so how was I supposed to know you were the one he was looking for?"

"You should have figured it out!" she yelled.

"Livia, be reasonable," Jacob snapped, then he abruptly stopped and made an effort to clamp a lid on his anger. She wasn't really mad at him; she just needed to lash out at someone because she was hurting.

"Come here," he said gently. When she did not move, Jacob went to Livia and put his arms around her. At first she kept her body stiff, then she gradually relaxd. In a moment he felt her arms come up around his waist, and he squeezed her tightly.

"I'm sorry," she said when Jacob released her. "I know I'm overreacting. I just don't know what to make of all this. You think your life is one thing, then you find out it's another."

Jacob knew exactly how hard it could be to adapt to sudden change, and he'd done some overreacting of his own, so he had a considerable amount of empathy for his wife. He silently wished he had some particular wisdom to impart that would help her make the adjustment. Almost as soon as he thought that, inspiration came to him, and he spoke it out loud.

"One time, right after we were married," Jacob said, "you told me that you and Gregory had always known that God had sent me to Caesarea for a purpose."

Livia nodded, and he continued. "At first you thought the purpose was simply to convince me to give up my obsession with Damian. Then you dared to believe that it was because you and I were meant to be together. Well, what if you and I were meant to be together, in part, so you could be reunited with Marcellus?

"Think about it. John, my family, Marcellus, the church here,

Polycarp and the church in Smyrna—they were all praying for my safety. Marcellus and John, and even Rebecca, were praying for you to be found. Gregory was concerned about your future and praying up a husband for you. And what happens? Damian leads me to the one spot in the world where God could answer all those prayers at one time. There's just no way that can be a coincidence."

Livia didn't respond, but Jacob could tell that she was weighing what he'd said.

"You should get to know Marcellus. He's a good man, Livia. Compassionate in the midst of brutality—that's how we came to know him. If it weren't for Marcellus, Rebecca and John would not have survived Devil's Island. You should be proud to have him for your father."

"I *had* a father," she protested, but her earlier vehemence was gone.

"And now you have another one. You've been blessed with two good fathers. That's something you should be grateful for."

Livia walked back to the window and stared out for a moment. "I'll give him a chance," she finally said. Then she asked, "Will you take me to the harbor today? I want to see the ocean."

"Tomorrow, I promise. I need to go see John this afternoon." Jacob both anticipated and dreaded the visit with his former mentor. "I have some fences to mend."

✝

Though Marcellus had tried to warn him, Jacob was not prepared to see John looking so frail. Even from a distance Jacob could see the changes. John had been old all of Jacob's life, but the Apostle had always been robust; now he looked his age.

John was sitting outside his house, on the old leather camp stool he had brought home from Patmos. His eyes were closed, and when Jacob approached, he thought the old man was napping. But without opening his eyes, John said, "It's about time you showed up, Jacob, my boy."

"How did you know it was me?"

"I recognized your step. Besides, I was expecting you. Marcellus came to see me early this morning, and he told me you were back. And if I'd guessed wrong, and it hadn't been you walking up the path to my house—well, who could blame a very old man for being wrong?"

"No one." Jacob couldn't help laughing. "It's good to see you, John."

"Come closer so I can get a good look at you," John said in return.

Jacob sat on the ground in front of John, who put a bony hand to Jacob's face. "There were times," the Apostle said, "I doubted I would ever live long enough to see you again."

"I'm awfully glad you did."

"I am too, son. I am too."

There was no trace of condemnation in John's voice, and Jacob was relieved and grateful.

"Help me up." John extended a hand, and Jacob stood to offer assistance. He folded the camp stool and carried it under one arm; John held on to Jacob's other arm as they went inside. The proud old man would never have done that a year ago, Jacob thought. He noticed that John was so hunched over that he appeared to have shrunk a few inches.

"Are you by yourself?" Jacob asked, worried that John shouldn't be left to fend for himself.

"Goodness, no. Marcellus has made sure there's always someone here—usually more than one person at a time. The fussbudget even made a duty roster and posted it." His laugh was low and raspy. "It gets so crowded in my own house, I have to go outside for some privacy."

John's house was a very modest, four-room structure that was as old as the man himself. But it was cozy and neat, and Jacob had spent many pleasant hours there. Sure enough, two ladies who were members of the congregation were inside, cleaning and cooking.

It was not that cold outside, but there was a small fire burning in the fireplace. When they had sat down on the short benches in front of the hearth, John asked, "So what did you learn on this grand adventure of yours?"

"I learned that vengeance belongs to the Lord, just as you tried to tell me. And that He is merciful to fools."

John grinned. "I had to learn that lesson the hard way too, I'm afraid."

Jacob paused, searching for the right words. "I know I disappointed you, John, and I'm sorry for that. I disappointed myself."

"I'll admit that I had high hopes for you, and that I was very disappointed when you went away without so much as a farewell. But I came to realize that my hopes for you might not equate with God's plan."

"I let so many others down too," Jacob said sadly. "I never went to Rome to work for the release of prisoners. Marcellus told me the Senate finally got around to voiding their sentences and most of them are home from Devil's Island now. They might have been home sooner, though, if I hadn't gone chasing after Damian instead of following through with my original plan."

John said nothing at Jacob's admission of failure, so he began to tell the story of his sojourn. "If I'd had any doubts that you were praying for me, they were dispelled the night I arrived in Cappadocia. I wound up in the home of a Christian who didn't even know me, but he told me the same things you'd already said."

Jacob recounted Gregory's prophecy, and John laughed until he had to wipe tears from his rheumy eyes. "You traveled hundreds of miles," he said, "just to hear someone else preach my sermon."

"That's the gist of it." Jacob relished John's laughter and the opportunity to share another lighthearted moment with his old friend and teacher. And he was grateful to God that their fellowship could be restored so quickly.

For over an hour, Jacob talked about everything that had happened since he'd last seen John.

"You did the right thing," John assured Jacob, when he told how he had let Damian ride off without following him. "The Lord will avenge the blood of His servants, in due time."

"Every now and then," Jacob said, "I wonder where Damian is. But I'm able to put it out of my mind. I know the Lord will bring him to justice, either in this life or the next—and I'm comfortable leaving it in His hands."

Antony and Tarquinius parted ways in the square outside the imposing three-story structure that housed the administrative offices for the city of Smyrna. The courthouse, library, and other public buildings were located around three sides of the square; a bath and gymnasium occupied the fourth side.

"I'll talk to the magistrate first," Antony said, "then I'll come get you if he wants to hear the story directly from you."

It would be a case of Tarquinius's word against Tullia's and Damian's, and Antony was not hopeful that the magistrate would even consider the scanty evidence against the conspirators. Still, he had to try.

He climbed the marble steps and pushed open the heavy door. The magistrate's office was on the ground floor, at the end of the long central corridor. Antony was deep in thought as he proceeded down the corridor. It was late afternoon and most of the day's business had been completed, so few people were around at this hour. He was surprised, therefore, when someone slipped out of the shadows and stepped in front of him, blocking his way.

A sudden chill tingled down Antony's spine. He had never laid eyes on Damian before, but Antony instinctively identified the man with the menacing stance and the glower on his face. Damian looked exactly as Jacob had once described him: short, scrappy, and sleazy.

Damian's florid features bore the evidence of advanced dissipation, but he appeared sober and his voice was steady as he said, "I thought you would have given up and gone back to Ephesus by now. Lawyering is not a very profitable profession, especially not with the kind of clients you've been meeting with at Polycarp's house."

Antony drew in a sharp breath. Damian knew who Antony was, where he was staying, and what he was doing in Smyrna. Had Damian even known the purpose of today's visit to the magistrate?

"I'm not in this for the money," Antony said slowly, attempting to hide his surprise both at Damian's sudden appearance and at his knowledge of Antony's whereabouts and business. "And I'm not leaving—not as long as Polycarp and his friends need my help."

"Perhaps Polycarp won't be around much longer . . . and perhaps you won't either, if you insist on staying. Haven't you noticed how bad things—really bad things—keep happening to the people around Polycarp?"

The implied threat was unmistakable, and while Antony couldn't completely suppress a shiver, he kept his face impassive. "What do you have against Polycarp? He's never done anything to harm you."

Damian spat out his answer. "He's a Christian. And Christians are vermin—the source of every evil that plagues the Empire. They deserve to be exterminated."

It was an argument Antony had heard before. Even as an unbeliever he'd known it was unfounded. Unfortunately, however, much of society held a similar opinion.

"As if that weren't enough," Damian continued, "Polycarp and his ilk are a threat to my son." Damian's face broke into an oily smile. "I'm sure your friend Tarquinius has reported to you about my newborn son. Sebastian is destined to be a great spiritual leader."

"That's odd. I wouldn't peg you for a religious person, or the father of one."

"I'm not religious, but the child's mother is. Power is my only god." Damian's eyes narrowed as he declared his allegiance. "Sebastian will worship at that altar as well. The oracles have spoken—my son will be a spiritual *and* political leader, and his influence will extend throughout Asia."

When Damian paused in his pronouncement, Antony offered no congratulations. He could foresee nothing but trouble from this child, the offspring of a witch and a notorious persecutor, and Damian confirmed Antony's fears as he continued, "And when my son rises to power, he will get rid of all the atheists—including the Christian ones."

Antony was quite familiar with the fine legal distinction. While being a Christian wasn't a crime per se, atheism was, and because Christians believed in none of the gods of Rome, they were often accused of atheism. For that reason, Antony was careful not to mention a client's religious beliefs in any legal proceeding. He never lied about it; he simply avoided the issue if at all possible so as not to subject the client to an official charge of *impietas*.

Apprehension overcame the anger that seethed inside Antony. Damian had waylaid him for the sole purpose of intimidation. But knowing what the man was capable of, Antony had to fight back a growing fear for his physical safety. The last thing he needed was to be involved in a public brawl, but he certainly intended to defend himself if necessary.

Antony swallowed dryly, trying to loosen the knot in his throat as he forced himself to speak calmly. "What do you want with me, Damian?"

"I want you to leave town—now. If you don't . . ." Damian shrugged, as if he couldn't be held responsible for the consequences.

"If I don't leave, then what?"

"Your career will simply . . . evaporate. Pffff!" Damian made a blowing sound, then laughed as if he'd made an uproarious joke. He lowered his voice and leaned closer to Antony. "Things are going to get very hot at Polycarp's house—blazing hot."

Hearing firsthand the threat of a fire at Polycarp's raised prickles on the back of Antony's neck. He had to get out of this place, had to

get some air—now. He quickly stepped to the side, but Damian
shifted with him.

Before Antony could move again, he heard a door open behind
him. He turned to see the magistrate leaving his office.

Damian suddenly clapped Antony on the shoulder. "It was good
to see you again," Damian said loudly as the magistrate approached.
"Give my regards to our mutual friends in Ephesus."

With a friendly smile and wave to Antony, Damian turned and
walked out with the magistrate, calling him by name. A moment later,
when Antony's knees unlocked, he followed them down the corridor
and out into the public square.

Tarquinius was still waiting outside, and his eyes widened in surprise as he watched Damian, who was laughing about something with
the magistrate, exit the building, then Antony. "What? . . . how . . .?"
Tarquinius stuttered.

"Damian accosted me in the corridor," Antony said. "He was
waiting for me."

Tarquinius swore and then quickly apologized. "I'm sorry. I
should have gone inside with you."

"It wouldn't have mattered. I didn't get to see the magistrate."

"I meant that I should have been there to protect you."

When he wasn't trying to gather information on Damian's
plans, Tarquinius had taken to accompanying Antony around
town. Without being asked, the innkeeper had appointed himself
as the lawyer's companion and bodyguard. Up until now, Antony
had been more concerned that Polycarp needed protecting, but
then Antony had never imagined that Damian would threaten him
personally.

"He didn't try to hit you or anything?" Tarquinius asked.

"No," Antony reassured him. "Damian just wanted to rattle me."

As they walked back to Polycarp's, Antony filled Tarquinius in
on the details of the encounter. Every time they turned onto another
street, Antony caught himself looking over his shoulder to make sure

they weren't being followed. Damian had accomplished his purpose; Antony was rattled.

That night he slept little. As he tossed and turned, he decided to meet with the church leaders the following day. Antony knew now that trying to get the authorities involved was probably a lost cause, so he would ask the deacons and elders to help persuade Polycarp to leave Smyrna for a while. Polycarp would not like the idea of going into hiding. In fact, the only place Polycarp would be even remotely interested in visiting right now might be Ephesus, in order to see John. But Antony didn't much like that idea; he would worry about Rebecca and Victor in the event Damian managed to follow Polycarp . . .

Rebecca. Antony threw off the blanket and sat up in bed. He still hadn't answered her last letter, the long ultimatum. He dropped his head onto his hands and groaned. *Lord,* he asked silently, *how did things get so complicated?*

Antony tried to pray coherently, but he was too weary and too worried. There had to be a resolution, some way to climb out of the quagmire that threatened to suck him under. This tribulation in Smyrna couldn't go on forever . . . could it?

Please, Lord, let it be over, he pleaded as he finally drifted off to sleep. *Please let me go home.*

35

FOR THE LONGEST TIME, Livia was speechless. She stared at the endless expanse of the brilliantly blue Aegean, searching for that almost-invisible seam where water met sky. Her husband had promised to take her to see the ocean, but he'd done better than that: on Saturday, two days after they arrived in Ephesus, Jacob took her out *on* the ocean.

He stood beside her on the deck of the *Mercury*. "Kaeso is going to bring her around and head back to the harbor now," Jacob said. "Next time we'll take a real voyage, not a quick sail. Today I just wanted you to have a taste of life at sea."

Livia nodded, and for a moment she watched the captain as he called orders to the skeleton crew, then she turned her attention back to her new fascination. She was enchanted and awed—and disappointed that their short excursion would soon be over.

She closed her eyes and inhaled deeply, trying to memorize the smell of the sea and the sound of the wind as the ship sliced through the water. Suddenly she leaned over the rail and stuck out her tongue, letting fine drops of ocean spray blow into her mouth.

"What are you doing?" Jacob asked.

"What you said—getting a taste of life at sea." She licked her lips and grinned. "It's salty."

"I already told you that," he said with a laugh.

"And I just proved you right."

Livia wiped her face and wordlessly studied the horizon again as the ship slowly changed course. "I feel so insignificant," she finally said.

"Insignificant? Why?" Jacob asked.

"In comparison to the ocean, I mean. It's so immense, and I'm so small. Somehow that puts everything into perspective." She pointed to the shoreline, now coming back into view. "It looks so tiny from here. A huge, sprawling city, but now it's just a speck on the horizon. Everything there seems so rushed, so important, so all-consuming . . . and out here, on the water, it all seems so inconsequential. I wonder . . ."

Jacob gazed at her with affection. "What do you wonder, my sweet philosopher?"

"I wonder if that's the way we appear to God. Not insignificant; we're made in His image. But all the things that worry us and loom so large in our minds—do they seem inconsequential from heaven's perspective?"

"I imagine they do," Jacob said. "The ocean is not exactly like heaven, though. Close," he added with a broad smile, "but not the same. When you're sailing, you eventually come back to shore, and you find that all the problems you left behind are still there waiting for you, still just as big."

"But maybe you can bring a bit of that perspective back with you, so the worries don't overwhelm you when you're back on dry land."

Jacob reached out and brushed a strand of hair off her face, tucking it securely behind her ear. "You're not still worried about what my family thinks, are you?"

"No, in just a couple of days they've managed to make me feel very welcome. I really like your family, Jacob."

"Then what's worrying you now?"

"It's not worry, really. I'm just trying to get over being very, very mad at Gregory for keeping the truth from me all those years. I know I should be mad at my mother, but she's not here to yell at. So I did a lot of yelling at Gregory yesterday. I don't want to let go of that anger—what they did was wrong, pretending that Marcellus didn't exist, as if he had never been a part of my life.

"But it's hard to stay mad at my uncle. I'm worried that he's getting sick again. And he's the only family I have . . . except for Marcellus. Maybe he'll seem like family too someday, but not yet."

"It will take time, but it will happen. He wants to be a part of your life now."

Livia nodded. "I'm angry at him too, though. I can't help thinking, if he really loved me, why did he leave me?"

"Apparently Marcellus didn't have much choice. I'm sure he'll tell you about it if you ask him."

"Oh, I intend to."

Jacob paused a moment, then said, "You'll have plenty of time to talk to him the next couple of days, actually. I have to go to Smyrna—"

"We've only been here two days and you're leaving already? How far is Smyrna? Why can't I go with you?"

"One question at a time," Jacob said, holding his hands toward her, palms out. "Smyrna is only a day's journey away, and I'm just going there and coming right back, so I wouldn't have any time to spend with you."

"But I'd be with you on the way." While Livia felt more comfortable with Jacob's family, she wasn't sure she wanted to be left alone with them just yet.

"There are a couple of reasons for the trip," he said, ignoring Livia's whining. "One is to do something for my sister. I've barely seen Rebecca in the last two years, and she's having a hard time of it right now. Her fiancé has been gone for months, and she's not sure what's going on. I intend to find out. But the main reason I need to go to Smyrna is to apologize to Polycarp for the way I left."

Jacob shook his head sadly and reached for her hand. "It seems I have a lot of relationships to restore. And I need to do that before we can truly start our life together here."

"You won't be gone long?" Livia hated the idea of being separated from Jacob for even one night; they hadn't been apart since they'd been married. But she understood that his sudden departure last year had created a rift not only within his family but within the church.

"One night," he promised, "two at the most. Then I'll be home. You'll barely know I've been gone."

✝

On Monday Antony decided to stay close to the house. Ever since he'd had the run-in with Damian on Friday, Antony had had the feeling that he was being followed. Yesterday Damian hadn't even bothered to be subtle about it; he'd trailed Antony through the public square and had even nodded and smiled.

Antony wasn't up to dealing with Damian's intimidation tactics today, and for once Antony had no appointments, no business that required his presence in town. So far Tarquinius had not been charged with a crime. And outside of that possibility, Antony had only one other case pending. A trial date had finally been set for the church member who had been falsely accused of theft. Just ten more days; Antony would be ready with his defense.

He was still concerned about Tullia interfering with the witnesses. It occurred to him that she might also try to bribe or threaten some of the approximately forty appointed *judices* who would hear the case and render judgment. There was little Antony could do about that except to be well prepared, argue the case brilliantly, and pray that he could persuade more of the *judices* than Tullia could sway.

The upcoming trial was easily crowded out of Antony's mind as he worried about Damian and Tullia's plot against Polycarp. Much as Antony had expected, the bishop had refused to leave town. Several of the church leaders were volunteering as watchmen, with one or more of them standing guard over Polycarp's house every night. Whether that would be enough to thwart a deranged arsonist, Antony didn't know. But as he was learning, with God all things were possible.

As had become his custom, Tarquinius arrived at an early hour, just as Antony was finishing breakfast. Today the innkeeper carried a large ax over his left shoulder and a short-handled hatchet in his right hand. He looked completely out of place as he stood there in the dining room, loaded down with cutting tools.

Bemused, Antony asked, "Are you planning to tear the house down before Damian can burn it?"

"No, sir," Tarquinius replied stiffly, then realized Antony was joking with him. He grinned as he propped the implements against the wall of the dining room. "I thought I'd chop some firewood later."

Tarquinius looked around, making sure no one could overhear him. "If you don't mind my saying so, I've noticed that the . . . uh . . ." He paused, searching for the right word and looking pleased when he remembered it. "The bishop and his followers don't pay much attention to practical things. Too busy with their religious duties, I guess. Not that that's a bad thing," he added quickly. "I just don't understand much about it."

"Until recently, I didn't either," Antony said. "But I suppose that's why God sends people like you and me to help them take care of the practicalities of life." He motioned for Tarquinius to have a seat. "So they can concentrate on spiritual matters."

Tarquinius carefully sat on the edge of the sofa but did not recline. "Running an inn for all those years, well, all you have time to do is take care of details like supplies and cooking and cleaning. I couldn't help noticing this household won't have enough firewood to last through the winter if somebody doesn't take care of it now." He paused and looked at Antony. His voice was quite serious as he asked, "Do you really think your God sent me to help Polycarp?"

Antony's reply was thoughtful as well. "Yes, I do. I can't explain it fully, but I believe you're supposed to be here—just as I am. And that it's part of God's plan, not just to help the bishop with mundane things like firewood and legal advice, but to protect his life so God can continue to use Polycarp to bless this city—and the world beyond."

Tarquinius reflected on that while Antony finished his breakfast.

When Antony rose from the table, Tarquinius quickly stood and said, "So, what should I do today? Stick with you, or stay here and watch out for the bishop?"

"I'm staying around here myself today," Antony told him. "Laying in a supply of firewood is an excellent idea, but let's go for a walk first. I want to see what we can do to better protect the house."

For the next hour, Antony and Tarquinius walked through the neighborhood, noting ways Damian might come in and out. The suburbs were not as crowded as the city proper, and the houses here were spaced a good distance apart. They were still close enough, however, that a major fire could be catastrophic for the whole neighborhood. Something else that concerned Antony was the house diagonally across from Polycarp—it was now vacant; the elderly man who lived there had died a few months ago. The empty house would make a good hiding place for someone who wanted to keep an eye on Polycarp.

Antony and Tarquinius were discussing whether to explore the other house when two men walked down the street. The men were dressed in hunting costumes, shorter-than-usual tunics with knee-length boots. As they approached, Antony recognized one of them.

"It's Damian," he said softly. "Do you know the other man?"

"Never saw him before," Tarquinius replied.

Antony wasn't surprised by Damian's appearance in the neighborhood, but the object Damian carried did come as a surprise. It was a military bow—the same weapon used by the archers of Rome's legions. The other man was similarly armed.

When Damian passed by, he raised his bow in a salute and called out, "Great day for target practice. The best season for hunting is just ahead." Damian's voice was loud and cheerful, and it was the kind of greeting one neighbor might call to another. Nothing threatening, nothing illegal, but disturbing nonetheless.

"Something tells me he's not stalking white-tailed deer," Tarquinius muttered when the pair had rounded the curve in the road.

"Be extra careful when you go out to chop wood later," Antony advised.

They walked around the perimeter of Polycarp's house. Like the other dwellings in the neighborhood, the modest one-story house was set back from the road. The only entrance to the home was through a walled, rectangular courtyard that opened to the street on one side and the atrium, or central room of the house, on the other side.

The rooms along each side of the house had windows with wooden shutters. There was barely room to walk behind the house; it backed up to a fairly steep ravine.

"No one is likely to approach the house this way," Tarquinius said. "Those brambles would cut you pretty bad."

Antony agreed. "I'll make sure all the windows stay closed, so it's mainly the front entrance we have to worry about."

They went back inside, and after fetching his tools, Tarquinius left. All afternoon Antony puzzled over when and how Damian would strike. He might watch the house for days, Antony realized, waiting for them to let down their guard, before trying anything. Damian wanted to instill fear, so he would play a waiting game.

When Tarquinius returned later with a cart filled with his labors, Antony helped stack the firewood behind the house. The physical exertion worked his muscles but allowed his mind to relax.

By the time they finished, Antony was feeling much calmer, and he enjoyed an early dinner with Polycarp and two of his students. Tarquinius joined them, and although he didn't say much, he appeared to enjoy their conversation, which was mostly a discussion of Scripture.

Afterward, Tarquinius told the bishop that he had brought a bedroll and planned on spending the next few nights in the front courtyard, if that was all right.

"You'd be a welcome guest," Polycarp said, "but there's no need to sleep outside. We'll make a place for you in one of the back rooms."

Over the years the house had been enlarged by tacking additional rooms onto the back, so the house was much larger than it looked from the front. The extra rooms were used as classrooms and bedrooms for the frequent guests—mostly pastors or deacons from other churches, who came seeking counsel, or young apprentices whose parents wanted them to receive doctrinal instruction from the respected young bishop.

"No, that's all right," Tarquinius said. "I prefer to sleep out front . . . to help keep watch, I mean."

"I see. In that case," Polycarp said, extending his hand, "consider the courtyard your bedroom." He shook hands with Tarquinius. "Antony told me about the firewood. Thank you for that. I appreciate your help—you're a godsend."

Tarquinius looked surprised and pleased. "That's what Antony said."

When Polycarp retired, Antony went to the courtyard with Tarquinius. They unlatched the wide door to the street and walked outside. It was just now dusk, and the neighborhood was quiet. Antony hoped it stayed that way all night.

He looked over at the vacant house. "When it gets dark," he said, "look to see if there are any lamps inside."

Tarquinius nodded. "Or anybody out on the street with a lantern."

"Verus should be here anytime," Antony said. "He's the church member who is on watch duty tonight."

"We can work together, one of us inside the courtyard, watching the entrance to the house, and one of us patrolling the outside. We'd be in shouting distance of each other if something happened."

"A good idea," Antony said. He'd feel more comfortable if there were several men watching the outside of the house, but at least Verus wouldn't be alone tonight.

Antony wondered how many more nights they would have to watch and wait before Damian tried to burn the place down. About to close the door and go inside, Antony stopped when he heard a horse trotting around the curve in the road.

"You expecting visitors?" Tarquinius asked.

"No." Antony watched the rider slow and pull off the road. He felt uneasy about the arrival, but told himself that it couldn't be Damian. An arsonist would not ride up to the front door.

The driver reined in the horse and dismounted. The man must have traveled a great distance; he wore some kind of foreign clothing Antony didn't recognize. But when the rider turned toward them, he greeted Antony by name.

Antony turned white as a bedsheet when he recognized the man. "Jacob!" he cried. "Jacob, is it really you?"

Jacob laughed, threw his arms around Antony, and clapped him on the back. "In the flesh, friend. In the flesh."

Antony took a step back and Jacob turned around to pick up the horse's reins.

Tarquinius suddenly screamed, "Get down!" He ran toward Jacob and shoved him. Gravel flew as the men hit the ground, facedown, in a hard landing. An arrow whizzed over their heads, barely missing them before impaling the open door to the courtyard.

The horse reared and Antony grabbed for the reins so the animal wouldn't trample its owner. By the time he'd gotten control of the horse, Jacob and Tarquinius had gotten to their feet, and they all made a run for the courtyard as more arrows rained overhead.

Tarquinius latched the door to the street behind them, and Antony opened the door to the atrium.

"Easy, girl." Jacob soothed the animal as he tied it to an iron ring on the wall. Before he could make it in the house with the others, yet another arrow lobbed over the courtyard wall and landed nearby.

The arrows had come from the direction of the vacant house, Antony realized. Whoever was firing at them—and Antony had no doubt who it was—was standing on the roof of the empty house across the street.

Inside the atrium, Tarquinius asked Jacob, "Are you all right?"

"I think so," he said, brushing gravel off his face and arms.

"Awful sorry I had to knock you down like that, but I'm glad I saw that arrow coming when I did."

"I am too," Jacob said. "I'm very grateful to you." He turned to Antony. "I wasn't sure what kind of welcome I'd receive, but I certainly did not expect to be shot on my arrival. What's going on?"

Antony stared at Jacob. He couldn't get over the fact that Jacob was here, in Smyrna, and he'd almost been killed.

"Antony?" Jacob repeated.

"Sorry," Antony said, running a frazzled hand through his hair. "For months I've thought you were dead."

"For months I *was* dead, in a manner of speaking," Jacob said.

Antony introduced the innkeeper, who had indeed been a godsend today, risking his life to save Jacob.

"We've met before," the beefy man said, as he shook Jacob's hand. "Last time I saw you, I was worried you were going to kill a man on my property. Now I wish you had. Things wouldn't be in such an uproar around here."

Startled into recognition, Jacob said, "The inn . . . Damian?"

"He's back," was all Antony said. "He's back."

"And the man we saw with him this morning, as well," Tarquinius added. "Too many arrows coming too fast to be a single archer—"

Tarquinius stopped and cocked his ear toward the door. "Did you hear that?"

They listened to the sound of someone knocking on the outside door at the street.

"Verus—" Antony suddenly remembered they'd been waiting for Verus when everything happened.

"You stay here," Tarquinius said to Antony. "I'll let him in."

Tarquinius returned with Verus, who was holding a broken arrow. "I found this stuck in the door," he said. "What happened? Hunters?"

"No," Antony said. "It appears we're under siege."

"Damian?" Verus asked grimly. Antony nodded.

"If it's just Damian and the other man," Tarquinius said, "we have them outnumbered. The four of us could overpower them—"

"But we don't know for sure," Antony said. "We could be walking into an ambush. On top of that, we don't have the kind of weapons they do, and it's dark now."

"You're right," Tarquinius agreed reluctantly. "We'll have to wait until morning."

Verus said, "I have a feeling it's going to be a long night."

Jacob was too stunned to say anything.

Verus took up his watch in the courtyard while the others left the atrium and went to find Polycarp—who, much to Jacob's relief, was overjoyed to see him again.

Jacob had felt physically ill ever since he heard the news that Damian was behind the attack, and his stomach felt no better after the hastily prepared meal Linus and Polycarp's other young pupil arranged. Over dinner, Jacob shared the sketchiest of details about his sojourn in Cappadocia and recent return, while Antony brought him up to date on what had been happening in Smyrna.

"When Damian showed up several months ago," Antony said, "but no one had heard from you—well, I thought he must have killed you."

"He's been back for several months and you never said anything to Rebecca about it?" His sister was right. Antony really hadn't been telling Rebecca much about what was happening in Smyrna if he'd left out that important detail.

"I didn't know how to tell her about Damian," Antony said. "It didn't seem right to put it in a letter, and I wanted to come to Ephesus to see her, but things kept snowballing here . . ."

"I know a lot has been happening, but you've neglected Rebecca—and worried her. She knows you've been holding something back from her, and fretting over what it was."

Antony sighed and said, "I will have to apologize to her for handling things so poorly."

"And you'll do it in person," Jacob insisted. When Antony agreed, Jacob said, "Now tell me what's been going on since Damian returned."

"For a long time he kept a low profile," Antony said, "but when the fires started, we suspected he was involved because he was staying with Tullia—"

"And because he fathered my sister's bastard child," Tarquinius interrupted, "and Tullia has some fool notion her baby is going to grow up to be some kind of high priest or something." He stopped, embarrassed at the outburst. "I'm sorry," Tarquinius said after an awkward pause, his face a study in dejection. "It really grieves me that my own flesh and blood has caused so much devastation, not just in my own life but in this town."

Polycarp gently reassured him, "Your sister's sins are not your responsibility."

"Do I have this right?" Jacob asked. "Tullia has given birth to Damian's baby?"

"Yes," Antony replied, and he related the pagan prophecies that the child would be a great spiritual and political leader and Tullia's ensuing threats against Polycarp.

Jacob thought of Rebecca. Damian certainly had a knack for fathering illegitimate children. Jacob couldn't help thinking that the births of both of Damian's offspring had been accompanied by prophecies: John had foretold that Victor would be a mighty man of God, while the godless oracles had predicted that the witch's son would be a powerful pagan priest.

"By killing Polycarp," Antony concluded, "Tullia thinks she can eliminate the Christian influence in the city and ensure her son's rise to power."

"If the Lord wants my life," Polycarp said evenly, "He is welcome to it. I have no use for this physical body other than His plan and purpose for me. But until He is ready to receive me into heaven—whether that be in a matter of moments or after I reach a ripe age, like my esteemed friend John—until it suits God's purpose for me, the devil and all his minions cannot kill me."

Polycarp excused himself then. While the others lingered in the dining room, discussing Tullia and Damian and their nefarious schemes, Jacob mentally revisited his original decision to pursue Damian and his subsequent decision to abandon the quest to avenge his family. Jacob could not escape the thought that if he had done what he had set out to do, Damian would not be here right now persecuting the church in Smryna.

Sergius and Plautius would still have their blacksmith business. Tarquinius would still have his inn, and his wife. So much suffering might have been avoided.

Did I make the right choice? Jacob wondered. He wouldn't be married to Livia now if he had killed Damian, and Jacob couldn't imagine life without her.

Just a few days ago John had reassured Jacob he'd done the right thing, but John hadn't known Damian was the one causing all the trouble here.

And what about Gregory's prophecy that Damian would destroy himself if Jacob left vengeance in God's hands? Jacob had walked away from Damian, but Damian had returned to continue destroying the church. Had Gregory given a false prophecy?

Jacob abruptly left the dining room, went out into the courtyard, and threw up his dinner. A few minutes in the cool night air revived him, and he went inside to find Polycarp. Jacob needed to apologize, and he needed some answers; perhaps the bishop had them.

What the bishop offered, however, was not an opinion, but prayer. The two men were still on their knees when the first rays of light heralded the dawn of a new day—a day that would seal their fate and bring a final, fiery end to the persecution in Smyrna.

36

QUINTUS AWOKE BEFORE DAYLIGHT and slipped out of bed without disturbing his wife. He would search by himself this morning; Aurora had been fussy during the night, and Agatha needed the sleep.

He quickly dressed, picked up his long walking stick, and headed across the hills toward his destination. It was a very strange thing to be doing, and Quintus would be hard-pressed to explain it. At first it was simply something he did for his wife because he loved her. But it had become his passion as well, and scarcely a morning passed that he didn't make the twilight trek.

Quintus smiled as he thought of his wife and daughter. How different his life was now. And how happy. It was an amazing thing, falling in love so late in life. The time had never seemed right for him before, so he had devoted himself to business without much thought of marriage—not until Helena had suggested it to him one day, and without the least bit of subtlety, steered him in Agatha's direction.

From the day he'd met her, the day Peter had found her shivering under the pier, Quintus had admired Agatha's fortitude and her fierce protection of her child. It hadn't been easy to win her trust or her affection, but he'd done both.

Now the two of them had a very quiet, contented life. He doted on little Aurora, and the first time she had called him Papa had been one of the happiest days of his life. If Agatha had her way, they would have more children, and that would suit Quintus just fine.

He was mentally picturing a houseful of children when the

familiar stench assaulted his nostrils. As always, he smelled his destination before he arrived.

And as always, Quintus spent the hour before sunrise searching the city dump.

He had a method: Approaching from the south, he started on the east side and worked his way around the perimeter, turning north, then west, and returning to the south. There was no plan to the dump, of course; it was an irregular shape, about a mile in circumference. Over time, the people who used it had worn a path around the stinking mountain of garbage. On hot days, steam rose from the rotting mess and the stench was even worse.

The walking stick was handy if Quintus wanted to poke through the heaps of refuse for some reason, but what he was looking for was more likely to be found close to the path that circled the dump. He wouldn't have to venture too far into the garbage; no one ever went that far to throw one out. Over the months he'd been searching with Agatha, they'd found three, but none of them had been alive. Quintus had taken each one of them home, though, and buried them in a grassy area behind the house. And he'd wept each time.

This morning he made a complete circuit of the dump without success. It was always disappointing when the search was fruitless, and he and Agatha had prayed about this often. But they believed God was leading them to do this on a regular basis, so they continued.

When he arrived back at his starting point, Quintus turned toward home.

Look again. He heard the voice in his mind and stopped.

Quintus looked back at the dump and saw a vulture swoop down. He ran toward the bird and shooed him away with the walking stick. But when he looked through the garbage near the spot where the vulture had been, Quintus found nothing but pottery shards, food scraps, and human waste. He gagged and turned back to the road.

He'd taken only a few steps when he heard the voice a second time. *Look again.*

He stopped and began to pray silently. *Lord, are you telling me to keep searching today?*

Quintus did not hear the voice again, but he felt something urgent rise up inside him, so he began the laborious process of circling the dump again, searching carefully along the sides of the path and occasionally poking into the piles of garbage.

The sun was way above the horizon by the time he neared the end of his second circuit, and still he'd found nothing. Perhaps he'd only imagined the voice telling him to look again.

You old fool, Quintus chided himself. He should have been at the harbor long before now.

He gave up and stepped back on the path, and then he heard it. Not a voice this time, but a tiny, mewing cry that sounded like a newborn kitten. Quintus looked around frantically, but couldn't see where the sound had come from.

"Please cry again. Please," he said softly.

The mewing started again in reply. And finally, in a place he'd already searched this morning—recognizable by the broken barrel staves that jutted out of a heap just off the path—Quintus found the source of the cry. He saw a minuscule movement under a wad of unbleached muslin that looked like discarded scraps of a tunic. The bundle hadn't been there earlier; he would have noticed it.

Quintus knelt down and carefully lifted the cloth, revealing a tiny, perfectly formed baby girl.

And this one was alive.

†

Agatha balanced Aurora on her hip as she walked up the hill to the villa. She and Rebecca were going to take Livia to the warehouse at the harbor today, and perhaps make some visits to the needy. Rebecca wanted her sister-in-law to see the relief operation and wanted to start introducing her to people. It would be wonderful to have additional help for the ministry, Agatha thought, even if it were only for one day. Perhaps it would even be something Livia would want to do regularly.

Hoping she might have a chance to talk to Rebecca alone, Agatha was arriving early. If it turned out that Rebecca was busy, then Agatha would entertain Aurora in the garden until they were ready to leave for the harbor. Aurora loved playing in the garden, where she could run free, and spending time at the villa was something Agatha always enjoyed—not because it was a mansion, but because, in a way, she regarded it as her home. She'd only lived there for a year, and she had merely been a servant, but it was the first place Agatha had truly felt welcomed and accepted. Every time she stepped over the threshold now, she had a feeling that she was coming home.

Even though she was not very good at making conversation, Agatha enjoyed talking to Rebecca. Quintus often told Agatha she needed more friends and would have plenty of them if she would just open up and talk more. She *had* made friends with Rebecca and found her easy to talk to. Agatha had almost told her about Aurora—would have, in fact, if they hadn't been interrupted that day by Jacob's homecoming.

That's what Agatha wanted to talk about now. Once she had said those first few words to Rebecca that day, it had loosened something deep inside. Now Agatha thought she might burst if she tried to keep it to herself any longer. She had to tell someone, and she thought Rebecca would be sympathetic and understanding.

When Agatha arrived at the villa, she was pleased to find Rebecca in the atrium, watching Victor play on the floor. He patted the colorful mosaic tiles and babbled as if explaining something to his mother, who listened attentively as if she understood.

Rebecca looked up, greeted Agatha cordially, and said, "I didn't expect you quite so early. Marcellus took Livia with him to see John this morning, and they're not back yet. I hope you don't mind waiting."

"Oh no, not at all," Agatha said, hoping she didn't sound too happy about the fact that Livia wasn't there. "Actually, I came a little early because I was hoping to talk to you, if that's all right."

"Of course, Agatha. I'd enjoy the chance for a talk."

Agatha was relieved that Rebecca seemed eager for the visit, and that she also suggested they go to the garden for privacy. They took the children with them as they went from the main part of the villa into the peristyle at the back. Three sides of the house opened onto the peristyle, with its colonnaded walkway around a large garden area. The fourth side was a waist-high stone wall that afforded a view of the hills.

Concrete benches were arranged around the two focal points of the garden: an enormous sundial and a beautiful, flowing fountain. It was a serene setting, one of Agatha's favorite places. She had known mostly chaos in her life, and had always longed for a place of retreat; she'd finally found it here. When she'd lived at the villa, Agatha would try to finish her work early and bring Aurora to spend a few quiet minutes in the peristyle garden. Heaven, she often thought, must be something like this.

Rebecca sat on one of the benches by the sundial and invited Agatha to join her.

"Down!" Aurora demanded as soon as her mother sat. Agatha obliged, setting the toddler on the ground. Aurora stood in front of Rebecca, watching as she dandled Victor on her knee.

Now that she had Rebecca's attention, Agatha was at a momentary loss for what to say, then realized that the children gave her an opportunity to begin. That was one of the few topics she felt comfortable talking about.

"Aurora is still tall and thin for her age," Agatha said, "but Victor is growing so fast."

"And getting into everything," Rebecca said. "I turn my head for one moment, and he's gone." Making a silly face at the baby in her lap, she said, "Isn't that right, you little rascal?"

Victor laughed and laughed, as if she'd said something uproariously funny, then he reached up and patted her face.

Beginning to relax, Agatha joined in the laughter. Her daughter, however, felt ignored and perhaps jealous. Aurora pouted and said, "*My* Victor." She stamped her foot and pointed to the ground. "Want my Victor down."

Victor reached for the little girl, and Rebecca put him down. Aurora gave him a big hug, which he endured for a moment before wriggling free and toddling off. Aurora chased after Victor and grabbed hold of his hand.

"She's very possessive of him," Agatha said, "and protective."

"She'll be a good mother someday," Rebecca said, "like you."

Agatha blushed. "I love kids." And wanted more of them, she thought to herself. She searched for a way to say just how much having more children meant to her, but the words wouldn't come.

Rebecca waited for a moment, then asked, "What was it you wanted to talk to me about, Agatha?"

"The other day," Agatha said slowly, "the day Jacob came home? We were talking . . ."

"We were talking about having more children."

"I was going to tell you something that day, but we got interrupted."

"I'm sorry we never had a chance to finish our conversation," Rebecca said. "We do now, though."

Agatha hated having such difficulty speaking. Rebecca was very patient with her, though, so she mustered her courage. "You said . . ."

Both women looked up briefly as the children yelled, then resumed talking when they were satisfied that Victor and Aurora were merely shrieking in delight.

"You said it would be good for Victor to have a brother or sister," Agatha continued. "I'm glad Aurora and Victor are close in age and enjoy playing with each other, in case . . ." Her voice faltered momentarily, but she recovered quickly. "In case Quintus and I don't ever have any more children."

"I hope you do," Rebecca said, "since that's what you want."

"I've always wanted children, and lots of them. But I nearly died giving birth, and now . . . now I don't think it's possible for me to have another child of my own. I even got up the courage to ask Marcellus about it, and he confirmed my fears. He said that if I did get pregnant again, I probably wouldn't live through it."

"I'm so sorry, Agatha." Rebecca's voice was full of compassion. "No wonder it made you sad when I said I wanted to have a big family."

The children are too quiet, Agatha suddenly thought, terrified. If they'd wandered off, at least they couldn't go very far in the enclosed garden. But when she looked up, Victor and Aurora were squatting down by some shrubbery, digging in the ground and patting small clumps of damp dirt into flat cakes. They would get filthy, but they would have fun and it would keep them occupied for a few minutes, so Agatha let them be.

"I'm sad for Quintus too," she said. "He's never had children of his own, and he's so good with Aurora. We talk about it all the time, and Quintus says we can adopt another baby—as many as we want."

"Adopt? A baby?" Rebecca looked puzzled. "How?"

"I'm sorry, *adopt* is not the right word." No wonder Rebecca was confused. Agatha had been too, when Quintus first explained it to her. Emancipation and adoption was a legal means of placing an older child—a son—with a wealthy family in order to secure an inheritance or advance a political career. It did not apply to their situation; girls could not be legally emancipated from their father's household and adopted.

She began again. "What I meant was that Quintus said we can *raise* another child . . . that is, we would treat it legally as our own, even though we couldn't . . ."

Agatha suddenly stopped and put her hands over her face. She wanted so desperately to unburden herself, but she couldn't do this to Rebecca. She couldn't. Fighting back tears, Agatha stood up. She would get Aurora and leave now.

Rebecca jumped up and put a hand on Agatha's arm. "Don't go, Agatha."

"I'm sorry, I shouldn't have said anything. You don't want to hear this."

"Of course I do. I want to hear anything you have to say. That's what friends are for—listening."

Agatha started crying then. "Oh, Rebecca . . . I can't involve you in this. What we're doing is . . . well, technically, it's illegal. It's the *right* thing to do," Agatha said forcefully, "but it's against the law."

Aurora heard her mother crying and came running over, with Victor waddling after her. She grabbed Agatha's skirt with grubby hands and looked up. "Don't cry, Mama."

Agatha knelt down and picked her daughter up. "It's all right, sweetheart. Mama won't cry." She turned to Rebecca. "Perhaps I'd better go now—"

The door from the dining room burst open and Quintus ran onto the colonnade, clutching a bundle under his cloak. "Thank God you're here," he called to Agatha as he stepped into the garden and came toward them. "I went home first, of course. I didn't know you'd left . . ."

Quintus paused for a breath, and a faint cry emanated from his arms.

Agatha gasped at the sound.

"She needs to be fed," Quintus said quietly but urgently. He looked around at the crowd that had followed him into the peristyle. Gregory, the steward, and some of the household staff stood gaping at the scene from the colonnade.

"Upstairs," Quintus told Agatha. "Quickly."

✝

Rebecca had never seen Quintus so agitated. She sprang into action. "Use my bedroom. I'll keep the children," she said, prying Aurora from Agatha's arms, "unless you want me to come with you."

"Yes, please," Agatha said, then she looked at Quintus, who nodded his permission.

Rebecca called for Gregory to take Victor. Then she turned to the
steward. "When Marcellus arrives," she said, "send him to my room
immediately."

Rebecca ran through the house as fast as she could with a toddler
in her arms, and climbed the stairs behind Quintus and Agatha. If she
had been surprised by Agatha's early-morning visit, Rebecca was completely stunned when she entered the bedroom and watched Quintus
place the bundle on the bed and unwrap it.

She had known it was a baby because she'd heard it cry the same
time Agatha did, but the sight of the naked newborn, dirty and whimpering, still shocked Rebecca speechless.

Aurora wasn't. She climbed out of Rebecca's arms and onto the
bed. "Baby," the toddler said happily. "My baby?"

"Yes," Agatha said, "Papa found us a baby—a girl, just like you."

Aurora crawled closer and wrinkled her nose. "Baby stinks."

Quintus laughed nervously. "I didn't take time to clean her up,"
he told his wife. "I was so surprised to find her alive, and so frantic to
bring her to you to nurse . . ."

Agatha loosened her tunic and dropped it to her waist, then
reached for the baby. Quintus propped pillows at the head of the bed,
and Agatha leaned back, holding the baby to her breast. It took several tries for the infant to latch on and begin to suck.

Rebecca was moved by the sight. Agatha, tears coursing down
her cheeks, nursed the tiny, smelly newborn, Aurora was curled up
contentedly beside her mother, and Quintus stood over them all with
an adoring expression on his long, thin face. What a picture they
made.

Where did Quintus get the baby? Rebecca wondered. Was that the
illegal part? She had a sudden, horrific thought that almost buckled
her knees. *Had Quintus* stolen *this child?*

Quintus knelt by the bed and gently stroked the baby's foot. "She's bigger than the other ones," he said. "I think that's why she was still alive."

"She looks like she might be a few days old," Agatha said. "Perhaps the father was away when she was born, so the mother got to keep her for a while before he came home and found out it was a girl he didn't want."

"I searched the garbage dump twice before I found her," Quintus said.

Rebecca couldn't stand it any longer. She sat down on the foot of the bed. "You found this baby in the garbage?"

"Yes," Agatha said, looking down at the discarded baby. "Just like I found Aurora." Lifting her chin defiantly, Agatha looked up at Rebecca. "And I'm keeping this one too."

Found Aurora? In the garbage? Rebecca could not comprehend the thought that Aurora was not Agatha's baby. Agatha had said she almost died in childbirth, and she had always nursed Aurora. How could that be?

The dump? That was where Quintus and Agatha had been sneaking off to in the early morning hours?

Nothing could have surprised Rebecca more. She had no idea what to say or do.

Quintus and Agatha were good people, she reminded herself. Even if they'd done something that was illegal, she wouldn't pass judgment on them without hearing their story.

At dawn on Tuesday, Jacob went to bed and slept for two hours. He woke feeling refreshed but sore. His ribs were bruised from hitting the gravel when Tarquinius had kept him from being struck by an arrow.

Damian's arrow. Jacob had no way of knowing for sure if it had been an assassination attempt, but that was his guess. Damian might have been shooting just to create panic among his intended victims.

Or he could have heard Antony shout Jacob's name and specifically aimed at him.

When Jacob went to the *triclinium* for breakfast, he found the table littered with bowls of half-eaten food, but no diners. Hearing voices, he followed the sound to the atrium.

"Good morning," Antony said, his voice weary with fatigue.

Jacob returned the greeting and took a seat on the bench next to Antony. Polycarp was seated on a low-backed chair, while Verus occupied the other bench. Tarquinius stood over Verus, wrapping a fresh bandage around his upper left arm.

"What happened?" Jacob asked.

Antony answered with a question. "You didn't hear the commotion?"

"No. My bedroom is at the very back of the house."

Tarquinius said, "The minute Verus here stuck his head outside this morning, Damian unleashed a barrage of arrows. One caught him in the arm. Nothing serious, fortunately."

"I'll say this," Verus said, wincing as Tarquinius tied off the bandage. "Damian is either a very poor marksman, or he's not shooting to kill."

"The latter," Antony said. "Right now he merely wants to instill fear in us."

"Intimidation would be his style," Jacob added.

Antony asked Verus, "Were you able to see the archers? Could you tell how many there are?"

Verus shook his head. "I didn't see anybody. But it was like Tarquinius said last night. The arrows came too fast for there to be only one man."

"It's probably just Damian and the man we saw yesterday." Tarquinius walked over to the door that led to the courtyard, but he didn't open it. "I wish we could see inside that vacant house across the street. That's definitely where they're holed up. We need to get in there and take them out."

"How are we going to get in there," Verus asked, "if we can't leave the house without getting shot at?"

Tarquinius pounded a meaty fist against the door, then turned back toward the group. "That man killed my wife," he said loudly, pointing in the direction of the house across the street, "and he's planning on killing the bishop. I heard it myself. He repeated the threat to Antony. We have to *do* something to stop Damian."

Polycarp had been silent to this point, but he spoke up now. "Let me make something clear. I will not have you—any of you—take a life in order to protect mine. Self-defense is warranted, not murder. Keep that in mind."

"If we can stop him without killing him," Jacob said, "we will. Agreed?"

One by one, the others agreed.

The group returned to the dining room to finish their meal, and as they reclined around the table, they continued to discuss Damian's plot and how to thwart it.

"It seems to me," Jacob said, "that if Damian wanted to destroy Polycarp by fire, he would do what he's doing now—keep us confined here, afraid to go outside for fear of being shot. And when he finally tires of that, he could shoot flaming arrows into the house and set it on fire that way."

"Except," Antony said, tearing off a piece of bread and passing the loaf to Tarquinius, "that hasn't been Damian's pattern with the previous arsons. He's been saturating the structure with oil and then throwing a lighted torch to create a tremendous combustion all at once."

As Antony explained how the fires at the inn and the blacksmith shop had been set, Jacob dipped his bread in the bowl and sopped up some porridge. He tried to picture the inferno the blazing oil would create.

"There's no way you can escape a fire like that," Antony said, "and no way to put it out. No way to keep it from spreading, either, without a miracle."

"Then we have to find a way to stop Damian before he can do that," Jacob said. "The only question is how."

At noon, long after Linus had cleared the dining table, they were still looking for an answer to the question.

Jacob finally made a suggestion he would never have considered a year ago. "What if we went to the authorities and asked them to stop Damian? I know they wouldn't have believed you," he said to Antony, "when it would have been just your word against Damian's.

"But now the whole neighborhood can see what he's doing—and they're in danger too. Anyone who ventures down the road could be hit by a stray arrow. The authorities *have* to step in now, don't they?"

"If it weren't a known Christian presenting the complaint, they would," Antony said. "You know how it is better than I do. Sometimes when we ask for help they don't take us seriously, and sometimes we wind up getting in more trouble than we were already in. It can be tricky."

"I think it would be worth a try, though," Polycarp said. "We owe it to the civil authorities to give them a chance to do their job."

Tarquinius sounded doubtful. "Verus said it earlier: We'd still have to get past Damian's arrows just to go for help."

"The ravine out back," Verus said. "It would be rough going, but if you follow it for about a half-mile, there's a place you could climb out by another road that leads to the main part of town."

Jacob stood. "I think we should do it. And I'll volunteer to go."

"I'll go with you," Antony said. "I've been dealing with the local government and know how to contact the proper authorities."

"Both of you are staying right here," Verus said firmly. "I'm the one who knows the way. I've lived here all my life, and I know where to find the constable. And besides all that, I'm a hunter. I have a couple of bows at home and plenty of arrows. I'll bring them back— just in case we need to provide the authorities with covering fire."

"Go, then," Jacob said. "The rest of us will pray you're able to secure the cooperation of the constable."

"I'll help you climb out a window and fasten it behind you," Antony said. He and Verus walked out of the dining room.

Tarquinius looked at Polycarp and Jacob. "I don't know how to pray," the innkeeper said. "But if you'll tell me the words, I'll say them."

Polycarp rose from the sofa. "When you know the one you're speaking to," the bishop said, "the words will come easily." He walked over to the innkeeper and motioned for Jacob to join them. "Come," he said to Tarquinius, "let us introduce you to the Lord to whom we pray."

The three men knelt on the floor of the dining room, and when they rose sometime later, a new name had been added to the Book of Life.

†

When the baby had finished nursing, Agatha asked Rebecca to help bathe her.

"There's fresh water in the basin," Rebecca said. She took the baby while Agatha refastened her tunic, then got a clean towel to spread on the washstand. Rebecca lay the baby on the towel and Agatha dipped a cloth into the water, wringing it into the bronze basin.

Quintus held Aurora, who watched the proceedings quietly but with intense curiosity. "My baby," she told her father several times.

"My baby too," Quintus said with a proud smile.

"Did someone really throw this little girl away?" Rebecca asked. She held the baby, who stiffened her tiny fists and wailed, while Agatha washed away the filth and stench of the garbage heap. "Who could do something like that?"

Agatha knew exactly the kind of person who was capable of such a heinous act. But before she could answer, Marcellus and Livia arrived.

The medical officer checked the newborn over carefully. "I can't say as I've had many babies for patients," he said with a grin, "but this one looks all right to me. She has no fever, her color is good, and she's strong enough to cry."

Rebecca went to the chest where she kept Victor's clothes and began to select some baby things for the little one. When the baby was dressed and swaddled in a blanket, Agatha laid her in Victor's crib. Clean and well fed, the newborn immediately went to sleep.

Her heart overflowing with joy and her eyes brimming with tears, Agatha turned her face upward and said, "Thank You, Lord. Thank You for giving me another baby."

Still holding Aurora, Quintus put a hand on his wife's shoulder and joined in her thanksgiving. "We praise You, Jesus, for this indescribable gift."

After a moment he said, "Agatha, it's time we tell our friends why we've been searching the dump for abandoned babies."

Agatha nodded. "All right," she said slowly as she sat down in the chair next to the crib. Talking about the past would bring back memories Agatha would rather not revisit, but she owed her friends an explanation, especially now that she'd involved them.

Quintus sat on the floor beside her, and Agatha instinctively reached a hand over to her husband. As he grasped her hand, Agatha took a deep breath and began to tell how she had lost one daughter and found another.

At the end of her long story Agatha concluded, "I named her Aurora because it was not long after dawn when I found her at the dump that day. And it was the dawn of a new life for me—for the both of us."

Quintus had held his wife's hand as she told the entire story. He asked her now, "Have you thought of a name for this one?"

"I was thinking of Dorinda. It means 'lovely gift.'"

"That's a beautiful name," Livia said.

"What will you tell people?" Marcellus asked. "If you suddenly show up with a baby, they are bound to ask questions."

"If it's somebody I don't know very well," Agatha said thoughtfully,

"I would just tell them that the baby's mother couldn't take care of her, so Quintus and I agreed to take her in. I would try not to elaborate beyond that."

She explained to Livia, "No one knew my background when Peter first took me in and brought me here. I got very good at being evasive when people would ask me questions. For the longest time I was terrified that someone would know I'd taken their baby and they would try to get her back."

"But they had thrown her away—left her to die," Livia said.

"Exactly. And I finally realized that if they hadn't wanted her to begin with, they weren't likely to change their minds."

Agatha paused for a moment, then finished addressing Marcellus's original question. "But when it comes to our Christian friends, I think we should tell them the whole story. You were right about that," she said to Quintus. "I should have talked about this before. I let shame keep me from speaking out, but I feel better for having said something now. Who knows? There may be other women, even women in the church, who have also been forced to give up a child. Maybe it would help them to know they weren't alone."

"Perhaps it would motivate the church to do something," Rebecca said. "You were right when you told me earlier that what you were doing was technically illegal but the right thing to do. We can't just sit by and let these babies die of exposure."

"So many times," Quintus said, "I would be searching the dump, and I would think of the story Jesus told about the shepherd who left the ninety and nine in the fold while he searched for the one lost sheep. When I would get weary, when I would think that finding another baby alive would be hopeless, I would remember that. 'Would Jesus quit looking?' I would ask myself."

He told them about the voice he'd heard that morning, the one that had said, *Look again.*

"So I kept looking. And see what happened?" Quintus gazed at his new daughter, still sleeping peacefully in the crib.

"You know something?" he asked Agatha.

"What?" she said.

"I'm going back to the dump in the morning and look again. I'll probably look every morning for the rest of my life. I'll bury the dead and rescue the living. And if, God willing, we find more children than we can raise, then we'll find good homes for them."

Agatha beamed at his vow to keep looking for abandoned children. "I wish there was a way we could convince society to give up this cruel custom. If people knew there were alternatives . . ." She trailed off and sighed. "Well, perhaps someday we'll put an end to it."

37

As the afternoon wore on, the men trapped inside Polycarp's house grew more tense. Tarquinius kept asking how much longer they were going to wait before doing something, and Jacob kept reminding him that Verus had not left to find the constable until noon.

"We just have to be patient a little while longer," Antony said.

The three men took turns pacing the flagstone floor of the atrium. Sometimes they all paced at once. Polycarp was closeted in one of the back rooms with his two students, beseeching God for deliverance.

Taking a break from marching back and forth, Jacob sat on one of the benches. To pass the time, he began to tell Antony all about Livia. "I never expected to spend so long in Cappadocia," Jacob said after he'd told the story of encountering the trade caravan and following Livia and Gregory to the cave house. "Never thought I'd fall in love and get married—not the way it happened, I mean. But God had a hand in it, and I couldn't be happier with the way things turned out."

"I can't wait to meet your wife." Antony was seated on the bench, leaning forward with his forearms resting on his knees. As he spoke, he cast a worried look at the door to the courtyard.

"We're going to get out of this alive," Jacob told him. "You'll meet my wife soon—and you'll marry my sister."

"I want that more than anything—I need that." Antony stood and stretched, rolling his head from side to side to relieve the tension. "I've been praying this would all come to an end so I could go home to Rebecca. I just never imagined the end would be so . . . so . . ." He shrugged. "I don't even know how to describe it."

Tarquinius quit pacing and took the seat Antony had vacated. "I've been thinking," he said. "Damian can't have an unlimited supply of ammunition. He has to run out of arrows sometime."

"Who knows what kind of supply he has?" Antony asked.

"Hear me out," Tarquinius said. "It's not like they've been stock-piling weapons over there for a long time. Yesterday was the first time anybody had seen Damian in the neighborhood. So, how much equipment could two men bring in with them? They were on foot— no horses or wagons."

"They looked like typical hunters yesterday," Antony said. "Each one had a quiver of arrows."

"And even if they'd had *two* quivers each—"

"I see your point," Jacob said. "If we could get them to fire all their arrows, it would lower the odds of one of us getting killed if we have to take action against them before the constable gets here."

"*If* the constable gets here," Antony corrected Jacob. "We don't know for sure Verus can persuade him to do something."

"Looks like they would have been here by now, if Verus had been successful," Tarquinius said.

"I just thought of something." Antony dropped down in the chair across from Jacob and Tarquinius.

"What?" the two of them asked simultaneously.

"Whoever is scheduled to watch the house tonight . . . we have no way to get word to them to tell them not to come. No way to let them know what they'll be walking into."

"They'll be ambushed," Jacob said. The thought sickened him.

"That settles it." Tarquinius stood. "I'm going outside to draw their fire."

"But you could be killed," Antony protested.

The stocky man regarded them with a resolution that was evident in his expression and his stance. "So? You two have wives—or will have," he said to Antony. "Mine is gone. Most of my business is gone. What do I have to live for?"

"Plenty," Jacob said. "You have a *new* life now, a life in Christ. Your life is not your own to dispose of as you wish."

"I never thought of it like that," Tarquinius said, looking flummoxed. "I heard Polycarp say something to his students yesterday. 'You are not your own,' he told them, 'you were bought at a price.' I didn't really understand what he meant." He sat back down on the bench beside Jacob. "I have a lot to learn about this new faith."

"I've been a Christian all my life," Jacob said, "and I'm still learning. Some of us are a little denser than the rest."

The three of them remained silent for a few minutes, then Jacob said, "Your idea has merit, Tarquinius. But rather than you walking out the front door and drawing Damian's fire, let's give him three targets at once—limited targets."

Jacob detailed his idea for them. "There are windows along the sides of the house. The ones close to the front should be visible to Damian from across the street. One of us can take a window on the east side, one on the west side, and the third can work from the front door. If we all stick our heads out at once, they'll have several targets."

They discussed the idea and agreed on a way to execute it. Tarquinius insisted on being the one stationed at the front door. "It's the riskiest position," he said. "And I really do have the least to lose."

Jacob offered to take the east side, the one closest to the house across the street. Antony would go to his bedroom, which was on the west side.

"I'll stick my head out and yell to get Damian's attention," Jacob said. "When you hear me, you'll know it's time to pop out. Don't stay visible too long, though. And wait for my signal."

As they moved to take their places, Jacob felt his pulse quicken. A bit of fear was healthy, he thought. At least it was a feeling other than the uncertainty and dread they'd been experiencing all day.

He went to the back of the house, where Polycarp and the students were praying. Quickly Jacob informed them of what he was doing, asked them to pray for protection, and warned them not to leave the room. Then he went back to the front of the house and entered the first room on the east side, the room Polycarp used as a library and study. The night before, the two of them had spent many hours in prayer here.

Jacob waited a minute, allowing time for Antony and Tarquinius to get ready. Then he unlatched the shutter, pulled it open, and rested his hands on the windowsill. Leaning forward slightly, he could see about half of the house across the street; he did not see any sign of Damian or his accomplice.

Jacob took a deep breath to calm himself, then stuck his head as far out the window as he could. "Damian!" he yelled in a loud voice.

In reply, he heard the high-pitched sound of an arrow in flight. He ducked as the missile whizzed by his head. Another followed, and Jacob jerked back inside.

He heard Tarquinius and Antony both shout, heard arrows fly in their direction, then leaned out of the window again, drawing more fire. The three of them repeated the tactic several times, but after a few minutes there was no further response.

Jacob waited a while longer, then he latched the shutter and went back to the atrium, hoping the others had fared as well as he had.

They had. Several arrows had come close, but none had hit their target. Comparing accounts of what they'd seen, they agreed that Damian had expended a couple of dozen arrows.

"He could have stopped because he was out of ammunition," Antony said, "or it could be that he caught on to our scheme and intentionally held his fire."

They had their answer shortly, when they heard a commotion in the street, then pounding on the outer door of the courtyard, accompanied by shouting. "Help! Somebody, help!"

"That's my cousin's voice," Tarquinius said. "Sergius!" He ran from the atrium through the courtyard and opened the door to the street.

Plautius had been hit; an arrow protruded from his chest, below the right shoulder. Sergius had hold of his brother under the arms and was trying to drag him. Tarquinius grabbed Plautius by the legs and helped Sergius get the wounded man into the house, while Jacob and Antony closed both the outer and inner doors of the courtyard.

"We were attacked," Sergius said, breathing with difficulty after carrying his brother. "Just walking up to the door when it happened."

"We had no way to warn you," Antony said grimly.

"How bad is he hurt?" Tarquinius asked.

"It's serious," Jacob said. "If we can get the bleeding stopped, he might make it." He wanted to hold out hope, for Sergius's sake.

They carried the unconscious man to one of the back bedrooms and began to tend to his wound.

"Get Polycarp," Antony said.

Tarquinius left to find the bishop. Jacob and Antony held Plautius on the bed while Sergius gingerly removed the arrow from his brother's chest. It was a good sign, Jacob thought, that Sergius was able to extract it, but Plautius had lost a lot of blood.

Polycarp brought some old cloths to tear up for bandages. "The important thing is to stop the bleeding," he said. "We can try to clean the wound later."

He began to wrap the strips of cloth tightly around Plautius's chest and shoulder. The first layer soaked through immediately, so Polycarp continued bandaging.

"Get some oil for anointing," he instructed the wide-eyed Linus. The young man nodded and ran out of the room.

When Linus returned, Polycarp anointed Plautius's forehead with oil, laid hands on him, and prayed for his recovery. The others stood around the bed and joined the petition.

It's in God's hands now, Jacob thought. *All our lives are in God's hands.*

Polycarp and the two students stayed with Plautius while the rest of them went to the kitchen. They found some bread and cheese and ate a light snack standing up, not bothering to go to the dining room.

After they told Sergius what had been happening, conversation dwindled. There seemed to be nothing left to say. The small kitchen

AVENGER OF BLOOD

was crowded with four men standing around, so they returned to the atrium to wait for Verus and, they hoped, the constable.

Jacob brought some bread from the kitchen, and he took it out to the courtyard, where the chestnut remained loosely tied to the far wall. "Here you go, girl." The horse nibbled the food out of Jacob's hand. There was some hay left in the corner, he noticed. Jacob had refilled the water trough earlier; there was still an adequate supply.

But the courtyard was not meant to be a stable, and he felt sorry for the animal, having to be confined to such a small space. "I know how you feel," he muttered sympathetically. It was a good thing the wall of the courtyard was tall, or the chestnut would probably have been killed by one of the arrows that had made their way over the top.

Jacob had been in Smyrna all of twenty-four hours, and he had no idea when he would be able to leave—if ever.

"A short trip," he'd told Livia. "One night—two at the most."

She would be out of her mind with worry if she knew what was going on. Jacob was glad she didn't. He understood why Antony hadn't been able to tell Rebecca. It was instinctive to want to protect someone you loved so much.

For a long time Jacob stroked the horse's mane and thought about Livia. He would have given anything to be with her at that moment. *Dear Lord,* he prayed, *please get us out of here. Please let me go home to my wife.*

At twilight Jacob went back inside. "We can't wait any longer," he told the men. "In less than an hour, the sun will be completely gone. Damian intends to torch this place, and he'll do it after nightfall. We can wait and try to stop him then, but if he manages to set the fire . . ."

He didn't need to describe for them what would happen if a blaze ever got started.

"So what do we do?" Antony asked.

"I'm with you, whatever it is," Tarquinius said, and Sergius added his agreement.

Jacob experienced a sudden clarity that had been building while he'd spent time thinking in the courtyard. What were they going to do? Stop the torment, that's what. He wasn't sure how, but he was sure it was time—God's time—to put an end to Damian's persecution.

All Jacob knew for certain was that he was going to face down his enemy—no, God's enemy. Jacob was meant to do it, had been destined to do it all along, just not in the way he had originally envisioned. This time he would face his adversary not as the self-appointed avenger of blood, but as a simple soldier of Christ, clad in the armor of God.

And Jacob had peace about it, perfect peace.

Within moments, Jacob had the outline of a plan. He would go out front to distract Damian. Antony would wait until Jacob was well out in the street, then ride the chestnut out of the courtyard and go for help. Tarquinius and Sergius would climb out a back window, go through the ravine, and come out on the other side of the nearest neighbor's house. Then they would cross the street and head for the vacant house where Damian and his accomplice were.

"You two will capture the other man," Jacob said. "I'll subdue Damian."

"But we don't have any weapons," Sergius said.

Tarquinius disagreed. "Yes, we do. I've got the tools I used to chop wood yesterday."

Jacob restated the bishop's earlier admonition. "Don't use them unless you have to." Then he added, "But if necessary . . ." He didn't bother to finish; they understood.

The men shook hands and went their separate ways. Tarquinius retrieved his tools and left for the back of the house with Sergius. Antony and Jacob went to the courtyard and saddled the chestnut.

"I'll find Verus or the constable—or somebody. I'll get help," Antony promised.

Jacob nodded and started to speak but couldn't find the words for a moment. "It'll be over soon," he finally said. "We'll be going home." It was not a delusion but a bedrock conviction.

He unlatched the door to the street and swung it open. His palms were sweaty and he could feel the pulse beating in his throat, but his spirit was calm. Jacob felt a stillness deep inside that steadied him.

As he stepped outside, a Scripture passage flooded into his mind:

For our struggle is not against flesh and blood, but against the rulers, against the authorities, against the powers of this dark world and against the spiritual forces of evil in the heavenly realms. Therefore put on the full armor of God, so that when the day of evil comes, you may be able to stand your ground, and after you have done everything, to stand.

The day of evil had come, and it was time to stand his ground. Jacob walked through the door of the courtyard toward the street.

Nothing happened. He looked at the house diagonally across the street. It was small, one story, with an outside staircase going up to the roof on the far side. No one was moving about, as far as Jacob could tell.

"Damian!" Jacob called in a booming voice. "Damian!"

A bump on top of the flat-roofed house moved, and a man stood up. He walked toward the front edge of the roof, which was about ten feet off the ground, and stood, fists on his hips.

It was Damian. Jacob noted the defiant stance and it reminded him so much of seeing Damian on Devil's Island that he could almost hear a whip cracking over his head.

"Looks like you spent too much time in Cappadocia," Damian yelled. "You picked up their peculiar ways."

"Better for riding," Jacob said, guessing the reference was to the trousers he'd worn for the ride from Ephesus.

He slowly took a couple of steps forward. Damian was not holding his bow. Was he out of ammunition?

"I want to talk to you, Damian."

"You have nothing to say that I want to hear."

"I have an offer to make."

Damian didn't reply. Jacob walked out two more steps and stopped. He wasn't out quite far enough yet for Antony to make a break for it, but Jacob didn't want to rush things. He had no idea where Damian's accomplice was.

"I'm the one you want. Let Polycarp and the others go."

"I want you all," Damian shouted. "Especially you—I owe you. But I want the so-called bishop too."

Jacob took another step forward. "Leave him alone, and I'll make it worth your while."

There would be no reasoning with Damian, of course. Jacob couldn't appeal to his conscience or moral sensibilities; the brute had none. But Jacob thought there was a possibility he could tempt Damian in one area where he was particularly susceptible.

"I'll give you money," Jacob said, "and passage to Rome."

"There's nothing there for me now."

"The money, then. Name your price."

Damian hesistated, and Jacob walked forward again.

"I don't believe you," Damian said.

"*Ride* into town with me, and I'll make the arrangements."

Antony picked up on the clue and burst through the open gate. As he spurred the horse into a gallop, Damian scrambled for his bow and fired, but he wasn't quick enough; the shot went wide.

Jacob ran a few steps toward the other side of the street, then saw an arrow flying toward him. He lunged to the left and hit the gravel. The arrow grazed his right leg, just above the ankle.

Damian had not fired the arrow that hit him, Jacob realized. He'd seen Damian get off a second shot at Antony, which meant that the other man had fired at Jacob. He looked up at the house and saw the accomplice leaning out of the window.

Jacob heard mocking laughter as he stood up and brushed himself off, and he felt a flash of his old anger then, and with it, a flicker of fear. But the emotions vanished as he heard the voice of the Spirit.

*Stand firm then, with the belt of truth buckled around your waist,
with the breastplate of righteousness in place, and with your feet
fitted with the readiness that comes from the gospel of peace.*

His ankle burned, and a trickle of blood ran onto his sandal, but Jacob
stood firm.

"I'm coming over there, Damian. I'm not armed."

Damian laughed again. "You're a fool if you think I believe that—
and if you really are unarmed, then you're an even bigger fool."

Jacob continued speaking as he slowly inched forward. "I could
have killed you several times but didn't, and for a long time I was
angry with myself for not doing it."

"You didn't kill me because you're a coward."

"No, I didn't kill you because I'm not a murderer."

Damian was silent as he fit an arrow into his bow. He raised the
weapon and aimed it at Jacob.

Jacob stopped where he was, possessed of a calmness he could not
have imagined.

"*You're* the coward, Damian. You don't have the courage to face an
opponent who's as strong as you. All you can do is prey on the weak
and vulnerable. You'll beat an elderly preacher. You'll rape a frightened, defenseless woman. You'll kidnap a baby and burn down buildings. But you're afraid of me right now because I have power—real
power—of a kind you can't even conceive. My *weakness* is my power."

"That's nonsense."

"It makes perfect sense when you know the One who is all-
powerful."

"You're talking in riddles."

Without turning his head, Jacob cut his eyes to the right. The
man who had shot him was no longer visible in the window. Had
Tarquinius and Sergius managed to reach the house already?

Jacob looked back at the roof. Damian held the bow pointed
directly at Jacob's chest, but still did not shoot.

"You can't kill me, Damian."

"You think not?"

Damian fired then, and although Jacob was less than a hundred feet away, the shot veered to the side and missed him by several inches.

Jacob remembered the earlier discussion with Verus. Maybe Damian wasn't a very good marksman after all. As a tribune, he had primarily held administrative posts; if Damian had ever seen a day of combat, it would have been many years ago.

"You can't kill me," Jacob repeated. "Oh, you can destroy my body—if God allows it. But you cannot kill my soul."

Keeping his eyes on Jacob, Damian knelt down and felt the rooftop for another arrow. He slowly stood, reloaded his bow, and leveled it at Jacob.

It's his last arrow. The thought came unbidden to Jacob's mind, along with a Scripture.

Take up the shield of faith, with which you can extinguish all the flaming arrows of the evil one. Take the helmet of salvation and the sword of the Spirit, which is the word of God.

Power surged through Jacob. He felt it in every fiber of his body as he spoke. "That's what you couldn't understand about all the Christians who refused to sacrifice to Caesar. You couldn't scare them into it because they knew you couldn't kill them—not forever. They loved God more than they loved their lives. You made their lives a living hell on Devil's Island, and some of them died there. Yet they're alive today, Damian. Alive!

"You killed my mother, yet she lives. Your father sent mine to his death, yet my father lives. Their spirits are alive by the power of Jesus Christ. He has won the victory over death!"

Jacob's entire body trembled from the force that propelled his words. "You have tormented and persecuted the body of Christ, but you cannot defeat the church triumphant. The gates of hell will not prevail against it. No matter what you've gotten away with in *this* world, Lucius Mallus Damianus, you will pay for your sins in the next. You will burn eternally in a lake of fire."

Damian released the arrow, and this one struck Jacob in the side. He felt a sharp pain as the shot ripped through his clothing and opened the skin. But the thickness of his long coat kept the arrow from completely embedding itself in his flesh. Jacob gritted his teeth and pulled the arrow out, then he held it up in front of him and snapped it in two.

Damian shook his fist and let loose a stream of vile curses. "I'll destroy you," he screamed. "And my son will destroy your sons. My seed will always be against yours."

He had stepped closer to the edge of the roof while continuing his tirade, and as Damian delivered his prophecy of destruction, he lost his footing and plummeted to the ground below. He landed in the weeds with a thud.

Jacob raced the remaining few yards across the street and through the yard of the vacant house toward Damian, feeling his side as he ran. Jacob was bleeding, but not profusely.

Falling ten feet hadn't killed Damian. He pulled up to his hands and knees, then struggled to his feet and stumbled toward the front door of the house. Jacob caught up with Damian and lunged for him, knocking him off balance. Both men went down.

Jacob grabbed Damian by the ankle but didn't have a firm enough hold to keep him down. In the process of getting up, Damian dragged Jacob a few feet before Jacob let go. His ribs were still bruised from his earlier falls, and the pain exploded in his side where he'd been shot.

He took a couple of deep breaths and got up, making it inside the house not far behind Damian, who ran toward the back, arriving in the kitchen only a few paces ahead of his pursuer.

Suddenly weak, Jacob leaned against the doorjamb for support. The fading light made the room dim, and he blinked to bring it in focus. Tarquinius and Sergius had made it through the back entrance, but Tarquinius was wounded. He was sitting on the floor, leaning back against the wall, with a broken arrow sticking up from his thigh. He was conscious, though, and he grinned at Jacob briefly. Sergius had knocked the accomplice out and was tying him with a rope.

Damian stood by the kitchen table. Several torches had been laid out there, and a small clay lamp had been lit. They had definitely been preparing to commit arson after dark.

He picked up one of the torches. "If I'm to burn in a lake of fire," Damian said, "you'll all burn with me."

With his other hand Damian reached for a jar on the table.

Oil! Jacob thought. *It's a jar of oil.* Damian was going to torch the place with all of them inside. With his last bit of strength, Jacob pushed away from the doorjamb and charged.

He fell into Damian, pushing him back against the table. When Damian raised up, he knocked Jacob to the floor. Jacob blacked out for a moment, then looked up and saw Damian tip the container of oil and pour it over the torch.

Jacob tried to get up but couldn't, then suddenly he was moving backwards and realized that Sergius was dragging him away. As Damian reached for the lamp to light the torch, an object sailed through the air toward him.

The hatchet, Jacob realized. That's what Tarquinius had been holding by his side when Jacob got there.

For an almost interminable moment, the hatchet flew end over end. Finally it reached its target, striking Damian in the side of his head with a sickening *thwack* that severed his ear and split open his jaw. Simultaneously with the impact, an arrow pierced Damian's chest. He fell back, hitting the table hard, then slumped to the ground, blood spurting from the gruesome wound to his head and more seeping from his chest.

The table tipped over when Damian landed. Both the lamp and the jar of oil fell on top of him.

✝

Jacob never saw the blaze ignite. He was lying in the yard when he came to and saw that the vacant house had become an inferno.

"We're safe," Antony assured Jacob as he tried to sit up. "Everybody got out—everybody except Damian."

"I got shot," Jacob said thickly. His head was spinning and he felt queasy.

"I know. We need to get you over to Polycarp's."

"Don't know if I can walk." Jacob's ankle throbbed and his ribs were so bruised, it hurt to breathe. But his other injuries paled in comparison to the pain from the hole in his side.

"When Verus and Sergius get back," Antony said, "we'll carry you across the street. They helped Tarquinius over. He insisted on walking, but it took both of them to steady him."

"How is he?"

"It will probably take a surgeon to get the arrow out of his leg, but I think he'll be all right."

Antony sat down on the ground beside Jacob, who watched the chaotic scene around him with a certain detachment. Neighbors had poured out of the surrounding houses and were beating the edges of the fire with blankets, trying to keep the flames from spreading.

"Where were they when all this was going on?" Jacob asked.

"Holed up in their houses, afraid. Or unwilling to help their Christian neighbors."

Willing to save their property, though, Jacob thought grudgingly. He watched them battle the blaze a minute, then asked, "What took Verus so long to get here, anyway?"

"He couldn't find the constable for a long time, and with all the harassment of Christians that's gone on here, none of the officers would agree to come to our help until they'd cleared it with the constable himself. Verus finally gave up and went to his house to get his bow and arrow, then decided to go back to the constabulary. The second time he persuaded someone to come with him. They had almost made it back here when I met up with them."

"It was Verus who shot Damian?"

"Yes," Antony said. "Verus took aim about the same time Tarquinius launched the hatchet."

Antony told Jacob how the fire had started, and how they had pulled him and Tarquinius out before the house was engulfed. "The officer who came with Verus even managed to drag Damian's accomplice out. Sergius hadn't injured him seriously, just knocked him out cold with the blunt end of the ax.

"Did a fine job of tying him up, too. We tossed the man over your horse, and the officer led him off to jail."

"You let him take my horse?" Jacob asked in amazement. "I worked for months to pay off that chestnut."

"Don't worry. I'll go get him tomorrow."

"Her. It's a her."

"All right, I'll go get *her* from the constabulary tomorrow."

Verus and Sergius returned, and they started to pick Jacob up. "I think I can walk now," he said. His head was clearing and he was beginning to feel a bit stronger.

"Tarquinius thought that too," Sergius said, "and he collapsed halfway across the street. He was so heavy it took four of us to carry him after that."

"I'm not that heavy, and I can walk," Jacob insisted stubbornly. "Just help me stand up."

They carefully pulled Jacob to his feet, and he surprised them by staying upright and steady.

Before they turned to leave, Jacob took a last long look at the fire. He thought of what John had said a few days earlier: "The Lord will avenge the blood of His servants in due time."

Damian was dead. He would torment the church no more.

Other persecutions would doubtless arise. But for now, for this place and for this time, the Avenger of Blood had wrought justice.

38

IT RAINED ON REBECCA'S WEDDING DAY, but no amount of precipitation could dampen her spirits as she and Antony stood before Theodorus and exchanged vows. In spite of the inclement weather, the lofty two-story atrium of the new home was packed with people. Rebecca had chosen to get married here rather than at the villa; it seemed appropriate to start her new life with Antony in their new house from the moment they became husband and wife.

Peter must have hired every delivery wagon in Ephesus to accomplish the move. With another shipping season just ending, he had put all the stevedores to work loading furniture at the villa and at Antony's house and transferring it here. In a few days Helena and Priscilla would move in; until then, Rebecca and Antony would have the place to themselves.

The month since Antony had first returned from Smyrna had flown by. He'd come back with Jacob, who had been injured. Looking haggard and harried himself, Antony had broken down and wept when he apologized to Rebecca for worrying her. He'd gone back to Smyrna briefly for the trial, which resulted in an acquittal for the accused church member, and then he had returned home for good.

Now Antony gave her hand a squeeze and said, "Excuse me while I speak to our guests from Smyrna."

She remembered Verus and Sergius from the time they'd helped rescue Victor. Sergius had told her earlier that his brother, Plautius, was expected to make a full recovery from his chest wound, but was not able to travel yet or he would have been there as well. The inn-keeper,

Tarquinius, had also come. He walked with a pronounced limp, but it didn't seem to slow him down much.

Rebecca looked over at her brother and caught his eye. Jacob lifted his goblet in a salute and grinned broadly. He mouthed something, but Rebecca couldn't make out his words over the noise of the celebration. She looked around for her other brother and found Peter sitting with Aurora in his lap. Quintus stood nearby, cradling Dorinda in his arms. The new baby was thriving, and as he'd promised, Quintus still searched the dump daily for other abandoned children.

Quintus was retiring from the shipping business, and Jacob would be taking his place. Rebecca was thrilled that her two brothers would finally be working together; how proud her father would have been.

Helena stopped long enough to kiss Rebecca on the cheek again. "You look lovely, dear. Such a beautiful bride," Helena said, then she was off. Rebecca's mother-in-law seemed to be in a footrace with Agatha to see who could flit around the atrium the fastest, each woman determined to make sure every guest was well fed and having a good time.

Priscilla was wagging Victor around; the baby's mouth was smeared with something sticky, and he was squealing with pleasure. Rebecca laughed at the sight.

Marcellus beamed with pride as he stood next to Livia. Rebecca knew the first few weeks in Ephesus had been rocky for her new sister-in-law, but Livia was adapting marvelously to her new home and her newfound father. She had even started referring to Marcellus that way. "I was blessed with a papa," she had told Rebecca, "and now I'm blessed with a father."

Rebecca was very grateful for John's presence. It would have been a far less joyous celebration if the Apostle had not been able to attend. John seldom left his house anymore; unable to walk more than a few steps, someone had to carry him wherever he went.

The booming, raspy voice was now feeble and tremulous. He no longer preached, and when he did address the church, his words were few but powerful. Two Sundays ago the deacons had carried John to the front of the congregation. The Apostle had looked at the people for a long time, then finally said, "Little children, love one another." That was all, but the simple words had been spoken with such pleading that people had begun to weep.

Rebecca saw that Theodorus and Polycarp were having a lively discussion. They were probably analyzing the finer points of theology; both men loved to dissect Scripture and glean every kernel of truth from it. When someone approached and asked Theodorus a question, Rebecca took the opportunity to go over and speak to Polycarp.

"We're so honored you came," Rebecca told him.

"Thank you for inviting me," the bishop said. "I'm deeply indebted to Antony for his service to our congregation. Attending your wedding seemed the least I could do to thank him."

"He's talked a lot about the students you disciple . . ." Rebecca instinctively looked around for Victor, then continued when she saw that Priscilla was still carting him around. "You know the prophecy John gave about my son before he was born."

Polycarp nodded. "I certainly do. When John was in Smyrna a year ago, he talked to me at length about you and Victor."

"I don't know exactly what the prophecy signifies," she said, "but I was wondering if you would train Victor. Someday, I mean."

"When you think he's ready," Polycarp said, "send him to me. I'll impart to your son all that I learned from John."

Relieved, Rebecca thanked the bishop. For some reason, Victor's future had been weighing on her mind lately.

"I should tell the Apostle good-bye," she told Polycarp. "I'm sure he'll be going home soon."

"I'm surprised he's stayed this long," the bishop said, "but he has always loved being around God's people. I'll say my good-byes too."

Later, Rebecca would think how significant that exchange had been. When she and Polycarp went to say farewell to John, she found

Marcellus and Gregory kneeling at the spot where John had been sitting.

A sudden knot in Rebecca's stomach told her that something was wrong, terribly wrong. She ran toward them and found John crumpled in a heap on the floor.

"He suddenly collapsed," Gregory told her.

At first Rebecca thought John was dead, then the old man opened his eyes. The left side of his face sagged, distorting his features.

"He's had a stroke," Marcellus said. "A major one this time."

John had had a series of small strokes over the last few months. There had been residual damage from each one, but it had been minimal. Marcellus had warned Rebecca that eventually John would have a massive stroke, and that one would kill him.

She knelt down beside John and touched his face. He looked up at her and blinked, and the right corner of his mouth twitched. She knew he was trying to call forth a smile, but the paralyzed muscles of his face would not let the smile break to the surface.

Fighting back tears, Rebecca said, "I love you, Apostle."

John blinked again and said something. It was only one word, and Rebecca didn't understand it at first. Then she choked out a small sound that was a cross between a laugh and a sob. He'd called her Scribe.

"We need to get him home," Marcellus said. "I've got some medicine there that will help relax him." He stood and waved Jacob over. "We'll make him as comfortable as we can," the doctor told Rebecca.

Antony was at her side now, and he helped Rebecca to her feet. As she watched Jacob lift John and carry him out, she let the tears fall, but they were tears of joy and gratitude as well as sorrow. God had allowed Rebecca to have John with her at every major event in her life. He'd been there for her birth and the birth of her child. He'd baptized Rebecca, had outlived both her parents, had lived to see Jacob's return, and now her wedding.

For a long time Rebecca had known this day was coming, but she'd been unable to accept it. Now, on her wedding day, she found the strength she needed.

"I can't keep John forever," she told Antony. "I have to let him go home. He'll be with Jesus soon."

✝

John lingered for almost three months. Even as his strength ebbed, he stubbornly clung to life with the ingrained tenacity that had seen him through decades of adversity.

As news of the Apostle's failing health spread throughout Asia, a steady stream of pilgrims flowed into Ephesus to pay their respects. With the final stroke, John had lost much of his capacity for speech, but his eyes lit up whenever he had a visitor.

Along with the pilgrims, other news reached Ephesus. In January, Rome crowned a new emperor when the elderly Nerva died, and his adopted son, Trajan, was elevated to the throne. Jacob prayed that the Empire would remain as stable under the son's leadership as it had the father's.

Toward the end of February, Jacob visited the elderly apostle, as he did most days. It was a cold but clear morning, and John indicated that he wanted to sit outside in the sunshine "one last time."

Jacob started to argue that it was too cold. But he'd never won an argument with the old man yet—and would probably lose this one, even though John could only say a few halting words at a time.

Giving in without a fight, Jacob took the old camp stool outside and placed it against the wall of the house; that way John would have some support to his back. Then Jacob went back inside to fetch the Apostle and carry "these old bones," as John had so often referred to his body, outside. It was not difficult; the old man weighed next to nothing.

When Jacob propped him up on the stool and bundled a blanket around him, John grinned his appreciation. For a while the dying man looked around at the bleak landscape; the trees, still bare from winter frosts, nevertheless held the promise of spring. Then John leaned his head back against the house, closed his eyes, and basked in the sunshine.

Jacob couldn't help smiling at the sight. He was glad he had honored the request. What harm could it do? John had precious little time left; he might as well enjoy it.

It was almost impossible for John to sit up unassisted; he tended to fall to the left. So Jacob stood at John's side, letting the Apostle lean against him. Within minutes John dozed off.

The familiar sight of John napping outdoors brought back memories for Jacob, and he swallowed a sudden lump in his throat. *I'll let him sleep a few minutes,* Jacob thought, *then I'll carry him back inside.*

Soon, however, he realized that John's breathing had grown too quiet. Jacob put his hand on the old man's shoulder and shook him lightly. "John? . . . John?"

There was no response. The Apostle's face was cold to the touch, and Jacob knew it was not simply from being outdoors. John had slipped into eternity while slumped against Jacob's side.

His heart as chilled as the wintry day, Jacob picked up the Beloved Apostle, carried him inside, and laid him on the bed. Before he realized what he was doing, Jacob pulled the covers over the Apostle's frail frame, as if putting him down for a nap. Then reality hit him: John was gone. He did not need to be taken care of anymore.

Jacob almost lost control of his emotions then, but there was too much to be done before he could allow himself to mourn. Some women from the church were there, and working through their tears, they began to prepare John's body for burial. Jacob left to find Marcellus and Quintus, so they could help him get word to the believers across Ephesus.

Following the Jewish custom, they buried John before sundown on the day he died. Most of the church members had been notified within a few hours, so the funeral was well attended. And the weeping on the hillside was so loud and boisterous that Jacob reckoned it could be heard all the way to the harbor.

The shrouded body was laid to rest in a niche in the inner wall of the private tomb that was adjacent to Abraham's sprawling villa. The rest of the family returned to the house, but Jacob remained in the mausoleum even after the last mourners had left. He couldn't bear to leave John just yet.

Dry-eyed during the funeral, Jacob wept now in private. He hadn't expected to be this emotional, but somehow the loss affected him even more deeply than the death of his father. Perhaps it was because he hadn't witnessed Abraham's death, but Jacob had been with John when he passed into glory. And perhaps it was because Jacob was a different man now, a more mature man, a man who understood more about life and death and faith and friendship.

The sun had not gone down yet, but it was always dim in the inner recesses of the burial chamber. Torches had been lit and placed in iron holders bracketed onto the wall. The cold marble crypt was an eerie place, yet there was comfort here. There was family here. John's funeral bier contained the only intact body tucked away in the crevices, but the bones of Jacob's mother and grandfather resided in carved limestone boxes, as did some of the servants who had worked for the family over the years. Eventually, "these old bones" of John's would be collected and placed in a similar ossuary.

Bleary-eyed from weeping, Jacob looked up at one of the wall sconces where the torches burned brightly, dispelling the gloom. *The last apostle is gone,* Jacob thought.

Did that mean the persecution was over? Would there be no more martyrs?

As Jacob stared into the burning torch, he suddenly saw Polycarp's image. Although it was Polycarp's face he saw in the flames, it was the face of an old man—a very old, white-haired man, like John.

Jacob blinked and looked again; the image was gone. Was his mind playing tricks on him? Or was it a glimpse into the future?

It was too close in the mausoleum. Jacob needed fresh air. He walked outside and sat down on the gently sloping knoll where the family tomb had been built. Sitting cross-legged on the ground, he stared at the sky. It would be a beautiful sunset; streaks of pink and purple had stolen among the clouds, their rich hues bringing a depth of color to the fading daylight.

What a sad day for the church, but what a glorious day for John. In his mind Jacob pictured the Beloved Apostle's reunion with his Master, and almost thought he could hear John's raucous laughter. All of Jacob's life he had heard John's stories of the Rabbi from Galilee. Jesus of Nazareth. Lord and Savior. John had told the tales so vividly that Jacob sometimes felt as if he'd been there with the Twelve.

Now these old stories floated into his memory, drifting through his mind like the clouds scudding over the hills. Jacob also recalled conversations he'd had with John and Polycarp about the lives and deaths of the original apostles. Polycarp had wanted to collect and preserve the accounts of their martyrdom, so he had talked about it extensively with John, and had communicated on the subject with church leaders across the Empire.

Odd, Jacob thought now, that while John had been the last to die, his older brother, James, had been the first. James had been beheaded in Jerusalem by Herod Agrippa, shortly before the king's own death.

Now John, the final member of the Twelve, was gone. And Jacob had been privileged to know him intimately. The Apostle's influence on Jacob's life had been, and always would be, profound.

Jacob was still pondering all these things when Livia found him on the hillside. She came up beside him and put a hand on his shoulder.

"It's cold out here," she said. "And you haven't eaten anything all day. Why don't you come inside?"

"I will in a minute. I'm just doing some thinking."

"Is it all right if I join you?"

"Have a seat," Jacob said, patting the ground beside him. "If it's not too cold for you."

"You forget, I'm used to the cold. And dressed for it." Livia sat down, spreading her heavy fur-trimmed cape underneath her. "You, however, are not."

"I'm fine," he protested. Actually, he felt a bit chilled in the light woolen cloak he'd thrown over his tunic, but once she'd pointed out the temperature to him, he felt obligated to deny it.

"So, what are you thinking about?" Livia asked. "The Apostle?"

"Yes," Jacob said. He paused and stretched his long legs out in front of him. "I'm also thinking about me, about the direction I'm supposed to be taking with my life."

It was something he'd discussed with his wife even before leaving Cappadocia. Jacob had not been sure what he should do when he returned to Ephesus. He'd been home for several months now, and even though he had agreed to help Peter manage the shipping business, Jacob still did not have a clear direction.

Not until he had sat down on the hillside, that is. With all the reflecting he'd done during the twilight hour, something was stirring in him. That something was *purpose*, and as he began to tell Livia about it, everything came together.

"I always thought I had to choose between my father's business and the ministry," Jacob told her. "I chose the ministry, yet it wasn't the right decision. I recently realized, though, that the shipping business *is* the ministry. My brother understood that long before I did. Last fall Peter and Rebecca sent a boatload of blankets for the prisoners on Devil's Island."

"And you arranged financial help for the Christians who lost their businesses in Smyrna," Livia pointed out.

"Yes," Jacob said. He and Peter had made interest-free loans to Sergius and Plautius, so the brothers could rebuild their blacksmith shop, and another one to Tarquinius for rebuilding the inn. "But there's so much more we could do. That's what I've been thinking about just now."

He drew his legs up and spread his cloak over his knees, speaking his thoughts out loud as they came. "Matthew said in his book that the gospel of the kingdom would be preached throughout the whole world before Jesus returns. I hope that will happen in my lifetime. It's already been seventy years; He's bound to return soon."

Excitement began to build in Jacob's voice. "He's coming back, Livia, and we must do whatever we can while there's still time."

"I agree, but I'm still not sure what you're talking about. More relief work for the Christians who are suffering?"

"Yes, definitely," he said. "But even more than that, we have to reach the lost. Do you remember what Paul wrote about evangelism in one of his epistles—the one to the Romans?" Jacob did not wait for her answer. "When he talked about winning the lost, Paul said, 'How can they hear without someone preaching to them? And how can they preach unless they are sent?'

"That's it, Livia. I'm not called to preach—I'm called to send preachers!" Jacob couldn't get the thoughts out fast enough now. "What's the fastest way to travel long distances? By ship. We can use the shipping business to launch missionaries. We won't just haul cargo—we'll transport preachers. We'll help them take the gospel not just to the far reaches of the Empire, but beyond . . ."

Jacob stopped because he was getting ahead of himself, but he knew that what he was sensing in his spirit was something with vast potential.

He stood and reached out a hand to help Livia up. "It's dark now. Let's get back to the house."

As they walked past the mausoleum, Jacob saw that someone had closed the heavy door, sealing the tomb, and had placed a torch on the outside wall. The flame reflected off the gleaming Italian marble. Jacob stopped and went to retrieve the torch, and as he removed it from the holder, he thought once more of John.

Jacob paused and made a silent vow to his mentor and friend. *I know my calling now, and I will fulfill it.*

Then he took Livia's hand and walked home, the torch illuminating their path, and the fire of the gospel burning in his heart.

DEVIL'S ISLAND
A Novel

Book One: The Apocalypse Diaries

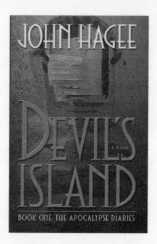

In his first novel, and the prequel to *Avenger of Blood,* John Hagee tells the powerful story of a Christian family caught in the persecutions of Rome—and how their lives interweave with the apostle John as he receives the book of Revelation on the island of Patmos.

> The apostle John pushed aside the incense. "I will not make your sacrifice," he announced to the Roman tribune. "There is one God, and his name is not Domitian." Standing next to John at the stone altar of the emperor's temple were other believers, including Asia's most wealthy citizen, Abraham of Ephesus, and his family. Will Abraham follow John's example? If he refuses to make the sacrifice, the shipping magnate's vast fortune will be confiscated by Rome, and he will either be executed or exiled to Patmos—*Devil's Island.* This exciting historical novel follows Abraham and his family as they make their choice to worship Ceasar or follow Christ, and it brings to life the days when Christians faced the lions in Rome's Colosseum—and when the exiled Apostle received the great visions of Revelation.

ISBN: 0-7852-6787-5